A DE...

As I crept through the main salon, it echoed an ominous void. Only the night wind stirred to enchant the flame of my lamp. On I went toward the courtyard, terrified of what I might find, yet unable to stay away. When I reached the archway, I found the light was gone. In its place was only the gentle murmur of the fountain and a jasmine breeze against my skin.

Suddenly, from out of the darkness, a hand clamped over my mouth. Another grabbed my lamp and threw it to the tulip bed where it sputtered and died.

"Call out and we both die," a man whispered, his lips pressed against my ear. Then I felt his grip slacken, his hand slide from my lips down over my throat to my breast. "Your heart races, Beautiful One." He turned me around in his arms. "It is I, Selim."

JASMINE SPLENDOR

Margo Bode

PUBLISHED BY POCKET BOOKS NEW YORK

A POCKET BOOKS/RICHARD GALLEN *Original* publication

**POCKET BOOKS, a Simon & Schuster division of
GULF & WESTERN CORPORATION
1230 Avenue of the Americas, New York, N.Y. 10020**

ISBN: 0-671-42431-9

First Pocket Books printing January, 1981

10 9 8 7 6 5 4 3 2 1

POCKET and colophon are trademarks of Simon & Schuster.

Printed in the U.S.A.

BOOK ONE

Chapter 1

A scrawny child elbowed his way through the crowd of seamen, stevedores and sightseers at the wharves in Nantes. A floppy cloth cap was raked jauntily over one eye, and an enormous greatcoat swept the ground as he walked. His bold stride hinted peasant origins, but a calculating gleam in his eye and a mouth tense with a ready sneer marked him as one of the thousands of waifs seeking any sort of life in the cities of France rather than face starvation on neglected country estates.

The little fellow had come to the harbor with a purpose. He wasted no time making his way to every woman in sight. Then he grabbed off his cap and asked, "Be your name Rivery, mademoiselle? Rivery or Fleury?" When the answer was no, he flipped on his cap again and picked a new target.

"Be your name Rivery, mademoiselle? Rivery or Fleury?"

"Yes," I replied, surprised to be addressed by a street urchin. "I am Mademoiselle Dubuc de Rivery."

"Here," he pulled an envelope out of his cap. "This is for you."

"Thank you." I took it and handed him a coin. He scampered away like a bandit.

"What is it, Aimee?" Adele Fleury asked, looking over my shoulder.

I broke the seal and opened it. "A letter from a Father Le Clerc at the cathedral."

"That's odd." Adele pulled at a corner of the page to have a look. "Oh no!" she said disgustedly.

"The little coward," I muttered. "What will we do now?"

Well might I have asked that question. As I stood in a cruel and unrelenting March wind near the water's edge, I anticipated an Atlantic passage that would end eight long years in France—eight from 1776 to 1784, with eight miserable winters, this one the worst. Perhaps it was the paralyzing morning cold that impaired my judgment. More likely it was the painful knowledge still tearing at my heart after almost a year that the man I loved, seemingly the embodiment of every human virtue, was actually an unscrupulous mountebank, the basest example of his self-seeking gender.

For whatever reason, I failed to recognize as I held the priest's letter in my hand that it was an augury to which I should pay special heed. Father Le Clerc had written at the request of a girl we had retained as a travel maid for our voyage. Her message was simple. She had boarded our ship, *Belle Gloire*, at sunrise in order to ready the cabin and see to our baggage. Recognizing the vessel's sorry condition, she refused to entrust her life to it upon the high seas and encouraged us to come to the same conclusion.

At that moment the choices were clear. Adele Fleury and I could decide to travel to our home in Martinique without the services of a maid, or we could remain in France until better weather and a superior vessel insured our safe passage. The serving girl certainly had grounds for apprehension. *Belle Gloire* must have been old before the American Revolution. She had seen no care in all the years of the conflict. While England had a death grip on the seas, no one chose to throw money away on ships that rotted in besieged French ports. The vessel wanted for paint and pitch. Lines hung about randomly while our departure was less than an hour away. The sails were soiled and patched, their flaws plainly visible even before the canvas was unfurled. More disconcerting, the vessel suffered a noticeable list toward the dock, but I reasoned it was due to poorly placed cargo yet to be secured.

"What shall we do?" I asked Adele at last. "Should we risk the passage?"

She clung to her cape as a vicious wind raked the harbor. "I bow to your judgment," she replied, shivering. "There is something to be said for staying here. The ship does not inspire confidence, and we'll have no servant. On the other hand, the weather in France is wretched, and we have waited such a long time for England to open the seas that the thought of another delay is maddening." She cast an uneasy glance toward the street leading to the dock.

"What is it, Adele? Are you expecting someone?"

"No, of course not," she replied hastily, then shuddered again from the cold. "Now, what is your decision? Shall we go or stay?"

There she had stated it: the two alternatives that would mark the crossroads of my life.

. . . Was it only a year and a half ago that I made my choice, and in choosing had catapulted myself into a foreign world full of perils I could never have imagined had I elected to remain in France?

"We shall go," I said, thinking only that soon we would be in Martinique, away from the cold, away from the stifling atmosphere of the convent where we had lived for so long and away from François de Marmont, the man who had almost taken my virginity in exchange for his lies.

No matter what life I found in the Antilles, it was certain to be superior to the mixture of pain and boredom that had become my lot in France, or so I thought as I made my decision. I stood on the Nantes wharf that cold March morning, refusing the wise counsel of an illiterate serving girl. When Adele asked, "Shall we go or stay?" I answered boldly, "We shall go."

"Pardon, mademoiselles." A footman dressed in full winter livery interrupted us. "Madame de La Fontelle asks you to return to the coach. She believes this weather will ruin your health."

"Yes, Jacques," I said, releasing the letter to Adele's custody. Then I pulled the hood of my cape closer around my face and shivered. My limbs ached from trembling in the cold as we walked back to the carriage. In spite of my resolve, I was apprehensive about our voyage, and a prayer to the Holy Virgin was on my lips as the footman opened the coach door.

"Quickly, quickly, get in!" ordered a brittle voice. "You're letting in the cold." Adele hurriedly climbed inside ahead of me and slid under a lap robe next to Marie de La Fontelle. I took my place with the other woman in the coach, the Abbess of the convent we had just left.

"What were you doing out there all this time?" the Abbess asked in the same unpleasant tone that had greeted us. I tucked the robe around the fullness of my cape and petticoats and tried to get warm without touching her.

Adele explained. "A messenger. The girl we hired as a travel maid won't go."

"That is unfortunate," Marie said, shifting her legs under her wrap. Even at that early hour Marie looked beautiful, though all of her thirty-seven years marked her face. She must have gotten up before dawn to dress. Her ensemble and wig were perfect in every detail, even to the replica of a sailing ship perched amid her powdered curls in honor of our departure.

"The girl had her priest write us," I explained. "It is more than one might expect from that sort, I suppose, but traveling such a distance with no servant . . ."

"We'll get on very well without her," Adele said

with forced enthusiasm. "Anyway, it's too late to find another. At least we won't be searching desperately for this one at the last second."

"I am glad you are so pleased with this wench and her consideration," the Abbess wheezed sarcastically. "But it still means you'll be alone. If you had allowed me to get someone from the workhouse, as I suggested, those girls they go where the director sends them."

"You know Aimee and Adele," Marie said, patiently tolerating the Abbess's ill humor in an effort to avoid arguing with her on the day of our departure. "They would have to share their cabin with the girl," she went on. "I'm sure they don't want to live with a common tart."

"Well, they've nothing at all now," the Abbess snapped. She was tired from rising so early; so were we, but unlike us, her fatigue was a constant condition. Supervising the Convent of Les Dames de la Visitation and the girls' school within its walls taxed her strength to its limits. She appeared overburdened while going about her duties, as if she were suffering a thousand years in purgatory for some sin God held against her by mistake. The weight of His wrath bowed her shoulders and made her steps slow and lifeless. She had the face of a woman who had never known youth. Not a tooth remained in the front of her mouth, and their absence made her look lipless and drawn. As a child she had had smallpox. It was not a bad case, but the beastly disease had left its tracks across the bridge of her nose and along the left side of her jaw. The scars were nothing like the cavernous wounds marking those wretched souls who populated secluded retreats in rural areas of France, where the horribly disfigured hid from the world.

The Abbess came from a titled family of the nobility of the sword, the kind of blood that could attract a wealthy husband looking for status, but her affliction poisoned her mind toward romance, and she took the veil. That was forty years ago. All those years of abstinence and regret had ill effects on her nature which became more pronounced whenever she saw Marie de La Fontelle. The two women shared responsibility for Adele and me while we were on the Continent. With their differences, they never could have been friends, but their disagreements over us made them mortal enemies.

"Did the wicked girl give any reason for why she deserted you?" the Abbess wanted to know.

"Yes." Adele pulled the letter out of her muff and reread it quickly. "She says she came down to the dock this morning to prepare our cabin, but one look at *Belle Gloire* and she knew she would never leave France on it."

"Pardon me, dear," Marie said as she reached in front of Adele and pulled back the window curtain to appraise the vessel as it was being readied to sail. "The girl has a point. It does not look seaworthy. Perhaps you should wait until later in the spring when the weather improves."

"I intend to leave today," I said firmly.

"And I with her," Adele added. "If we don't leave on *Belle Gloire,* it might be months before we can book passage on another ship. Now that the seas are open to French ships again, half the populace seems to want to go to the Antilles. No use being put off by one frightened maid's suspicions." Adele pulled back the window curtain herself and looked at the ship. "I have seen worse wrecks sail out of this harbor."

"Sailing out is not my concern," Marie countered. "It's sailing into port on the other side of the Atlantic that worries me. I know both of you are anxious to leave. You've had to wait six years for peace between France and England, but a few more months and we may find a safer vessel. Open your curtain, Aimee." Marie reached in front of Adele once more and pulled back the drape. "Look at it."

The Abbess spoke up, "If you decide to stay, there is always the convent. You could take your vows."

Marie wanted to respond to that suggestion, but she held her tongue and let our silence refuse the offer as gently as possible. "I know you haven't the vocation, either of you," the Abbess went on sourly. "But go or stay, shut those curtains. It's too cold for an old woman to be exposed to this weather." She pulled the lap robe to her chin as if to shut us out along with the chill.

We obediently closed the curtains and allowed ourselves a few moments of silence. In the coach that morning were the three women who had influenced my life most.

Marie de La Fontelle was a noblewoman, her heritage as old as France itself. She and my mother were closer than sisters while they were growing up. Both of them attended school in Nantes at the Convent of Les Dames de la Visitation. Then my mother sailed off to Martinique to marry. The two never saw each other again, but in a letter my mother wrote just before she died, she asked Marie to see to it that my time in France be spent in her care attending their old school. My intentions were to be away from Martinique for two years, but the plans went awry with the rebellion in the English colonies and King Louis' meddling in the affair, taking the colonists' side and provoking the English, bullies that they are, to vent their wrath on us for their impotence against the faraway rebels. After eight years, I had gotten my fill of the old school, and my fill of France, but I loved Marie and saying good-bye was painful.

Beside me in the coach sat the Abbess of the convent and director of our school. Throughout my adolescence she represented adult authority, so it was against her that I directed my resentments and defiance. In spite of that, in spite of the times I openly disobeyed her or subverted by stealth her rules and pronouncements, disrupting her quiet world, I knew she loved me. And in a strangely frightened yet disrespectful way, I loved her too, for her gruff manner, her predictably miserable humor and her constant and sincere concern for my virginity and my immortal soul.

Adele sat next to Marie, as much my sister as if we had shared the same parents, which we most certainly did, at least by half. Her mother, a mulatto slave on our plantation in Martinique, died in childbirth the same year I was born. My father brought her baby into our house to be raised as one of the family. He died not long afterward, but in his will he gave little Adele her freedom and a respectable trust to pay for her education and maintenance. As I learned years later, this caused a lot of talk in Fort Royal. Noble French blood flowed copiously through the dark population there, but rarely did any gentleman acknowledge his illegitimate offspring with an inheritance.

After my mother died, Adele and I went to live with my father's sister, Louise, and her husband. They raised us as their own daughters, with little room for doubt that we shared the same heritage. Aunt Louise, Adele and I all have the same green eyes and identical moles just under the right corner of our mouths. Marie says I look a great deal like Adele, though neither of us admits a resemblance. I'm blond, of course, and she's dark, a warm copper color with an abundance of black hair. She usually wears it in tight ringlets framing her face, with thick braided coils in back. Her neck is longer than mine, and she's very lean, which makes her look much taller. She moves with a fluid grace that suggests the pride of a doe, but when she dresses for the theater in jewels and wig and gown, she is like a spring flower dancing joyously on the breeze.

We have always loved each other, trusted and protected each other, bonded more closely than blood, comfortable in the unspoken awareness of our mutual affection. When my guardians prepared to send me to France, I refused to set foot on board ship unless Adele accompanied me. Then, when I found living on the Continent no longer bearable, she would not allow me to return to Martinique alone, even though life for a woman of color promised to be much more interesting in France than among the slave-owning provincials of the Antilles.

These are the three women in my life. They join one other to make the four points of the compass that guide me: the fourth is the Holy Virgin, as alive to me as any of the others. I will always carry her in my mind as I saw her at the chapel of the convent, her gently smiling countenance warming the stone of her likeness as she looked down every day when I went to her with my prayers.

She was my true confessor. Of course, I went to the confessional as often as necessary to satisfy the Abbess, but I refused to reveal my innermost thoughts and damnable transgressions to any ordinary man behind a screen who had purchased his vocation to gain the revenues it provided from church lands. Most of the priests who said Mass at the convent were degenerate bluebloods, no more the servants of God than are lice the disciples of the dog that nourishes them. These disreputable fellows rarely studied the Scriptures. The façade of celibacy was their license to father bastards whenever a willing female could be found. And their Latin was a scandal. The Mass became a mockery. To cover appalling inadequacies, these men of the church perfected what we called the "liturgical mumble," a slurring of speech and variation in tone, heavy on the vibrato, with enough Latin words thrown in to convince the unlettered that they were witnessing the Mysteries. Any girl over the age of twelve at the convent, however, had studied Latin and knew the charlatans for what they were. As the only men we saw in those days fell into that unattractive category, we had a very low opinion of the entire male gender.

It seemed to me that the four fine ladies in my life certainly demonstrated feminine moral superiority. That morning, looking at the faces of three of them, I whispered a prayer of thanksgiving to the fourth, trusting she would convey to God my gratefulness for being born a woman.

My thoughts were interrupted abruptly by a tap at

the speaking door in the coach wall. The driver told Marie that an officer from the ship was outside.

"Tell him to come here," she replied. Then to us, "I intend to find out something about this *Belle Gloire* before you trust your lives to it."

A cold winter gust accompanied the officer's appearance as he opened the door. "Your pardon, ladies." Leaning inside, he looked quickly at each of us until his eyes met those of Marie de La Fontelle. Then it was as if the rest of us did not exist. "Madame." He bowed as formally as he could, considering the confines of the door frame. "The captain sends his respects and requests Mademoiselle de Rivery and Mademoiselle Fleury be on board in a quarter of an hour." Any common seaman could have delivered the same message to our footman, but here was an officer delighted with this opportunity to meet the famous Marie de La Fontelle, who was the talk of Nantes. He studied her intently, trying to determine if she were as beautiful as her reputation suggested.

There was contempt in the Abbess's eyes as she observed the young officer's eagerness. Perhaps she was jealous and cloaked her emotion in disapproval. Of course, she felt only disgust for the weak-willed seaman. Her condemnation was reserved for Marie alone, a woman of intelligence and strength who chose to soil her immortal soul by tempting others into sins of the flesh.

Marie knew she could never win the Abbess with piety, so occasionally she lived up to the woman's most vivid expectations just to keep the Abbess alert and properly self-righteous.

"Thank you, young man," Marie said with a bit of coquetry in her voice. "I want to ask you a question, but please lean into the coach a bit first. Let me have a look at you." Such eager and designing young men deserved little more than scorn, but making sport of this one could provide a bit of fun to take the sting out of our farewell.

"I hope this conversation will be short," the Abbess

sighed. "If no one else is aware of it, we are in the throes of a winter gale."

It was terribly cold with the door open, but Marie ignored her. "I was going to ask you, my young ship's officer, if you thought these two ladies would be safe on their voyage to the Antilles, but now that I see the look in your eye, I know the answer."

"And what is it you see, madame?" the fellow asked playfully.

"I see that no woman is safe with you." She took her arm out from under the lap robe. The presumptuous officer must have given her a devilish look, for she laughed wickedly as he kissed her hand. "Tell me," she went on. "You seem a man who knows what he is about. Is the ship safe?"

"She's a tired old girl, madame. But she will take us to Martinique. I'm sure of it."

"And will she get you back to Nantes?" Marie brushed a bit of dust off the front of the officer's coat. Her suggestive manner was unmistakable, but to make certain, she tweaked his chin.

"I'll be back in the fall, madame. May I call on you?"

"Until then your absence will leave me desolate."

He took her hand again, kissed it and prepared to leave. "Until the fall then." He forced his boyish voice an octave lower, affecting the grand seducer.

The Abbess ignored him, focusing on Marie. "You are despicable, madame," she blustered, enjoying a healthy rage. "And to think you conduct yourself so shamelessly in front of these children." Marie smiled victoriously, but made no response to the old woman.

"I am Marie de La Fontelle," she said to the officer. "You may call on me at—"

"Of course, madame. I know who you are and where to call. Everyone in Nantes knows you. I am Jean-Claude Dupierre, at your service."

"You'll be back in the fall, Jean-Claude? You are certain?"

He smiled wistfully and struck a thoughtful pose. "As certain as any man can be about the sea, madame."

"You sound like an experienced seaman. How many crossings have you made?"

"In my mind, dear lady, I have traveled the world under sail. There is no danger I have not met and mastered."

"Get to the point, man," the Abbess interrupted. "You're little more than a boy. How many passages have you made?"

"This is the first," he responded, quite embarrassed by the confession. "Now, if you will excuse me, there are pressing matters aboard ship that require my attention. Your servant, ladies." He hastily took his leave.

"Wonderful. Simply wonderful!" Marie threw up her hands and tossed her head back in disgust so that the toy ship on her wig dipped precariously. "You are going to cross the Atlantic Ocean in the dead of winter in little more than a chamber pot with officers who travel the world in their dreamy heads while navigating a cake of soap in the bath tub."

"We know you want us to stay here, Marie," I said gently. "And we love you for it. But let's have no more talk about the ship or the officers. I plan to be on board when *Belle Gloire* catches the tide."

"So do I," Adele added.

"So be it, then," the Abess sighed. "May the blessings of the Virgin go with you, children." Her tone was gentler than I had ever heard it before. "Now I have something for each of you before you go." She opened the wall compartment under her window and took out two small packages wrapped in silk. Then handed one to Adele and the other to me. "Open them," she said softly. Her gift to each of us was a new missal with delicate miniature paintings illuminating almost every page of the Mass.

"Oh, thank you," Adele and I said, almost together.

She presented her hands to us. When I kissed them, I could feel how icy cold and bloodless they were.

"See that you open those books now and then," she barked. Surely, the woman would go to her grave giving commands. "And remember me in your prayers, girls." Her voice softened again. "I know I'll remember you both."

"We'll miss you," I said sincerely, and leaned over to kiss the old woman on the parchment of her cheek.

"You're sure you want to go?" Marie asked once more.

"Yes," I replied.

"Then kiss me, both of you, and be off. I cannot pretend this composure a minute more." Tears shimmered in her eyes as she reached out toward me. I could feel her quake as we embraced. "If, after all, Martinique is not what you want, come back to me, Aimee."

"I love you, Marie."

She squeezed me desperately for an instant, then broke away. "Adele, come here, dear."

As the two of them said their farewells, I kissed the Abbess's hand once more. Then she took mine. "At last my life will be peaceful again with you two troublemakers far away." She paused. "Ah, whatever will I do with my days?" The hint of a smile touched her mouth and was gone.

Marie signaled the driver, and a footman opened the coach door. Adele climbed down and I followed, fighting with every breath not to sob. Glancing back into the coach quickly, I saw the two dear ladies wave farewell, then I stepped aside and permitted the footman to close the door.

Adele slipped her arm through mine as we walked away. There was some turmoil on the street behind us. She turned to see what it was, but I was too upset to take notice of it. We were almost to the ship when I heard him.

"Aimee! Aimee! Wait!"

My heart leapt and the tears I could no longer hold back started down my cheeks.

"Aimee!" It was his voice. I looked back. He was running toward me, pushing people aside, dashing around stacked barrels on the dock.

I felt Adele squeeze my arm. "Aimee, it's François!"

Chapter 2

When I turned, I saw François de Marmont push past
a sailor and hurdle a wooden crate. His cape caught
the wind, billowing behind him. It thrilled me to see
him, so tall and lean in his army uniform, urgency
and determination upon his face, so perfectly framed
by his dark hair and military tricorner.

Then from nowhere, a stevedore with a wheelbar-
row cut in front of him. François was moving too fast.
He tried to evade the fellow, but could not. They col-
lided, and François landed on his back. As he sat up,
his eyes met mine. Then he smiled helplessly, and it
was my undoing. Instead of turning away and board-
ing the ship, I waited. The unfettered warmth of his
smile led me to hope he would say the words that
would keep me in France. As he brushed himself off
and came toward me, I remembered the first time I
saw his face.

In Paris, just after the new year of 1783, Adele and
I attended one of Marie de La Fontelle's Thursday

17

salons. Once we reached the age of eighteen, Adele and I were allowed to attend such gatherings, but we rarely chose to do so. This time we extended our holiday visit a few days, because Marie promised it would be more in the spirit of the grand days of the past. By that she meant her guests would discuss intellectual topics. They would be witty and intelligent instead of droning and buzzing endlessly about politics and taxes. Several men from the Academy of Sciences were invited, including the renowned chemist Antoine Laurent Lavoisier.

Unfortunately, Marie's predictions about the event were a bit off the mark. Lavoisier did appear. He did stay for the entire afternoon and through dinner. There was no denying the man was a scientific genius, but he had other interests as well. He was a tax farmer, one who buys the privilege of collecting the king's taxes in exchange for a share of the booty. His techniques for collecting and recording revenues kept the conversation wallowing at the miserable level of politics and the treasury. I suffered an attack of the kind of monumental boredom experienced only on high holy days with Mass morning, noon and night.

"I fear I grow faint," Adele sighed aloud, then whispered to me behind her fan, "get me out of here before my head falls into the punch."

"My dear, let me help you," I replied full of concern. "You will pardon me." I tried to excuse myself from a small group of popinjays and clerics who were discussing finance.

"Tell me then," a sallow archbishop asked the others as I rose to my feet. "If we do not increase tolls on the highways across ecclesiastical lands, how will we be able to maintain them well enough for the commerce you value so highly? This winter is going to create havoc on the roads. Repairs will cost thousands, but everyone says more taxes will break the back of the peasantry. Devil take them."

"I have a solution," said a slack-jawed young man I recognized as the youngest and most decadent blossom of an old and noble family tree. "Reinstitute the *corvée*," he said matter of factly.

"You make light of this, monsieur," the archbishop replied disgustedly. "The *corvée* would mean revolution."

"Hardly," the young man said arrogantly. "French peasants have labored for their lords under the *corvée* for centuries. It costs the peasants nothing to work a few days, and you will have men for repairs without having to lay on heavier tolls."

"Work without pay?" I queried, hating myself for responding to the imbecile. "Certain people, quite uneducated types, I am sure, seem to think that work without pay is the most onerous tax of all. Something about losing what they might have earned elsewhere. I take it, monsieur, you do not agree."

"Of course I do not agree," the young man responded in a condescending tone, thinking himself of superior intellect. "What can a peasant earn in a day? A few cents at best. Nothing at all really. Forfeiting it now and then is hardly an onerous tax, as you call it." He lifted a pinch of snuff to his nose.

"Now that you explain your logic, it is all very clear." I opened my fan and played the coquette in the same way I had observed Marie do it so many times before. "But there is a certain measure of intelligence required for someone to make sense out of what you say," I went on. "That must be the reason why simple peasants and goatherds will never take your side in the argument." The young man smiled his acceptance of my view while his companion, the archbishop, chuckled to himself at the fellow's stupidity.

"My advice to you, monsieur," I said soberly, "is that if you are looking in the countryside for converts to your position, bypass the peasants. You'll find your comrades among the goats and asses."

"I beg your pardon, mademoiselle," the young man stammered angrily.

"And well you should, monsieur. Good evening." I took Adele's arm and led her away.

"Why did you insult that poor fellow like that, Aimee?" she asked disgustedly when we were in the antechamber.

"He's a pompous buffoon."

"Of course he is, but Marie invited him here. Can't you ignore such people?" I made no reply, but wished I had done just that.

We went through the hallway and up the servants' stairway to the library. A maid sat outside the door. She stood as we went by. Inside, a fire was burning low, and a single candle on the pedestaled reading table played its light along the bookcases.

"We should have gone back to the convent last week," Adele muttered half to herself. "I knew this would be a waste of time. Marie goes on and on about the old days, Madame Geoffrin, Madame de Tencin. . . . The wonderful days when women ruled Paris! Sweet Mother of God, could all their socials have been as boring as this?"

"It's the times, Adele." I poured her a brandy from the decanter on the table. "Here." I handed it to her. "Who can speak cleverly about abstract matters when no one knows from one day to the next if the country will come crashing down on our heads?"

She sighed and began looking along the shelves. "We wouldn't be in such a mess if the king had not let Franklin and the Americans talk him into fighting the English. What business is it of ours, I ask you that?"

"Don't ask me. I haven't any idea, and you can go downstairs right now if you've an itch to argue politics. I have had quite enough for one day."

"Not that group again, thank you. As soon as I find something to read, it's to bed for me." She pulled a volume down from a high shelf and began to leaf through it.

"If you see any Molière, give it to me, will you?"

I filled a brandy glass for myself and started toward one of the wing-backed chairs facing the fire.

"Is *Le Misanthrope* all right?"

"Perfect."

She handed it to me. "Hmm, this looks interesting." She tucked a book under her arm, added a bit more brandy to her glass and then gave me the play. "Good night, Aimee."

"Sleep well," I responded, looking forward to an evening alone after the long afternoon. It didn't matter that I would miss dinner. A brandy, some reading and then early to bed would be good preparation for our trip to Nantes in the morning. There were two chairs near the fire with a small console between them. I set my brandy down, lit a few more candles and then moved the candelabra closer. The large chair was warm and comfortable. I nestled in it, enjoying the exquisite pleasure of relaxation and silence.

"Good evening, mademoiselle." A masculine voice jarred my senses and I jumped. The darkly handsome face of a man I had met earlier in the evening emerged from the depths of the other chair. "Oh, forgive me," he said. "I should have announced my presence when you came in."

"That would have been the courteous thing to do, monsieur." The rudeness in my tone offended even me, and I regretted it. Still, he had startled me into an unguarded retort. I did not offer apologies. Instead, I prepared to leave.

"Please stay," he protested. "I've had the fire to myself a long time." Something about him was not like the others. "I couldn't help hearing what you said to your friend," he admitted. "These salons are deadly affairs, aren't they?"

"The hostess, Madame de La Fontelle, is very dear to me, monsieur. What I said to Adele was not meant—"

"Of course. I know what you meant," the fellow interrupted. "My father loves these afternoons too, but he spends a lot of time at Versailles. If you aren't

involved in government these days, no one has any
time for you, and if you are, your entire existence
depends on politics." He reached over and picked up
my brandy glass. "May I?" he asked, then took it to
his lips without waiting for my answer. I found his
boldness exciting.

"You're the Comte de Marmont's son, aren't you?"
I asked, finally remembering.

"Yes, François de Marmont. We met downstairs,
Mademoiselle de Rivery." He smiled again as he
spoke my name. François de Marmont was a very
handsome man, dark and masculine, clearly not a
saloneer. Without his smile he would have appeared
arrogant, for his blue eyes seemed cold. But when he
smiled, his eyes danced. If he never said another
word, I would have enjoyed just looking at him by
the firelight.

But the empty silence following his introduction
made me uneasy and I tried to fill it. "If you aren't
interested in salons or politics, monsieur, why did you
come this afternoon?"

"Lavoisier, I wanted to meet him."

"Ah, you are a scientist then."

"No, not exactly. I'm an artillery officer in the
army." I noticed the cuff of his coat as he reached
for my brandy glass again and remembered he was
wearing a uniform. He went on, "Monsieur Lavoisier
is an expert on gunpower, chief of the state gunpowder
commission. Thanks to him there have been many
improvements. Our powder almost always ignites now,
and there's enough of it for more than one volley.
With new guns and his powder, artillery will be the
key to a French victory whenever we take the field."
He spoke with a good deal of forcefulness.

"You do sound convincing." I laughed with delight
to hear a man speak about something of which he
had some knowledge. It was so refreshing after the
salon.

"Pardon my zeal, mademoiselle." Although the light
was poor, a hint of a blush was detectable on his

cheek. "It's just that my entire family is cavalry. They haven't any use for cannon and treat me like the village idiot because I don't choose to saddle myself to a horse for the rest of my life. Why, one cannon is worth a division of cavalry, slashing their blades, striking nothing most of the time."

"And you say that Monsieur Lavoisier knows a great deal about gunpowder? You two must have had a fine discussion downstairs. I should have enjoyed hearing part of it."

"Monsieur Lavoisier?" François replied cynically. "We had no discussion at all. I had hardly met the man when someone asked him about the national debt. From that moment until right now, I suppose, he has talked of nothing but what the king and his new minister of the treasury should do."

"But you'll have other opportunities to speak to him. He will be in Paris until the spring. I know Madame de La Fontelle expects him to attend her salons regularly."

"He may be in Paris, but I will not. Tomorrow I leave for Nantes."

"Nantes?" I repeated. "Why are you going to Nantes?"

"There is a new cannon works on an island in the Loire near the city. An Englishman named Wilkinson, quite sympathetic to the American colonies I believe, is setting up his sheds there. All the latest techniques —solid cast iron, bored barrels, everything. I'm going to spend a year learning his methods."

"Adele Fleury and I are going to Nantes tomorrow also." I found myself very pleased that this François de Marmont would be living near the convent.

"You are?" He looked at me with unguarded delight. "That is wonderful news." His smile stirred a strange feeling within me.

"Yes, we are students at the Convent of Les Dames de la Visitation. Do you know it?"

"No. I've never been to Nantes before, but I'll find

the convent. May I call on you? If the sisters allow visitors, that is."

"Please do. We receive guests every Sunday afternoon. Perhaps we may even see you tomorrow along the road somewhere. Adele and I will watch for your carriage."

"I'll be traveling by public coach," he said directly, without fearing to admit that his family had no vehicle to carry their son on such a journey. Hard times affected more than just the peasants and the treasury. Income from estates had dwindled, especially for those noblemen like François' father, the Comte, who neglected his lands to spend almost all of his time at court.

"Then why don't you ride with us. Our berlin is large enough and we will feel safer with a man inside in case of highwaymen."

"That's very kind of you, mademoiselle, but I'm sure you'll be more comfortable without me." His refusal was only a courtesy. I could sense he wanted to accept.

"Oh please come! Adele is the worst traveling companion. She takes a dose of laudanum every morning and then sleeps through the day. It's almost like being alone to go with her."

"In that case, I wouldn't dream of allowing you to make such a long and tedious trip unescorted. What time do you plan to leave?"

"Early. Eight o'clock in the morning, I believe. We'll pack a breakfast so you won't have to eat first. Can you be ready?"

"Yes. I'll be here at eight exactly. Thank you very much." We smiled at each other, then François took my glass again and finished it. "May I pour you a brandy?" He acted the host.

"Yes, please," I replied. "But only if you'll join me."

He disappeared behind my chair. "Where is it? Oh, I see." When he returned he still had only the one glass.

"I thought you were going to have one too?"

"Let's just share this one. Do you mind?" He drank slowly from the crystal. As I took it from him, his hand touched mine. An intimacy enveloped us, the darkened library, the fire and our single glass of brandy.

"No, I don't mind at all."

Chapter 3

In the days when Adele and I were students at the convent, it was said that the highways between Nantes and Paris were among the best in France. If that were so, an assertion I found impossible to believe, the country's roads were in a sorry state indeed. We traveled to Paris at least four times a year. I knew every bone-jarring wheel rut and unsavory inn along the way. Although I enjoyed the change of scene our holidays provided, the dread of moving from place to place took the joy out of our anticipation as the date of a departure approached.

The first and only exception to my otherwise uniformly disagreeable experiences along the Nantes Road was the journey I made in the company of François de Marmont.

He sat beside me in the carriage as it rolled along. Adele was secured to the seat opposite with a stout leather strap so that she would not be thrown about by our vehicle's violent bumps and lurches as she slept. Never had I enjoyed travel so much. The time flew by. Whenever I gave a moment's thought to our progress, the driver was pulling up to the door of an inn for a meal, preparing to change teams or making ready to stop for the night.

As we talked, I learned that François was troubled about his family. He came from the nobility of the sword, of course, or he never would have qualified as an army officer. The Marmont estate perpetually tottered near bankruptcy, but the old Comte insisted on keeping up appearances. He signed so many promissory notes they were almost a second state currency in Paris. Two sons in the military brought no wealth to the family coffers. On the contrary, they incurred huge expenses for servants, lodgings, uniforms, equipment and entertainment for their comrades. François seemed very worried about the pressure that their indebtedness was putting on his father.

Such discourses about the situation left us in somber moods for short periods of time, but we did not pass the entire journey in dreary litanies of our own problems. For the most part, we were flamboyantly gay and witty all the way to Nantes, though after we crossed the Loire River, east of the city, François became pensive. At first I assumed he was simply disappointed that we were soon to part company. Then an unusually nasty stretch of road sent us sprawling. I was thrown across the coach and bumped my head on Adele's temple.

"We're like dice in a cup," François laughed as he helped me up. Adele opened her eyes, smiled drunkenly, then drifted off again. "Amazing how she can sleep no matter what happens."

"It's the drug," I explained as I straightened my bonnet.

"You're all right, aren't you?" he asked.

"Yes, of course."

"Good." He hesitated. "I have something to tell you." The tone of his voice suggested I was not going to like what he had to say. "I'm not free," he went on. His statement, coming from nowhere as it did, caught me off guard. When I made no response, he tried to explain. "This is terribly presumptuous of me, but I feel you and I mean something to each other. I want to call on you at the convent whenever I can. Next Sunday will not be soon enough. Aimee, you mean a great deal to me, but I must tell you this. My father has arranged a marriage for me. Quite a bit of property and a good income go with it. My family desperately needs the money."

His revelation was a shock. I had begun to fancy the idea of a courtship. He was like none of the other men I had met. He seemed sincere, intelligent. I genuinely liked him, and what was more disturbing, I realized that he aroused in me the dangerous yearnings that I knew should never be awakened until a woman is safely married.

"I understand," was all I could say. Then I felt a rush of burning embarrassment. Disappointment flushed my cheeks, and I reached into the wall compartment next to me for a fan. His eyes were on me, studying my reaction. "I understand," came out of my mouth again, quite against my will. Mercifully, the fan covered my discomfiture.

"I've met my betrothed only three times," he explained. "She is just fourteen. It is strictly a financial arrangement, her father's money for my family's blood."

"Under the circumstances, I wonder if it would be prudent for you to call on me socially. Your betrothed might object. I know I would."

"I am not married yet. It will be at least two or three years. The girl is nothing more than a child. She has no maturity. I can see nothing at all about her that is the least bit attractive or desirable."

"For your sake, I certainly hope you find some qualities in her to admire. Your father obviously needs a wealthy relative."

"Then you do understand."

"I suppose so."

"And I may call on you next Sunday? We can be
. . . friends?"

"Yes." I smiled, knowing full well we were more
than friends already. The other woman in his life,
child of wealth but not position, did not seem real. I
had never seen her. François conducted himself as
if she did not exist. It was difficult to take his betrothal seriously, and I allowed myself the luxury of
believing something important could grow out of our
evening by the fire, our journey across France and the
visits that were to come.

On the Sunday following our return to Nantes, Mass
was even more excruciating than usual. For one thing,
I had to face it on an empty stomach because it was
time I took communion. The Abbess told me so herself. The dry wafer at the rail was just enough to start
my stomach churning so noisily that Adele thanked
me later for drowning out the sermon. My nerves
were on edge. François said he would come to visit
that day. I tried to pretend that if he failed to appear
I would not be too disappointed, yet I could feel
anticipation tingling through me. I knew if he did not
come, my feelings, and most probably my heart, would
be deeply bruised.

The afternoon hung heavily in the stale air of my
little room as I waited, trying to read, but every few
seconds stealing glances out my window toward the
path from the main gate. There was a knock at the
door.

"Come in."

It was Adele. "Not here yet?" she asked. "I hope
he doesn't come. This matter of a betrothal, it's not
good at all!"

"You don't have to worry. We're just friends."

"Yes, of course," she taunted. "That's why you have
been sitting here for an hour watching the path."

"I have not. I felt like reading today."

"I don't believe that for a minute, but anyway you
can put your book away. Look!" Adele pointed out

the window. There was François walking briskly, with
the dark cape of his uniform swept back by the cold
February wind. Quickly, I went to the closet to get
my heavy cloak.

"Sweet Mother of God, Aimee! At least wait until
someone brings you word."

"You're right. I mustn't appear too eager. After all,
we're just good friends." Adele laughed and so did I.

"Have a good time," she said. "But remember what
he told you. If you fall in love with him, it will be
your undoing."

"My heavens, Adele. You sound so grim."

"I intend to. A man in his position usually wants
more than companionship when he comes calling.
Some people consider you very beautiful, you know.
A bit pale perhaps." She grabbed my cheeks and
pinched the redness into them. "There." She smiled
at me maternally. "We know this fellow doesn't have
marriage in mind, don't we? What does that leave?"

"Aren't you rushing things just a bit?" I grew irritated.

"Perhaps, but I've never seen you this way about
a man before. You keep telling me how much you
want to go back to Martinique as soon as it is safe
to travel. Well, if you want to make any kind of
match in the islands, you'll have to be a virgin when
you get there."

"I am a virgin, and I intend to stay one until the
day I marry."

"I know your intentions, Aimee," she said earnestly, then pointed toward the window. "It's his intentions that worry me. Have a lovely afternoon with
him, but keep a guard on your emotions." She left,
but almost before the door could close I heard another knock.

"You have a visitor, Mademoiselle de Rivery." The
message was delivered by one of the serving novices.

"Thank you. I'll be right down."

There were several guests in the Abbess's formal
reception room that Sunday. François sat on a deli-

cately ornamented chair next to a collection of porcelain saints near an archway leading to the dining room. When I saw him I realized how out of place he must have felt, entering this world dominated by women. There he was, in complete military regalia, awkwardly balanced on a tiny stick of furniture and surrounded by female celibates and their families in a place where the worship of God was conducted almost totally through feminine intermediaries.

"Captain de Marmont." I presented my hand.

When he stood to greet me, the scabbard of his sword knocked a likeness of Saint Genevieve off her shelf. The statue's head shattered as it hit the floor. "Oh damn!" he muttered and tried to pick up the pieces. I bent down to help him.

"Perhaps you'll venture into our den unarmed next time, captain." The voice of the Abbess, intolerant and biting, was worse than the sound of the breaking glass.

"I'm terribly sorry. Please allow me to replace it."

"I would never dream of stopping you," she smiled sarcastically.

"May I present Captain François de Marmont," I said, hoping she would leave us alone.

"We have met." She looked at him as if he were a toad while she spoke to me. "Perhaps you would like to take your young man for a walk in the garden."

"The weather is cruel," I protested.

"I would love to see the garden, mademoiselle. Let's go."

"You see," said the Abbess. "I know an outdoorsman when I see one, and so does Saint Genevieve. Have a nice walk." She returned to her other guests.

I took François' arm as we made our way past a dozen curious faces, each wearing the superior look of sacrifices sought and endured. "What a collection of gargoyles." François rubbed his forehead in disbelief when we were safely outside. "How can you stand living among them, and with that Abbess in command?"

"She does seem terrible when you aren't used to her," I agreed.

"And she's ugly. Did you see the look she gave me when I broke that doll? I'd sooner face a regiment of Hessians."

"But for a devout Christian, she doesn't simper around here looking for opportunities to martyr herself like so many do. That's the worst part of the church. It attracts weaklings who substitute submission for piety. They are forever searching for their own personal cross to bear."

"You're right about the Abbess. She's not one of them. To tell you the truth, Aimee, I believe I'm afraid of her."

"I am too, but I hope she never finds out. It would ruin all our games."

"What do you mean, games?"

"I think the Abbess actually enjoys Adele and me because we don't twitch and whimper every time she scowls. If she knew my heart almost stops whenever I see her coming, what would be the point of disobeying her?"

"I can see that you are very daring for a convent girl, and I won't be less so. If you can face that old gargoyle every day, I can face her on Sundays. But I will bring my sword, no matter what she says."

"Then the least I can do is not keep you waiting."

Our walk took us through the rose garden. All the bushes were wrapped carefully with brown sackcloth to protect them from the weather. As they swayed back and forth in the winter wind, they looked very much like shuffling files of penitents making their way to the chapel.

"See there." I pointed to my window in the student quarters. "Mine is on the second floor, the third window from the corner. I have a view of the main gate. When I see you, I'll come down and we'll meet in the garden."

"Then I won't have to see the Abbess at all."

"Oh, yes you will. There is quite a bit of etiquette

and ceremony around here. But you won't have to face her alone. That will help, won't it?"

"It certainly will. With you beside me, I could face a thousand gargoyles." François drew his sword with a flourish. "Take that!" A swathed rose bush felt his blade. "I'll save you, Aimee. Stand back, you devils, or I'll run you through!" He grabbed my hand and we raced off to the orchard beyond the chapel.

François and I endured the winter in such outdoor diversions. Each Sunday we presented our compliments to the Abbess, then spent the rest of the afternoon in the frozen garden or walking among the trees. With every visit my feelings for him grew stronger, and so did Adele's concern. Hardly a day passed that she did not caution me about François' commitments elsewhere. His betrothal allowed me no peace, yet my dearest friend kept the subject at the forefront of my mind. There were even occasions when she threatened to tell the Abbess the entire situation and thus end our assignations. As it was, François was welcomed as an acceptable suitor. Marie de La Fontelle could have enlightened the Abbess about his entanglements, but the two women rarely corresponded and so the Abbess remained ignorant of my indiscretion.

Marie intended to return to Nantes in the spring. Certainly then, when she was in residence, we could not keep our secret from her. She would terminate our Sundays even if she had to lock me in the bell tower to accomplish her ends. François and I realized we had only until her arrival, but long before it threatened, we knew we were in love. Constrained by François' situation, both of us silently vowed never to reveal our true feelings, and we never did, never until the month before Marie's return. It was April. From my window I saw François as the gatekeeper bid him welcome. We met in the garden near a budding jonquil bed.

"Hello, Aimee." He kissed my hand and I felt the warmth of his lips on my skin as he lingered there an instant longer than was proper. "You look beautiful."

"Thank you, François." I tried to appear gay as I spun around to show off my new ensemble. "Do you like it?" The gown was white satin with delicate green flowers printed on the fabric. There were bountiful petticoats underneath, a pleated bodice and a low neckline, made acceptable for convent attire by a fluffy white fichu draped around my neck and tucked down in front.

"I like it very much. The green matches your eyes."

"I'm going to wear it next month at Marie de La Fontelle's estate. There is to be a lawn party the day before the ball. Will you attend?"

"I think not." François' expression betrayed the same sadness I was striving to conceal. "The celebrations will outlast the weekend," he went on feebly, "and I must not be away from the cannon works for such an extended period."

"Yes," I responded. "It's just as well, though I'll miss you, especially on Sunday." I ached to let him know how I dreaded Marie's arrival, but I could not.

"You do look beautiful," he said tenderly. "The gown is magnificent."

"I wanted you to see it."

We went inside for our few moments with the Abbess and then slipped away to the orchard. Thoughtfully, Francois brought a bottle of wine with him. I borrowed a glass from the kitchen, and we shared it, just as we had on the night we met.

"Let's sit down and finish the wine," François said, indicating a shady spot under a flowering cherry tree. A gentle breeze pulled petals from the branches and made a soft down of blossoms for our couch.

"If I were at La Fontelle for the ball," he asked, "would you dance with me?"

"Every dance," I replied, trembling on the brink of a confession of my feelings.

I took a sip of wine and then offered it to him. He reached out but instead of taking it, wrapped his hand around mine and tipped the glass to his mouth. His touch frightened me. I knew I should pull away, but no power in heaven or hell could force me to it. He set the glass aside and kissed my fingers, my palm, my wrist.

"François," I whispered in feeble protest.

"I love you, Aimee." His eyes shone with an intensity that stirred my own emotions to dangerous heights.

"I love you, François." At last I had said it.

Still holding my hand he pulled me to his embrace. "François." I became frightened. "Do we dare?"

His answer was a kiss. His hand touched my cheek, my neck. He kissed me again. For an instant the thought entered my head that I should resist him, but it disappeared quickly in the heat of my passion, and I yielded to his arms as they enveloped me. Nothing in my life had prepared me for the ecstacy of his embrace. The excitement was so intense it made even the simple act of breathing a struggle. My cheeks burned, my heart pounded and the thrilling sensation of his lips against mine aroused longings in me I understood only too well. The pressure of his body forced me down. Then his weight slid over me. Even through the dense shield afforded by my petticoats, I could feel his body pressing against my femininity. Terrified, I recognized my own desire, pushed him away and sat up.

"Darling," he whispered breathlessly. "I love you so. Please forgive me."

"This is so new to me," I sighed.

"I know." He took my hand. "And to me as well."

"What shall we do?"

"We shall get married." His statement was totally unexpected.

"What of your betrothal? Your father?"

"It no longer matters. Nothing matters except that I love you. Will you marry me?"

"Yes, François." His arms were around me again, pulling me to him. The same feeling began in my thighs, surging upward. "Stop! Please, François. Stop! Not like this." He released me.

There was a tense silence. Then he said, "Let's walk a while." He helped me up. "I'll write to my father tonight. By next week he can have me out of that ridiculous contract in Paris. Then we will wait a respectable interval and announce our engagement. I don't suppose there is any chance you are wealthy? It would make everything so much easier."

"Sorry, darling. I have some land in the Antilles, but with my income you could keep little more than a carriage and horses in the capital."

"Then Father will have to marry the girl himself. I have other plans." He kissed my hand.

Smoothing the skirts of my gown, I turned away from him. "How I regret showing off my ensemble to you like this. I never suspected you might actually come to La Fontelle for the ball, but now you must be there."

"And so I shall be, my darling." He placed my arm on his. "Now walk me to the gate. I must take my leave if I am to catch the ferry to the cannon works."

When I told Adele of François' proposal, she was delighted. At last she stopped pestering me about my inperiled virtue. Both of us agreed to keep the information from the Abbess until François was actually free of the Parisian, but upon Marie's arrival, I told her everything. She was less than pleased because of François' financial situation, but she recognized my happiness and acquiesced.

In the weeks that followed our expressions of love, François visited me as always, and each time our desires became stronger. We alluded frequently to the secret delights we would enjoy as husband and wife. Whenever he touched me, even in the most formal manner, I could feel my passion rise.

"Next weekend I will see you at La Fontelle," he said, as I walked him to the gate on the Sunday before the ball.

"The parties begin on Friday. Will you be there?"

"Yes, I have already made arrangements at the cannon works to be free for the entire weekend. You will be staying at the château, won't you?" he asked.

"Yes, Adele and I each have a room."

"And I will be in the guest house." He smiled and I realized what he was thinking. "You may hear a knock at your window in the dead of night, but don't be frightened. Just let me in."

"Do you think it wise?" I asked, knowing I should tell him to stay away. "You will need a ladder or something."

"Leave it to me." He kissed my hand. "Until Friday night."

Chapter 4

Adele and I arrived at Marie de La Fontelle's château on the banks of the Loire near Nantes early on the following Friday afternoon. The long tree-lined lane leading to the mansion was one continuous celebration of spring. Flowers bloomed and nodded to one another, exchanging compliments on the magnificent colors they had chosen. A batallion of gardeners were rolling the lawns and completing the last transplant of tulips near the central fountain in front of the house. At the edge of the wood in the distance, a family of deer grazed peacefully, enjoying new shoots of grass and the warm spring air. The trees were just beyond the bud with tender leaves, like a verdant down, on their branches. Behind the château the river shimmered like a diamond with a thousand facets. The setting was beautiful. Life was beautiful. I was loved and I loved in return. "Sweet Mother of God," I whispered. "Thank you."

Marie was occupied with arrangements for the

weekend when we entered the château. She greeted us quickly and sent us off to our rooms.

"I'll have a bath now," I said to the maid who was waiting in the hall. In my room freshly cut lilacs filled the air with their fragrance. Light blue floral wallpaper and yellow curtains on the east windows overlooking the fountain made the place fresh and clean as the season. "Have the tub put near the window," I told the maid as she unpacked for me.

When my bath was ready, I locked the door and slipped off my clothes.

François may be here tonight in this very room, I thought.

At the convent there are only a few small mirrors in the student quarters, mostly hand mirrors because the sisters do not use them, and we girls must bring our own. But in my room at the château, long mirrors decorated the doors of the armoire. A warm breeze from the south windows tingled on my bare skin and gave me the sensation of being outdoors. I looked at my reflection and wondered if François would find me beautiful.

There was a knock at the door. It startled me and I blushed as if someone had found me out in some act of debasement.

"Who is it?"

"Adele." She turned the knob. "Why is the door locked?"

"I'm going to take a bath."

"Are you in the tub yet?"

"No."

"Then let me in." I pulled on my calico bath dress and opened the door.

"You know you don't have to wear a dress to take a bath here. Only at the convent," she said as she walked in.

"Yes, but I'm so used to it now. It keeps me from catching a chill."

"If you are worried about that, get the tub out of the draft." She stepped to the windows and pulled them shut. "It's only May, too early for bathing at all, in my opinion. I was going to ask you to go riding with me, but I don't suppose you will want to go outside after being in the tub."

"No, I think I'll spend some time getting ready for the dinner party tonight. François is coming."

"Yes, I know," she said, with a hint of amusement in her voice. After his proposal, she began speaking of him in a kindly fashion. "You really love the fellow, don't you, Aimee?"

"Yes. I think of nothing but him. What is your opinion of an autumn wedding?"

"It will be lovely, but what does Marie think?"

"She is far from delighted. A good match means a wealthy one to her, but she likes François and she knows we are in love. She won't try to change my mind."

"We both know you well enough to realize that would be impossible. You are as stubborn as she is."

"In this case you're right. Now before my bath water gets cold, I'm getting in the tub. Out of here, if you please."

"Very well, I'm leaving." Adele went to the door. "But take off that bath gown. The Abbess will never know."

"Enjoy your ride," I called to her as she walked toward the stairs. Once the door was locked, I opened the windows again and went back to the tub. Thinking of François and the possibility that he might actually find his way to my room that night made me feel so audacious that I did as Adele suggested—slipped off my gown, let it fall to the floor still dry, then stepped into the metal tub and lowered myself into the warm water. The sensation was exquisite.

At the dinner hour that evening, François sat across the long banquet table from me. Forty other guests were in attendance. The occasion was very festive with a good deal of loud talk and merrymaking. But for the two of us there was no one else in the room.

"What did you send me in that wooden chest?" I asked, referring to the box delivered to my room early in the evening.

"You read the note, didn't you?" He smiled and raised an eyebrow in his special way that should have sent me straight to confession.

"It said something about books. You sent me books?"

"That's right. There are books inside. I know what a scholar you are. It's the perfect gift. Don't you agree?"

I felt his foot touch mine under the table, and I smiled. "That may be, but it isn't what I expected. Besides, the thing is locked."

He reached into his waistcoat pocket. "Here is the key. I didn't want you opening it in front of anyone."

"What kind of books are they that no one else may see?"

"There's something else too." His foot slid up along my leg and I opened my fan to cover a blush.

"François, stop it." He didn't stop. "What else is inside?"

"Just take the key and find out."

After dinner, when all the ladies escaped the dining room, I went upstairs and unlocked the chest. There were books, quite an assortment of badly worn leather volumes lined up on the first shelf, all of them about cannon and gun-powder.

"What on earth will I do with these?" I asked aloud. When they were all stacked next to me on the floor, I lifted up the inner shelf. Seeing what François had sequestered beneath the volumes made me laugh with delight. The books were an elaborate deception to cover a coiled rope ladder in the bottom of the chest.

My bed was not turned down, and I knew the maid would be coming soon, so I returned everything to the chest and fastened the lock again. Then I went downstairs. François was waiting for me in the antechamber.

"Did you find it?" He was almost giddy with excitement.

"Yes. How clever you are. I never suspected a thing."

"Just so no one else does." He leaned closer to me. "Do you think it is too early for you to retire, darling?"

"The maid hasn't come yet. Let's stay here a while. We'll have a brandy and talk."

"What are you two plotting?" Marie's voice was full of music as she came out of the salon. She was very happy. Her dinner party was a success, and her house was full of people she enjoyed. "You aren't planning to run off together, I hope."

François and I looked at each other knowingly, then broke into laughter. "No, Marie. We aren't running anywhere," I said.

"Then go in and join the party." She waved her arm toward the salon, but a handsome young man took her hand and led her off toward the garden.

"I am a bit tired, Marie," I called after her. "I think I'll go upstairs soon."

"Get a good rest, dear. You have been studying far too much." Her voice tapered off as she turned a corner in the hallway. There was laughter and I knew she wouldn't miss me when I left.

François kissed my hand after a half hour had passed. "Good night, darling. Listen for a stone at your window."

"Mine is the corner room, remember. But don't come to the windows overlooking the fountain. Call at the ones around the side of the house. No one will see you there."

"I'll be careful." He smiled assuringly. "Good night, Aimee."

I ran up the stairs to my room, breathless with excitement when I got there. Then, with the door safely locked, I emptied the chest and unrolled the rope ladder. Next, I took off my wig, undressed and put on my spring nightgown. It was of pink cotton, very innocent, with a high neckline and a white embroidered bodice that tied in a broad bow in back. I let down my hair, brushed and perfumed it, tied it with a ribbon and I was ready. Then came the waiting.

I tried to read, but every noise from the party downstairs, every creak of the old house and every whisper of a breeze had me on my feet and over to the south windows to see if François was below. Then, just as a carriage rolled around the circle to the front door, summoned by guests departing early, I thought I heard a pebble on the glass. Looking out I saw François' eager smile. I secured the ladder to the stout window mullion and threw the rope down to him.

When he had reached the top, he pulled the strap of a leather pouch off his shoulder and handed it to me. "Here, take this before I drop it."

Raising himself from the top of the rope into the room was no easy task. François could not lift his foot to the height of the sill. Finally, in frustration, he grabbed the ledge and rolled inside head first. His leg caught the edge of a small console. It tipped over, and the vase of flowers resting upon it crashed to the floor. We both froze. The dreadful sound of shattering glass would surely bring footsteps in the hallway and someone to see if I were alright.

While we waited, expecting the worst, I heard the sound of galloping hooves as they approached the château, and I silently crossed the room to look down on the drive. There, illuminated by the lantern light of the entrance, a lone horseman dismounted his hard-driven bay and drew what looked like a dispatch case from his saddle pouch. Then he hurried inside.

"Do you think we're safe, darling?" François asked in a whisper.

"Yes." I turned to him as he stepped clear of the broken glass.

He took me in his arms. "I know I shouldn't have come. If we are found out it will be your ruin."

"It will be your life," I said, only half teasing. "Marie might well have you killed."

"I suppose so," he responded gravely.

"But never mind. You're here now."

"Yes, and I could use a drink."

"Oh, there isn't a thing," I confessed.

"Yes there is." He picked up the leather pouch I had dropped to the floor when he arrived. "Would you care for a brandy, darling?" He pulled out a bottle of Marie's best stock and a large linen napkin cushioning a crystal goblet.

"My nerves could certainly use it," I said. "Here, let's sit down." I led him to a satin loveseat across the room from my bed. When he was comfortable, with his feet up and the glass in his hand, I sat down next to him and nestled against his chest. For a time we sipped the brandy, saying nothing, simply enjoying its warmth and the anticipation of our stolen night together.

"I'm sorry about the vase, Aimee," François said as he took my hand and kissed it gently, first each finger, then the palm.

"It isn't important, darling," I responded, delighted with his touch. "The noise frightened me, but no one downstairs seemed to hear. Fortunately, your timing corresponded closely with the arrival of a messenger that must have distracted everyone. Probably word from Paris to one of the guests. Many of Marie's friends speculate on the Bourse. They gain or lose fortunes in a day. I imagine there's a good deal of excitement downstairs right now, depending on the news from the capital."

"Either way, that courier was good news for us, occupying everyone downstairs as he did," François said with an embarrassed smile. "I had no idea how difficult it would be to get off that rope." He paused, then sat bolt upright. "Good God! The rope!" It was still there, tied securely to the frame separating the two south windows. "We might as well hire a crier." He slid off the loveseat to his feet. "I'll get it."

After he pulled the rope inside, he shoved it under the bed. "There. Now we are safe." He turned to me and smiled. "Come here, darling. Let me have a look at you in your pretty nightgown."

It's beginning, I thought as I walked toward him, my heart pounding in my breast.

"You are so beautiful, Aimee." He took me in his arms and kissed me. It was a different kind of kiss, not like the ones in the orchard, stolen quickly when no one was around. This started softly, tenderly, but then our feelings grew. François held me closer, tighter, and I yielded to his every move.

"Oh, François."

He must have thought my sigh a protest for he released me: "Are you all right?" he asked anxiously.

"Yes."

"I love you, Aimee." He kissed me again and stroked my neck. "May I?" He pulled at the ribbons on my gown.

"Perhaps I should." I began to untie them. He took off his coat and waistcoat, then his shirt. At first, I was almost embarrassed to look. I had not seen a man naked to the waist since my childhood when half-dressed slaves walked to the cane fields along the road near our house.

I could see that François was strong. The muscles of his arms were long and smooth. It pleased me to look at them, but I was startled by a thick mat of black hair over his chest. The Abbess often said men were beasts, but I never dreamed she referred to a physical resemblance. I found this to be very attractive, even compelling. I wanted to touch him, feel his chest against me.

"Is there anything wrong, darling?" he asked in a tender voice.

"Oh no, François, but I never . . ."

"I know." He took my face in his hands, kissed my cheeks, then undid the back of my gown. Slowly he slipped it off my shoulders and eased it down until I felt it brush against my legs and fall to the floor. His hands glided over me, thrilling me with every caress. My emotions soared.

Neither of us spoke a word, but I felt his arms around me as he carried me to bed. He lay me down and pulled up the counterpane. Then he took off the rest of his clothes and slipped under the cover himself.

"I love you, Aimee," he whispered. I trembled as I lifted my arms to embrace him. Every second's passing increased my exhilaration as I felt the soft touch of his hand along my hip and down over my thighs.

Suddenly we heard a knock at the door. "Aimee, Aimee, dear. Are you asleep?" It was Marie. Her voice conveyed concern but no hint of agitation. She did not suspect François' presence.

"Don't say anything," François whispered. "Maybe she will go away." The panic that gripped me at that moment so contracted my chest that I doubt I could have spoken to save my life. François' breath on my hair came in shallow spurts. He was frightened too.

"Wake up, Aimee. I have to talk to you." She knocked again, louder this time. Only the dead could have slept through it. The doorknob turned against the lock.

"Get dressed and get out of here," I whispered. "She isn't going away."

The bed creaked as François got up. He grabbed his britches, but one of his shoes was caught up in them and it fell to the floor causing more racket than if it had come from a draft horse.

"Aimee, why is the door locked? Open it at once and let me in." Marie sounded irritated.

"I'll be right there. Let me put on a robe," I called. Then softly, "Hand me my nightgown, François."

"Who are you talking to in there? Is someone in there with you? By God, I'll have his head!" I heard her footsteps trail off.

"Hurry, François! You have to get out of here!"

He pulled his britches on. "Where did I put the rope?"

"It's under the bed." I fell to my knees and tried to pull it out, but he pushed me aside and got it himself. There were more noises in the hall.

"Break it down." It was Marie's voice again, followed by the muffled thunder of shoulders crashing against the hardwood door. François was still struggling to tie up the rope when splinters around the lock crackled and the door flew open.

"Seize him!" Marie ordered. Four of her husky servants lunged at François. There was no point in attempting to flee now. He submitted without a struggle. It made no difference to them, however. While two men held him defenseless, the others began to pound him with their closed fists.

"Stop it!" I screamed and threw myself upon them. "Make them stop, Marie!"

"That's enough," she said harshly. "Leave us alone."

As quickly as the men had come, they disappeared through the broken door. François was still standing in spite of their attack, but he was stunned and bleeding from a cut above his eye.

"Marie, how could you let them do such a thing?" I demanded as I helped François to my rumpled bed where he could sit down. "François, are you all right?"

He had no time to answer. Marie spoke out. "He's a lot better than he's going to be. I'll have him drawn and quartered for this.

"Nothing happened," I said disgustedly. "You interrupted us before there was time."

"Are you sure?" Marie was still standing in front of the door with her hands on her hips as though she were defending her castle keep, but her voice softened at the news.

"What kind of question is that?" I snapped. "Am I sure? Don't you think I would have noticed?"

"You'll not use that tone of voice with me, young lady."

"What will you do? Call your henchmen and have them beat me as well?"

"You had better hear me out before you say anything more," she cautioned. "This man was going to take advantage of you."

"We are going to be married, Marie. That makes it a bit different, don't you think?"

"If that were true, the fellow would still be a scoundrel for seducing you like this, but it isn't, is it, monsieur? No, this is rape, or would have been, had I not come up here when I did."

"What do you mean, we aren't going to be married?" I demanded.

She turned to François. "Perhaps you should ask Captain de Marmont." Her eyes narrowed as she looked at him. "But before you answer, you disgusting blackguard, you should know that I wrote your father when Aimee told me of your gallant proposal. A message from him just arrived."

She held a letter in her hand. "I want you to hear just part of it."

Madame, I am well aware that my son has been conducting an indiscreet flirtation with your ward, Mlle. de Rivery. I have written to him about it several times, and he assures me it will not interfere with his marriage plans. Just this week I received confirmation from him that he will be present in Paris for a reception to be held at the estate of his future parents-in-law on the second weekend in June. Sometimes young men like François are swept up by their own manhood and make inconvenient vows, but he is much too responsible to throw away his entire future and that of his family for the hand of a penniless island girl.

I am sending you this letter by the fastest possible post in order to spare Mlle. de Rivery what pain and embarrassment I can. Please encourage her to break with François at once. Nothing good can come of their liaison.

I was stunned by what I heard and waited for François to give some explanation, but he said nothing. "François, you told me your father knew we were going to be married. He does know, doesn't he? Doesn't he?"

"No, not yet." François sat on the edge of the bed where we had almost consummated his deception. His head hung down with the weight of his guilt. "I didn't have the nerve to tell him. His health is not the best. I wanted to wait until the right time presented itself."

"After you've married the child in Paris, I suppose." My voice was sharp to cover my humiliation.

"I planned to avoid that reception somehow," he offered feebly. "And I swear to you, Aimee—"

"Make him leave, Marie." I turned away from him to hide my pain.

"Aimee, please let me explain." His voice was desperate. "I love you. Believe me, I love you."

"Marie, make him go!"

"Get out of here," she bellowed. "And use the back stairs. I know you have no regard for Aimee or her reputation, but if you show yourself to my guests as you are, I'll have you horsewhipped."

"Aimee, please." He grabbed my hand, but I pulled away from him and turned my back. "I'll come to the convent. You have to let me talk to you."

"Just go, François," I said defeatedly. "Go and never come back."

Ten months passed after that night, ten months of anguish as I tried to forget what had happened. But François would not let me forget. I refused to see him, but there were his letters. Whenever we went to the opera, he appeared at the door of our box. When we traveled to Paris, he hired a horse and dogged our path. I spurned his every effort, but he kept on.

While Adele and I stood on the dock together the day our ship set sail, I said, "After today, I'll be rid of François de Marmont for good," but the thought chilled me to the quick. I still loved him in spite of everything, yet pride prevented my admitting it, even to myself. Each time I sent him away my heart ached. Only the slenderest strand of self-control kept me from clasping him to me and forgiving all. Now was the last test. If I succumbed, my life was ruined. With him lay the short but pampered existence of a favorite concubine, with an apartment in Paris, a place near him in Nantes, gifts and affection until I had squandered my youth. Then he would desert me and I would face the rest of my life a fallen woman completely alone. But when I saw him hurrying along the pier, I wondered what my life would be like if I tried to live it without him.

"How did he find out we were leaving?" I wondered aloud.

"I told him," Adele confessed.

"You! You never even liked him! How could you have done such a thing?"

"You still love him, and he loves you."

"I don't love him." My face flushed with the lie.

"I know you do, and you'll waste both your lives if you live apart. He'll work things out with his father. Just give him time."

"Then you have been the one all along, keeping him informed of our travel plans, letting him know when we would be at the theater." I glared at her as if she were a traitor.

"You needn't turn your emerald eyes on me like that. I did it for your own good. Now let François talk to you. I'll go to the ship." She walked away quickly, with a determination in her step I recognized and chose not to counter.

"Aimee," I felt a hand on my arm. François spun me around. "I'm so glad I happened to see you."

"Your confederate has confessed, monsieur. Don't pretend this is a chance meeting."

"That doesn't matter now. Marry me. Marry me, Aimee. I beg you."

I was speechless. In all the past ten months he had never suggested that he was free. If he had told his father about me, if he had quit the ridiculous engagement in Paris, then I could let down my guard. I ached to fall into his arms and weep.

But then I remembered Marie. She warned me that a man would say anything to have his way. The only promise a woman could trust was given in front of a priest.

"Your father, have you told him that we would wed?"

François did not answer at once, but he kissed my gloved hand so tenderly I almost swooned. "Father does not know yet. But I promise I will tell him." If he had not been so timid about it, if he had not said "promise" I might have had faith in his word. But it was another deception. I felt used and degraded as if he thought I had no more sense than a naïve milk-maid.

"You rely too heavily on promises. I cannot believe you."

"What can I do? I'll do anything to keep you in France."

"You cannot keep me in France now."

"I won't live without you. Surely after all these months you know at least that much about me."

"Then tell your father, and tell the little girl who waits for you in Paris. When you are at liberty to ask for my hand, I'll be waiting to offer it."

"Do you swear you will wait?" His hands held my arms so tightly they hurt.

"I swear I'll wait . . . for six months. No more."

"Thank the Lord." He swept me up in his arms and spun me around. "You won't have to wait that long. As soon as I have talked to Father, I'll come to the convent to get you."

"François, I told you I'd wait, but not immured in that nunnery like a moldering corpse."

"Where will you be then? I'll fly to your side."

"Surely you have noticed we are at the wharves," I said bitterly. "There is a ship waiting."

"But you aren't going to leave now after all we've said."

"Nothing has changed as far as I am concerned. You have asked me to marry you before. Nothing came of it. Perhaps it will be the same again. Six months will tell. If your proposal is serious, you'll find me in Martinique. Now, good-bye."

I walked toward the gangplank, refusing to look back no matter how much I regretted what I was doing. Still, he had made a fool of me once. I could not submit to his wiles again. It was a desperate gamble, and every step I took made me more fearful that I had gone too far.

Chapter 5

A nasty wind whipped about me as I climbed the
gangplank of *Belle Gloire*. Against it my heavy winter
clothes seemed no protection. The terrible cold together with my anguish over leaving François made
my misery complete. Yet there was one more facet to
my desolation. Once I was on board, I hurried to join
Adele and go below, but as I approached her, I overheard M. Dupierre, the officer we had encountered
earlier, as he spoke to her. Their exchange filled me
with guilt.

"You must forgive me, mademoiselle," Dupierre
said. "The law requires that I see your identity paper
and notify the authorities of your departure." The
young fellow cringed visibly when he made the request, fearing that an insult to one of La Fontelle's
friends could jeopardize what future he had with that
great lady on his return from the islands.

"I have it," Adele replied unperturbed. "You will
see by the documents that I am a free Negress, a fact
which permits me to travel without encumbrance any-

where I choose." She presented her papers, proof she was subject to no laws applicable to French colonial slaves.

Dupierre took it from her, glanced over it nervously, hardly seeing it at all, then handed it back as if it were plague-ridden. "The law is satisfied. I have seen it. You should have no difficulties concerning your status during the voyage, but we will be carrying slaves, and someone may mistakenly think—"

"I trust you will look after my interests in that regard," she interrupted him.

"Rest assured, mademoiselle. You may call on me at any time."

Just as she turned away from the officer, a jailer from the Nantes prison came aboard. Behind him filed a dozen or more Negroes, all of them well dressed and refined. Anyone who had ever been in the islands would know them to be domestic servants, personal maids and valets. They had traveled to France with their masters, but because they were slaves they could not enter the country and had been imprisoned temporarily until return passage to Martinique could be booked for them.

This discourteous reception was the result of a law passed the year after Adele and I arrived. Slavery was illegal in France. The institution was unnecessary in a country where so many idle people milled about the city streets and languished in the countryside without work. But the colonies were a different matter. Not enough French hands could be found to tend the fields and care for the households of the island nobility. In Martinique, slavery was necessary, so it was accepted. This presented a real dilemma to any wealthy colonial landholder who wished to visit his ancestral homeland. Of course, he would bring servants with him when he traveled, but as soon as he reached French soil, his slaves became free. So many Negroes bolted at the first opportunity that certain of the King's ministers feared for the purity of the French race. The total number of Negroes scattered through all of France at the time was less than a thousand, hardly an invasion of serious proportions. Still, there were government officials who viewed their presence as a threat, so a law was passed. All free Negroes had to register with the authorities and carry identity papers. These people could not marry or mix their blood with whites. Any slave traveling with his master to France could not accompany him ashore, but had to remain under guard at the port of entry and return to the place from which he had come at the earliest possible time.

It was because of the law that these miserable wretches coming aboard *Belle Gloire* had to endure another winter passage with little time to recover from their first. They were quartered in the bowels of the ship in one small cabin. I learned later that there was absolutely no regard given the four unhappy souls in the group who were women. They were afforded no privacy during their time below deck, and lived in confinement with all the others, having to dress, sleep, eat and attend to those physical requirements of daily life that are best accomplished without witnesses.

Being free, Adele was spared such humiliations. In France her beauty and intellect won respect and admiration among the nobility. Although marriage to one of them was forbidden, several suitors were willing to swear to Negro ancestry in order to be eligible for her hand. But now she was returning to the islands, solely on my account. She would find no acceptance in noble society there. People of her own race, uneducated as they were, could provide no companionship for someone of her culture and abilities. Except for me, she would be totally alone.

My eyes followed the last of the slaves as he walked along. His expression mirrored the desperation and fear in his soul as he looked down into the pit where he was to live. Adele was completely different from those slaves, but when she stepped off the ship in Martinique the people there would see her only as another Negress, hardly a human being at all.

"It isn't too late, you know," I said to her as I took

her arm. "You have no reason to go back to the islands."

She seemed startled to see me. "Nothing has changed?" she asked.

"No, nothing. But please reconsider. It will be terrible for you in the islands."

"If it is, I'll come back to France, but I'll see you settled first, and I'll see the old house and Aunt Louise and Uncle Claude. We can ride along the beach together as we used to do, and I'll be warm." She shivered and grabbed her bonnet when a strong gust from the north tried to rip it away. "This climate is dreadful."

"But Adele," I protested. "You are certain?"

"I'm freezing out here. Let's go below."

Our quarters were dark and damp. An eager cabin boy hurried to remedy the situation by lighting an oil lamp which hung from the low ceiling. He was another of the crew on his first voyage, but for a novice he was competent. In no time at all he had glowing coals in the small brazier suspended from a metal post on the wall near the door. The design of the little stove, the boy explained, allowed it to swing freely with the movements of the ship without spilling hot embers onto the wooden floors. It was a clever gadget and put out copious amounts of heat for its size. We could take off our heavy capes and be comfortable, but the dampness and musty smell of the place never left.

All went well until the ship quit the protection of the Loire and stood face to face with the winter Atlantic. We gave up our attempts to unpack and took to the single bunk the two of us had to share. It was either that or crash about the cabin, for the vessel began to shudder and jump violently.

Then the sickness began. A penetrating odor seeped from the oil lamp. There was no vent for the brazier and its smoke began to accumulate, nowhere quite so densely as around my nose and mouth. To make matters worse, both of the diabolical devices swung back and forth in unison. My eyes could not find a single place to rest where I would not see those nauseating movements, and if I closed my eyes completely, the contents of my stomach automatically rose to my throat.

"Lie flat for a while, Aimee," Adele counseled. "This discomfort will pass." She felt fine, of course, a fact I quickly grew to resent.

But Adele was mistaken. As the hours went by I became sicker, and I found no consolation in observing that she too had begun to suffer. There was a small receptacle for the products of our misery, but no one ever came to empty it because the cabin boy himself was much sicker than either of us. Together we tried to take it on deck and rid ourselves of its stench, but the ship took one of its violent lurches before we reached our door, and the contents of our chamber pot spilled over the floor. The vileness of that little accident occasioned our filling the receptacle again, and then we faced the same situation as we had before—a full pot and nowhere to put it. By that point both of us were so wretched from our illness and the putrid atmosphere of the cabin that all we could do was go to bed and pray for calmer seas.

Calmer seas did not meet us. Instead, a fierce late winter storm wracked the already treacherous Bay of Biscay, throwing the ocean into continuous tumult for two days and two nights. We should have expected such weather. The entire year had been one storm after another. Many coastline villages and towns were in ruins as wind-lathered tides broke over them. So terrible was the suffering that King Louis himself supplied three million in relief funds, an act of generosity which undoubtedly created a good deal of suffering around Versailles when his fine Austrian queen discovered her husband had been giving money away to people who were not her court favorites.

Throughout the storm, Adele and I heard strange rumblings below us in the ship's hold, as if the old vessel's innards were as afflicted as our own. Later we found out their cause, and the blame can be heaped on the heads of the English. After their unfortunate encounter with the Americans at the Battle of Saratoga, when the rebels were victors at last, France cast her lot with the colonists, and England blockaded our ports. Few French ships lifted anchor in the years that followed. Men of the sea either died trying to run the blockades or emigrated to sail under neutral flags. After the war, when the seas opened to us again, there was a dearth of qualified seamen, but an abundance of peasants looking for any kind of work. Such farmers and herdsmen made up the crew of *Belle Gloire*.

It was from haylofts and root cellars that they gained their experience in stowing goods. Believe me, I do not mean to speak ill of those fine men who earn their livelihood from the land. But I cannot think of a time when I have seen a root cellar groan over on its side and then swing back again as does the tossing belly of a ship. The country bumpkins who loaded *Belle Gloire* knew nothing about how to pack a vessel for ocean travel. No casks were secured. No ropes bound the bales and boxes. When the Atlantic had its merry way with us, the cargo roamed around the hold with the freedom of fish in the sea, but with very unfortunate results.

"Aimee, wake up!" I felt Adele's hands on my shoulders. "Wake up!"

"What is it?" I groaned, without opening my eyes.

"We have to get out of here!" she shouted as she pulled at me. "Help me undo the straps on the bed." We had tied ourselves down to keep from falling out.

"Let me sleep, Adele."

"Aimee, wake up!" she demanded. "We are sinking. Look about, will you?"

Her words roused me only slightly. When she finished untying us, I lifted up on an elbow to see what it was that so concerned her, and my eyes met my travel trunk as it floated next to the bunk. "Sweet Mother of God! We'll drown!"

An instant later we both scrambled out of bed and

into the cold sea water. Although it did not reach my knees, the clothes I had slept in, petticoats and all, acted as a wick and soaked me to the waist in no time. Within seconds my legs ached as the cold penetrated to my very bones. "Are we going to die, do you think?"

Adele tried to cover her fears with a lighthearted tone. "I believe so," she said casually. "But let's not dwell on unpleasant prospects. We might have a chance if we can get to the deck. Perhaps longboats." She struggled to open the cabin door while I just stood watching her, feeling myself turn to ice.

"Help me, Aimee," she snapped.

I made my way to her side. The water behind the door worked against our efforts.

"If it's much deeper out there, we may drown when the door opens." I tried to reason, but by now I was near panic.

"Then we'll drown, but if we don't open the door, what do you suppose will happen to us?"

Even in my frenzied state of mind I could see she had a point, and I redoubled my efforts. With that the door began to yield. As it moved, water rushed in, but still it was not yet waist high. We knew we would get out.

When the water levels were equal, the door opened easily and we half pulled, half swam our way to the companionway and up the stairs. On deck we found a cold but beautifully clear morning, calm seas and a pack of unruly sailors gathered around their captain near the bow. As Adele and I inched toward them on the icy and badly listing deck, we could see in the distance a single longboat with about a half dozen men working the oars. The fellows on deck seemed to have no interest in saving their ship, but divided their time equally between two apparently useless activities—screaming profanities at the longboat and demanding some sort of violent action toward it from their commander. The presence of two ladies in their midst did nothing to diminish their tempers. They kept right on bellowing their foul oaths without even a protest from the once chivalrous officer Dupierre who raised his voice with the rest.

The air was frigid. My clothes were soaked. I was freezing and terribly afraid, but the danger cleared my head in no time and made me forget my illness.

"Captain!" I called out in what I thought was a strong voice. He ignored me, bombarded as he was with demands of a more pressing nature. "Captain!" I shouted. Still no response.

Adele, trembling with cold, tapped a sailor on the shoulder. "May I pass?" She wished to move closer to the captain to get his attention.

The seaman looked around at her. "Ah, so you got out. Good for you, girlie."

"Yes I did," she responded indignantly. "No thanks to you. We should have been notified when the ship began to sink."

"The storm kept us hopping, dearie. A crate of iron rods stove in the hull. Even the paying passengers had to save themselves. You are the only slave what didn't drown."

"You mean you didn't let them out."

"Didn't think of it at the time. None of us did. Lost some livestock in the hold as well." Adele's hands went to her mouth in shock as she heard that so many men and women had died during the night. The sailor seemed unconcerned.

"Have you no feeling for those poor souls?" she demanded.

"They was just slaves," he replied. "And besides, we're all going down. Them bastards out there took the only longboat what wasn't busted up in the storm."

Shortly, two sailors took out muskets and began firing on the longboat, but those escaping were too far away to fear the shots. They paid them no heed, but just kept on working their oars, crawling over the surface of the sea like a great wooden spider.

After a while the men on board *Belle Gloire* lost interest in the disappearing longboat and turned to the fact that we were all in imminent danger of drowning.

That provided an opportunity for us to gain the captain's ear.

Adele spoke up. "Captain, a moment please."

He turned from his vigil at the bow, a tired man of about forty years with a heavy lineless face and frightened eyes. "My God!" he exclaimed. "I forgot about you women."

"Yes, well, we managed to get out of our cabin," she said.

The poor man looked embarrassed as he confronted us. "I am terribly sorry, ladies. All is lost."

"Is there nothing we can do?" I asked. "Build a raft from pieces of wood, something like that?"

"Nothing that would keep our carcasses out of the sea, I'm afraid. It would be good enough if this were the heat of the summer, but any length of time in the water now and you'll freeze to death."

"And there are no boats?" Adele sounded incredulous.

"Gone," the captain shook his head. "All of them ripped away in the storm. All save that one out there. If I could get my hands on those cowardly blackguards, I'd tear them apart and feed them to the sharks." He looked back out to sea and cursed helplessly into the wind. We left him alone.

The ship carried no sail that morning, the masts being casualties of the storm. Because we lay dead in the water, every swell even on a calm sea rolled us about. The ship's timbers groaned ominously, and the deck listed more and more as loose cargo shifted below and we continued to sink. There were six other passengers, all men, and the crew sharing the same doom. Several wept. From time to time someone knelt in prayer. The captain simply went on cursing.

I turned to Adele. She was shivering. So was I. "This is my fault. If we had only remained in France."

She put her arms around me and I rested my head on her shoulder. "No it isn't, Aimee."

We stood embracing each other for a long time. The ship kept sliding lower in the water and the list

grew worse, forcing the opposing side higher into
the air. How I wanted to blame François for what was
happening, yet I could not. Weakness was a part of
his nature. It was I who failed to recognize that fact
in time. He had been straightforward in the beginning. He told me about his betrothal. I chose to ignore
it. I allowed him to call at the Convent. I compro-
mised myself. Then, when his lack of character was
revealed in such a way that I could not deny it, I
chose flight, entrusting my life and Adele's to a vessel
unfit for the open sea. Undeniably, I hated François
at that moment, but the responsibility for my desperate
situation rested squarely on my own head. *Mother of
God! Forgive me for bringing Adele down with my
folly!*

"A ship! We are saved!" A hysterical voice interrupted my silent confession. "Bring the muskets here!
Signal them, for the love of Jesus!" Dupierre cried.
Clearly a man who knew his own interests, Dupierre
had climbed to the uppermost part of the listing deck
in the hope thereby of extending his life for as long
as possible. While he perched up there, he scanned
the horizon praying and hoping for a reason to hope.
Suddenly, he glimpsed the form of a sail. If we could
draw their lookout's eye, indeed we might be saved.

"Wait there you!" shouted a rotund merchant, once
jolly and overbearing, now reduced to sniveling more
over his lost riches than his lost life. "They could be
pirates." He clutched at the buckle of his moneybelt,
which protruded like a tumor on the dome of his belly.
"We'll be robbed!"

Sarcastic laughter came from one of the sailors, the
same one who had spoken so rudely to Adele. "We'll
be robbed!" the sailor mimicked. "If they be pirates,
we won't notice their stealin'. We'll all be missin' our
heads and other vitals before they take your gold.
And the ladies there." He lifted his gnarled hand to
point at us. Then he said no more. Every man on the
slanting deck turned his eyes in our direction. Each

knew his fate if the far-off ship carried pirates, and each knew a woman could expect much worse.

Recognizing the danger, no one made a move to signal. Fear of the unknown paralyzed them. Not one had ever seen a pirate before, but there were stories, terrible stories. Dupierre turned back toward the sea and watched the other ship, but he said nothing more. The captain gave no order. Even the sailor with the facile tongue failed to put it to use.

"I believe these men are going to let that ship pass us by," Adele observed, her voice filled with disgust.

"We have no chance now without help," I added. "Surely they can reason that much."

"I see no evidence that these men can reason at all."

"Then we must do it for them. If it's a pirate ship, we die. If it isn't we live," I said to myself. Then I raised my voice. "Signal them! Fire the muskets!"

"It's our only chance!" shouted Adele.

The crewmen holding the weapons looked at us curiously, as did everyone else aboard, but they did not respond.

"Do as I say!" I tried to duplicate the tone that the Abbess used when reprimanding the gardeners. Pointing to the promontory where Dupierre kept his vigil, I forced my voice low and loud. "Go up there and fire those weapons!"

The men hesitated, but finally they began to pull their way along the rail to the uppermost part of the deck where they discharged their muskets.

"Reload and fire again!" I ordered. They did as they were told and continued until Dupierre shouted, "They've altered course. They've seen us!"

A cheer went up from all hands, but it subsided quickly. Then the waiting began. Our vessel continued to sink. I recognized the possibility that the approaching ship, friend or foe, might not reach us in time. At last, Dupierre announced his recognition of a Spanish flag, and I allowed a sigh of relief to escape my lips.

A pock-marked sailor glared at me malevolently,

"Could be a pirate's ruse to keep our guard down," he said.

"Keep our guard down!" Adele laughed. "What guard? We're almost under water."

"If it's pirates, they'll blame us for the signals," I whispered to her, feeling the weight of responsibility for whatever happened.

"It won't matter," Adele replied. "We'll be dead."

"They're pirates!" screamed the whimpering merchant. "I know they are. They'll kill me and take my money!"

"They're Spaniards!" shouted the captain. He had climbed to the promontory with a glass. "The ship carries cargo, and the officers are in uniform. We are saved!"

"Sweet Mother of God!" I said as Adele and I huddled under a blanket upon the dry deck of the Spanish merchant ship. "I'll never be warm again."

"You would be if these Spaniards had their way," Adele laughed quietly. Around us stood a cluster of officers resembling little boys awaiting a sweet. "Were you brought aboard the same way I was?" she asked with a smile.

"I felt a hand on my limb under my petticoat as I climbed up," I confessed. "And an officer put his arm around my waist to lift me over the rail."

"Then he crushed you against him before he let you go, didn't he?"

"They are Spaniards, after all. We must expect some of this sort of thing."

"Oh, I'll have no complaints as long as they know how to sail a ship. By the look of this vessel, we'll be in good hands."

Just then the Spanish captain approached and delivered his compliments. Then he hurried us below.

Our destination was now Majorca in the Mediterranean. The captain was the second son of a landholding family in Andalusia. Like so many second sons in Spain and France, he had nothing to show for his family's riches except a name long enough to be bound in leather. His older brother was heir to everything else. Don Rafael Domingues, a shortened appellation, was a man in his middle thirties, seasoned by the sea yet still youthful. There was a lot of the Moor about his face, especially his dark haunting eyes. A sadness abided there, as if he mourned all those long dead Muslims who fled Spain centuries before.

Unlike the designing Dupierre, Captain Domingues was chivalrous by nature. He gave Adele and me his own cabin during the voyage and provided us with dry clothes, sailors' clothes though they were, while his sailmaker mended and cleaned our own. It was his sincere regret that he could not take us all the way to Martinique himself, but the owner of his ship had dispatched him to Majorca. Fortunately, vessels left there regularly for the Americas, and he assured us we could book passage easily.

The day after our rescue, Adele and I reluctantly followed instructions to avoid seasickness and took some of the frigid air on deck. The seamen's togs we wore kept us comfortably warm. I felt lighthearted and a bit wicked dressed as a man. It was exciting and even festive, like being disguised at a Paris masquerade. While we walked about and had a gay time speaking our school-girl Spanish, a small sail was sighted in the distance. It did not take long for the French captain to recognize it as belonging to the longboat that had escaped him. He hurried to Captain Domingues and explained what had transpired the day before. Although there was a stiff wind whistling around my ears and I could hear nothing of their conversation, I saw clearly that the Spaniard was outraged to think any men of the sea would have committed the unpardonable crime of abandoning their vessel while innocent women had to face death by drowning.

Domingues shouted several orders to his men, and the ship began to come about. As we approached the longboat, the men aboard her waved and cheered, thinking themselves rescued. Only after they were directly alongside did they recognize French faces looking down at them with malice from the rail. This dampened their spirits hardly at all, for now everyone was out of danger. What they had done could be forgotten.

"Throw us a line there, man," shouted one of the longboat crew.

Captain Domingues responded in French. "Of course, a line down below." He turned to signal two of his crew who hurried to the rail. Then each of them dropped a cannonball down on the hapless Frenchmen. I did not see the immediate result, but as I understand it, one ball crashed through the bottom of the longboat and the other crushed the chest of a fellow who reached up in the foolish expectation of catching a rope.

"May your souls burn in hell for what you did," one French officer called out from the safety of the Spanish deck. Other Frenchmen shook their fists and shouted insults. The Spaniards took the entire thing as a fine joke.

"That poor devil who caught the ball looked quite surprised. Did you see the stupid expression on his face?" Don Rafael mimicked the dying man while his crew laughed until they wept.

"Those men will drown," I said to Adele. "We should do something. Do you think Captain Domingues will save them if we plead for their lives?"

She thought for a moment. "He is a Spaniard. They are a cruel race. But he is a Catholic. Yes, I think he'd save them if we asked him to."

We climbed the narrow steps to the upper deck at the stern and looked back toward the men who would die in the icy waters of the bay unless Adele and I spoke up. The day before, those same men had left us to die.

"It's very cold on deck, Aimee," Adele said with a shudder as she stood by my side.

"Yes, it is. Let's go below and get warm."

Chapter 6

The remainder of our passage was uneventful and pleasant. Long before the garden isle of Majorca emerged on the sea's edge, warm spring breezes caressed our ship, bearing a perfume of the fresh herbs and flowers that flourished on the island's hillsides.

The night before our planned arrival, Adele and I were eager to tread upon solid ground again after what seemed an eternity at sea. The weather was dry with no hint of winter in the air, and our Spanish officers had promised to escort us about while we waited for a westward passage. Two women recently pulled from the deck of a sinking ship could hardly hope for a better fate. François was on my mind a good deal, of course. There had been many idle hours for pondering. But in all candor, I cannot say I was in poor spirits as the ship gracefully cut the waves in its approach to Majorca.

Certainly, I slept well. A light knock at our cabin door hardly roused me. Then the knocks turned to pounding and the door flew open.

"Don Rafael!" Adele gasped in surprise. I awakened quickly and sat up in bed, the counterpane pulled to my chin.

"Senoritas!" The captain rushed in, his eyes wild. He wore no coat and his blouse was disheveled. Two pistols were stuffed in his belt. From his threatening appearance and strange manner, I imagined that his Spanish blood had gotten the better of him and he intended to molest us, but I was in error. He threw himself to his knees next to our bed. As Adele lay on the outside, he grabbed her hand and pressed it to his forehead. "Forgive me, dear ladies," he said. "I have failed you."

Just then there was an explosion in the distance. The captain reacted to it without hesitation, jumping to his feet and throwing his body over us. I was almost bent double by his weight, and he nearly smothered Adele. Seconds later, we heard the splintering of wood above our heads, shouts and scrambling feet on the deck and what sounded like the collapse of the mainmast.

"What's happening?" I demanded as I pushed the captain off me and sat up again.

"Barbary pirates, we are under attack. They crept up on us during the night, the blackguards. We are completely cut off from the port."

"Can we outrun them?" Adele asked.

"Not now. We'll have to stand and fight."

"Surely, help will come from Majorca," I reasoned.

"Oh no, senorita. Every Spanish ship of the line in the Mediterranean is deployed along the African coast, hoping to cut off the pirates before they reach our sea lanes. No one is going to help us."

"What will happen?" Adele's eyes held those of the captain, demanding the truth.

He pulled the pistols from his belt. Just then another cannon blast came from the east and he once again threw himself upon us. A splash just beyond the stern reported the pirates had missed. When Don Rafael got to his feet, he thrust his pistols into our hands. "Take these. They are primed and ready to fire."

"I have never shot a pistol in my life, Don Rafael," I confessed, trying to hand the weapon back to him. "And I doubt I could hit the floor under my feet let alone defend myself.

"No, senorita, keep it."

Adele's voice was subdued. "Keep it, Aimee. It isn't for pirates."

"Stay here and bar the door," the captain instructed. "By the Holy Mother, I swear we will fight to the last man, but if we fail, turn the pistols on yourselves. You must not be taken. My soul would burn in torment if I died thinking that those fiends . . ." He could not bring himself to continue.

"We have faith you will save us, Don Rafael." I did not believe my own words.

"Pray for a miracle, senoritas."

A frightened young Spaniard appeared at the door. "Captain," he called. "The guns are ready."

"Very well," Don Rafael responded. With that the sailor turned and was gone.

"I must leave you now. Lock the door after me. Let no one pass until the battle is over and you hear my voice."

"You have our prayers, captain." I tried to sound confident.

"And you have mine," he responded, making the sign of the cross as he prepared to leave. "But keep those pistols at hand." He disappeared.

Adele swung her legs over the edge of the bunk and stood up. She was wearing only a shift, and I could see the outline of her delicate body silhouetted by the morning sun through the stern windows. In her hand was a pistol. She held it almost reverently but with more than a hint of revulsion, the way one might take up the putrified remains of a dead saint long preserved as a relic.

"Take this away, Adele," I said and passed my pistol into her other hand. She looked at it strangely, as if through a haze, not quite able to distinguish its features. "Get rid of them," I directed her. "Put them on the table." She moved in a stupor, depositing the weapons with great care on Captain Domingues' writing table. "Adele?" I questioned. She did not seem to hear me. "Adele?"

She stood next to the writing table and allowed her empty eyes to gaze out the windows to the sea. There were shouts overhead, sharp commands. Then the Spanish cannon fired and our ship rolled in the water from their recoil. Adele grabbed the edge of the table to steady herself. I could see tears glistening on her black lashes, but her voice did not tremble when she spoke.

"I refuse to wait here to die." There was a long pause while she looked out at the sea and searched for composure. "This is outrageous. Men make such an unforgivable muck of everything they do. And who pays the price for their follies! We do.

"Had your spineless François faced his father with the truth long ago, we would be safe in France right now. Had that imbecile of a French captain known the least detail of sailing the Atlantic or even selecting a crew, we would be almost to Martinique. And now Captain Domingues has sailed directly into the murderous clutches of Barbary pirates. He regrets he has failed us and suggests that given the situation, we should kill ourselves so that he can rest in peace. A pox on all of them."

Above us cannons continued to belch missiles into the sky. More frequently than ever balls struck the ship, bringing down essential sections of the rigging without damaging the innards of the vessel where valuable booty lay waiting to be taken. Screams pierced the air from the lips of men caught under falling timbers. There was a rising gale of panicked voices as the Spaniards and Frenchmen on deck watched with dread the unrelenting approach of the malevolent pirate ship.

Amid the cacophony of violence that played on the

cabin ceiling, Adele kept her eyes on the stern window. "What can we do?" I asked finally. "The pirates will prevail. How can we save ourselves?"

"I don't know yet," she said sharply.

"We can pray, Adele. Come sit down with me. Let's pray together."

"The devil take praying and beseeching and waiting for our salvation. By the Holy Mother, we are out of the convent now. There is nothing to protect us. We'll save ourselves, Aimee, or die." She slammed her fist down on the table.

"Get out of bed," she ordered. "We'll build a barricade. Help me with this table." She was already straining at it when I threw my weight into the effort, discovering that doing something, anything, gave me courage.

We worked quickly, lifting the table from the niches in the floor which prevented its sliding about. Once it was against the door, we piled up everything else that would move.

"That should slow them up a bit," I said with a sigh when we were finished. Out the stern windows I could see Majorca. "Now, look out there." I pointed toward the island. Adele walked to the windows. Just then the ship lurched in the water and immediately after came a crescendo of men's voices, a mixture of terror-filled screams and the bloodthirsty raving of killers as they swarmed onto our vessel.

"There can't be much time now, Aimee."

"I know. But look how close we are to the island. If we could break out these windows and get to the water—We can swim." I slipped my arm around Adele's waist and we both looked toward the coast.

"Do we dare, Aimee?"

"We must save ourselves. Now get something and start breaking out the windows."

"What?" She paused. "The pistols!" I grabbed mine and holding it as a bludgeon prepared to hammer, but before my first blow fell, the rumble of running feet came from the companionway. Then there were shouts.

Among them we recognized the voice of Captain Domingues.

"This is the hour!" he called out in Spanish over ringing sword blades and the grunts of his assailants. An instant later we heard an agonizing scream. The weight of a body fell against the door. It had to be Don Rafael. As he slid down to the floor we could hear him cry, "The shots! Let me hear the shots!"

Adele and I stared at each other, reluctant to comply with the captain's last request. Then there were shots, but they came from outside. Don Rafael was dead, and I knew that the one remaining barrier between us and the pirates could last only moments more.

"The windows, Aimee!" Adele shouted, and began to break out the glass. Our pistols worked well against the heavy panes, but they met strong resistance from the wooden skeleton that held each window in place. Outside, the pirates began pounding on our door. They could not have known we were on the other side, but they must have assumed anything so staunchly defended by the Spaniard had to be a prize worth their efforts.

"We won't get out in time, Aimee!" Adele sobbed.

"Keep on, Adele! Keep on!" I threw my pistol to the floor and yanked at the window frames with my bare hands. Daggers of broken glass clinging to the wood gouged my flesh, but in my frenzy to escape I felt nothing. A chair behind us on the barricade fell to the floor. The rest of the furniture began to groan and shift while the door inched open.

"Aimee, we still have the pistols!"

"Do you think they'll go off after all this?"

"I don't know." She looked at the weapon in her hand.

"Will you shoot me? I could never do it myself."

"Adele!"

"And I'll shoot you," she offered, pleading. "We can do it together. Please, Aimee."

"Yes, yes!" I agreed. I might not have the courage

to take my own life, but I could not fail Adele and leave her in the hands of the pirates.

The barricade was falling away rapidly. It was only a matter of seconds before our lives would end. The panic that gripped me before while I struggled with the window melted away. A calm sadness overtook me, but I did not weep.

"When the moment comes, Aimee," Adele said in a trembling voice. "Don't look at me. Just do it. If I see your eyes, I'll not be able to shoot."

"Yes, you're right. I couldn't either. Here." I reached for the barrel of her pistol. "Rest it here!" I placed it between my breasts. She guided mine to a like spot on her own body, and for the first time I saw that her hands were bleeding badly. So were mine. It did not matter.

We were ready none to soon. There was only time for one whispered farewell when the door gave way. Two savages flew into the room, filling it with a sickening stench of gore and sweat. In an inkling they realized where their treasure lay and lunged at us. My heart raced, but I knew my duty. Adele's breast heaved under the weight of the pistol in my hand. My dear Adele, I wanted to look at her just once more before the end. Our eyes met. Then I pulled the trigger. When I looked again, Adele was still next to me. Horror distorted her features. One of the pirates had her by the arm. She screamed and pulled away from him, but her efforts were to no avail. I dropped my gun, grabbed the loathsome devil's wrist, ripped him off her and let his arm fall to the floor with the rest of his lifeless body. I had killed him. The other pirate lay dead near my feet, the recipient of the pistol ball meant for me.

In a heartbeat's time every horror imaginable flashed through my reeling brain. Adele and I were still alive. Both pistol balls were spent on the first two pirates that came upon us, and I could hear more of them rushing down the companionway.

"Quickly," I screamed. "The table back against the

door." Adele and I hurled it in place, but it was no use. An animal force on the other side of the door exploded through it and drove the table into us, almost pinning me to the broken stern windows at the other side of the cabin.

Now there was only one thought in my head. I had to keep those men from laying their filthy hands on me. Death seemed a certainty, but I fought with the strength of ten to avoid being ravaged.

There were six of them, six or perhaps more. The cabin was not large, and the pirates flooded it with their reeking bodies. They were unspeakably hideous, disfigured by sword or dagger scars of one sort or another. Gore dripped from their weapons, their hands, even their mouths.

"Sweet Mother," I cried when I beheld the evidence of the awful carnage on deck. Then Adele grabbed my hand. She had leapt to the table top and pulled me up after her. When the first pirate made a grab at us, she swung her pistol like a club and brained the fellow. I brought down the second in the same fashion. With that I became a raving Amazon, mad with panic and bloodlust, screaming, kicking and brandishing my cudgel. Any one of the pirates could have killed me with a single pistol ball, but not a shot was fired. After we laid open two heads, the men remaining fell back. Each held a bare blade, a gigantic deadly looking thing, long and curved, with glistening edges where blood had not sullied the blade. They were a devil's horde. Four of them were left, and a door wide open to any number more. Fires danced in their eyes from the fighting they had left on deck. Their mouths, framed in long black mustaches like scimitar blades, were hateful and twisted. Their heads were swathed in bulky turbans. Balloons of bloodstained fabric enveloped their legs. It was a company of monsters about to run amuck.

The pirates stood at bay in a narrow crescent just outside the range of our weapons. "Why don't they kill us?" Adele asked in little more than a whisper.

"I'm afraid I know why, and so do you," I whispered back.

Adele cast a quick glance in my direction. "Aimee, you are covered with blood."

"What?" I looked down at myself. "My hands!" I moaned, and remembering the wounds felt them throbbing. "It was the window glass."

"I'm bleeding too!" Adele cried. When I looked, I saw her hands and blood-streaked shift. There were pools of blood on the table from her cuts. Her face was drawn from fear and exhaustion.

The men around us kept staring, waiting for something. Then suddenly one of them spoke. We could not understand him, but I assumed he issued a command, for immediately another ran out of the cabin. Those remaining kept their eyes on us.

Agonizing moments went by. Each second increased my terror and further paralyzed me with images of what would happen when the pirates grew tired of their wait. Next to me, Adele was growing weak. Her body swayed much more than could have been caused by the ship's movements.

"Adele, are you all right?" I asked, and, hearing my own words, recognized the stupidity of the question.

"I feel faint," was her response.

Sounds of men descending the companionway meant nothing to me now. My fate was sealed. The pirates in front of us looked back toward the door expectantly. When new intruders swaggered in, the others moved aside deferentially. There were three of them, but two were the subordinates of the third. It was clear he was the commander of the entire barbarian mob. A man takes on a certain look about the eyes and mouth when he expects obedience. It matters not what race he is—French, English, Barbary pirate or even Hottentot, I suppose. Leaders have an aura of power, and it is as distinguishable as the badge of a royal society. Perhaps such men are born with that demeanor, but I believe they must practice it in the

mirror. This fellow was a master. He could have been
a Bourbon or Hohenzollern monarch the way he
looked around the place, all pomposity and arrogance,
with his men hugging the walls to get out of his way.

The sight of him left no room for doubt that he
had been in a fight. His outlandish garments were
torn and spattered from the mayhem on deck. Still,
his clothes were elegant in their foreign way—black
pantaloons and a flowing white silk tunic. The curling
scabbard hanging from his waist was engraved and
encrusted with gems, and the close-fitting turban
around his head was decorated with a great spray of
jewels. What added immensely to his air of command
was a defiant, seemingly ageless face, and the fact that
he stood more than a head taller than any other man
in the room. He was a giant.

"Good morning, senoritas," he said, shattering the
terrible silence that had reigned in the cabin. I made
no response. Neither did Adele.

After a brief pause the commander went on. He
filled the air with fluent Spanish, yet in a peculiar
Musselman cadence. More often than not he accented
the wrong syllable of his words, reversing the parts of
his sentences. This made his speech difficult to understand, but listening intently I gleamed that he
claimed the title of Captain Pasha and was named
Ibrahim Ben Raza, a pirate very proud of his oc-
cupation. He and his band owed their allegience to
an oriental potentate called the Dey of Algiers. Ben
Raza insisted on listing every title of the Dey, with
"Son of and Conquerer of" repeated time after time.
All of it was totally lost on me until he hit upon "Successor to Barbarossa," then my heart froze. Every
French child from Ile-de-France to the Antilles knew
horror stories of the fiend Barbarossa. White Christians manned the oars of his galleys, Christians
snatched from their homes and families by raiding
pirates who attacked the coast of Europe. His corsairs
laid waste to entire cities, enslaving their populations,
raping, dismembering, killing. The name Barbarossa

was as hated as any in the history of the world, and now Adele and I had fallen into the hands of a bloodthirsty cutthroat who spoke it as though he were petitioning a martyred saint.

Pasha's introduction finished, he tossed about a profusion of empty compliments. When I sifted through his rococo monologue, I found that in the main what he said was a simple guarantee. If we put down our weapons and offered no resistance, we would not be molested.

"Now, senoritas, hand me your pistols," he said at last. As anyone might imagine, we did nothing of the kind. There we were, confronting an assortment of pirates with their weapons at the ready, while one of their number, a devout disciple of history's most infamous villain, offered a feeble assurance that they intended us no harm.

Patience was not one of Captain Pasha's virtues. No sooner did he realize we would not comply with his request than he reached up to snatch my pistol. His audacious move after such a long period of inactivity in the cabin caught me off guard, and I failed to react. Adele was much more alert. She stepped in front of me on the table and took a swing at the fellow's head with her own gun butt. He jerked out of the way agilely and laughed. His men laughed as well, while they tried to cover their surprise at our refusal to obey their master.

Ben Raza studied us. Then suddenly he turned to his men and issued a sharp command. Perhaps he ordered them out of the cabin to underscore his promise. Whatever it was, they had already begun to move toward the door when Adele collapsed. Added to everything else, that last effort to beat back the pirate was too much for her. As she began to fall, I slipped an arm around her waist and supported her weight as best I could, but the pistol fell from my hand. Suddenly, my bargaining position had deteriorated to nothing. Knowing that, the pirates grew restless.

With no other alternative, I kicked the pistol from

the table while I struggled to keep Adele from rolling to the floor. Just as I looked to the Pasha for assistance, one of his men, an ugly fellow, his face marred by gaping livid scars, charged at me like a lusting animal. I clutched Adele close and shrank from him. There was a flash of reflected light, the sound of air and flesh being cleaved in two by the Pasha's blade, followed by a dull thud as the grotesque head of my attacker flew free of its moorings and bounced against the wall. Only as it slowly rolled across the cabin, one way and then the other with the rise and fall of the ship, did I realize that Ben Raza had saved us. I looked at him in amazement. His face was stern as he slowly and deliberately wiped the blood from his sword and replaced it in its scabbard. Then I fainted.

Chapter 7

When I awoke, my head felt as though a formal wig had been fastened to it with stakes. As I looked about, there seemed to be no one else in the room. Everything was unfamiliar and bizarre. Tapestries of strangely intricate design hung from the walls and billowed, almost breathing with the wind. Even the door was partially covered by a rug tied to one side like a tent flap. Rugs and pillows lay about on the floor. An oil lamp swung back and forth from a ceiling hook, its motion telling me I was still at sea. The salt air mixed with a fragrance I could not identify, an incense of some sort. My shift was gone, and I found myself in a loose-fitting silk gown with floppy sleeves and a drooping collar. Bandages covered my aching hands. The foreignness of the place, the undeniable evidence that a stranger had disrobed me, dressed my wounds and done who knows what else gave me a sense of being violated, as if someone had trespassed on my soul. I felt terribly alone and helpless.

"Adele? Adele, are you there?" I called into the half light of the lamp.

"Aimee, you're awake at last," she responded in a weak voice.

"Where are you?" I lifted my head to see her, but the effort made me feel faint.

"Don't strain yourself. I'll be right there."

From behind me I could hear the sigh of silk sliding on silk, then the whisper of Adele's feet on the rug. She sat down on a pillow next to my low bed and touched me. Her hand was bandaged too. "Does your head hurt, Aimee?"

"Yes, awfully, and no wonder. Unless I have some pillows, I'll surely die during the night. They're barbaric to lay a person down perfectly flat like this."

"Your head aches from the fever. Both of us have been terribly ill. The wounds from the window glass festered."

"You look fit," I observed. Adele's gown was similar to mine. She had belted hers at the waist and wore it with a flair.

"They are taking good care of us."

"Who are?" I wanted to know.

"The pirates. There's a slave named Raol. He's the ship's doctor. We owe him our lives."

"But my hands still throb," I groaned. "Give me that cushion, will you?" I motioned toward one on the floor.

"The cuts were deep, but look at those bandages," Adele said, as she picked up the pillow gingerly to avoid opening her wounds and propped it behind me. "Have you ever seen anything so white? Raol is a fiend for cleanliness. He changes them four or five times a day. In another week I'll have my dressings off."

"In another week? How long have I been asleep, Adele?"

"Six days. Your fever was much worse than mine."

"Six days!" I was shocked. It seemed like just a few hours had passed since I saw that severed head roll on the floor with its tongue lolling out. The thought of it made me shudder.

"Do you have a chill?" Adele asked when she saw me quake. "There still may be a touch of fever."

"No, I think not. But the memory of what happened is so fresh. I can't believe it has been six days."

"I know. Every time I close my eyes I see the hideous faces of those pirates."

"Are we in their clutches now?" I asked.

"Yes," Adele said, and then turned toward the sound of the opening door behind her. A raisin-skinned old man came in. When he saw that I was awake, he smiled warmly, revealing three brown teeth. Two lean Negro boys followed him, carrying a tin cooking pot and some bowls.

"This is Raol," Adele explained as the fellow prepared to feed me a bit of soup.

"Thank you for caring for us, Raol," I said sincerely. Hearing his name, the old man looked up, but evidently he had not understood my words.

"He doesn't know French or Spanish, Aimee," Adele said. "And he never speaks. I'm beginning to doubt that he can."

When Raol finished redressing our wounds, he left us alone. "I've seen no one else since the pirate chief brought him here, just the old man and his servants," Adele said.

"And the pirate?" I asked. "He gave you no clue about his intentions?"

"Not a word."

The next day our futures became clear when Captain Pasha Ben Raza came to call. Raol accompanied him, and sat on a pillow near the door. The Pasha was in full regalia, wearing a costume that made even the most flamboyant Versailles courtier seem drab by comparison. That day his balloon trousers were green silk. Above them he wore a brilliant red vest over a white blouse. Jewels on every one of his fingers sparkled even in the dim light of our sick room. His turban was a halo of white.

"Praise Allah you are well again," he said as he bowed and salaamed. "Raol is a magician, is he not?" The Pasha sat down on the rugs as he spoke.

"He has cared for us very well," Adele responded.

"By the beard of the Prophet he had better!" The Pasha exclaimed. "He knows that your health means his own."

Perhaps it was the Spanish, but I failed to understand what he meant by that remark. "Is it plague or some other contagion?" I asked.

"No, Senorita de Rivery."

"Thank the Holy Virgin for that," I sighed. "But if there is no contagion, the old man's health should not be threatened at all?"

Ben Raza smiled as he would at the question of a confused child. His arrogance irritated me in spite of the fear that was my predominant emotion at the time. "You misunderstand," he explained. "Two such beautiful women as you and the Senorita Fleury are precious to me. If harm should befall either of you, I would be disconsolate. My grief would be such that I would strike out against those responsible. While you are ill, Raol is responsible. I would kill him."

The logic behind his explanation seemed quite elementary to Ben Raza. Old Raol, perched on his pillow, grinning like an idiot, had no apparent objections to the arrangement either, though I cannot help but wonder if he would have been so docile had my condition taken a turn for the worse. Such death threats seemed barbaric and I said as much. "That is barbaric! You would kill a doctor because one of his patients dies."

"You are a woman and do not understand such matters," Ben Raza continued in his infuriating tone of condescension. "But do not concern yourself. After all, it is in the hands of Allah, is it not? Long ago it was written when you would live and when you would die. Perhaps coaxing Raol to his best has helped achieve the Great One's design. You are alive. Praise Allah for that."

"Why are we so important to you?" Adele asked.

"A question that cuts to the essence, and so soon."
He chuckled. "Clearly you are of the West and have
no patience with the refinements of civilization. I had
hoped we would converse for a while. It would have
pleased me to explore your minds. Though you are
only women, you seem to have character. I would
have tested it with the devices of the eastern eye and
ear."

"We have been tested quite enough, thank you,"
Adele responded, and I found myself admiring her
courage. "Our lives are in your hands, and we wish
to know your intentions."

"Ah well!" The Pasha looked upward as if to seek
understanding. "I will begin with you, Senorita
Fleury." He reached into his sash and pulled from it
a string of perfectly matched pearls. "Please accept
this gift from a humble admirer. The creamy glow of
these pearls will be beautiful against your amber
throat." Adele looked at the necklace, making no effort to hide her surprise at the unexpected turn of the
encounter. Then after a long pause she spoke. "This
is no explanation. You may keep your pearls."

"But you must learn to accept gifts from me, loveliness," the Pasha protested. "You are going to join my
harem in Algiers." He smiled as if he had just bestowed a great honor upon her. Then he rose to his
feet, stepped much too near Adele and clasped the
strand around her neck. "I was right," he proclaimed,
delighted with the touch of her body as he let his
hands play over her shoulders. "You look magnificent."

Adele glared at him, then she slowly raised her
bandaged hand until her fingers wrapped around the
pearls where they draped near her breast. Her touch
was not that of a woman examining an expensive gift,
but more like that of a prisoner about to rip away her
bonds. I saw her grip grow firm, the strand of gems
draw taut. Adele's eyes and the Pasha's were locked

together in a test of wills. Finally the necklace broke and the pearls cascaded to the floor. Raol rushed to gather them up, but the Pasha said something to him and the old man hurried back to his pillow.

"This is madness," I cried. "Surely you can see you will never subdue Adele. Neither of us will be of any use to you. Let us go. We have relatives in France. They will pay a ransom, any ransom. There must be a price high enough for you to let us go."

"A ransom?" he responded as if the idea were a novelty. "Perhaps for the Senorita Fleury, after a few years when I tire of her. Who can say?" Then he turned sharply to look at me. "But you, Senorita de Rivery. There will be no ransom for you. Not now. Not ever."

Since the days of my childhood I have been taught that men rarely mean what they say when dealing with women, and my experience with François proved that to be true. But Captain Pasha Ben Raza was an exception. I knew from his confident air and aura of strength that he did not trouble himself with deception. This gave me all the more reason to be struck dumb with horror when he pronounced that I would not be released for the rest of my life.

Adele's unequivocal rejection displeased him, but he was not insensitive to the unnerving effect that his refusal of a ransom had on me, and he grew concerned for my weakened condition. "Do not distress yourself, senorita." He spoke in the gentlest tone he could muster. "Your future is a wonderful one. You will be a gift to my master, the Dey of Algiers. Jewels will be yours, and servants and great wealth. There is no woman on earth who would not weep with joy to enter his harem."

I looked at Adele, not knowing what to say or do. "Don't worry, Aimee," she said in French. "We'll escape somehow."

Seeing no possibility of it, I lost heart. "It would

be better if you killed me," I said to the pirate bitterly.

He smiled. "You simply do not understand. You are a treasure, like a rare coin of great value. No one but a fool would find such a coin and then throw it away." He reached out and took a lock of my hair in his fingers. "Spun gold. That is what you are. With you I will purchase the esteem of my master. In his harem you will be the happiness of his old age. You will rekindle the fires of his manhood and bear him sons and more sons."

The Pasha, savage though he was, quickly noticed that his description of my future did not fill me with delight. On the contrary, every word he uttered made me more terrified, and the fear on my face urged him to further explanations.

"The Dey's coffers are filled with gold and precious stones, and he will lay it all at your feet. For every infidel vessel we take in the name of the Prophet, one fifth of our booty goes to him. That is a great fortune. Still, when I find some object of special value, a treasure of unsurpassed beauty, nothing gives me more joy than to carry it to the Dey personally to see the pleasure in his eyes and to repay him in small part for his kindness to me.

"Do you see now, senorita. You are such a gift, a virgin, a woman of gold, so young and beautiful. He will be pleased beyond words, and that is my fondest wish. For it is my happy destiny to serve the Dey. Kismet placed you in my hands. Praise the Mighty One for his wisdom."

Hearing all this I was filled with revulsion. Harem meant prison to me. All I could think of was a small cell with barred windows where I would waste away in an idleness interrupted only when an old Musselman came round to violate me.

Suicide seemed the only alternative. The Pasha wore a dagger on his belt. I saw the thing and thought to snatch it and stab him, though I knew I would die for my efforts. Adele must have understood my desperation.

"Don't do anything foolish," she said, again in French so that the pirate could not understand her. "We'll get away."

"Captain Pasha," she went on in Spanish. "Is it only virgins that you give to this Dey of yours?"

"Yes. There must be no possibility that his heirs could be questioned."

"Where did you get the idea that Mademoiselle de Rivery is a virgin?" she asked in a calm tone. "If it is a virgin you want, you'll have to look elsewhere. You have not got one there."

Immediately I recognized the cleverness of her ploy. If he could not give me to his master, then at least Adele and I might be able to stay together.

"She is telling the truth," I confessed.

At that news the Pasha's countenance changed markedly. He was no longer supremely confident, and his smile disappeared. A tower of impatience, he glared at Raol and questioned him. The old man seemed undisturbed. He bowed his head almost to the floor and responded at length, revealing at last that he had a tongue. What he said satisfied Ben Raza.

"The Senorita de Rivery is a virgin. Raol swears it upon his own life." The Pasha looked at Raol and the fellow nodded his head. Then Ben Raza said to Adele, "It is you who are impure. But because of your beauty I will overlook your indiscretions."

"And how does your magician know such things," Adele demanded indignantly. "Can he see it by looking in my eyes?"

"He knows, senorita. He knows. And it is not in the eyes that one looks to find out. You slept for a long time, both of you. Raol took certain liberties. He knows the truth."

Seeing by the shock in our faces that no further explanation was necessary Ben Raza turned and left. Raol followed him like an obedient spaniel leaving me with my legs firmly crossed and my cheeks afire to contemplate what the old scoundrel must have done and to wonder if he was correct about Adele.

Alone, she and I spent the rest of the day trying to comfort each other and make plans to free ourselves, but when we considered our fragile state of health, escape seemed impossible. Still, we swore to each other we would resist Ben Raza at every opportunity.

Later that afternoon, Raol returned. By that time the humiliation I felt for his outrageous exploration of my body was so mixed with anger that I drew an empty pitcher from the cabinet near my couch and threw it at him. Unfortunately, he danced out of the way with little difficulty. Ignoring our displeasure, he gave each of us a goblet of cloudy brown liquid and pretended to drink from one of them. Then he feigned slumber to tell us it was a sleeping potion.

"What will he do to us while we sleep this time, Aimee?" Adele asked, a sharp edge on her voice.

"I don't care any more. If this makes me sleep, at least I won't be thinking." I drank down the foul-tasting liquor without hesitation. Adele did the same, and both of us slept dreamlessly through the night to awaken the next day feeling reasonably well.

That morning, soon after Raol once again changed our bandages, Ben Raza called on us with news that our ship was moored at the harbor in Algiers.

"The slaves of my wives are here now, Senorita de Rivery. They will prepare you for your presentation to the Dey." As he explained, I could hear in the background the sounds of happy voices and light footsteps in the companionway. "They speak no French or Spanish," he continued, "but they know well the ways of women and the secrets of beauty. Let them have their way with you."

I could say nothing in response. It had never occurred to me the day before that we would be in Algiers so soon. The rush of events was too much.

Ben Raza took my silence as acquiescence and

turned to Adele. "Please, Senorita Fleury, step outside for a moment. I wish to speak to you alone about a matter of great importance."

While I was paralyzed with trepidation, my friend kept her wits about her. "I will not go with you," she said defiantly. "Aimee and I will stay together. Say anything you have to say to both of us and be done with it."

"Please, senorita. I beg you to reconsider."

"Why should I?"

"We will speak of the ransom."

"There will be no ransom for me without Aimee."

"Both of you could be saved, but we must talk about it."

"I don't believe you," Adele continued to resist.

"Senorita," the Pasha protested. "I swear it before Allah."

Adele looked at me. It seemed that this was the first time since our capture that the pirate spoke any sense. Certainly there was some ransom he would consider. All men, expecially pirates at sea, have a price. "Go with him, Adele," I said in French. "I know he is a pirate, but he has protected us thus far and he did give his oath."

"I can't explain it," Adele responded. "But I feel we are being duped. Why a ransom now?"

"I don't know, but I'm sure he can be bought. We must take the risk." Reluctantly she followed him out.

I lost sight of Adele in a flood of olive-skinned girls who streamed into the cabin as soon as the door opened. All of them smiled and chattered in their foreign tongue. Their clothes were elegant, unlike any I had ever seen. Many of them wore jewels on their fingers and ears. Nothing suggested bondage or enslavement, but it was their gaiety that caught me off guard. I tried to draw away from them, but they kept reaching out to me. Several tried to embrace me at once, all the while jabbering. I was terrified.

"Get out of here!" I screamed, pulling away. "Get out!" I violently pushed the nearest one, the effort aggravating the pain in my hands. My victim fell to the floor and cried out. Then the covey of slave girls fell silent.

"Now leave me alone," I ordered. They looked at each other stupidly, not having the slightest notion why I was upset.

"Go! All of you." I pointed to the door. Still, they stood motionless. "Out of here!" None caught my meaning. "Sweet Virgin, how can all of you be so stupid?" I grabbed a woman close at hand by her flowing black hair and began to drag her toward the door. She struggled and let out a piercing shriek. Her friends came to her aid, all of them screaming and shouting.

In the ensuing struggle, I was greatly outnumbered, but I fought for my life in spite of my wounds. Medicine bottles spilled on the rugs as cabinets were overturned. I bit and gouged whatever flesh presented itself, but the Africans managed to force me to the floor and held me there until the Pasha returned to discover the cause of the commotion.

He shook his head as he looked around the ruins of the cabin. "By the beard of the Prophet, you are slow to recognize your destiny, Golden One."

"Tell them to let me go," I demanded.

He so ordered. The girls released me and I sat up on the floor. "Get rid of them." Again he spoke a few words and the women left in a noisy cloud of cries and chatter.

"Are you all right?" Ben Raza asked, sounding genuinely concerned. "Your hands? Should I call Raol?"

The pain in my hands did not matter to me. "I won't have those women in here again. I refuse to go to this Dey of yours like a sacrificial lamb. You can kill me or let me go. It is as simple as that."

The Pasha stood in front of me, his arms folded, his feet slightly apart against the ship's gentle motion. The man's height inspired awe. Behind him the oil lamp swung slightly. Its light danced off his white turban and made it glisten like a crown. "Listen to me now, Golden One." He spoke slowly so that I would understand every word. "You will do as I say."

"Where is Adele?" I demanded, fearful that Ben Raza had lied to us about the ransom.

"She is safe, but you will never see her again."

"What?" His words staggered me.

"She has been taken to my home. If all goes well, she will stay there. Disobey me and she will be sold into slavery."

"You must let me see her," I pleaded, and felt all my defiance melt away.

My grief at that moment could have been no worse had Ben Raza told me she were dead. She and I were like two limbs of the same body. One without the other made a cripple of us both. Since the cradle we had been together—and now I had to go on alone, perhaps forever.

"You never intended to bargain with us for our freedom," I said to him coldly. "You broke your holy oath."

"There will be no ransom. That is true. As for my oath, senorita, Mohammed's followers are never bound by any oaths given to infidels. Allah knows unbelievers cannot be trusted, and he would not put us at a disadvantage. Allah is not a fool, after all."

"Then how can I know you will keep your word about Adele if I cooperate with you?"

"For this simple reason," he explained. "You will please the Dey or the enmity of one of his favorites can lead only to disaster. I am not a fool either."

"I know very well what you are," I said, hating my impotence even more than I hated the man who had rendered me so.

"And I know you will do as I say, senorita. You will because you love your friend. I will send in Raol to bandage your hands. Then my women will return. This time you will treat them with respect."

Being without Adele was a prospect too horrible to bear. I could not face it. I swore I would free myself and find her. Somehow we would escape to France.

It must have been my desperate need to believe it that allowed me to see any hope in such an impossible scheme, but I clung to it through all the days that followed. I would escape and find Adele. That was all that mattered. And after I found her I would kill Ben Raza for his treachery.

Chapter 8

At sunset on the day I arrived in Algiers, I found myself in a tiled antechamber of the Dey's throne room.
Earlier, I had been stripped naked by the Pasha's
women, most of them sullen after our first encounter.
They scrubbed me all over, demonstrating a flagrant
disregard for my modesty. I found this particularly
shocking for a race of women who make a habit of
covering their faces in public. While I was completely
bare, they crushed rose petals on my skin and rubbed
oil into every part of me. Then I was dressed in oriental clothes.

As I waited for my audience with Baba Mohammed, Dey of Algiers, I wore a gauze chemise and pantaloons that tied at the knee. Over the pantaloons I
had on outer trousers, silk ones gathered at the knee
and falling loosely around my ankles. Then there was
a waistcoat with a cutaway front, and over it a brocade
gown fitted very tightly and opened to the waist. It was
quite an elegant costume but for the fact that the
chemise was transparent as window glass, and the

outer gown provided no covering for my bosom at all.

None of the women with me were so exposed, but when I objected to such a display, they misunderstood and tried to rub rouge on those parts of my breasts they wanted to be most distinguishable through the gauze. That outrage I resisted with such vehemence that they gave it up, fearing another brawl.

The costume sparkled with jeweled buttons and decorations, but I did not spend a great deal of time contemplating their beauty. My mind was too full of dread as I awaited my confrontation with the man who was to be my master.

Ben Raza's words on board ship still echoed in my ears. I had no intention of offering any resistance that might jeopardize Adele. The Dey of Algiers could have his Musselman way with me and so be it. I planned to bide my time. When I regained enough strength, I would escape.

The idea of losing my virtue in such an indelicate manner filled me with chagrin. In my situation, however, it was miraculous I had any virtue left, considering I had been in the clutches of Barbary pirates for over a week. Thinking about the ordeal ahead, I admitted some relief mixed with all my other emotions. It had to come sometime. Putting it behind me would end the terrible anticipation and free my mind to make plans.

Now I was too afraid. Whenever I let myself think about this Arab and what he was going to do, doubts seeped around the edges of my resolve and ugly visions danced in my fantasy.

"If only I were not a virgin," I said aloud. But then I thought of François and how much I resented him. It was just as well he did not have the satisfaction of deflowering me before I found out the truth. I would sooner be ravaged by a Musselman against my will than have to live with the humiliation of having given myself to that coward François de Marmont.

I cannot say how many hours I passed there in speculation and fear. Certainly, the place of my confinement was not intended to cause such chargrin. It was small, like a convent cell, but as perfect as a jewel. The complicated patterns of the mosaic on the walls created an airy impression, as if a breeze were ruffling a leafy glade. Rugs more beautiful than any I had seen in France covered the floor. They were woven of bold reds and blues in floral patterns bordered with interlacing branches. The line of the archway that crowned the chamber was so fine and delicate that it suggested a bird in flight.

In spite of my lovely surroundings, the wait was agonizing, but I found no relief in the sound of footsteps outside nor the voice of Captain Pasha Ben Raza as he spoke to the guards. His entrance made me more aware of my near nakedness and I grew uncomfortable. At first, he seemed titillated by my embarrassment and sought to increase it by inspecting me carefully, paying special attention to my transparent chemise and what lay beneath it. His motive was not lust, however, but an overwhelming desire to please his master. He was eager for the audience and quickly began my instructions.

"He will see you," Ben Raza announced sternly. "Now, follow me. Say nothing. Do nothing. Just stand still after I lead you in. Do not move at all unless I tell you to, no matter what happens. The Dey may touch you. He'll want to see your teeth. Europeans often have terrible teeth, but yours are sound." He paused for a moment, then grabbed my jaw. "Show them to me."

Without thinking, I tried to jerk my head free, but his grip was too powerful. "Show them to me," he demanded. "Remember Senorita Fleury!" I drew back my lips in a grimace. "They're pearls, praise Allah." He released me. "Now put on your veil and come along."

He spun around and charged through the archway. I drew a fine opaque cloth over my face as I had been shown and fastened it, feeling relief that the length of the veil allowed it to cover my breasts. Even so, I was not eager, and I did not hurry after him. Impatient, the Pasha came back, took a firm hold of my wrist and dragged me down the long corridor toward a double archway flanked by two gigantic Negroes who dwarfed even Ben Raza.

Just outside the arches, the Pasha stopped. "Understand, Senorita de Rivery. This audience is very important. I'll remind you once more—"

"You don't have to remind me. I know what you can do."

"Very well. We will go in. Stay close behind me."

The throne room was large with a high ceiling. The walls were a mosaic of gold and dark tiles. The rugs on the floor were dark as well, and very little light crept into the place from the high windows or the open courtyard beyond two tiers of pillars. As my eyes adjusted to the dimness I saw the royal divan in a far corner, and on it a fragile old man almost smothered by his royal raiments and mushrooming turban.

"Now, senorita," the Pasha whispered. "You are in the presence of Baba Mohammed, Dey of Algiers. Walk to the divan with your eyes cast down, then kneel and place your forehead on the rugs." I did as I was told, and while I was in that position, I heard the Dey speak to Ben Raza. The sound of his voice surprised me. I expected something deep and terrible to merit the fellow's power over the Pasha, but what I heard was paper thin, almost a cackle.

"Stand up now, senorita," Ben Raza commanded, and I did. Then I beheld the Dey of Algiers. Here was the scourge of the Mediterranean, the successor to Barbarossa, the lecherous Musselman who intended to deflower me—a shriveled old man so decrepit that it was a struggle for him to stand.

The Pasha took Baba Mohammed's arm to help him walk over to me. Then the old fellow reached out with a quivering hand, pulled away my veil and stroked my cheek. Resisting a strong urge to flee, I looked into his face. His skin was the color and texture of a dried apricot against which the bones of his skull were outlined. His eyes were couched in heavy folds.

He cackled something more at Ben Raza. "He wants to see your teeth," the Pasha told me. I opened my mouth obediently, and Baba Mohammed scrutinized every tooth in my head.

When he was satisfied that they were adequate, he let his fingers slide down my neck and along my shoulder until he cupped my left breast in his hand. I revolted instinctively at that and knocked his fragile arm away, forgetting for a moment all the horrors that could befall Adele in an African enslavement as punishment for my misbehavior.

The Dey was staggered by my blow and might have fallen but for a fat Negro standing behind him who prevented it. Ben Raza responded like lightning with a backhanded slap across my face that sent me crashing to the floor. Baba Mohammed's strength was overtaxed by the excitement, and a coughing fit overtook him. It racked his dry old bones so violently that I thought he might not survive. Attendants rushed to his aid and helped the Negro and Ben Raza carry him back to the divan.

A few moments later the Dey recovered, but the spasm left him exhausted. It was clear even to a woman of my inexperience that if the Dey of Algiers were to launch an assault on my virginity, it would be as secure as the ramparts of Mont-Saint-Michel.

There was very little time for me to take comfort in that observation, however. As soon as Ben Raza saw the Dey had recovered, he marched toward me with murder in his heart. I tried to scramble to my feet and get away, but he grabbed me and threw me over his shoulders. As he carried me off, I could entertain no doubt that I would be dead within the hour and Adele would be on her way to Timbuktu, the property of some miserable desert nomad. Then I heard the old man's voice again. He was calling Ben Raza back.

The Pasha tossed me to the floor and bowed to the Dey. He sat down quickly on a pillow next to the royal

divan, and the two men fell to talking. While I tried to
rub away the pain where Ben Raza had hit me, I
watched their exchange. Every now and then they cast
a look in my direction, but for the most part I might
have been another of the stone pillars in the courtyard.
Finally they finished. I could not help but notice that
both of them looked self-satisfied to an offensive de-
gree, and that fact encouraged me in my hopes of seeing another sunrise.

"Bow to the Dey, senorita." Ben Raza's voice had
softened. I bowed as before. "The audience is over.
Please follow me out."

When the Pasha and I returned to the antechamber,
I did not feel well. Naturally, after what had just happened, I feared for my life. My cheek throbbed. At
least two of my teeth were loose, and I could taste
blood in my mouth. Considering that Ben Raza was
the culprit responsible for it all, I found him to
be amazingly solicitous after we left the throne room.

"Please sit down, senorita," he said as he took my
arm and eased me onto the divan. "Are you comfortable?"

Shocked at his concern, I said nothing, but my hand
against my reddened cheek told him enough. "Senorita,
did I hurt you?"

I was still very afraid of him, but there are certain
questions so utterly stupid that they do not merit ci-
vility. Under the circumstances I considered this to be
one of them. "Of course you hurt me," I snapped.
"You struck me across the face. You may have broken
two of my teeth. You most definitely hurt me, Senor."

"Oh, no!" he lamented with an intensity I found
difficult to understand. Then he raised his right hand
to the heavens. "May Allah cleave this arm from my
body if it has caused you permanent harm." He stood
in that pose for quite a while. I think he may have
expected something to happen along the lines of his
petition, but Allah had not taken him seriously. Certainly I did not.

Finally he gave it up and directed his attention to

me once again. "Is there anything I can provide to ease
your suffering?" he asked.

The taste of my own blood as it oozed around my
wobbling teeth was making me ill. "I would like some
wine to cleanse my mouth," I replied.

Ben Raza looked distressed, but he went to the
guard at the door and said something. The fellow left
his post. While we waited for his return there were
more apologies. The Pasha propped pillows here and
there to make me comfortable, and I became increas-
ingly apprehensive and puzzled about his change of
demeanor.

When the guard appeared with a pitcher, Ben Raza
filled a pottery cup for me. "Senorita, this will make
you feel better." He handed it to me.

I looked at the liquid, expecting a reassuring ruby
color to meet my gaze. "What is this?" I asked.

"We have no wine here, senorita," he responded.
"It is forbidden by the Koran."

"But this looks like water."

"It is water."

"I do not drink water." I tried to hand it back to
him, but he would not accept it.

"The water is pure, senorita. I swear it by the beard
of the Prophet."

"Oh you do! Well, your oaths mean nothing to me."

"Please, senorita. You should drink it."

"It does not agree with me, senor. No thank you."

"This is not France, senorita. We drink water here."

"Then drink it yourself. After I see you down a cup,
I promise to drink some as well." At that point I hoped
the fellow would come down with a vicious case of the
bloody flux.

He downed it as if it were liquor. "Now you," he
said, handing me a full draught. I took it and threw it
onto the rugs. "Senorita, you said—"

"I lied. You know how we infidels are."

The Pasha was clearly disgusted with me, but for
some reason he controlled his tongue, and his fore-
bearance told me I had the upper hand, at least for

the moment. "Perhaps some tea then?" he suggested with a forced smile.

"I prefer wine," I said haughtily, "but if you have none, tea will do."

When the tea arrived, I found it sweetened with honey and quite delicious. It eased the pain in my jaw and freshened my mouth. The Pasha could see its salutary effect and was so encouraged that he began to explain his intentions for my future.

"Senorita, I have wonderful news for you," he began. "Unfortunately, it brings great sorrow to many others. Surely you noticed, the Dey is dying. You saw the condition of his health."

"He did not look well," I agreed.

"An old wound," he went on. "I never suspected. It has been several months since I saw him last." Ben Raza shook his head sadly. I could see that he felt a great deal of affection for the Dey and was genuinely distressed at his condition, but I was unmoved. "Allah will take him to his bosom soon," the pirate muttered.

And good riddance, I thought, almost aloud.

"You pleased him," he continued. "In spite of everything, you pleased him very much. But he does not wish to waste your youth in the harem of a dying man."

My heart almost leapt into my mouth at those words. "You'll set me free then!" I blurted out. "And Adele, I can arrange a ransom for her! You'll free her too?"

"What?" the Pasha looked startled. "No, no. You are going to Istanbul."

"Istanbul?"

"Yes, the Dey is going to give you to the Grand Turk himself, the Sultan of the Ottoman Empire."

My shoulders slumped. Tears came to my eyes, and my face must have reflected bitter disappointment.

"Please, senorita. This is magnificent! It is your glorious fate to live in the palace of the great one. If you bear his son, you could become the most powerful woman in the world. You are blessed. I kiss the hem of your garment." He knelt down and drew my skirt to his lips.

I jerked it away. "Stop that!"

"But senorita, you are going to the seraglio of the Grand Turk. You will see him with your own eyes. You will lie beside him on his sacred couch."

"Why?" I screamed. "Why are you doing this to me? Haven't I endured enough? You have taken Adele from me. Do you think some Turk will take her place? Do you think it's pleasant for me to wait around to be raped? Well, I'll tell you. It's horrible. I've never been raped. I don't have any idea what it's like. I suspect it is just as nasty to be raped by a Turk as by anyone else. I don't know. I just sit and wait, dreading it, wondering about it. This suspense is more cruel than the deed."

"But senorita. It is your fate—"

"I will not hear one more word from you about my fate. You said my fate was here in Algiers, and now I'm to be shipped off again. You don't know anything about my fate."

I caught my breath and went on. "Sweet Mother of God! Adele was right. Men make such a muck of everything. You, you're a pirate! Have you no pride? Pirates are supposed to rape women. For the love of heaven, why don't you rape me right here and now. Why this endless delay?" I buried my face in the pillow by my side and sobbed.

Pasha paced back and forth in front of me, watching me cry. He tried to speak, but he could not seem to find a way to begin. At last several women came to the chamber to take me away. I was weak with sadness and offered them no resistance.

"Senorita," Pasha spoke at last. "Allah has blessed you in so many ways. To go to Istanbul, to serve the great caliph of us all. What more can any woman want in this life?" he asked as the servants directed me toward the archway.

"I want to be free," was my reply. "And I want to see Adele." Then I was led away.

Chapter 9

The month of May passed while I stayed in the Dey's harem. During that time, his craftsmen worked day and night to prepare a ship to take me to Istanbul. I was not the·only cargo, however. The hold carried my dowry, an immense fortune in captured European booty.

The Dey of Algiers was rarely so generous without design. This act of munificence was carefully planned to purchase the Ottoman Sultan's favor and erase some old debts. Baba Mohammed desperately needed munitions for his war against the Europeans, and Istanbul was his only reliable market. Without the Sultan's goodwill that source could disappear, and at the time there was reason to wonder about the Sultan's disposition on the subject. For years Baba Mohammed had been delinquent in sending the tribute expected in Istanbul from vassel princes of the Sultan's dominion. This insult went unpunished because the empire did not have the military strength to challenge the Dey's forces.

Now there were dangerous rumors. The Sultan's grand admiral had led Turkish armies against several rebellious regions on the fringe of the empire. He had conquered them and ruthlessly returned them to taxpaying status. Recently, Baba Mohammed's name had been on the admiral's lips. If the Sultan cut off the flow of munitions and then sent an army to Africa, Baba Mohammed would lose his throne, and the Europeans would sweep through his kingdom like vultures after the Ottomans dealt their death blow.

Baba Mohammed needed to regain the Sultan's favor in order to secure his position. For that reason my dowry and I were consigned to Istanbul. On the day of my departure the morning sun was white hot, but the air did not cling to me like the French summer heat. Instead, it drank the moisture from my body and left me with a constant thirst. I took that thirst with me as I left the Dey's palace and stepped into an enclosed sedan chair. The vehicle was sumptuous but its interior was stifling, and I soon envied the loosely robed men on horseback who were my escort.

After us followed a grand procession. My entourage included armed guards, eunuchs, cooks, maids, body servants, hairdressers, seamstresses, a masseuse, a storyteller and four large dogs in oriental costume. A train of pack animals laden with baggage stretched far behind my servants, kicking up a cloud of dust that enveloped much of the city. When I looked through my curtains, I could see curious crowds of dark-skinned people lining our route in much the same way that Frenchmen gather to catch a glimpse of King Louis or his Austrian queen.

Time and again, swarms of little children ran toward my vehicle and cried out for charity. Alms givers walking on either side of me threw coins, and the children scattered to catch them. It had been explained that Musselmen are directed by the Koran to give alms to the poor as a means of tithing, and beggars are considered the servants of Allah for providing their wealthier brothers an opportunity to follow the Prophet's commandments. As a result beggars are constantly under foot in every Islamic city, much the way lawyers are in Paris. You cannot move ten paces along any street without being accosted by ten or a dozen.

Our long and meandering column finally reached the harbor, and my guards cleared away the rabble so that I could emerge from my sedan chair in safety. As I stepped outside, the bright African morning blinded me momentarily, but the sea air was refreshing, and I savored its bouquet.

The ship waiting for me might have been wrought by a silversmith the way it glistened in the sun. It was the largest vessel I had ever seen, much bigger, it seemed, than some of the inhabited islands off the coast of France. The trees felled to make the masts were such giants they must have grown for a thousand years. The ship had been built for beauty, but it was deadly as well; three banks of cannon ports eyed the sea in an unceasing vigil. Above them, crewmen scrambled over the rigging to make preparations to catch the next tide.

The smell of the sea, a pirate ship and another passage to another potentate—all of it brought on a rush of horrible memories of my last disastrous voyage and filled me with foreboding as I stepped aboard. There an incongruous reception greeted me. As soon as the ship's crew was notified of my presence, they left their duties and formed well ordered ranks on the main deck.

"The blessings of Allah upon you all," called a familiar voice. I turned toward it and saw Captain Pasha Ben Raza striding toward my women and me with a broad grin on his face. He salaamed formally.

"Captain Pasha," I said, trying to hide my surprise at seeing him again.

"Ah, Senorita de Rivery," he bowed directly to me. "I knew you in spite of your veil. Your golden hair peaks from beneath it. I hope you have been well," he went on. "Your hands?"

"They have mended," I replied. "How is Adele?"

"She thrives, senorita. She thrives." He beamed as he spoke, and I resented the happiness in his face. "We will speak of her later," he said, "but now, may I suggest that you send your women to their quarters. I must see you alone. There is a message from the Dey."

I did as he asked, and he led me to my cabin. It was in the stern of the ship, quite spacious and decorated in Turkish fashion. There was a divan to one side; rugs and cushions, everything dark and cool. In the center was a Moroccan leather travel trunk I assumed to be part of my baggage.

"Senorita," Ben Raza began. "The Dey wishes you the blessings of the Almighty. His poor health keeps him from delivering his benediction personally, but he has commissioned me to present you with a token of his devotion.

"The Dey is a fine ruler," he went on. "Very fair and just. His people prosper. They love him. When you are at the Grand Seraglio in Istanbul, it will do the Dey no harm for you to speak well of him."

The Pasha reached into his sash and drew out a key. With it he unlocked the trunk. When he threw back the lid, I could see a honeycomb of golden hexagonal boxes fitted perfectly into a wooden frame. He pulled out one of the boxes, and below its place another container, identical to the others, became visible.

Ben Raza handed the first box to me. When I lifted the lid I found a velvet bed covered with diamonds. There were at least twenty stones, all different in size, all winking in the lamplight as if they had lives of their own.

The Pasha drew box after box from the trunk and opened them. Each contained a fortune in precious stones—pearls, rubies, emeralds, sapphires, and more diamonds.

"Am I to deliver these to the Sultan?" I asked, awed by the beauty of the gems.

"No, senorita. These stones belong to you. They are a gift from Baba Mohammed."

A wave of elation swept over me when I heard those words. So many terrible things had happened, but now this. My heart raced and my hands began to tremble. I could not think clearly.

"You are certain?" I asked, trying to regain my composure.

"Yes," Ben Raza assured me. "Baba Mohammed will not have you go a pauper to the Grand Turk."

"Captain Pasha, tell me the truth, why is he giving me all this?"

"I did tell you the truth. He hopes you will speak kindly of him to the Sultan. He needs Ottoman support."

"And he thinks I can get that for him?"

"Yes."

"But how? I'm a prisoner, little more than a slave. I know nothing of politics, and I am a woman in a realm where we rank as chattel. How can I influence a sultan?"

"Come, senorita," the Pasha took my arm and led me toward the divan. "Sit down and I will explain." I made myself comfortable and took off my veil. The metal key in my hand was warm. I held on to it tightly.

"You are beautiful," Ben Raza said when he looked at me. "That is very important, but it is not all. You see, the Grand Turk lives in his seraglio and speaks with very few people. There are his viziers, his religious leader, the Mufti, some eunuchs and a few of his pashas. The word *pasha* means 'sultan's foot,' but they are more like his eyes and ears. All he learns about his empire comes from the small group who are his advisers. These eyes and ears of his are not always true. They distort and color everything to suit their own purposes, yet the Sultan can rely on no one else for he speaks with no one else. No one, that is, except his women.

"Of course, there are hundreds of women in his

harem. He buys them by the score. He receives them as gifts. Most of them he has never seen. But you, senorita, you will be one of his favorites. We have no doubt of it. You will please him."

"But Captain Pasha," I interrupted. "If there are so many women in the harem, he may never notice me. Then what will Baba Mohammed's fortune buy for him?"

"The Sultan will notice you," he responded confidently. "The Dey has seen to that. Messengers have been sent ahead to spread news of your beauty. The Sultan will be expecting you."

"But all of his women must be beautiful," I said.

"Yes, yes. That is true." Ben Raza smiled cunningly. "There is something else though. Your dowry is quite handsome. There is enough treasure in the hold of this ship to interest even a sultan. I know I'd look upon the snake-headed Medusa to make it mine."

"Ah," I smiled. "You aren't gambling a fortune on something as simple as the color of my hair."

"Your hair is magnificent, senorita. And so is the treasure. We know that your special kind of beauty will give you influence with the Sultan, but what we have in the hold will finance a holy war against Russia, and that has a certain beauty all its own."

"Then I suggest you send the treasure and let me go. I'll do you no good in Istanbul."

"You underestimate yourself, senorita," the Pasha protested.

"You underestimate me, senor," I responded sharply. "How can you imagine I will forget that it was you and the Dey who have held me prisoner? Do you think so little of women that you imagine I will not seek revenge?"

"Revenge?" The Pasha sounded shocked. "But we are not to blame for what has happened to you. It is the will of Allah. You were destined to go to Istanbul. Why should you seek vengeance against the instruments of the Almighty?"

"I am a Catholic. I do not believe in destiny. God intended that we choose our own paths."

"All right, senorita," the Pasha responded. "Do you choose to accept this treasure chest?" He motioned toward the trunk with his arm and then admonished me. "Know this before you choose. If you accept it, you must pay the price. You must go to Istanbul and enter the Sultan's harem."

"If I refuse it, you'll let me go?" I asked.

"If you refuse it, your brains must be addled. The Koran speaks of such people as being visited by God. I will let you go in the name of the Prophet."

"I refuse it." A surge of excitement rushed through me as I held out the key to him.

"Allah, be merciful," Ben Raza cried. "You would give up such a treasure?"

"In exchange for my freedom? Of course!" I tried to give him the key. "Now I'd like to see Adele. Tell me how I can find her."

"You cannot leave," Ben Raza said, still amazed at my decision.

"But you can have the trunk. Here, take the key. You said that if I refused—"

"You will go to Istanbul."

I squeezed the key in my hand. It represented a fortune, but I was still a prisoner. I had been a fool to take the word of a Musselman the second time, knowing it meant nothing to him. My disappointment brought tears to my eyes, but I forced them down.

Ben Raza saw my grief. "Be reasonable, senorita."

"Be reasonable?" I shouted back at him. "I think it's very reasonable for me to want to cut your heart out, and if you send me to Istanbul, I'll see to it that someone does."

"Then it will not go well for your friend, Adele." Ben Raza responded. "She is happy now. Let her remain so."

"You say she's happy. You liar. She may be dead."

"She is not dead."

"Prove it," I demanded. "Bring her to me before we sail."

"You disappoint me, senorita." He stood up, walked to the door and left.

I knew then I would never see Adele again. All my dreams to escape and free her were lost. My only purpose for staying alive was gone.

I looked at the chest. If I had had its contents just two months before, I would have been welcomed into François de Marmont's family as his wife. Now it would not purchase anything, not a single passage to Martinique nor a bottle of good wine.

I heard the cabin door open behind me, but I did not turn to see who entered.

"Senorita," Ben Raza said softly.

"Leave me alone!"

"Aimee!" The voice that spoke my name was familiar music.

I spun around, "Adele!"

Her arms opened to me as she came into the cabin. I felt my limbs weaken as I rushed to her. She embraced me warmly, and all the misery and fear that I had tried to hide for so long came pouring out in a flood of tears.

"Senorita de Rivery," the Pasha tried to speak over my sobs.

"It's all right now, Aimee," Adele whispered. Her arms tightened around me and I felt safe.

"Senorita de Rivery," Ben Raza persisted. "I had hoped it would please you if I delivered your friend. It was to be a gesture of goodwill, but you were so determined."

"That's enough, Ibrahim," I heard Adele say to him. "Please leave us now."

He turned and left the cabin.

Chapter 10

"Adele, you're alive!" I cried and hugged her.

"Of course, I'm alive, Aimee." She held my face in her hands. Her smile was warm and happy as she wiped the tears from my eyes. "Ibrahim must have told you I was all right."

"Ibrahim, is it? Well, if you mean that barbarian Ben Raza, who can believe him? He's lied to me more than once."

"Yes, I know," she looked amused. "But you've done the same to him. I enjoyed the episode of the water and wine."

"You know about that?" I was surprised. But seeing Adele again and knowing she was safe was too exciting, and I gave little thought to the gentle tone of her voice when she spoke of the pirate. "Here, let's sit down."

Reluctantly we let go of each other long enough to make ourselves comfortable with pillows on the floor, assuming positions that would have been difficult for us had we been dressed in French petticoats and stays.

"Tell me what happened to you, Adele." I held her hands and noticed that several of her fingers were decorated with valuable gems.

"There's a lot to tell, Aimee, but before I begin, I have a present for you." As she spoke, I could not help but notice that even under our dire circumstances, she was as lighthearted as if we were chatting in her room at the convent. "I understand you have a terrible thirst," she went on.

"I'd kill for a glass of good wine, if that's what you mean."

"That is precisely what I mean." She got to her feet and went to a wall cabinet under the stern windows. "My dear, I am here to save you from that mortal sin." She pulled open the cabinet doors and revealed four shelves of bottles.

"Wine!" I shouted. She took a bottle out. I could see its strong shoulders and dark color. "Bordeaux?"

"Yes, and very good," she answered. "There are tumblers over there." She pointed to another cabinet near the door. I found them. She opened the bottle, and we sat down again.

"To us, Aimee," she said and raised her glass.

"Together again," I added. Then we drank. "Wonderful," I sighed, delighted with the taste. "How did you get it in this uncivilized wasteland?"

"Ibrahim took it from a ship last year. Even with the war he entertains a few Europeans now and then, and he keeps wine and spirits for them."

"I'll wager he takes a drink himself," I said as I drained my glass.

"He may," she responded. "But I doubt it. He seems rather devout."

"There are several words I could use to describe Captain Pasha, but devout is not one of them. Now tell me, what has happened to you? You look wonderful, but did he hurt you?"

"No, he isn't really that sort."

"I know his sort. He's capable of anything."

"I don't think so. He's basically good."

"You can't believe that?"

"I can believe my eyes, Aimee. I was taken to his home after I left the ship. It's a villa high up in the hills overlooking the harbor. There are children. He loves them. He's well educated, and he has wives."

"I know about wives. The Dey has more than thirty."

"Ibrahim has only two others," Adele explained. "One is Algerian and quite a bit older than he. They were married when he was a boy, and she bore him three sons. His second wife is Maltese, younger and very pretty. Her children are a boy and a girl, six and four. The children are very happy and they adore their father."

"About the wives," I asked cautiously. "You used the word 'others.' Does that mean you . . . ?"

"Yes. There was a short ceremony, and he considers me his wife."

"I don't care what he considers. I want to know what you think."

"I don't know." A half smile came to her lips. "You'd think I'd want to kill him for what he's done to us, but I don't. I enjoy being with him. He isn't like any Frenchman I've ever known."

I was shocked by her attitude. "He's certainly no gentleman," I pointed out.

Adele looked at me strangely. "You say he's no gentleman as if I'd consider that a condemnation."

"Well it is," I responded, impatient at her obtuse manner. "Can you imagine any French gentleman bullying us like this? I'm virtually a prisoner—and you. He dragged you off to his lair, took you by force and threatened your enslavement if I didn't cooperate with him. Gentlemen don't carry on like that."

"No, they don't. They're much worse."

"Come now, Adele. Talk sense. The man raped you."

"No he didn't," she said flatly.

"What?" I couldn't believe she had escaped him.

"That's right. There was quite a lovely courtship.

We spent several days together getting acquainted. I even met his mother."

"Then you went to his bed willingly?" I was stunned. "You and that animal?"

"That's enough, Aimee." There was anger in her voice. "I won't have you talking about him that way."

"He's going to ship me off to Istanbul and give me to a Turk!" I shouted. "I'll talk about him any way I please."

She paused. "Yes, but you must understand. After I had a chance to reason with him, he wanted to set you free. He even went to the Dey and offered to buy you from him, but the Dey refused. Ibrahim did everything he could."

"Then why doesn't he let me go once we leave Algiers?"

"He's devoted to Baba Mohammed. He'd never disobey him."

"Oh, so he's a man of principle, is he?" I sneered. "Well, if he's so generous, why are you still here, still a prisoner?"

"I'm not a prisoner," she said matter of factly. "He offered to return me to France if I want to go."

"Then go, for the love of heaven."

"I don't think I want to."

"You must be mad."

"Believe me, Aimee, if I thought I could raise a ransom and get you out of this, I'd go back. But I know about the jewels." She motioned toward the travel trunk. "King Louis himself couldn't match what the Dey has invested in you. A ransom is impossible."

"Forget about me, Adele." I set my wine glass down and knelt in front of her. "You can save yourself."

"I need time to think about that," she said.

"You don't mean you could live with that barbarian, do you?"

"Yes, I could. And he isn't a barbarian. He's quite civilized in a Musselman's way."

"But Adele, there are a half dozen Frenchmen who begged for your hand. You could have any of them."

"A Frenchman," Adele said disgustedly. "I suppose you mean all those sons of the nobility that pass their time in boudoirs and at gaming tables while they wait for their fathers to die. I don't consider any of them worthy of my attention. If I did, I would have stayed in France and married."

"But they aren't all popinjays," I protested. "You could find someone with character. Look at François!" I was shocked because that statement was nonsense, and I knew it. But after my imprisonment in the Dey's palace, I found Adele's acceptance of Ben Raza intolerable and bewildering. In my confusion I grasped at any straw to bring her to her senses. "I was such a fool to leave him," I went on, "but I'll find a way to get back. I'll escape!"

"I don't want to hear about François de Marmont," Adele said sharply.

"Why not? He has his weaknesses, but he's proof that every gentleman in France is not as shallow as you say."

"Let's not discuss him now," she insisted. "I can feel the wine, and I don't want to say anything I'll regret."

"We *will* discuss him now!" I walked to the cabinet and took out another bottle. "What you have to say will come out sometime. You know yourself well enough to realize you won't keep it from me for long." I pulled the cork.

"All right," Adele held out her glass and I filled it. "The man is a swine."

"Adele, that's a terrible thing to say."

"I knew I shouldn't have started this after so much wine. Forgive me for being so blunt. I don't want to hurt you. Let's talk another time."

"No! You'll have to tell me now, so out with it."

"All right," she said and took a sip from her glass. "I probably could have kept my peace if I didn't think you might throw your life away trying to reach him. But if you escape from Istanbul, and the Turks recapture you, they'll kill you."

"I'll be better off dead than a prisoner for the rest of my life."

"You don't know that. All you do know is that you'll be very rich. Everything else you imagine about a harem is just that—your imagination. You may find its a good life."

"I know that if I were free I could go home and marry François."

"No," Adele said forcefully. "François never intended to marry you."

"Yes, he did. I know he did." Tears filled my eyes, but I managed to keep from crying.

"There's no doubt in my mind that he loves you," Adele said, trying to soothe me. "If I didn't think so, I never would have helped him to see you. It seemed just a matter of time before he would straighten things out with his father. At least that's what I thought, but he let you go without making one move in that direction. I couldn't believe my eyes when you came aboard that ship and told me nothing had changed. I sent him the date of our departure at least a month in advance. He had plenty of time to go to Paris and make the proper arrangements, but he did nothing.

"I had a reasonably high opinion of François until that day. But then I realized he never intended to marry you at all. If Marie hadn't foiled his plans at her château, you would have been at his mercy. He would have taken your virtue, then kept you dangling and married his father's choice."

"I'm afraid you may be right," I confessed, hoping to put an end to it and wishing I had not forced her to speak her mind.

"Of course I am, and you know it. Otherwise you would never have left France."

It was true. I left because I was frightened that such a thing might happen, and I would end up as nothing more than a well-kept mistress. Paris is full of such women, inhabiting elegant apartments, living from day to day with the certainty that they will one day be old and alone, their beauty and youth squandered on lovers who have lost interest.

Adele put her arms around me. "Aimee, don't you see? What is so damning about the entire affair is that François actually loves you. He loves you and he was willing to deceive you so cruelly. You may consider him the cream of French manhood, but I believe he has no character at all."

"Oh Adele," I sighed on the brink of tears. "How could I have been so wrong about him?"

"You were in love with him and that blinded you to his faults, but even then you were clever enough to spare yourself the humiliation that would have come if you had stayed in France."

"Clever?" I laughed bitterly. "Hardly. If I had stayed in France, I might have ended up as a kept woman, but at least I'd have my freedom. What am I now? A prisoner."

"Aimee, you call this a prison, but here we are, drinking fine wine. A dozen slaves are waiting outside to serve you. The largest, most luxurious ship I have ever seen is transporting us along some of the most beautiful and historic coastlines in the world. There are safe harbors all the way to our destination. When we get there you'll probably be greeted as a queen, and you have a treasure in gems to ease your path wherever you go. My dear, if there were bars on this prison of yours, they would be to keep the rest of the world out."

Chapter 11

Throughout our passage, Adele and I never spoke of François again, and I struggled to keep him out of my thoughts. In spite of my bizarre imprisonment, there were compensations. I was surrounded by oriental luxury. My companion, Adele, was full of high spirits and optimism and I had escaped the boredom that had plagued me at the convent. If nothing else, my life had become an adventure.

The last day of our voyage started with a ritual to which I had become accustomed. My servants arose early and took their places on the stern deck for morning prayers. When they were finished, Lydia appeared. She was a healthy looking Moor of about twenty-seven years. Her face was broad and cheerful, her eyes so dark and distinctly outlined by heavy lashes and cosmetics that they always seemed full of wonder. She was a slave in the Dey's harem. Because her mother was French, another unfortunate victim of Barbary pirates who captured her and sent her into Algerian slavery, Lydia could speak my language, and the Dey sent her with me as a translator.

"Good morning, mademoiselle," she said musically. "I have your breakfast."

"Good morning, Lydia." I sat up and smiled. She set the tray on the rugs next to my bed. "On deck it is said that Istanbul will be sighted soon. Would you please do me the kindness of excusing me from your presence this morning. I hope to catch the first glimpse of the city." She looked at me anxiously, but she already knew my answer.

"Of course. Go, by all means. Adele will be here soon to keep me company."

"Oh, thank you, mademoiselle." Lydia embraced me, kissed my cheek and then ran out the door. I smiled after her, still a bit uncomfortable, yet pleased with the warm affection women show one another in Musselman society.

While my door was still open, Adele called to me from the companionway. "Aimee, are you still in your cabin?" She no longer shared quarters with me, as she went to Ibrahim Ben Raza's bed every night.

"Yes," I answered. "Come have coffee."

"Not now. Put on your veils and come up on deck. We've reached Istanbul."

It was a measure of the peace I had found aboard ship that I met the news of our arrival in the city of my future captivity with excitement as well as apprehension. Adele and Ibrahim had comforted me with the opinion that it would take weeks after my arrival to gain an audience with the Sultan. Every bureaucrat and functionary from gatekeeper to royal turban bearer would have to record my name and be paid in gold, and each one would keep us waiting an appropriate length of time before he would agree to a meeting. My carnal payment for all the luxury I had enjoyed was still far off. Adele had even suggested that my part of the bargain might not be as terrible as I had supposed. So I could breathe in the sea air without a tight feeling of fear in my chest. I called my servants, hurried to dress and went up on deck.

Istanbul is one of the most beautiful cities on earth. Approaching it from the Sea of Marmara in early morning is the best possible introduction to it. It balances gracefully on the very edge of Europe like a terraced garden of blossoming flowers that have turned their faces toward an Asian sun. Dozens of minarets support the sky's blue canopy over mosques, bazaars, bustling activities and all the races of the world. Brilliantly painted houses and shops are arranged in irregular ranks that ramble up and down every hillside. Yet water dominates the setting. Life seems to burst forth into the sea with schools of small boats that ferry people and their goods between two continents.

Neither Adele nor I spoke as our eyes drank in the magnificent sight, but all around us I could hear my servants whispering to each other. None of them had ever seen the city before, and they were awed by its grandure as well as its religious significance. It is a special place to the people of Islam because it is the home of the Ottoman Sultan—the grand caliph of all the faithful—something like a Musselman pope.

Captain Pasha joined Adele and me when our ship approached the clear blue finger of water known as the Golden Horn. As our vessel turned westward into its mouth, he pointed to our destination—the Grand Seraglio, the palace of Abdul Hamid, the Sultan.

Seeing it for the first time made me shudder. Its size was overwhelming. The palace walls crawled like a serpent over the entire southern point jutting into the Horn. Dark cypress trees gave it an ominous, evil appearance, the suggestion of a shroud. In spite of the warm Mediterranean sun, I felt a chill, and I turned to Adele for security. She was not beside me.

"Adele," I called out, thinking she must be watching the city from a different vantage point on the vessel.

"There, mademoiselle." Lydia stepped near me and

pointed down. While I had been looking at the palace, Adele had descended to the main deck. Ben Raza was with her. A boat had come alongside. There was a messenger. Ben Raza made a noisy protest. He appeared very upset. The messenger pulled a document from a leather case. Ben Raza looked at it and threw it down. Then he took Adele's hand.

I called to her. She looked up and waved. After that she was helped over the side to a ladder, and she slipped out of sight. Moments later the boat carried her away.

I ran to the steps leading to the main deck, but Ben Raza met me there on his way up. "Where have they taken her?" I demanded.

"I don't know." His voice was desperate. "It was by the Dey's orders. The envoys he sent to the Ottoman court with news of you were also told to meet our ship. They've taken her. I don't believe it."

"But why?" I asked, frightened by what I saw in the Pasha's eyes.

"Baba Mohammed fears you. If you were to be uncooperative, his cause could be severely damaged. He intends to keep Adele against the chance you should try to escape."

"You scoundrel!" I screamed helplessly. "You knew he would do this!" As soon as I spoke, I realized I was wrong. The fear in Ben Raza's face was one oath I could believe.

"No, senorita," he protested. "I knew nothing. But I understand. The Dey is cunning. He knows I can no longer bargain with the life of a woman who is so dear to me, and he knows that Adele is the only lever he can use against you.

"Please, senorita. You must cooperate. If you don't, Baba Mohammed will kill her."

Chapter 12

Ibrahim Ben Raza escorted me to my cabin soon after
Baba Mohammed's men took Adele away. There I
found my servants waiting to prepare me for my entrance to the Grand Seraglio. Because Lydia had explained to them that Adele was being held prisoner,
the women were subdued as they helped me into my
trousers and gowns. They were very fond of Adele
and fearful I might commit some act of desperation
that could jeopardize her life. Their apprehension was
due to the wild reputation I had earned as a result
of the brawl involving Captain Pasha's women on the
day of my arrival in Algiers.

"You must conduct yourself with decorum," Lydia
said over and over again. "Remember Mademoiselle
Fleury."

I did not respond to her directions, knowing full
well what I had to do. In my silence the other women
coaxed her into more exhortations until I was near
hysteria for fear I might do something accidentally
that could bring Adele harm.

A knock at the cabin door finally turned the admonishing eyes away from me.

"Enter," I called, relieved to be temporarily free of their scrutiny.

"Your veil," Lydia chastised me. I pinned it in place.

The Pasha came in and salaamed formally. "Your entourage is waiting." His face mirrored the same concern I saw everywhere else, and my anxiety increased.

"Senorita," he continued. "I know you are afraid, but believe me. I have entered the seraglio many times bearing gifts for the Sultan or instructions from the Dey. No matter how urgent, nothing moves quickly among the Ottomans. It is the bureaucracy. Not a mouse or a flea enters that palace without being recorded in the registers. Your name will be written half a hundred times before you will see the Sultan, and every scribe who marks you down will detain you long enough to demonstrate his importance and collect a payment for his services.

"This is the way of the Ottomans, and I have never known it to vary. You will see at least another month go by before you will have to do your duty. Then, when it is finished, Adele will be released. I'm certain of it."

"Thank you, Captain Pasha," I said, suddenly feeling very close to the man who had caused me so much grief. "I know you're trying to comfort me, but these delays only increase my anxiety and lengthen Adele's imprisonment."

"Ah, but it is the way of these Ottomans, senorita. The delays are unavoidable."

"Then I will have to bide my time, I suppose, and try to keep my imagination in check. But how will I be sure Adele is safe?"

"I will send word to you. The Kislar Agha of the harem accepts gifts in exchange for his assistance. He is the eunuch in charge of all the Sultan's women, and he can deliver my message."

"Then I'll never see you or Adele again?" I asked, already knowing the answer.

"Who can say, senorita? That is in the hands of Allah." He bade me farewell with a compassionate smile. Then he bowed and in European fashion kissed my hand. "May the blessings of Allah fill your heart with serenity, Golden One." He turned and left the cabin.

"It's time to go, mademoiselle," Lydia urged. "The Sultan must not be kept waiting."

"We'll be the ones who will wait," I explained to her, realizing that Pasha had spoken in Spanish, and she could not understand a word. "But let's make a start. We'll hurry these reluctant fellows along as best we can."

My ride to the seraglio was far from pleasant. No matter how much I wished to be finished with the conjugal initiation that lay ahead, I was filled with trepidation as it approached, and my stomach was aflutter. Adele's situation caused me even more anxiety. My performance in the Sultan's bedchamber would determine her fate as well as my own, and my inexperience in that arena was a matter of public knowledge.

In the excitement of our arrival in Istanbul, Adele's abduction and all the lengthy preparations to come ashore, I had forgotten to eat anything. Soon after we left the ship, that omission had the predictably disagreeable effect of giving me a dull headache and a sour taste in my mouth. Lydia and I rode to the seraglio in the same carriage, a miserably sprung contraption that transmitted the irregularities of every paving stone through my spine to my throbbing brain. Ours was the place of honor in the caravan, in front of the baggage but behind the beasts and vehicles conveying gifts. The air was filled with dust kicked up ahead of us on sections of the thoroughfare where the cobbles were missing and the roadbed exposed. Lydia insisted that the carriage curtains remain closed tightly to keep out the dirt, and so we saw nothing of historic Istanbul. I was in no mood for a tour and did not protest until the heat of the closed carriage oppressed me. By that time the caravan had come to a stop in the shade of a plane tree outside the gates of the seraglio. As long as I was veiled, Lydia made no objection to opening the windows.

After a quarter of an hour had passed, one of our eunuchs came to the door. "There is a delay," Lydia explained after he had spoken to her. "These Ottomans must record the goods we carry, and the guards cannot find the proper official with the register." Thinking that this lived up to Ben Raza's description of the palace bureaucracy, I tried to prepare myself for a long wait.

An hour passed, perhaps two. I grew impatient. My stomach and head had not improved, and it was still very warm in the carriage. Finally, I heard the vehicles ahead of us begin to move. Then our carriage inched forward into the sun. When we stopped again, the eunuch reappeared and spoke to Lydia.

"The Kislar Agha, the chief eunuch, mademoiselle," Lydia explained. "He extends his greetings to you and offers his apologies for this unforgivable delay. He advises you that a *palanquin,* a sedan chair for one, awaits just inside the Imperial Gate to carry you to the harem of the seraglio."

"Then I can get out of here?" I asked, hoping a bit of fresh air might clear my head and improve the condition of my vitals.

Lydia spoke with the eunuch and then answered. "The Kisler Agha awaits your pleasure, mademoiselle. You may leave the carriage whenever you choose."

"Open the door," I ordered, and Lydia repeated it to the eunuch.

Readjusting my veils, I stepped out behind a wall of palace eunuchs into the shadowless noon of a Levantine summer day. Its brilliance struck my eyes like hammer blows and added temporary blindness to my other afflictions.

"Are you ill, mademoiselle?" Lydia asked as she took my arm to steady me.

"I don't feel at all well," I replied. "But let me walk about for a moment or two. I need some air."

"Of course, madmoiselle. We'll walk to the gate. Then you can rest in the *palanquin*. You'll be all right." Still firmly holding my arm, she led me toward the entrance to the palace. I walked slowly, one hand shielding my eyes.

It was no more than a few paces before we reached our destination, the Imperial Gate. Lydia tried to hurry me into the *palanquin* that waited inside, but I resisted, still a bit queasy from my earlier confinement.

"Please, honored one," she almost begged me. "This is no place for you." Her tone had changed. No longer did she assume the role of governess. There was fear in her voice. As the pain in my eyes took up residence further back in my head, I caught a glimpse of her making a furtive sign against the evil eye.

"What is it?" I asked, but she had no time to answer before I saw for myself. To the right of the open gateway, along broad niches in the palace wall, staring at me like sentries of the damned, was a company of severed heads—grotesque, reeking and blackening in the sun.

"Mother of God!" I exclaimed, terrified. Then the fetid air surrounding the corrupted flesh enveloped me, strangled me, and I fell to the street in a faint before Lydia or the eunuchs could come to my aid. Twisting away from the hideous sight, I cracked my head against the front wheel of the carriage, and mercifully passed out on the cobbles.

When I began to come around, I heard Lydia's voice. She was kneeling beside me, cradling my damaged head in her lap. Expecting to see her, I opened my eyes, but I was greeted by the terrified countenance of one of the eunuchs who had thrust himself forward to determine that I was still alive. In my daze, his black face, distorted with fear for his own future, was so ugly that I thought it one of the severed heads on the wall come to life. At the sight of him I let out what must have been a blood-chilling scream which so frightened Lydia that she jumped to her feet, taking her lap with her, and sending my head to an unfortunate meeting with the pavement.

"Oh, mademoiselle!" she cried, dropping to her knees again. Then she spit a few nasty words at the eunuch who had caused the new mishap, and he shrank away. "Honored one," she helped me to sit up. "Forgive me. Forgive me. I would sooner be devoured by scavenging dogs than cause you harm."

"It's all right, Lydia," I said feebly as I got to my feet. "But those heads? Why are they there?"

"I don't know, mademoiselle." She turned to the eunuchs, one of whom spoke to a palace guard who had watched the entire episode with curiosity.

The translation completed, she explained, "They are men who have fallen from the Sultan's favor. After their executions they are displayed to the people as an example. Do not be afraid. The guard said there is no evil eye." Lydia was very relieved by that piece of information. I was not, but I managed to walk through the gate in spite of my revulsion.

The large courtyard inside was crowded with people in outlandish dress, many prancing with the arrogant demeanor of the military. There was no time for further observation, however. Lydia hurried me to the *palanquin*. Once I was seated in it, she looked in. "Is your head all right, mademoiselle?"

"I think so." I reached up and winced when I touched the bump.

"There will be a bruise," she said. "But I know ways to hide such things. Rest now. Your journey is almost over." She patted my hand and withdrew, pulling the curtains across the door, sealing me up again.

The ride was very comfortable this time. My bearers were so expert in their work that I could have built a house of cards inside my compartment and it would have stood like Gibralter. Outside, I heard their booted footfalls as they carried me along, but beyond that all was quiet. Remembering the crowded court-yard, I wondered at the silence. It soothed my aching brain, and I relished it.

"Mademoiselle de Rivery." I heard a voice of inde-terminate sex call through the curtain of the litter af-ter we had come to a halt. Then a fleshy black hand separated the fabric of the drape and presented itself. "May I assist you?" I hesitated, but took the hand and stepped out.

"Your servant, mademoiselle." The speaker sa-laamed reverently. He was the biggest man I had ever seen, as tall as Ibrahim Ben Raza, with a huge bee-hive of a turban on his head. Even more striking than his height was his girth. He was huge and an enor-mous belly protruded from his ermine-trimmed *pelisse;* its broad green sash around his middle brought to mind the globe and its equator. Over the *pelisse* a voluminous flowered robe with sleeves to the ground completed his ensemble and intensified the sense that the fellow was more a geographical wonder than an anatomical one.

"In the name of the Sultan Abdul Hamid, Allah's Shadow upon the Earth," he said formally and in surprisingly clear French. "May I bid you welcome to his well-protected domain." He bowed as deeply as his bulk would allow. "Praise the Almighty you have arrived safely."

"The Kislar Agha," Lydia whispered as she stepped up behind me. "Chief black eunuch of the harem. Say something to him."

In spite of her instructions, I made no reply, dumb-struck as I was by the beardless giant before me. In a high, gentle voice he went on. "If you and your slave will follow me, I will show you to your apartments."

"Thank you," Lydia whispered and then squeezed my arm.

"Yes, thank you," I said tardily, my mind catch-ing on the phrase "your slave." Lydia did not belong to me.

We passed under a portico and through a gate that the eunuch identified as the Gate of Felicity. "There is the Grand Turk's throne room," he informed me, with a wave of his massive floral arm in the direction of a pillared building in the middle of a wide green. A walkway led us through a smaller gate and into a passage. Turning this way and that, we came to still another gate, a guarded antechamber and then into a long corridor. "This is the Golden Road, mademoiselle," the Kislar Agha said. "It is the thoroughfare of the harem. Now we have entered the women's quarters."

"You may remove your veil, mademoiselle," Lydia whispered as she pulled hers away.

"Not yet," I responded. A fan would have been useful at that moment, for I needed something to hide behind so that others could not read the fear in my face. Without one, I elected to remain veiled a while longer.

The corridor through which we walked was a delicate lacework of mosaics. At irregular intervals, pointed archways led to double doors recessed behind them. Tiers of balconies like the loges of a theater rose overhead, in some places reaching as many as six levels. More striking than the vast size of the place or the ethereal beauty of the architecture was the vitality that filled the air. Women were at work everywhere. As I walked past one open door I could see seamstresses bent over their needles. At another, lithe figures swirled in what appeared to be a dancing practice. Other women scurried about carrying trays of food, ledgers, coffee urns and paraphernalia I could not identify. Where there was no work going on, ladies wearing exquisite costumes rested near fountains in open courtyards and chatted together, laughing, holding hands and often caressing each other affectionately.

As the Kislar Agha passed by there were friendly exchanges. Everyone smiled at him and spoke, but it was clear that the harem's population had a special

interest in me. I sensed their eyes on my back long
after I had passed them by, and their scrutiny let me
know I was an outsider. I felt unwelcome and alone,
but as much as I wanted to flee I held my head erect
and strutted along, trying to duplicate Marie de La
Fontelle's most formal gait while the veil concealed
my fear.

Two black boys sat on their haunches on either
side of an archway ahead of us. As we approached,
they jumped up, bowed to my escort and then to me.
After the Kislar Agha acknowledged them, he walked
into the vestibule and opened the ornate double
doors which led to an apartment. "These are your
quarters, Mademoiselle de Rivery. Please accept my
apologies for such humble accommodations. Even now
we have slaves working day and night to make ready
apartments that will be more worthy of a woman of
your beauty and courage."

Lydia and I stepped inside as he finished speaking.
"Ah," I heard my companion sigh when she saw the
main salon. The room was magnificent in every detail.
Openness pervaded the atmosphere created by an expansive triple archway leading to a courtyard which
allowed sunlight to fill the room. The floors were
covered with silk rugs, all of them in shades of cream
and white with blue accents that suggested the rippling
waters of a brook. The walls were tiled and covered
with tapestries, each decorated with artful designs and
enriched with precious stones that caught the sunlight.
On a dais opposite the archways was a canopied divan
strewn with rugs of a rich ruby color. Posts at the
corners of the couch were encrusted with gems, and at
the back a drape created from strands of pearls was
suspended and attached to the canopy posts as one
might tie back window curtains.

"It is beautiful, monsieur," I said, feeling more
confident now that I was not on display to the entire
harem.

"I hope you are pleased, mademoiselle," the Kislar
Agha said formally as he walked to a low table near

the divan, picked up a tiny bell and tinkled it gently in his massive hand. From a stairway that curled down along the far wall, eight young women descended. They were very silent, their slippered feet making almost no sound on the stone steps. All of them were dark, well dressed, even down to jeweled rings on their ears and fingers. They all seemed afraid.

As each one reached us, she bowed to the Kislar Agha and then to me. When they were assembled, the eunuch presented them. They smiled timidly as their names were spoken, and then kissed my hand.

"Guselli and Aishe, step forward," Kislar Agha ordered after the introductions were complete. They did, two young women, each perhaps fifteen years of age. Guselli had a long thin face with high cheekbones and the look of the Orient about her. Aishe had fuller features with a rosy complexion and a dazzling smile. "Once these two lived in the house of a French trader," the eunuch explained. "They know your language and will be able to assist you until you have mastered our tongue.

"Now I will send them away to show your other slaves to their quarters."

He referred to "my slaves" again, and it irritated me. Because of my close relationship with Adele and her feelings about slavery, I had grown to oppose the institution. It was time I made myself clear. "Lydia and the other women are not my slaves, monsieur. They belong to the Dey of Algiers. Am I to understand that they will remain here with me instead of returning to their master?"

"Yes," he replied. "If that is your wish. Of course, if you do not find them satisfactory, I will have them taken away immediately."

"No, no," I protested. "They are lovely people and I want them to stay. But I do not own slaves. If they remain, I will set them free and pay them for their labor."

"If I may be allowed to explain, mademoiselle. One does not free slaves in the seraglio. To be a slave—"

"You misunderstand me, monsieur," I interrupted him. "I will not have slaves, and as these women have been given to me, I set them free as of this instant."

"Go slowly, mademoiselle," Lydia cautioned. "If there are customs here . . ."

"It makes no difference."

As I spoke, Aishe and Guselli turned to the other women and explained what had transpired. One, then another, then all of them burst into tears, embraced and tried to console each other.

"They think you are not pleased with them," Lydia surmised.

The Kislar Agha spoke and they hurried up the stairs and out of sight, the sounds of their unhappiness lingering after them.

"With your permission, mademoiselle," the eunuch began, "I will explain something."

"Very well," I responded, somewhat confused.

"To be a slave in the seraglio of the Grand Turk is a great honor. The Grand Turk rules and protects all of his domain through his slaves. They are his ministers, his bureaucrats, his soldiers. Everything of importance in the Ottoman state is performed by a slave to the Sultan. Freeing these women is a terrible thing. They will have to leave the palace. They cannot remain."

"But I will provide for them."

"The Grand Turk provides for everyone here. He who eats the Sultan's bread does the Sultan's bidding. It is the way of the seraglio, the way of the Ottomans. Everyone living within these walls is a slave to the Sultan, even those that belong to you. I am a slave. The mother of his child is a slave. Even you. You are a slave from this day on. Praise Allah for such a gift." He paused. "Do you understand?"

"I am a slave?"

"Yes," he said with a condescending smile. "You will see that being a slave here is a blessing. Being near the Grand Turk, our Padishah, serving him—it gives life meaning. Truly, Allah has smiled upon you.

Now, may I tell your women that they are slaves once more and welcome in your household?" I hesitated. "If you send them away, there will be great shame for them, and they will suffer for it."

"All right," I said reluctantly. He rang the bell. The women appeared, cautiously descended the staircase and listened quietly until they understood that I wanted them to stay. Then they clapped their hands and thanked me, all of them trying to embrace me at once until the Kislar Agha had to order them away so he could get on with more important matters.

"Lydia will stay," I corrected him when he indicated she should join the others.

"Very well," he said. "May I suggest you recline on the divan, mademoiselle. This day will be a long one for you. There is a chair under the stairs," the eunuch said to Lydia. "Will you bring it to me, please? I am not built to sit on the floor," he explained with a self-deprecating smile.

After the Kislar Agha was seated and Lydia had taken her place near me, his remarks began. He explained that the Dey of Algiers had sent emissaries to the Sultan telling him of my arrival. "It was Abdul Hamid himself who gave orders for us to prepare your apartments. There have been rumors of your beauty. The story of your capture—the way you fought for your life—it is the talk of the harem, and all of it has further aroused the Sultan's interest. He has requested that you be presented to him at the earliest possible moment, and so I have arranged for you to have an audience today. Your women will return shortly to help you—"

"Today!" I gasped, astounded. "That's impossible!"

Lydia hastily concurred. "The lady is exhausted from her long passage."

He looked at me curiously. "Then she is not eager," he concluded. "That explains much. Baba Mohammed's emissaries made mention of a certain young lady they hold prisoner. You understand, mademoiselle, her life depends upon you." I nodded but did not speak.

"Of course she understands," Lydia said sharply. "When she's fit, she'll show the Sultan a glimpse of paradise, but she must have rest." Turning to me, she went on, "Take off your veils, dear one. Pull them away from your forehead as well. Look there, eunuch. See the lump above her eye. Do you intend to present her with such a blemish?"

"How did that occur?" he demanded, very concerned.

"A better question," Lydia countered. "How long will it remain?"

"There are women in the harem who know treatments," he said anxiously.

"I will take care of her."

"You have only until tomorrow. The Grand Turk will not be put off."

"It will require two days."

He examined the lump more closely, the worried expression upon his face growing more intense. "Two days you have. It is an unsightly bruise. But she will be presented one hour after noon on the day after tomorrow. Further delay will cost her friend's life, and your own, woman."

Lydia looked at him angrily and spoke in Arabic. Her voice had the sting of a slap as it struck him, and he left without saying another word.

"Kislar Agha or not," she muttered. "He's got no more between his legs than I do, and by the Prophet he won't threaten us as if he were the master here."

Chapter 13

After the Kislar Agha departed, Lydia stormily turned to me. "Have you no pride, child?" she demanded. "A eunuch says you will do a thing today, and you look as though you'll faint. Showing such fear to a eunuch! How will you control him if he knows you are so weak?"

"But aboard ship everyone assured me I would not meet the Sultan for weeks," I whimpered.

"Enough!" She was unsympathetic. "Those people do not matter now. We are in the Grand Turk's harem. Have you no eyes to see what confronts us? The kitchen slaves here are as lovely as Baba Mohammed's favorite wives in Algiers. You are beautiful, mademoiselle, but here you'll find beauty without strength is as valueless as a grain of sand on the desert. While you learn the order of things, you must not lead others to underestimate you. Command your servants and eunuchs firmly or they will take command of you.

"Now, I am going to see about some ointments for

133

your forehead. While I'm doing that, you will take a bath." She called up the stairs to the serving girls. One of them came to the landing and gave her the information she had requested. "The *hammam,* our bath, is through that archway." Lydia pointed to a portal under the staircase. "Go in there and relax. You must get hold of yourself soon. Remember, if your audience with the Grand Turk goes well, you'll go to his bed, not to execution. Don't be so afraid."

She put her arm around me as I walked to the bath. "Would you like a servant to attend you?" she asked gently.

"No," I responded, not wishing to endure a stranger. "I'll feel better alone."

"Very well. I'll join you as soon as I can. Now relax and let the heat and water do their work." She had great confidence in *hammams* as a cure for almost every ailment from monthly discomforts to headaches or a touch of the plague. "A bath and all will be well." With that she departed.

I had discovered in Algiers that the *hammam* is among the Musselman's most ingenious inventions. It is a three-chambered haven devoted to the pleasures of bathing, and it is such a delight that if the Convent of Les Dames de la Visitation had had one within its walls, I might have considered taking my vows. Of course such a thing could never exist in France, where the average Frenchman is forever fearful of the effects of night vapors and disease upon a human body debilitated by frequent immersion in warm water.

Exhausted and near tears, I sat on a couch in the antechamber for a while, soothed by my solitude, but the temptation of the hot room soon led me to undress and prepare myself. There were several long white towels called *pestemals* resting on shelves built into the wall. I wrapped myself in one and then selected a pair of *takouns* for my feet. They are bath shoes with high wooden blocks attached at toe and heel so that one stands several inches off the ground while wearing them. In the baths of the Orient they are used to prevent people from falling on the slippery marble or burning their feet on the hot floors.

Properly attired, I pulled open the door leading into the bath, and a reassuring burst of hot moisture surged around me. The hot room was decorated in white tile with a large fountain at its center. There were smaller basins built into the corners. Running water babbled into all of them and filled the air with its song.

I made myself comfortable on the wide marble bench that formed the lip of the central fountain. There I found a silvered copper pitcher which I used to ladle warm water over my body after I had removed my *pestemal*. My head still throbbed, and I was always aware of the painful bruise over my eye, but the sound of the water, the heat and solitude gave me strength enough to examine my situation.

One fact overshadowed the others. Baba Mohammed's men held Adele and would kill her if I did not satisfy the Sultan. That alone meant I would have to give myself to him willingly. I was certain that my actions could not jeopardize my immortal soul, but it was for my body that I was immediately concerned. I took little comfort now from Adele's reassurances that the mysteries of the bedchamber are less to be dreaded than savored, for I knew she spoke as a woman in love. Still, every matron in France had endured what awaited me, and most of them seemed to survive their initial encounters, frequently with husbands as much strangers to them as any Turk could be.

Lydia was right, of course. I was not going to my execution. I would endure the Sultan. My only choice in the matter was whether I would preserve some dignity through the proceedings or behave like a foolish child.

As I turned to fill my pitcher again, Lydia entered the bath, a *pestemal* around her waist. She carried a wet silk sack in her hand. "You will be well soon," she said confidently. "Just place this on your head over the bruise."

I took the sack in my hand. "It's freezing cold!"

"It's filled with snow," she explained with a delighted smile. The Ottomans bring it down from Mt. Olympus in velvet bags. They flavor it with honey and rose water and eat it as something called sherbet, but it will be a perfect remedy for that swelling."

I did as she suggested and placed it against my wound. "It almost burns," I laughed. "But it does feel better."

Just then the *hammam* door opened and a middle-aged woman entered. She spoke to Lydia in Arabic. Though I could not understand the exchange, I heard the word Sultan several times, and it made me uneasy. Then the woman gracefully bowed in my direction, her hand almost touching the floor before it swept over her knee, heart, lips and forehead in a formal greeting. From her appearance I guessed she was about forty years old. A pleasant, almost motherly smile lit up her countenance. Her face was round and her contours full, a fact I determined with little difficulty for she proceeded to drop her *pestemal* as soon as she entered the room.

I had already learned that Musselwomen make bathing a social event, even celebrating special occasions like birthdays in large groups, all the participants being completely naked. So enlightened, I was not as shocked as I might have been had I come here directly from the cloistered life where I remained clothed even when alone in the tub. Still, I was a bit taken aback, for this shameless matron and I had not so much as been formally introduced.

"Lydia, what's happening?" I asked, trying to sound unperturbed.

"She's going to bathe with you, mademoiselle. I tried to tell her you weren't up to company, but she refuses to listen."

"Then bid her welcome. I've decided to take your advice and not be frightened, or at least try not to show it."

"Praise Allah for your wisdom," she replied. "It's a blessing that you recognize your destiny."

"There will be no talk of destiny, Lydia. I've chosen my own path through this."

The intruder walked to the fountain and sat down beside me. She looked under my ice pack quickly, indicated satisfaction with the treatment, then she directed Lydia to fetch an urn of oil.

"Who is she?" I asked when Lydia returned. There followed an exchange which came to me in translation. The woman's name was Mihrishah, and she bore the title of Sultan because she was the mother of the heir to the throne. Mihrishah Sultan was not a concubine of Grand Turk Abdul Hamid, however, but had belonged to his predecessor, who was also Abdul Hamid's brother. Because Ottoman laws of succession state that the oldest surviving male of the line always inherits power, her offspring, Prince Selim, though Abdul Hamid's nephew and not his son, would be the next Grand Turk.

Mihrishah reached over and poured a bit of oil from Lydia's pitcher into her palms. As she listened to the translation of her words, she slowly rubbed the ointment into the skin of her legs and hips. By her affected manner, I assumed she enjoyed an audience. She was a proud woman, pleased with the kindness that time had shown her and proud of her position in the harem. As Lydia spoke, I learned that when Abdul Hamid died and Prince Selim ascended the throne, Mihrishah would become Sultan Valide, Queen of the Veiled Heads. Her description of that post created the strong impression that once she assumed the title, she would become the despot of the harem.

"Mademoiselle, may I tell the lady that you are greatly honored by her visit?" Lydia asked me.

"Yes, that's a good idea," I replied. "But why did she come?"

"As a welcoming gesture, I suppose. You don't want me to ask her, do you?"

"No, but I'd like to know."

After Lydia translated several niceties, I found out
the answer to my question. A person named Poppy
had sent her. For some reason, Poppy and Mihrishah
had been very eager for my arrival. They viewed my
unwillingness to wait upon the Grand Turk with chagrin.

"There are forces against you here, beautiful one,"
she said through my servant. "Abdul Hamid must not
learn of your reluctance. His favor is vital to your
success, and there are those here who would see you
fail."

"What do you mean—fail?" I asked, surprised to
think that the woman beside me was an ally of the
Dey and knew his motives for sending me to Istanbul.

"You must warm the heart of the great one," she
responded, innocent of my suspicion. "There is much
to tell you before you understand. I know you have
had a long journey. Your first day here has been a
difficult one, but you must be told these things. Poppy
is certain of it, and I am as well."

"Who is this Poppy you refer to?" I asked. "You
speak as though I should know her, but I've met no
one in the harem but you."

As Lydia translated my question, Mihrishah's earn-
est expression melted into an amused smile. "Poppy
is not a woman of the harem. Poppy is the Kislar
Agha."

"Poppy. The name does not suit him," I observed
drily.

"Oh, but it does. You see, every eunuch that comes
here is given the name of a flower. The custom dates
back even before the time of Suleiman the Magnificent, when the royal harem was located in the old
palace. Eunuchs are usually brought to the harem
when they are young boys. They are so soft and gentle
then, like flowers. Many women grow quite motherly
toward them. As a matter of fact there are no bounds
to the affection that sometimes grows between a
woman of the harem and her favorite eunuch. Poppy
was a handsome boy when he arrived. Of course, I

was not here then. I only know rumors of the reputation he achieved in his youth.

"He was very popular with the harem women, and skillful at pleasing them with all sorts of artificial devices."

A puzzled look crossed my face as Lydia translated Mihrishah's words. "Oh dear," the woman said, shaking her head. "You know nothing of these matters, do you, beautiful one?"

"I'm afraid I don't."

"Then I will tell you. Even a virgin must know what goes on in the harem. Innocence is too dangerous." She hesitated. "Where to begin. Do you know what happens between a man and a woman when they lie together?"

"Yes," I said with a blush. Never in my life had anyone ever spoken to me so openly on this subject before. While in the convent, Adele and I had speculated about romance, but only once had an experienced woman ever broached the subject. That embarrassing discussion occurred when I had reached the age of eighteen. Marie de La Fontelle took Adele and me into her library one afternoon to explain the basic act. The interview was awkward. All of us were uncomfortable in spite of our affection for one another, but Marie felt it her duty to end our ignorance before some unscrupulous cavalier had the opportunity to do so.

"As you will learn soon enough," Mihrishah went on shamelessly, "women as well as men have strong appetites for the act of love. There are hundreds of women here in the harem, but there is only one Grand Turk. Because of this, most of our community go through their entire lives unsatisfied. Rather than completely deny themselves, many find substitutes. You will see sapphists here, women who love other women. Some of the bolder ones may even approach you. Others find their pleasures with young eunuchs. But the black eunuchs of the seraglio are unequipped to please them. Unlike the white eunuchs of the Second

Court, who are simply rendered impotent, black eunuchs are cut clean. Nothing of their masculine parts remain. They cannot even make water as a man would. You will notice that many of them carry small silver quills in the folds of their turbans. A eunuch must insert that where his manhood used to be in order to relieve himself while standing in the masculine manner."

"How horrible," I cringed. "Musselmen are barbarians to mutilate anyone like that."

"Oh no, beautiful one," Mihrishah corrected me. "Those of the true faith do not commit such abominations. Castration is forbidden by the Koran. Eunuchs are purchased from Christians in North Africa. Christians do the cutting. Then they bury their victims to the waist in hot sand until the bleeding stops. The ones who survive are sold.

"Of those who arrive here, the cleverest find substitutes for the manly staffs that have been taken from them. Of course, the Grand Turk condemns these unnatural acts. As one preventative there has always been a law that zuccini and cucumbers may not be brought into the harem unless thinly sliced. In spite of such obstacles, the eunuchs continue their practices.

"But I was telling you of Poppy." She brought herself back to my original question. "He was a very clever young eunuch who warmed so many hearts and beds with his clever use of vegetables that he became wealthy with the gifts his women gave him. Much of what he received went to buy opium because it was so popular with his fellow eunuchs who were less affluent than he. Each time a superior ordered Poppy to work, he went to his cache of opium and gave some to a friend. This person did Poppy's task. In time almost all the eunuchs in the harem entered his employ. They called him the Poppy Master, referring to the source of the wages he paid them. Harem women simply called him Poppy.

"Quickly, the number of his followers grew. His wealth increased. He became very fat from so much luxury, and at the same time he built a network of followers throughout the palace, later throughout the Ottoman domain. His power grew through the wise use of the information he gained from them. Now little happens that is kept secret from Poppy. He was the first in the seraglio, even before the Dragoman of the Porte—the government interpreter—who knew you were coming. Poppy spoke to the Dey's emissaries himself."

"You say that as if it were a major coup," I observed. "But why is knowing about me so important? Certainly, women must arrive here all the time."

"Yes they do, but most of them come as children. For example, I was eight years old when Ottomans raided my village. They kidnapped me and gave me to the Sultan as part of his share of their booty. I've been here ever since. As a novice I was educated in the Ottoman languages of Arabic, Turkish and Persian. I learned to sing and tell stories, I was taught the art of pleasing the Padishah and I was trained in a productive skill. When I was older, I went to work in the harem as a seamstress, but then my turn came to wait on the late Sultan in his apartments. He took me to his bed. That elevated me to the rank of qadin. After I bore his son, the title of Sultan was bestowed upon me, and now I need only wait until I become Sultan Valide. This is the traditional life story of a woman of the harem, though most of them never progress beyond their working days.

"You see, you are not like the rest of us. You have lived differently. You have been tested in the world of men and have survived. We have been trained since childhood to be gentle and submissive, and so most of us do not do well in the face of adversity. Sad as it is for the fate of my son, I am one of the weakest. Until he is on the throne I must protect him, but a strong voice raised against me and I dissolve like spun sugar in a rain.

"But you, beautiful one. You are unique among us. It is said that when you were captured by Baba

Mohemmed's men, you snatched a sword from one of them and chopped his head off."

"What?" I interrupted the translation. "What was that?"

"She thinks you killed one of the Dey's men with his own blade," Lydia said, demurely covering the smile that curled her lips.

"Well, tell her that isn't true." Lydia hesitated. "Go on and tell her," I insisted. "I'll not have these people thinking I'm capable of such a thing."

Lydia spoke for several moments. Her monologue was quite animated considering my instructions. At one point she jumped to her feet and slashed an invisible blade across Mihrishah's neck.

"What are you doing, Lydia?" I demanded when I saw that.

"I'm trying to explain what happened just as you once described it to me, mademoiselle." She talked on. Soon the Mihrishah, then Lydia, looked in my direction and shook their heads.

Mihrishah patted my hand softly, "We won't speak of it again. Let us say simply that you are a strong woman, and Abdul Hamid needs strength more than anything else. These are hard times for him and his domain."

Lydia noted that I had begun to perspire heavily from the bath. "Perhaps you should go into the cool room soon, mademoiselle," she suggested. "I'll bring in your dinner."

Her mention of food reminded me that I had not eaten all day. "Yes, I'll finish bathing myself." The steaming *hammam* had begun to make me light-headed, and I stood up to splash some water from the fountain over me. Mihrishah sighed with approval.

Lydia was still near us and translated, "You are very beautiful. Just what Abdul Hamid needs to inspire him." Then she pulled my hand toward her and pointed to the skin on my forearm. "That will have to go, of course."

"What does she mean?" I asked.

After a short exchange with Mihrishah, Lydia responded, "The hair on your arms will be removed. It is the custom here."

I had noticed from my first glimpse of the woman in her natural state that aside from what was on her head, she had no hair, but I assumed that this was a characteristic peculiar to the Ottomans. Then the woman let go my arm, reached down and unabashedly stroked the modest patch between my legs. Shocked, I pushed her hand away.

She laughed. "Tomorrow that comes off too."

Chapter 14

"Food at last!" I exclaimed when Lydia finally found Mihrishah and me in the cool room. She carried a large tray covered with Turkish delicacies. Most of the dishes were strange to me, as foreign as my naked guest on the next couch. But I could recognize skewered meat and reached for it hungrily.

To my surprise, Mihrishah grabbed the sleeve of the *caftan* I had slipped on and slapped the skewer out of my hand. Seeing its succulent deliciousness bounce on the marble, I almost wept. "What did she do that for?"

A few sharp words were exchanged. Lydia was not overawed by Mihrishah Sultan's high station. Outrage would better describe her reaction as she picked up the fallen morsels of lamb and began to pop them into her mouth. "She thinks I'll poison you, mademoiselle." Her last words were garbled by chunks of meat as she angrily demonstrated that the food was safe.

"Don't be ridiculous," I laughed, almost too hungry to be civil. "Give me one of those."

As Lydia passed a skewer to me, Mihrishah cautioned, "Forgive my abruptness, beautiful one. This abode of felicity can be a wonderful place to live, but there was a serpent even in the garden."

"Lydia is hardly a serpent, Sultan," I replied, wiping my mouth with a large velvet napkin.

"No, but there is one who would rejoice at your death. Kiusem Sultan is your enemy."

"I don't even know this Kiusem Sultan."

"You threaten her position."

"But how? I don't understand."

"Let me explain. It is complex, but we live in the land of the Byzantines. Like them, we find nothing concerning the powerful is as it appears.

"Kiusem is the mother of Abdul Hamid's only son, Mustapha, a very strange boy, weak-minded, violent and easily influenced by his mother. Rumors abound that the Grand Turk can no longer bring forth the Ottoman seed, but those of us in the harem know this is not true, for time and again we see the court abortionist walk along the Golden Road. This is because Kiusem has convinced Abdul Hamid to beget no other sons. In this way Mustapha's right to succession will not be threatened.

"Kiusem is very anxious to see Mustapha ascend the throne. Only one obstacle stands between him and a clear path. That is my son, Selim, who will be the next Sultan. Kiusem has made several attempts on his life, but in spite of my delicate nature, I have managed to foil her each time. Poppy has been invaluable to us, ever watchful, with his spies bringing him information from wherever it is to be had."

"If this is going on," I asked, "why doesn't Abdul Hamid do something about it? Does he favor Mustapha over Selim?"

"Oh no! He hates the son of his loins because the boy is unworthy of his destiny. But Abdul Hamid fears Kiusem."

"Why should the Grand Turk fear anyone, especially one of his harem women?"

"He is afraid because Kiusem and Mustapha have the support of the palace troops, the Janissary Corps. The Janissaries do not want my son to take the throne because Selim favors important reforms that will undermine their power. He wants to modernize the army, improve the administration of the sanjaks, or provinces, and end the corruption that exists between the palace bureaucracy and the suppliers of goods. Without these reforms the Ottoman dynasty is doomed, but every change that Selim contemplates will weaken the position of the Janissaries."

Mihrishah went on at great length to explain how Selim's reorganization of the military would put command of all troops back in the hands of the Sultan. "Long ago, when the Janissary Corps was formed, it was made up of Christian boys taken from their homes, forcibly converted to Islam and educated in the palace school. They were the Sultan's personal slaves, dependent on him for everything. They owned no property, could not marry and lived in a disciplined manner. They were fiercely loyal to the Grand Turk, and as swift and relentless as the sword of the Prophet when thrown against an enemy.

"Because of their education, their loyalty and their knowledge of newly conquered lands they became the governors and administrators of many border territories. During times of peace some of them went to work in the bureaucracy. The followers of Mohammed living in the Sultan's domain saw these Christian Janissaries become rich and powerful as slaves of the Sultan, and they demanded the right to such positions for themselves. Weak Sultans succumbed to their pressures and opened the Corps to them. Next was demanded the right to marry and pass on positions from father to son. This was also granted. Discipline broke down. Loyalty to family outweighed loyalty to the Sultan.

"Then the Ottoman star began to fall. Instead of expanding, the borders began to tighten around us. There were no more conquests, only defeats. Janissaries fought defending their own soil. They could claim no booty and they became sullen, turning against one Sultan after another, assassinating some, forcing others to abdicate in favor of Janissary selections.

"During idle years between wars some of the troops became artisans. Others invested in commerce, becoming connected with suppliers of material sold to the Ottoman government. Their profits grew whenever there was war, and so they opposed peace. Victory or defeat mattered little to them. As long as we fought, they had a hungry market for their military goods.

"You see," Mihrishah continued, "the Janissary Corps has spread its poison like a sickness throughout the state. They do not see that their evil practices will destroy the dynasty. Their greed makes them blind.

"Kiusem is aware of this. With her dwarfs as messengers she has let the Janissaries know that Mustapha opposes reform. She leads them to believe they will thrive under his reign, for she cares nothing about the people or the dynasty. Her son must take the throne, and she will do anything, promise anything, to achieve that end. As a result, if Abdul Hamid acts against Kiusem, he fears the Janissaries may revolt, and he no longer has the strength of will to put them down.

"Prince Selim and I know that Kiusem must be stopped. Poppy is with us. We believe that if the Ottoman house is put in order, our armies can go forth like the great Ghazi warriors of the past to conquer the infidel. We have a small group of allies in the military who favor reform. Most of them are among the Sipahis, the Ottoman cavalry. All of us see Selim as the hope of the future, but we are fearful because the present is in such jeopardy. Every day that passes without the beginnings of reform, the Ottoman people suffer and our enemies grow more dangerous."

When Mihrishah had finished speaking and Lydia had completed the translation, I was still confused. "Sultan, your cause is a noble one, but I don't see what role you would have me play in it, or why Kiusem would consider me an enemy."

"Abdul Hamid needs a woman of your strength if

he is ever to challenge Kiusem's power. You could give him a son to carry on the blood of Othman the Conqueror even if Mustapha were eliminated. The Padishah wants to end Kiusem's dominance in the seraglio. He knows she is dangerous to the dynasty. If it should fall, so would end the entire Ottoman state. A woman like you, a woman who could disarm a seasoned corsair and cut off his head with one blow, you could lend courage to Abdul Hamid, and with the blessings of Allah, you could save us all."

Lydia's cheeks were flushed with excitement as she finished translating Mihrishah's words. "Praise the Almighty, mademoiselle. Think of it. Allah's vice-regent upon the earth is in peril. His palace guard threatens. The mother of his son intrigues against the heir to the throne, and you have been sent to set things right. You are blessed, mademoiselle, to have such a destiny. At evening prayers I will send a thousand thanks up to Heaven for allowing me to serve you." She knelt next to the couch where I lay and kissed my foot.

As she babbled on, I did not listen. I could no longer ignore her Musselman superstition. There did seem to be a guiding hand that had brought me to the Levant, yet the true Church teaches of free will. I thought of Martinique. One day when I was a child, my cousin Marie Josephe-Rose and I decided to visit the tumbledown shack of a fortuneteller. We were frightened by talk of voodoo and witchcraft, but it was an adventure so we went inside.

The old fortuneteller's prophesies were grand. She said both of us would reign as queens. We laughed at her fantasies, but some of the things she said came true, strange things that no one could have expected. She said that when Marie Rose left the islands, a magic light would descend from the heavens to mark her way. I was already in France when my cousin sailed from Martinique, but she wrote me later about her departure. Some sort of heavenly flame fell from the sky and illuminated her ship as it left the harbor. Everyone could see it. They called it St. Elmo's Fire.

It was just as the fortuneteller predicted. And her marriage! The prophesy was that her marriage would be unhappy, and it is. Her husband is a scoundrel.

Marie Rose and I swore never to tell anyone about the fortuneteller. As good Catholic girls we denied predestination, and we believed that such things as reading the future in coffee grounds were black magic and a devil's device. *Could it be that the time will come when Marie Rose is a queen by the name of Josephine? And could it be that I was sent here by God just as Lydia believes?*

My servant's moist lips against my foot brought me back to the present. "Stop it, Lydia." I swung my legs around and stood up. She remained kneeling as I spoke. "There will be no more talk about destiny, Lydia," I said gently. "God gave every human being the freedom to choose her own path." She nodded her head obediently. "Now," I went on, "about cutting off the head of a pirate with one blow? I told you to silence that rumor, but Mihrishah keeps repeating it. Why?"

"Please, mademoiselle, sit down. You are tired and you should not excite yourself." Lydia reached toward the food tray. "I know you did not like the yogurt of Algiers, but you have not yet tasted it here. This is the best in the world. What you had at the Dey's palace is like the dung of afflicted vultures compared to this." She handed it to me hurriedly, obviously trying to change the subject. "Pardon, mademoiselle. I will eat some first. Mihrishah Sultan is wise. We cannot be too careful." She shoveled a spoonful of the noxious paste into her mouth. "It is safe, mademoiselle. Here. Taste it."

"The pirate with no head, Lydia. What did you tell her?"

"Trust me, mademoiselle." Lydia set the dish of yogurt on the tray and stood up. "I told her you cut off his head. When one enters the den of strangers it is better to go as a lion than a lamb. I disobeyed you, I admit, but Baba Mohammed commanded me to do it. His emissaries planted the story for your protection. Later, when you know your friends and your enemies, you may want to reveal the truth, but from what Mihrishah Sultan has said, I gather that a headless corsair could prove to be a valuable ally."

"You may be right," I conceded, recognizing the cleverness of the tactic. "But you were speaking with my voice, translating what were supposed to be my words. I have to be able to trust you." Lydia cast her eyes to the floor as she listened to my rebuke. Next to me Mihrishah shifted uneasily on her couch, irritated at not being able to understand what we said. "We'll talk of this later," I said, breaking off the discussion. "And tomorrow you will begin giving me lessons in Arabic. If I stay here, I want to be able to speak for myself."

"You will stay, mademoiselle." Lydia's eyes danced under the dark canopy of her lashes. "I know you will stay. You are too wise not to see Allah's will in all this."

"Lydia, not a word about destiny or I'll set you free. I swear I will."

She clapped her hand over her mouth and then laughed, "Not a word, mademoiselle. I promise."

Chapter 15

After Mihrishah Sultan left the apartment, Lydia led me up the marble staircase to the second level. There, off the main hall, I found a lovely bedroom with a high gilt dome overhead, a silken couch and a latticed balcony overlooking the immaculate courtyard with its regimented banks of flowers around the central fountain.

"You will rest now, mademoiselle?" she asked.

"Yes," I replied.

"You saw the water closet downstairs." Lydia referred to an invention very popular in the Orient to which I had become accustomed in Algiers.

The water closet in this apartment was just off the *hammam*. It was a small tiled room with a convenient receptacle for human waste and a system of water pipes by which it was carried away. I had never seen such a thing in France, though two or three are said to exist in Paris. French architects do not usually dwell upon the baser aspects of human existence when they conceive their grand designs. It is considered unseemly to ponder systems by which excrement might be contained and transported efficiently. As a result of this prejudice, no modern buildings in France have quarters specifically designed as latrines. The more practical Musselmen with their water closets seem to have avoided some of the unpleasant problems of living in close quarters. For example, there are no disgusting odors lingering in hallways of the Ottoman seraglio, and no piles of coiled filth hiding behind furniture and next to potted plants as one might find even in Versailles.

"I'll leave you to sleep now, mademoiselle," Lydia said as she walked toward the door.

"I am tired," I confessed. "But with all the excitement of the day, I don't think I'll be able to close my eyes."

"Lie down on the couch and relax. I'll bring you something." She went out but returned in a few moments with three small caskets on a tray beside a pot of tea. "How long would you like to rest? If you choose, you can sleep until tomorrow, but I fear you'll be besotted if you do."

"Just a few hours and I'll feel better."

"Then it will be the green box." She set the tray on the floor and selected a golden pill from the green container. "This will give you four restful hours."

"What is it?"

"Just opium. All three boxes are opium, but the women here told me the green are coated with a thin membrane of gold. It dissolves quickly in your stomach and lets you sleep. Those in the red box have two layers of gold. Take one, and by the time its covering is gone, the power of the green pill has been spent and the red one begins to work. Those in the yellow box have three coats. They do not begin until the others are finished. If you take one of each, you can sleep for a long time. Ottomans are clever, are they not?"

"The pills must be very valuable," I observed. "It seems such a waste to swallow something covered with gold."

"But you are much more valuable, mademoiselle. Especially if you please the Grand Turk." She handed me a pill. "Please take this and get your rest."

I swallowed the drug with a sip of tea and lay back, feeling Lydia's gentle touch as she brushed a lock of hair from my face. Soon I was asleep.

The sun had set when a noise downstairs roused me. As I awoke, I heard the comforting babble of the fountain below my window. My eyes opened to the gentle glow of an oil lamp casting its rays against the golden dome that haloed the room. Then the sound of a harsh voice jolted me alert. It came from the main salon. Feeling sluggish from the drug, I arose clumsily and went to the top of the stairs.

Below, in the blue and white salon, were two young girls I recognized as my servants. While I watched they threw themselves to their knees, foreheads on the floor, before a bizarre looking creature who placed her foot on the neck of one of them. The intruder was dressed in red from her slippers to the spangled cap on her dyed black hair. An abundance of jewels decorated her costume. A scarf as long as I am tall that was draped around her shoulders was one wide mantle of precious stones.

Her gown was strewn with them, her sleeves, every part of her attire. The sheer weight of the ensemble must have been substantial, but the wearer appeared undaunted. She was a big woman, tall and heavy from many luxurious years in the idle life of the harem. Her face, vulgar from copious quantities of rouge and powder, was round, almost swollen, and there was the suggestion of jowls below her chin.

Just behind her stood a gaunt, wrinkled, black eunuch, elegantly outfitted, but pale in the shadow of his mistress. By his side was another woman, quite young, dressed in dark shades of blue with diamond accents. She seemed pretty from a distance, with oriental features and a lithe body. Pulled taut against her wrist was the loop of a jeweled leash attached to the collar of a dark-haired whippet. The dog, wearing a mantle of gems that covered her chest, was a perfect companion to the woman in blue, both of them sleek and dark, both of them restless and poised to dart after the slightest movement.

I took in the scene only an instant before the people downstairs noticed my presence. When my eyes met those of the woman in red, her arrogance was like a gauntlet in my face. "You there," I called out. "Take your foot off my servant!" She did, but only to turn and speak to her eunuch. He then went to the door and gave a signal. Shortly, an old woman entered. She was well dressed, with a colorful shawl tied around her hips, but she wore no jewelry. Her hair was gray with age, but her face was gray as well, the color of fear. When I came downstairs and approached the group, I could see that. Each time the woman in red spoke to her, she cringed.

"Good evening, mademoiselle," the crone whispered in such heavily accented French that I could hardly understand even a simple greeting. "The Sultan Kiusem welcomes you here." She turned back to her mistress and spoke. Then the women in red, Kiusem Sultan, bowed to the floor and performed the same ritual salute Mihrishah had done that afternoon. I nodded my head.

Remembering what Mihrishah had said about Kiusem, I was frightened. There seemed a possibility that this company might dispense with further formalities and do away with me. I turned to my servants. "Get up!" I motioned with my hands. "Where is Lydia?" They did not understand. "Lydia? Lydia? Go find her." If nothing more, they recognized my need for a translator. I waved them toward the door and they hurried out. "No! No!" I called out tardily. "One of you stay here with me." Too late. They were gone.

When I looked back to my visitors, Kiusem was far from happy. She snapped at the old woman.

"Please, mademoiselle. Please. *Temena*. You. Now. *Temena*."

I shook my head to let her know I did not understand. This seemed to anger Kiusem further. She instructed the crone nastily, then spoke to the woman in blue.

"Trouble now. I know French only little. Please! *Temena*. It is bow." The old woman bent to the ground and touched her knees, heart, lips and forehead. "You, mademoiselle. You."

At last I understood. I was to return the Sultan Kiusem's greeting. "Of course." I copied the old woman's movements. Kiusem was satisfied. She began to speak rapidly. The crone paid close attention but trembled with fear.

"She wants . . . she says . . . I do not know the words." The artless translator struggled on but I understood nothing. Finally she grabbed my hand in desperation and tried to pull me toward the door. I resisted, fearing the Sultan's intentions. Kiusem glared at me. Then she, the eunuch, the woman in blue and her whippet marched out of the apartment.

"Good night, mademoiselle," the trembling slave said as she bowed, her tired bones creaking with the effort. After she had righted herself, she hurried out behind the others.

The briefness of the encounter, its disjointed and nonsensical nature made it seem like part of a narcotic nightmare. I could still hear Kiusem's angry voice, and mixed with it the old woman's whimpering, but now the sound came from behind me. I went back to the archway and out into the courtyard. Through one latticed wall I could see the Golden Road. All along it oil lamps burned through the night. They illuminated a grisly scene. Kiusem appeared insane with anger, perhaps because the old woman had not performed adequately as a translator. There in the open where people on the path could see it all, the Sultan railed at her helpless slave. In a frenzy Kiusem raised her hand like a jewel-studded mace and struck the old woman across the mouth. The crone screamed in pain. I could see red slashes where the Sultan's rings had gouged away flesh. The vicious hand rose up to strike again.

"Stop hitting her!" I shouted through the grill. "Stop it!" Kiusem paid me no heed. She swung and the slave staggered. Her accomplice, the woman in blue, had heard something though. She looked around nervously at the people along the path. They had pulled back against the walls, withering from the sight of the violence. Through lattices, shutters and doors opened only by cracks she saw watchful disapproving eyes. Her whippet jerked at the leash uneasily. The eunuch whispered something in his mistress's ear. Kiusem looked at him angrily, almost as if she might turn on him next. Then she spat upon the old woman and stomped away. The others followed.

They left behind a silent void, everyone on the road still too disconcerted by what they had witnessed even to exchange glances with one another. I had never seen such a display of uncontrolled temper in my life. At the convent if a nun so much as raised her voice in anger, the Abbess ordered her to a cell for a week to contemplate her sins.

Slowly, life came back to the Golden Road. There were rumblings of concerned voices that blended with the gentle rush of water in the fountain behind me. People began to move about, and I turned to go inside.

"Mademoiselle!" I heard Lydia call out in panic from the salon. "Mademoiselle! Where are you?" When I saw her she was running up the stairs. "By the Prophet, if that sorceress had done anything to hurt her . . ."

"Lydia, where have you been?"

"Mademoiselle, you're safe. Praise the Almighty." She rushed down the steps and threw her arms around me. Shaken by the scene in the apartment as well as the episode on the road, I took comfort in her embrace. "When I heard Kiusem Sultan was here," she went on breathlessly, "I ran all the way."

We sat down on the divan and I told her what had transpired in her absence. As she listened, she shook her head. "Kiusem wanted you to go with her?"

"Yes. It appeared that way."

"I have been asking questions, mademoiselle, and I have learned much. You were wise not to go. It is said that Kiusem has murdered many women of the harem. They go to her suite and they disappear. There are those who will not eat the *pastromani*, our preserved meat prepared in the harem kitchens, because they believe Kiusem has it made with the bodies of her victims."

"Blessed Virgin!" I made the sign of the cross. "No one could be so evil."

"She is evil, mademoiselle. It is said that with her own hands she once strangled an infant son of the Grand Turk and threw his body into the sea. It is said that she casts spells and turns people to stone and that she sleeps with a scorpion. It is said that she can fly like a vulture over the rooftops of the harem, and even that—"

"Enough!" I interrupted. "This is more than I can believe. We must remember it is also said, and by you, that I wrested the sword from a fighting corsair and cut off his head with one blow. Perhaps Kiusem Sultan wanted you to hear these stories. No one sleeps with scorpions. I think she is trying to frighten us."

"If she is, mademoiselle, I pray she tries no harder. I'm frightened enough right now."

"So am I, Lydia. So am I."

Chapter 16

At sunset on the second day of my Turkish captivity I sat alone on the couch in my dressing room. Outside, the voice of the palace *muezzin* called the faithful to prayer. Five times each day the *muezzin* climbed to his perch in the fluted minaret of the palace mosque and set his message upon the air. Five times a day every *muezzin* in the city followed the same ritual, all of their voices joining until Istanbul itself seemed to proclaim in the mysterious language of the East that there is no God but Allah and Mohammed is his Prophet. My servants were gone to the courtyard for their sunset rites to mark the start of a new day. *How fitting for benighted Musselmen to have their days begin in darkness.* For me sunset marks an end, and that day it was especially so.

The Sultan waited on the other side of twilight. As I lay dreading what was to come, it seemed that my entire life had been a preparation for this one horrible encounter. I could no longer think beyond it. I would endure the Turk and then the abyss.

That last day of my innocence had been grueling. I was prayed over, massaged, perfumed, oiled, scrubbed and finally depilated. There was something oddly religious about the way my servants readied me, almost as though I were a postulant about to take her final vows—the ritual bath, the white gown and the hair cropping. What made my experience so different from that of the Catholic sisters was that my new lord ruled in this world and not in the next. The Grand Turk was a man, and so my preparations dealt with matters of the flesh. The ritual bath was a sensual experience of exotic fragrances and ointments. My white gown was an elaborate ensemble of exquisite fabrics and jewels designed to complement nature's gifts and stimulate the Sultan's desire.

As for removing my hair, the experience was dreadful. The Turks used a depilatory of lye and perfumes, a very hazardous concoction. For my protection one of them applied some to her own arm several seconds before it was dolloped on me. Because I was considered too important to be damaged and at the same time dangerously ignorant of how much pain the caustic might cause without doing real harm, the first woman was to be an indicator. When she could no longer tolerate the stuff, they washed it off my body. My hair would be gone but my skin would remain. The theory was sound but for one factor which confounded it. The Circassian who preceded me missed her true vocation. With her capacity for suffering, she should have become a Christian martyr. While she sat like the Sphinx with lye devouring her, I screamed in agony.

Of course, she only had the paste on an arm, first in one spot, then another between her wrist and elbow. Arms do not hurt so much, but there are other places. When the caustic went to work on my private parts, the servants had to restrain me. Even then, slippery from the steam and the ointments, I managed to wriggle away and once free, I plunged my entire

bottom into the fountain to insure I would have some
of my femininity left to present to the Sultan.

After the lye I was as smooth as a piece of glass
when my women began to paint. My nails were lacquered, fingers and toes. They tinted my cheeks and
lips with rouge, darkened my eyes and rubbed color
onto my nipples and knees. It offended me to be
handled so intimately, stroked and kneaded by several
people at once, most of them intentionally placing
their hands on parts of me I rarely touched myself,
but their attitudes were far from carnal, and I tried
to present a stoic façade to their numerous outrages.

These preparations took most of the day, interrupted only by the calls to prayers which took my
servants away for a while. I came to look forward to
the *muezzin's* song as the announcement of a respite.
Then I realized he would chant only once more that
night, and at that time I would be with the Turk.
Whenever that thought occurred to me, it was accompanied by a sickening wave of apprehension and fear.

In contrast, Lydia and the others were full of high
spirits when they returned from their ritual. Guselli
brought me a small loaf of white bread and some
sweet butter to keep my stomach from rumbling. No
other food was permitted in order to avoid a sense of
fullness which supposedly impeded romance and inter-
fered with conception.

While I dined on the meager fare, I heard sounds
of confusion in the hallway. Lydia went to investigate.

"What is it?" I asked, frightened of any unexpected
occurrence.

"Poppy's slaves are downstairs. I'll go see about it."
While she was gone I finished eating. Then the servants began to dress me in my nuptial costume, or so
I called it. In fact, the Sultan did not marry. His
consorts were slaves, every one. Even the dead Sultan
Valide, his mother, had been a slave, probably not
even a Turkish one. To the Ottomans, the maternal
bloodline of their Padishah is of no consequence. Only
the sire is important.

Lydia called orders down the stairs as she reappeared in the doorway. "It's a present, mademoiselle. Something from Captain Pasha Ben Raza." A look of devilment danced in her eyes.

"A present?"

"Yes, something you'll enjoy." She waved two husky eunuchs into the room. Between them they carried a huge copper cauldron, its tin surface frosted and cold.

"Snow?" I asked, surprised at the contents.

"More than that," Lydia laughed as she scraped away the surface layer of white to reveal a dozen or more bound corktops. "It's champagne!"

"Champagne! Wonderful! Open a bottle quickly." She could not. Because of her faith, she knew nothing of spirits and was baffled by the corks. I took charge myself, and the merry sound of popping soon vibrated through the room.

After the eunuchs were sent away, two of the women found a crystal goblet. As each servant took her turn adding a new piece to my ensemble, I toasted her health. Soon I had tempted several of them into sampling the forbidden liquor.

In addition to the trunk of gems Baba Mohammed had given me, he sent a small chest of ornamental jewelry that I might wear for this occasion. Had I been decorated with every piece in the collection, I would have toasted myself senseless before I ever met Abdul Hamid. However, Lydia suggested that simplicity better suited the attire of a virgin. I agreed, selecting only a necklace of emeralds set in gold, each stone the size of my thumb nail and surrounded by diamonds.

"You are magnificent, mademoiselle," Lydia whispered, tears glistening on her black lashes. She took a drink of champagne. "This is against the Koran, you know."

"Yes, but you can confess tomorrow." I refilled her glass.

She was very inexperienced in the wonders of wine

and felt its effects quickly, jabbering happily as she tried to translate whatever my servants said.

"They are praising you, mademoiselle, as the most beautiful woman in the harem," she explained. "They pray you have a son who will be their Padishah, and they look forward to serving you when you are the Sultan Valide."

"Optimistic, aren't they?" I laughed. "Abdul Hamid has not even seen me yet, and already they have me the queen mother."

"Not optimism, mademoiselle. They believe it is your destiny."

"Destiny! Not now! Just champagne!" I handed Lydia a freshly opened bottle.

She lowered her voice. "If you'll pardon my boldness, mademoiselle. These women are very proud to be your slaves. They ask no more of life than to serve, but if I might make a suggestion."

"Yes, of course."

"The trunk from Baba Mohammed that was brought to your suite this morning."

"It's in my bedroom." Through my chemise I touched the key that hung from my neck on a tiny gold chain.

"You are a woman of great wealth, mademoiselle. You can afford to be generous, and generosity can only strengthen the affection these women feel for you. In the days ahead, their loyalty will be beyond price. Now would be an auspicious occasion for presenting gifts."

"You know the ways of a harem, don't you, Lydia?" I smiled my approval of her thoughtfulness. "I'll go and get a box of jewels."

"Nothing too large, mademoiselle. Lest they think you a fool."

"Yes. I'll choose carefully."

When I returned from my errand, I presented each woman with a diamond. All the stones were of a like size, about as big as the eye of a cat. Even Lydia received one, though I took her aside a few moments later and gave her a sapphire ring from the nuptial collection.

The effect of my gifts upon the room was tumultuous when added to the excitement of the occasion and the champagne. In the general high spirits my anxiety subsided until it was announced that the Kislar Agha was downstairs.

He was dressed in his official finery, complete with ermine trim on his *pelisse,* one of the designations of his office. As I approached him, I noticed for the first time the small silver quill that protruded from one of the folds of his turban.

"Your beauty is beyond description, mademoiselle. With the blessing of Allah a son will be made this night." Although the wine had helped to lighten the moments before the eunuch's arrival, his reference to the evening's objective—the conception of a child and all the necessary processes by which that is accomplished—started a trembling in my limbs that quickly spread through my entire body.

"The blessings of Allah upon you!" Lydia called from the top of the stairs. I looked back and saw all of my servants who had crowded onto the landing to wish me well. Then I followed the eunuch through the door.

When I stepped outside, I saw that except for the two gelded children guarding my door, the chief eunuch and I were alone in a silent corridor. The thought occurred to me that I could easily run from the fellow, hobbled as he was by his own obesity. But through Lydia's inquiries and my own, I had learned something of the lay of the palace, and I realized escape was impossible. The place was built in three major compartments or courts. The First Court, the Court of the Janissaries, takes its name from the soldiers who are housed within it. Along with them live the many artisans and craftsmen required to support the five thousand people of the seraglio.

The Second Court, enclosing an expansive green lined with trees, houses the Divan, the Ottoman deliberative body. Across the courtyard are the dwellings of the palace cooks and the kitchens where food for the palace inmates is prepared.

Five gates lead from the Second Court to the Third Court, but the most important portal is the one through which I had passed, the Gate of Felicity. By contrast to the first two courts and their public functions, the Third Court is a private place, the home of the Grand Turk and his women. The Golden Road links the harem, the women's quarters, to the selam, the men's domain. Were I to flee that night, I would have had to run the length of that road, make my way through a warren of harem corridors, then traverse the entire Second Court and finally try to pass through the realm of the Janissaries undetected. Instead, I chose to meet Abdul Hamid.

What I had learned about him in the two days before our encounter revealed little about the man. Few women knew him well. But it gave me some insight into Ottoman traditions. He was close to sixty years old and had reigned for twelve years. Prior to his accession he had lived within the walls of the harem in a suite of apartments known as the Cage. In essence, that meant he had been a prisoner for over thirty years, never venturing out of his luxurious dungeon, never receiving guests or news of the world. His only companions were deaf mutes, eunuchs imprisoned with him, and a cohort of sterile concubines who satisfied his physical appetites but were as ignorant as he of what went on in the realms which he would one day rule.

Thus it was understandable that those slaves Lydia and I asked to describe their Padishah were quick to praise him for his clear mind. Many of his predecessors, similarly immured for decades, had gone completely mad before they ever took the throne.

The reason for this peculiar apprenticeship to the sultanate was originally a humane one, although its practice had degenerated over the years into cruel barbarism. Before the Cage was developed, a prince,

upon the night of his ascension to Grand Turk, ordered his deaf mutes into the halls of the palace to
find all the other male heirs and strangle them to
death with silk bow-strings. No exceptions were made.
The Sultan's own brothers were slain, as well as infant
nephews and cousins. Even the unborn were eliminated by drowning their mothers. Only when the new
Sultan was the sole surviving bearer of the Ottoman
seed was he safe from assassination, because then his
death would end the bloodline, and everyone believed
that would doom the empire to immediate collapse.
After generations of such slaughter, the Cage seemed
a benevolent alternative that would still effectively
prevent conspiracies, though the debilitating effects it
had upon the dynasty were impossible to ignore.

I would pass the terrible Cage as I walked toward
the site chosen for my audience with Abdul Hamid.
But as I stepped out upon the Golden Road, I gave
no thought to Mihrishah's son, Prince Selim, who was
then imprisoned there. I was only aware that I could
no longer hear the reassuring voices of my servants,
and I grew fearful. The Golden Road was deserted,
yet just as two days before when Kiusem struck the
old woman, I sensed eyes behind every lattice and
window drape. The guards at my apartment door
quietly knelt when I passed by. There was not a sound
to be heard along the entire harem path except the
cascading water of the fountains.

"Where is everyone?" I whispered timidly, feeling
as though I marched to my death.

"Never mind," my escort replied. "Abdul Hamid
is waiting."

I realized that the women of the harem must have
hated me. After all, I had not followed the prescribed
path or spent years in preparation. I was a newcomer
who had usurped their privileges. The emptiness of
the corridor and its deserted loges echoed my every
step, but behind it I could sense envy and hostility
harbored against me.

A slight movement from the second balcony caught

my eye. A door had opened. Then one on the other side. Still, I could see no living soul. My heart raced. The Kislar Agha continued ahead of me, his manner all pomp and formality. Several doors had opened, but just by cracks. A fist emerged from one of them. It clutched a missile. I saw the hand draw back, then with a rapid motion hurl the object at my head. Protectively, I threw my arms over my eyes and rushed forward. In my flight I could hear shouts, yet nothing struck me. I felt only an occasional gentle touch like the wings of a butterfly against my arm. Looking up, I feared more attacks, but to my amazement the air was full of rose petals. Hundreds of women had streamed out of the doorways, filled the balconies and begun showering me with flowers.

"They are wishing you well, Mademoiselle de Rivery," the Kislar Agha explained. "This is a custom of the harem. They pray you will give Abdul Hamid a son."

"How beautiful!" was all I could say.

The Golden Road soon became a carpet of pink and white. Its walls rang with cheers from the harem sisterhood. Only one section of the balcony remained silent and deserted. The Kislar Agha, rose petals clinging to his turban, looked back to see if I had noticed. "Kiusem Sultan's suite," he said soberly. I understood.

Along the corridor on the left was a solid wall with windows only in the upper levels. I surmised it was the Cage. Beyond that was a pillared hallway which led to a tulip garden and a porticoed kiosk.

"You will wait here, mademoiselle." The Kislar Agha's voice was muted as we stood in an antechamber. "I will announce you to the Padishah." He smiled in a warm, almost fatherly way. "Praise Allah you have come to us." He disappeared through the doorway.

Had the eunuch been gone more than a few seconds, I would have panicked. Fear choked shut my throat as if it were on a drawstring. Try as I might I could not fill my chest with air. The sound of my own heartbeat terrified me as I struggled to breathe. No thoughts entered my head while I waited, nothing except the realization that my body was on the verge of an uncontrolled rebellion.

"Abdul Hamid, Allah's Shadow upon the Earth, bids you enter," the Kislar Agha said when he returned. Trembling, I took a step forward. "Don't be afraid, child." He put a massive hand on my shoulder. "He is the Padishah, the caliph of us all, but he is also a man. Now go inside and kneel before him. That is the only ritual. I'll wait out here."

The golden domed room I entered was softly lit with oil lamps. The rugs and tapestries were in rich shades of blue and red. On a silk divan under a gilt and jeweled canopy sat the Grand Turk. I walked toward him, then knelt as I had been instructed. When he spoke, I looked up. He signaled me to stand. I did, and my eyes met those of the man to whom I belonged. He wore his age well, but he was an old man. A close-fitting white turban wrapped around a small black hat covered his head. At the front of it was a spray of jewels which held in place a tall *aigrette;* that magnificent plume swept the air above him. His skin was sallow parchment upon which were drawn eyebrows distorted into high arches. His beard and mustache were dyed black.

Without the cosmetics and finery he could have been any man at all, for he did not have the look of a monarch. Only his mouth betrayed an infamous ancestry. There was a cruelty about it, a natural sneer. In it I could see the savagery that had led the Turks of ages past to slaughter crusaders and desecrate their Christian shrines.

Abdul Hamid extended a jeweled hand toward me. I was slow to take it, but he was patient. In signs and gestures he bade me sit down beside him. He brushed his hand across my face and touched my hair. Though he smiled approvingly, his expression could not erase the evil inheritance in that Ottoman mouth.

Perhaps sensing I was afraid, he retreated toward a gilt device near his couch. I recognized it from my experience in Algiers. It was a *nargileh,* a waterpipe. He opened a case on the small table next to it and offered me a choice of several finely crafted mouthpieces. At first I refused, having no taste for tobacco. He insisted however, and I obliged him as I knew I would have to oblige him throughout the night.

The smoke was cool and fragrant. I breathed in some of it as Lydia had shown me and found it less offensive than on other occasions. The Sultan spoke now and then and took a sip of the pipe. A gentle breeze from the courtyard carried the scent of jasmine and caused the lamplight to dance upon the golden dome. I relaxed. The smoke was soothing.

Time passed. Abdul Hamid took my hand in his. I watched him as he lifted it to his Ottoman lips, but it was as though the hand were not mine. I floated somewhere at a distance, an invisible observer. Then the Sultan called and the Kislar Agha appeared. He helped me to my feet and led me away.

"Is that all?" I asked drunkenly when we returned to the antechamber. "I hardly noticed. Did he do anything?"

The eunuch laughed softly. "He is pleased, mademoiselle. He is most pleased. It was just as I told you. Now follow me. You will go to his bedchamber."

I felt almost giddy for some reason, perhaps from the champagne. At least I was no longer terrified. "Off we go then, Monsieur the Kislar Agha." I took his arm. "It's time for bed."

"Ah, beautiful one. You feel the hashish?"

"I feel something. If you call it hashish, so be it, and let there be more of the same."

"Whatever you desire, mademoiselle," he said delightedly. "By the Prophet, a son will be made this night, and then you will want for nothing the rest of your life."

We walked outside and through a garden of blossoming jasmine. My mind was miraculously free of care and I felt a warm affection for my companion. "Where did you learn to speak French, Poppy?" I paused to take in the fragrance of the night.

"You call me Poppy," he chuckled. "I am pleased, but we must not dally. The Sultan will follow shortly." He coaxed me toward a broad stairway on the far side of the courtyard.

"I'm coming, but tell me. Where did you learn to speak French so well?"

"When I was a boy. Soon after I came here. There was a Frenchwoman in the harem. Nothing like you, of course. She was a favorite of the Sultan Mustapha, but just one of many. In her lonely times we talked together and she taught me her language. Later, Mustapha gave her to one of his generals and she left the harem. Since then I have practiced with the Dragoman of the Porte. He and I usually take coffee together and exchange gossip after morning prayers. Often we speak in French."

"Dragoman, I've heard that word before somewhere. What is a dragoman?"

"He is an interpreter. Istanbul is the crossroads of the world. Almost every tradesman and merchant needs a dragoman to speak for him when he conducts business with foreigners. The Dragoman of the Porte is the Grand Turk's official translator. He is a Greek fellow by the name of Cantopolis Effendi, and he is a master of more tongues than you'll find on the Janissary tree."

His reference was curious. "How many tongues are there on this tree?" I asked as we started up the stairs to an ornate kiosk built into the palace wall.

"There are many. You see the Janissaries perform summary executions whenever the mood strikes them, and they hang the heads of their victims on a tree in the First Court. The tongues swell and blacken like overripe fruit." The Kislar Agha noticed me wince at his description. "An unfortunate choice of words. Please forgive me, mademoiselle."

"It reminded me of what I saw at the main gate

when I arrived. Did the Janissaries kill those poor wretches as well?"

"Perhaps, but by Abdul Hamid's order. Those heads belong to the Grand Turk."

Two eunuchs opened the doors of the kiosk and we entered. My spirits had taken a bad turn as a result of my recollection of the events surrounding my arrival, but Lydia was waiting for me inside and I had no time to think.

"Hurry, mademoiselle." She rushed up to me and started to undo my *entari,* the long overgown.

"I'll leave you alone now." The Kislar Agha bowed and went out.

"I must be gone before the Sultan arrives," Lydia explained nervously. "It is the law of the harem that when I hear the Grand Turk's silver-nailed slippers on the steps, I must run. Tonight he should see no woman but you."

"Then go now," I urged her. "You need take no risks for me. I'll be all right."

"You must change." She held up a pale blue sleeping caftan. "Quickly. Out of your clothes."

Together we attacked the jeweled buttons of my gown and the ties at the knees of my pantaloons. There was a wall of mirrors behind the canopied divan. "Sweet Mother of God, Lydia!" I half whispered when I saw myself in the nightdress. But for the little rose embroidered on the front between my breasts, I may as well have been completely naked.

She hardly noticed, frantic as she was to pack up my other clothes and leave. Then her mirror reflection paused and cocked its head. "I hear his footsteps," she gasped. "I must flee." Just before I could grab my white shawl to cover my nudity, she snatched it up and ran out the side door.

An instant later there was a flurry of activity at the main entrance to the kiosk. Abdul Hamid entered with the Kislar Agha at his side and twelve black eunuchs trailing behind.

The abrupt arrival of such an entourage turned me

to stone. As I stood in the lamplight wearing little more than the night, I felt their eyes like hands upon my flesh.

"Make them leave!" I cried and ran to the couch where I hid behind a pillow. "Does Abdul Hamid require an army for this conquest?"

The Kislar Agha spoke to the Sultan and then translated the response. "These are eunuchs, mademoiselle, creatures of the harem. They are here to serve, and they will remain."

"Eunuch or not, they have eyes. How could anyone be expected to go through with this if there are a dozen men in the room?"

"You will do wonderfully, mademoiselle." The Kislar Agha tried to reassure me. "Just remember we are trained to hear nothing, to see nothing, to say nothing. We are here simply to serve the great one." The chief eunuch came over to the divan and affixed a mouthpiece to one of the tubes of the *nargileh*. "Smoke a while. Relax. All will be well."

One of the other eunuchs turned down several of the oil lamps so that the royal couch was illuminated by only a small circle of light. Darkness enshrouded all the men in the room.

A few moments passed. Then Abdul Hamid stepped into the light wearing a simple white *caftan*. With his turban gone, he seemed even less regal, for his head was shaved, but still his silent mouth spoke of barbarism.

I breathed in the cool smoke of the pipe and it strengthened me. Again I withdrew from my body to watch what followed unmolested. The Sultan sat down and pulled a finely stitched silk coverlet over both of us. He gently eased away the pillow I had clutched as a shield.

His hands were soft, more finely groomed than any French courtier's. As he stroked my skin, he began to speak. I did not understand a word, but I read something in his eyes, something I had seen before. It was not desire or what I might have taken for Ottoman lust. It reminded me a bit of Mihrishah Sultan when she spoke of her son, and even of the Kislar Agha as he talked of the Sultan. Abdul Hamid was not thinking of the pleasure of the moment. He had a grand design for his empire, just as the others did, and I was the key to its success.

Abdul Hamid coaxed off my *caftan* and embraced me. His lips touched my neck, my breast, the unshielded nakedness of my femininity. Still safe outside myself, still the observer, I watched his manhood seek a home within my body. I saw myself grimace with pain. Then a strange force racked the Sultan. He called out. His weight collapsed upon me, and he pulled himself away.

The Kislar Agha was at his side seconds later. They spoke briefly, then the eunuch explained to me that he would go at once to the harem register and record the date and time of the event so that if a child were born nine months hence, no one could doubt it was from Ottoman seed.

It was done. What had hung over me for months like a sentence of death was finished in just a few moments. Surprisingly, it was not so terrible as I had expected, though at the same time there was no insight to be gained from the experience that might discredit the practice of abstinence. I wondered at the man who lay next to me, so quickly asleep after discharging his dynastic responsibilities. The Grand Turk. "An inflated epithet," I said out loud as I reached for the pipe. Soon I slept too.

At daybreak when I awoke no one shared my bed. Consistent with tradition, Abdul Hamid had risen early and slipped away, leaving behind the clothes he had worn the night before.

"Good morning, mademoiselle." Lydia greeted me with a pot of coffee and an eager expression. "You look radiant, beautiful one." As she pulled back my cover to help me up, she exposed a red stain on the bedclothes. "Praise Allah!" she cried, delighted.

"Praise Allah for your good fortune, mademoiselle."

"And for the coffee, Lydia." I struggled to shake off my slumber. "I'll have it now."

"Of course." She filled a cup. It was thick and black, even stronger than what I had learned to enjoy in Algiers, but with milk, the perfect tonic after my drugged sleep.

"Here are the Sultan's clothes, mademoiselle. Shall I search them for you?"

"Certainly not!"

"But it is a custom. Whatever money he has left behind is yours to keep."

"Considering the trunk in our apartment, I don't believe we need his spare coins."

"But it could be seen as an insult."

"I have done my duty. The Dey of Algiers gave his word to another of his own faith that Adele would be released. Insults are no longer my concern, unless of course, they are directed at me. Whatever is in the Sultan's purse will remain there."

"Very well, but what can I tell the servants? They will measure your success by the prize you bring home."

"Tell them anything. Trot out the Dey's trunk if you like and claim it is from Abdul Hamid."

"What a wonderful idea. You'd be worshiped as a love goddess once that story spread through the harem. How unfortunate everyone saw the trunk when it was delivered. I told them it was from the Dey. Of course, they don't know what's in it."

I could see she was scheming to transfer the Algerian jewels to another chest and then make outrageous claims in my name. "Put whatever you're thinking out of your head, Lydia. Just help me to dress."

The Kislar Agha was seated on his personal chair in my main salon when I returned to the apartment. He seemed even taller than usual when I saw him, all puffed up with pride from the success of his night's work.

"The blessings of the Prophet upon you, mademoiselle." He beamed at me as he salaamed.

"Good morning, monsieur. It is early for callers, but you are welcome." After his assistance during my ordeal, I could not deny a certain affection for him.

"I bring you gifts from Abdul Hamid." He clapped his hands and two of his slaves who had been in the courtyard carried in an immense mahogany chest.

"It's bigger than the other one," Lydia whispered excitedly. "It's half again the size."

She ran out of the room and came back with the entire household in tow, all of them silent, all of them with their eyes on the chest.

Poppy pulled a key from the folds of his waist sash and handed it to me. I passed it to Lydia, who quickly unlocked the box and threw back the lid. "Silver!" she exclaimed. "Thousands, millions of pieces of silver." The other women rushed up to examine it.

"Abdul Hamid is very generous, monsieur," I observed, realizing now that such gifts were in fact purchases of one sort or another.

"There is more." The eunuch pulled back the sleeve of his robe to reveal a golden medallion suspended on a heavy chain from his arm. "This is the seal of one of the richest *timars* in Anatolia. It is yours." He placed the medallion around my neck.

"What is a *timar?*" I asked as I looked at the seal.

"It is what you might call a fief. Holders of *timars* are vassals of the Sultan. Many provide troops for his military campaigns."

"And I am to provide such troops?"

"Oh no. The revenues from your lands will be nothing more than slipper money."

"But there's enough wealth in that chest to last the rest of my life. Does the Sultan believe all French women have the appetites of Marie Antoinette?"

"If you bear a son, you will need even more, believe me. And Abdul Hamid will see that you have it. But there is something else."

"What more could there be?"

"You are very important to us, mademoiselle. I myself would guard your every breath if I could, but it is said that a loving friend is Allah's strongest shield against all evil. You have such a friend."

"Aimee!" I heard Adele's voice as if from a dream. "Aimee!" When I turned, I saw her standing in the courtyard, the morning sun glistening off her silk garment.

"Adele! You're all right?" My voice quaked with emotion. We rushed to embrace each other.

"Yes," she cried in my arms. "I'm all right, but you —I'm sorry they used me against you like this."

"That's over now. You're safe."

"But there will be another time, and then another. They'll use me whenever they find it necessary."

"No, never again." I took Adele's arm and led her toward the *hammam*. "Poppy, thank you very much for delivering her safely. You may call on us tomorrow."

'Whatever you wish, mademoiselle. Tomorrow." He bowed and departed.

"I have so much to tell you, Adele, but now I believe it is time to bathe."

"A bath by all means," she laughed as she dried her eyes. Her voice was full of life. "Will it be *à la turque,* this bath of ours?"

"Most assuredly *à la turque,*" I responded. "You see, I left my bathing gown in France, and I fear I shall never go back to retrieve it."

BOOK TWO

Chapter 17

Dark centuries before Byzantium fell, Turk tribesmen —the marauding ancestors of Osman and his dynasty —dwelt in a wild expanse of emptiness known as the Asian steppes. After these nomads captured Constantinople, the city became their master, instilling in them irresistible aspirations of greatness. In the shadow of Greek, Roman and Byzantine monuments the Ottomans established their domain. And from their new capital, which they called Istanbul, rugged warriors and disciplined armies extended their despotic tentacles to create a vast empire. Such is the way with this race of people—no matter how far the Turks strayed from the source of their heritage, they still felt the lure of the steppes.

Part of that heritage must harken back to the days before the smaller and efficient provinces, called sanjaks, dominated Ottoman territory. Long ago, forebears of the Turks endured bitter winters in tent encampments swept by cruel winds over a land that offered no shelter. Hardy souls venturing into the cold met only slate gray skies that drew the horizon in upon them.

The coming of spring was a joyful release for such miserable wretches. What comfort they must have taken from a warm sun, a gentle breeze and renewed pastures for their flocks. As a crown to all their other blessings, the spring earth was covered with a beautiful mantle of wild flowers nourished by the melted snow.

Perhaps in memory of those days, the Grand Turk's seraglio is bedecked with blossoms during every season that will sustain them; roses, carnations, lilacs, jasmine and a hundred other varieties can be found, but the wildflower of the steppes, the tulip, holds the place of honor. Tulips are an Ottoman passion. Westerners developed innumerable varieties, and the Turks paid such high prices to obtain them from Europeans that the tulip became known as "the gold of Europe."

Outside my new harem apartment the ground glistened with that European gold. In early May an intricate parterre of tulips arranged by color created an eight pointed star around a small marble fountain at the center of my courtyard. It was larger than the courtyard of my previous suite. Everything about the new place was more spacious. The vestibule outside the main entrance now had to accommodate several eunuch guards and a servant who screened callers. The formal salon was decorated in the same white and blue colors with red accents that pleased me earlier. But now there was room for my entire household, grown to over fifty women, whenever I had reason to assemble them. Most often they gathered to watch dancers or perhaps a traveling group of Jewish players. Frequently, we listened to storytellers or musicians furnished, from the ranks of the harem, who used the three broad steps leading from the entrance into the salon as a stage for their performances.

Upstairs were bedrooms, dressing rooms, a water closet and a sitting room where I spent most of my time. In the midst of all things Turkish and strange, I had created a small world of my own where I preserved the flavor of France.

Not long after I arrived at the seraglio, Poppy discovered a sealed storeroom full of exquisite furnishings that had been presented to Sultan Mustapha by the Baron de Toth. The Baron was a military adviser who served the Porte for several years. Although Hungarian by birth, he represented France, and if I may judge from his selection of gifts, he demonstrated an excellent eye for the rococo style.

In my more daring moments, when I hungered for the culture of my childhood, I studied the lovely pieces that had been presented to the Grand Turk. I found that they had allowed some of the finest woodcraft the world has ever produced to molder and rot in damp cellars while their cavernous chambers cried out for furnishings of any variety. In spite of my strong desire to master the Ottoman way in every detail, I could not resist decorating my sitting room and boudoir with whatever could be salvaged.

By the arrival of spring my new apartment was complete. One May afternoon as I looked through a lattice balcony off my French sitting room at the array of tulips below, I called down to the eunuch gardeners and praised them for creating such a display. Certainly the flower beds at La Fontelle were more extensive than those of my small courtyard, but they were not so detailed and perfect, nor did they demonstrate so much affection on the part of their husbandmen for the wonders of nature. Although the Ottomans may be a people of undistinguished heritage and peculiar customs, there is much about them to be praised, and that beautiful day I saw only their best qualities. A west wind carried the fragrance of lilacs. The sunshine was warm and cheerful as it wended its way through the grill. And Adele was with me again.

One week before, she had moved into the bedroom next to mine after having spent the winter in a villa on the Bosporus with Captain Pasha Ben Raza. When fair weather signaled his return to the sea, Adele elected to remain in Istanbul. The Grand Turk extended the protection of his household to her, and in so doing, provided me with the companionship of my friend for a bit less than half the year.

It was wonderful to turn and see her studying at a delicately carved escritoire as if we were still at the convent. Yes, it was quite the same except that now she did not wear the cumbersome petticoats of a French lady of fashion, nor the modest fichu draped around her neckline. Instead she dressed in harem trousers, tied at the knee and flared around her ankles, with a lightweight chemise above and a long gown called an *entari* covering the ensemble. Her hair was much the same as it had always been, though now it sparkled with jeweled pins embedded in the braided bun at the back and encrusted upon the small cap she wore at a saucy angle on her forehead.

Not long after we had arrived in the Levant, both Adele and I decided to adopt Ottoman fashion, realizing that we would be more welcome among the women of the harem if we respected their customs. We even took up the practice of using *surma,* a black cosmetic dust applied to the eye with a thin copper wire. It seemed that in the Orient everyone used it, even the oldest crones who worked in the slave kitchen. Many men wore it as well. I know Abdul Hamid did, and so did the eunuchs.

"Naksh Sultan," Lydia called to me as she entered the sitting room. She always spoke in Ottoman Turkish now, a language she acquired with little difficulty, and she called me Hanoum or Naksh Sultan, the name Naksh being given to me by the harem sisterhood and meaning "beautiful one."

"I am here on the balcony," I responded as I walked inside.

"The new supplies have been recorded in the kitchen register," she explained. "These Turks keep records of every single thing that enters the palace."

"The bureaucracy is large," I said with a smile.

"And there must be work for everyone, and for their children that will come after them."

"Soon there will be a scribe to record each piece of garbage we send out as well," she grunted. "But such things should not concern you now, Hanoum Sultan. Now is the hour of your nap."

"But I am not tired, Lydia."

"You must rest during the warmest part of each day to preserve your beauty. Please, Sultan, just an hour or two."

"Not today," I responded as I sat down at a parquetted card table and prepared to practice my calligraphy. "I have not yet mastered a single Ottoman script, and I am told there are over twenty used in the palace."

"They are devilishly hard," Adele agreed, looking up from her studies. "I prefer Persian or Arabic to these Ottoman dots and curls. Every time a speck of ink flies from my quill, I find I have changed the meaning of an entire sentence."

"Such things are best left to the bureaucrats, Hanoum Effendi. Both of you have mastered the spoken word. Harem women are not expected to know more than that. Now please, Naksh Sultan should get some rest and so should you. Your Captain Pasha hopes to find you beautiful when he returns from the sea."

"Our studies are more important, Lydia," I explained. "If I am to succeed here, I must become Ottoman in every way, and it is said that an Ottoman knows the written word."

"But that is not meant for women, Hanoum Sultan. Ottoman women are not scholars, they are mothers of sons."

"But the mother of a prince must be more than a mere ornament to her husband's bedchamber. I will adopt the Ottoman way as best I can, and that means more than simply donning the habit."

"Do you think that your enemy, Kiusem, spends

hours in study, risking the remains of her loveliness upon calligraphy and books?"

"I doubt she can read a clock," Adele said sarcastically. "And it baffles me how a woman who appears so dull witted can be a danger to us."

"She does seem to lack the polish of a courtesan," I agreed.

"Yes," Adele went on. "I saw her at the harem banquet two days ago. While everyone else ate with their fingers, she seemed to maul the food with her hands."

"But it has not always been so," Lydia said in a perplexed tone. "I have spoken to women who have lived here for years. They say Kiusem Sultan has behaved strangely for several months."

"Perhaps she has some affliction," Adele responded. "But still, the woman is not bright. If she were, she could see that the Janissaries are as much a threat to her son, Mustapha, as they are to Mihrishah Sultan's son, Selim. When Aimee counsels Abdul Hamid to strengthen his control over the army by creating a new corps trained on a European model, Kiusem believes it is an attack upon her."

"In fact it is, Adele," I said. "She and Mustapha need the Janissaries. She knows that Abdul Hamid will not live long. Then Selim will take the throne, but he is a young man. He may rule for forty or fifty years. By that time her own son could be dead, and she will have lost any chance to become Sultan Valide. The Janissaries will be her means to eliminate Selim soon after his ascendency. They will need a pretense, of course. But one day they will turn over their kettles and declare a revolt. They will make demands of Selim until he can yield no more. Then they will throw him back into the Cage or put him to death. Either way, Kiusem's son will become Grand Turk before his rightful time. Her key to power is the Janissaries, and she knows it well."

"But does she not realize that the Janissaries can do the same thing to Mustapha if he does not give himself over to their control?" Adele asked. "For a woman who has lived with the history of Rome all around her, she is dangerously ignorant of the lessons it could teach. The decline of the West began with emperors who rested their thrones upon a praetorian guard."

"Ottoman decline has already begun," I pointed out. "Even with the treasure ship Baba Mohammed sent, Abdul Hamid is incapable of mounting an effective assault against the Russians. He has no modern arsenal and few weapons factories. His military exists as if it were the seventeenth century."

"But there is time to modernize. You told me so yourself. With military reform and a few more years of peace while we rearm, the Ottomans can defeat Russia."

"Yet every day there is more pressure for war," I responded. "The Janissaries clamor for it. Catherine of Russia continues to fortify her southern frontier and allows her troops to violate Ottoman territories. Whenever I speak with Abdul Hamid he tells me of new insults to our sovereignty, but I continue to remind him that a war would bring disaster."

"Surely he realizes that," said Adele confidently.

"Yes, but the Janissaries do not. Their officers want war in order to fill their own purses. Kiusem speaks for them. During her audiences with the Grand Turk she opposes every word I say, and she still has influence. After all, she is the mother of his first born."

Chapter 18

The next day at midmorning I paid a call on Mihrishah Sultan. Once or twice each week I took coffee with her, often in the company of the Kislar Agha. During our conferences, both of them manifested great interest in anything I could reveal about the West. They had a special curiosity regarding the thoughts of the great philosophers. I introduced them to Rousseau, Montesquieu, Voltaire and Locke, lecturing my colleagues by the hour as if they were students. In exchange they described in detail the political situation in the Ottoman domain and sketched as best they could the main characters who dominated events outside the harem.

A comfortable friendship evolved between the three of us as time passed, based upon a sense of shared interests in the future of the realm. Poppy was devoted to Mihrishah's son, Selim, "The finest flower of the Ottoman seed," as he called him, and "the last hope of the dynasty." Mihrishah was eager for him to take the throne as well, knowing that through Selim, she would exercise vast influence within the palace. Both of them believed that the introduction of western military methods was essential to the survival of the state. They saw me as their means of bringing such ideas to Abdul Hamid's attention, thus smoothing the path for future reform.

The Grand Turk had grown very fond of me during the year I lived in the harem. As Poppy had hoped, I replaced Kiusem Sultan in his affections although Abdul Hamid's attitude toward me resembled that of a doting parent more than a lover or husband. Nonetheless, we spent many evenings together while he strove to teach me Turkish. On such occasions I had the opportunity to speak on the subject of western monarchs and a modern military.

Admittedly, I knew very little about such subjects that were more suited to the French salon society I had assiduously avoided during my later years in France. Still, compared to the inhabitants of the harem, or to any Turk for that matter, I was an expert on the West, and my counsel was sought frequently.

That day as I walked to Mihrishah Sultan's suite along the now familiar Golden Road, past the harem mosque on the left and Kiusem Sultan's apartment on the right, there was no reason to suspect that this gathering would differ greatly from any other. When I reached my destination, one of the eunuchs who trailed behind me stepped forward to make my presentation to Mihrishah's guards. The ornately carved doors swung open and a double file of apprehensive slave girls greeted me. I drew a tense breath and walked inside.

"Peace be upon you, Naksh Sultan." Poppy rose from his chair and salaamed.

"And on you be peace," I responded. "Where is Mihrishah Sultan this morning?"

"Here I am," she called from the top of the stairs. "I will be down in a moment." She was dressed in cool shades of apricot and green over a white chemise and pantaloons. She was always attractive, but this morning she seemed unusually lovely, and I told her so after our exchange of *temenas*.

"Thank you, dear," she smiled with satisfaction. "Coming from such a beauty the compliment is even sweeter."

As Poppy took his chair again, he reached into his robes for a string of worry beads, then cast a furtive glance toward the courtyard. "What is it, Poppy?" I asked, sensing his disquietude as I sat down on a cushion. "I noticed something unusual as soon as I came in the door."

"You are very astute, Naksh." He rolled the beads, a type of Musselman rosary, between his massive palms. "Yesterday I spoke with Abdul Hamid about this. He has given his approval, but still I do not like it."

"You are here to see to it that all is proper," Mihrishah reminded him. "Both of us agreed that it was time the two of them met."

"You will please tell me what this is about," I insisted.

"There is someone on the way here who has heard a great deal about you," Mihrishah said. "And you have heard of him as well. My son has expressed a desire to speak with you, and the Padishah has no objections."

"Selim is here?" I was quite surprised at such a breech of Ottoman law. "But I understood that no man is to lay eyes on me as long as Abdul Hamid lives."

"But the Padishah has given his permission," she explained. "By law Selim should never venture outside the Cage, but Abdul Hamid knows how unprepared a prince can be if he enjoys no freedom whatever before he takes the throne. Selim cannot roam the provinces at will, of course, but within the palace he moves about without being suspected of treason."

"Then why are you so worried," I asked Poppy. "If we are doing nothing wrong?"

"When one departs from tradition there are risks. We are judged by appearances here, and I do not like the way this could be interpreted. You are Abdul Hamid's favorite, yet he allows you to be seen by Selim. Does this show weakness or strength? Will it encourage our enemies or fill them with despair? I do not know the answers, and what I do not know frightens me."

"But no one outside my servants will know of Selim's visit," Mihrishah assured him. "He is not marching down the Golden Road after all."

"Kiusem will find out, I promise you. Whenever the Prince steps outside of the Cage, she hears of it."

"Every time you mention that Cage, it makes me shiver," I said, repulsed by the barbaric imprisonment forced upon Ottoman heirs to the throne. "From my bedroom window I often look out at its solid stone wall and wonder how many princes have gone mad during their years of isolation there."

"Too many, Sultan." The answer came from behind me. "Fortunately, I am not among them." When I turned I saw the Prince, who had just arrived through the courtyard. "Allah's blessings upon you this fine morning," he said jubilantly.

"Prince Selim, son of Grand Turk Mustapha III, and future Padishah of all our well protected domains," Mihrishah Sultan spoke formally. "May I present Naksh Sultan."

Before I could stand or kneel or make any demonstration of obeisance, the Prince strode across the salon and planted himself before me. "At last we meet," he said warmly, extending a delicate hand. I offered my hand in return, and in an exaggeration of continental ettiquette, he bowed and kissed it.

"Selim!" his mother gasped.

"My Prince!" Poppy exclaimed. "This is a woman of Abdul Hamid's harem. I am shocked. The audience is over. Naksh Sultan, please come with me." The Kislar Agha clicked his worry beads in agitation and groaned to his feet, but I did not move. Everything surrounding Selim's arrival had happened so quickly, I did not know what response to make to any of it.

"Poppy," Selim tried to explain. "Take no offense in my uncle's name. No harm was intended. I spoke to my European physician, Dr. Lorenzo, this morning. He instructed me in the French manner of greeting."

"I shall have a word with him then," Mihrishah said angrily. "He is to attend to your health, not your deportment."

"Your salutation was a great kindness," I said to the Prince, hoping to end the embarrassment. "Thank you." Turning to Mihrishah, I sought to soothe her with a question. "Tell me, Sultan, how does one properly address the heir to the throne? Is there an Ottoman term I should know?"

Unfortunately, her son gave her no time to reply. "My name is Selim," he said lightheartedly. "Please call me that. We will have no formalities among friends."

"Allah be merciful," Mihrishah gasped again. "What has possessed you, son? You are to be Grand Turk. I demand some propriety."

"Please Mother," he protested. "This woman has come to us from the great land of France. I would not have her bow and simper in my presence. She and I will be friends. Poppy calls me Selim. She will as well, and I will call her Naksh. No. I will call her by her French name." He turned and looked directly into my eyes. "What is it?"

The intensity I saw when I looked back into his unsettled me. "Aimee," I said, hardly above a whisper. Then speaking more clearly, "My name is Aimee."

"Selim." Poppy sounded apprehensive. "All of us are agreed that it will better serve our cause if Naksh strives to become more Ottoman. One way she can do this is to answer to her harem name and no other."

"You are wise," the Prince replied. "But I wish to learn of the West from a woman of the West. During our interviews I will call her Aimee. It can do no harm."

"Very well," Mihrishah said, greatly disturbed. "Let us be seated and take coffee." She nestled on the divan and then signaled her servants who brought in our refreshments.

Selim reclined next to his mother. Adoringly, she took his hand in hers and toyed with his fingers while the coffee was being served. The Prince paid no attention to her maternal fondling. His eyes never left me, and I found I could not look away from him. His aura of fragile beauty was fascinating. It suggested a nobility of spirit that surpassed even his exalted birthright. His body was lean and strong as a willow branch, his unbearded countenance clear and intelligent, his long black mustaches fascinating. No voluptuary was Selim. He had not succumbed to the innumerable temptations offered by his luxurious prison, yet the Cage had had its effect upon him. He seemed to thirst for the life that had been denied him, drinking it in with his eyes. As I began to sip my coffee, I felt as if he would consume me.

When the servants had gone I spoke up. "Tell me about the Cage," I asked, trying to gain some control over the awkward situation.

Selim smiled at my request, and I caught a glimpse of his ancestors in the cruelty of his mouth. "It is not so bad as you must imagine, Aimee." Mihrishah shifted uneasily at the mention of my French name, but Selim ignored her. "The Grand Turk is very concerned about my education. After all, he spent many years in the Cage himself, and he knows of its dangers. If I am to rule wisely, I must learn the ways of the world. To increase my knowledge, Abdul Hamid allows me certain visitors. My physician, Dr. Lorenzo, attends me every day, and there are others.

"When I am alone, I read the books they bring. I study the Koran, and of course, there are my women."

Unexplainably, I felt myself color at the mention of his concubines. "Still, it seems so terrible," I said struggling for composure. "That your uncle finds it necessary to keep you imprisoned within the palace. Surely he does not believe you would intrigue against him."

"Oh, but he does, Golden One," Selim responded. "And with good reason. Many princes have conspired to take the throne even from their own fathers. To prevent civil strife they had to be killed or locked away."

"You see, Naksh Sultan." Poppy addressed me formally. "In many respects we can be thankful for the Cage. Without it, Selim would have been strangled when Abdul Hamid first strapped on the ceremonial sword. Then Kiusem's son, Mustapha, would be the only heir."

"We must be grateful to Selim's father, as well," Mihrishah explained. "He began Selim's education in the affairs of state. When he was little more than a child, the Prince was allowed to attend sessions of the Divan and meet with foreign ambassadors. Abdul Hamid's small gestures would be of little value had Selim not acquired some knowledge of the world."

"That is true, Mother," Selim leaned over and kissed her on the cheek. "My father was wise. It was at his side that I met a great emissary from France, a military genius who demonstrated rapid fire artillery. I was only a boy then, and I imagined everyone in France must be as brilliant as he."

"Perhaps you still think so, my son," Mihrishah said pointedly.

"Perhaps I do." Selim looked at me and smiled.

"Certainly French girls learn nothing of artillery from their tutors," his mother said. "Is that not correct, Naksh?"

"Yes, Sultan," I replied. Irritated by her condescending manner, I tried to remember some of what François had told me about the cannon works near Nantes. "I know only that modern weapons are cast of iron, their barrels bored with machines driven by steam or water. They far surpass anything made of bronze. A scientist named Lavoisier has improved gunpowder. Now, many experts are certain that artillery will become the determining factor in future conflicts on the European continent."

"Aha!" Selim sprang to his feet, spilling his coffee on the rugs in his excitement. "By the beard of the Prophet! The French are a race of geniuses. Could our bombardier agha tell us as much? I think not."

"You are a remarkable woman, Naksh Sultan." Poppy smiled in surprise at my knowledge of such a subject. "How is it that you can speak with authority on the science of artillery?"

"Living in France, one learns many things," I said recklessly, knowing it would offend Mihrishah. "Of course, I could never construct a weapon myself."

That remark only further delighted the Prince. "Such a confession!" He laughed as he walked toward the courtyard archway. "A woman of Abdul Hamid's harem offers apologies that she cannot arm his batteries for him! We forgive such a deficiency, beautiful one. Now come with me." From across the room he held out his hand. "I wish to see your golden hair in the sunlight. Its color is the talk of the harem."

I saw Mihrishah and Poppy exchange worried glances. "It is time you returned to the Cage, Selim," his mother warned. "We do not wish to anger Abdul Hamid."

"He has encouraged this meeting, Mother. You told me so."

"He did not intend you to take Naksh into the garden. You are to talk to her in the presence of the Kislar Agha."

"That is correct, my Prince," the eunuch confirmed.

"And so it shall be." Selim was unperturbed. "You will accompany us, Poppy."

"And leave me here to drink my coffee alone?" his mother sulked.

"Out of the question!" Selim returned to the divan and took his mother's hand, helping her to her feet. "We will all take the air together. It is a beautiful morning, and the perfume of jasmine dances on the breeze." He turned to me. "Aimee, help Poppy up, if you will." Clearly, Selim was not to be denied.

"This is unwise," Poppy whispered to me as he groaned out of his chair.

"Why is the Prince behaving so?" I asked softly.

"We will speak of it later."

Selim's mother hung on her son's arm like a shield as he walked toward the courtyard, but halfway across the room Selim stopped, lifted her hand and placed it upon the arm of the Kislar Agha. Staggered, she drew back, but Selim insisted. "This is how it is done in France," he explained, seemingly oblivious to the root of her protest. "Dr. Lorenzo showed me this morning. When men and women stroll about, they walk so."

"I must personally thank the good doctor for taking a hand in your education," Mihrishah said sarcastically.

Undeterred, the Prince took my hand and placed it where his mother's had been. "Is this correct, Aimee?" His voice was seductive. His eyes engaged mine.

"Yes, it is," I answered softly, realizing in an instant that this latest move was more than a breach of Ottoman etiquette. Unmistakably, Selim intended to cuckold his uncle.

"Mother. Poppy. Won't you two lead the way?" As they passed us, I could see that Mihrishah's face was white with rage, the Kislar Agha visibly shaken by the Prince's conduct. "This is delightful," Selim went on. "We will imagine we are in Paris."

While our two chaperones walked ahead, the Prince allowed his hand to rest upon mine. His increasing boldness amazed me, yet I understood it. The fires of youth had been burning within him during all the years he spent locked away with his books and his sterile concubines. Considering his passionate nature, his apparent fascination with all things French and the stories he must have heard about me from Poppy and his mother, it was clear that his imagination had run away with him.

More troubling and unexplainable was my own reaction. At his touch, I actually trembled and grew short of breath. His fragile beauty aroused me, his youth excited me. While I knew no good could come of transgressing Ottoman laws of the harem, I found I could not force myself to leave his company. I was helpless even to stop the shaking of my hand upon his arm.

"Your hair is more beautiful than sunlight upon a fleece of white clouds," Selim whispered when the babbling courtyard fountain prevented our companions from hearing. "I would touch it and ask no more of paradise."

Just then Mihrishah turned and saw the blush upon my cheeks. "You must leave here at once, Selim," she said, her voice quivering with indignation.

"No, Mother. I will stay a while longer." Selim did not even deign to look in her direction as he spoke.

"There is danger," she went on, desperate to end her son's indiscretion. "Kiusem Sultan knows that Naksh is here. This foolishness yields her a dangerous advantage. The Janissaries will be told. Who knows where that may lead?"

"Your mother is wise," I forced myself to say, knowing all the while that the oafish Kiusem was hardly capable of such a complex plot.

"You wish me to leave then?" he asked, unable to mask his disappointment.

"I wish only that no harm comes to you or to any of us. We will meet again another time. More carefully."

"Go now, Selim," Poppy advised also. Then he went to the far corner of the courtyard. "Is anyone about?" he asked Mihrishah.

She walked to the salon and looked in. "No," she replied. "It is safe." The eunuch quickly lifted a large section of tiles from the walk. Beneath it was a steep stone staircase leading under the wall.

"Ah, that is how you avoided the Golden Road," I said, surprised. "How clever to have a secret entrance."

Selim looked at Poppy strangely, and then to Mihrishah. "Surely you have told her, Mother?"

"No, Selim. We thought it wise to wait a while longer. But now she must be told."

Selim began to speak, but Poppy interrupted him. "Allow me to explain. You see, there have been times in the past when violence against a Grand Turk spilled over into the harem. Such times may come again, and we believe it would be dangerous for women like Mihrishah Sultan and yourself to live in quarters which do not allow some means of escape. Mihrishah has this tunnel. When your new suite was built, a similar one was constructed for you. It is in the courtyard and is connected to an underground passage that winds through various stove chambers under the *hammams*. It runs from the Cage at one end to the old Sultan Valide's apartment and then to an exit near the suite of the harem laundress. From there it is only a short distance to the Fifty-Three Steps and then out the Shawl Gate."

"Who knows about this passage?" I asked.

"Only we four," Poppy assured me.

"But what of the workmen who opened the entrance? They must have realized what they were doing."

"Yes," Selim smiled. "But they will tell no one."

"You are certain?"

"Only the fishes," he replied grimly.

"They are in the Bosporus, Sultan," Poppy said. "We did not tell you about the passage sooner because we feared you might use it as a means to escape."

"And now?" I asked.

"And now you are one of us," Selim said with more emphasis than was prudent.

"You have remained here too long," Selim's mother's eyes flashed with anger. "Now be gone."

"Very well, Mother. I'll come again soon." He reluctantly let go my hand and then kissed Mihrishah's cheek quickly. "Thank you, Poppy, for arranging this meeting."

"I am your servant, my Prince."

"Aimee." My name upon his lips told his mother and the eunuch what they most certainly had suspected, and I saw their distress. "May Allah keep you safe from harm until we meet again."

"God be with you," I replied with all the coolness I could muster. Then the Prince descended the staircase.

"I do not feel well," Mihrishah said coldly after the tiles had been replaced. "I am going to bed." She glared at me as she spoke, making it clear that I was the cause of her discomfort.

"We will leave you then," Poppy said soothingly. "You will feel better after a rest."

"Good day, Mihrishah," I called as the Kislar Agha hurried me out the door.

My eunuchs, who had been waiting in the vestibule, fell in behind us as we returned down the Golden Road. Passing Kiusem's apartment I could hear the voice of her companion, Safiye, the one I always remembered from my first day in the harem as the woman in blue. She was singing a romantic ballad, perhaps serenading her mistress before they lay together, for the two of them were unabashed sapphists, and all the harem knew it. Beside me Poppy still clicked his worry beads. His concern over Kiusem's finding out about our meeting seemed groundless. After all, a woman who so frequently squandered her energies in base practices with her serving girls could hardly constitute a danger to any of us.

"You must understand Mihrishah," Poppy explained as we approached my door. "Understand and reassure her. She loves her son very much and has invested her entire life in his future. It was she who selected the women of his harem. All are beautiful, yet none is bright enough to win his lasting affection. She has no intention of allowing someone to steal his heart and usurp her place as the only woman of importance in his life. You must not cause her concern, Naksh. We three must remain allies if we are to prevail over Kiusem and the Janissaries."

"You should not have brought the Prince to Mihrishah's apartment today," I told him. "Years in the Cage have given him strong appetites."

"Yes, I know, but he insisted that all of the reformers should sit down together, and his mother agreed. Believe me, it will not happen a second time. Mihrishah will never allow Selim to see you again." The certainty in his voice sent an unexplainable chill through me. I knew Poppy was right. The stakes were too high to allow anything to interfere with the alliance between Mihrishah and me.

"May Allah guide your path, Naksh," he said when he left me at my apartment.

"God be with you," I replied.

Chapter 19

When I returned from Mihrishah Sultan's apartment, Adele was in the courtyard where she sat against the garden wall enjoying a light repast of fine Turkish white bread, fruit and contraband wine. I sought her out there and made myself comfortable on a rug by her side. We sent the servants away, and then, speaking in French to avoid being understood, I told her what had transpired.

"You are attracted to him?" she asked. My response was an embarrassed smile. "Of course you are." She called for another glass and offered me some wine. It was a heady Cyprus vintage popular in Istanbul ever since the reign of a sixteenth-century Sultan, coincidentally named Selim. The Sultan Selim thirsted for it so intemperately that he ordered a war waged against the Cypriots to insure a regular supply.

"I cannot explain my infatuation, Adele, but it is a fact nonetheless. I know it can only cause unhappiness. Mihrishah was furious when she saw the attention Selim paid me. She will never allow us to see each other again, but even if she did, it would be no different from today. Hands touching, poetic phrases, nothing more. We'll never be alone together."

"Just as well then that you won't see him," Adele reasoned. "No use torturing yourself over something like this."

"And it is torture," I agreed. "I'm falling in love with him."

"Aimee, you don't really believe it's love."

For an instant I was angry that she doubted my word, but when I saw her amused expression, I had to smile. "All right," I confessed. "It's not love. Selim isn't the only one who's been locked up. I lived behind the walls of a convent for eight years when most women our age were being courted and wed. Now I've exchanged that confinement for this one. The Grand Turk is the only man I've known. He's old enough to be my father and behaves as if he were. I don't need a father, Adele. I need a lover. Selim is the only man I've seen in a year who has his manhood intact and can hoist it without risking a stroke. I may not love him, but I want him desperately."

"I don't like it when you're desperate, Aimee. You take terrible risks. Remember what's at stake. Your friendship with Mihrishah Sultan is very important and will be even more so when she is Sultan Valide. From your description of this morning's fiasco, I gather that any liaison between you and her son would win her undying enmity."

"She does keep a close watch on his affections," I agreed. "Best we remain separated. In my sorry condition any available tumescence should suffice. Perhaps I should pass a few gold sequins to the harem inspectors so they will spare me an occasional cucumber. They are comely vegetables, not particularly noted for their conversation, but I understand that as far as endurance is concerned, they are unsurpassed."

"This is no life for a woman like you, Aimee." Adele set down her wine glass and leaned against the garden wall. "You need a man to love."

"I need something."

"What about this tunnel?"

"Yes, it's out here somewhere. We'll find it later."

"Have you thought lately about escape? You could return to France, find a husband, live a decent life. The tunnel would make it so much easier."

"I can never leave here, Adele. You know that as well as I."

She picked up my glass and filled it. Just then my servant Seriphina, came to the doorway. "Your pardon, Hanoum Sultan."

"Yes, Seriphina. What is it?"

"Mahmoud is awake and he hungers."

"Bring him to me."

Moments later she placed in my arms my infant son, the son begotten by Abdul Hamid on the first night I went to his bed. There was much of the Ottoman about the child, his mantle of dark hair, his shining black eyes. But from the moment of his birth, I could see that his mouth was mine and so would be his spirit. He nuzzled close. As I put him to my breast, I felt the reassuring tingle as my body released the milk that would sustain him. "One day my son will be Grand Turk. I cannot carry him off and rob him of his destiny, and neither can I run away and leave him behind. Until he takes the throne, I must protect him. Without me he would not live to see tomorrow."

Adele and I finished our wine in silence, Mahmoud, his hunger satisfied, fell asleep and Seriphina took him away. Since his birth two months before, my full vigor had not been restored, and so I retired to my bed for a rest. Later in the afternoon, Adele managed to slip a quill into my hand, hoping I would practice calligraphy, but it was to no avail. Images of Selim kept drifting in and out of my mind.

The day ambled away before my eyes as I thought of him. That night the *muezzin's* last call to prayer found me alone in my sitting room enjoying a bittersweet melancholia. It seemed impossible that I should ever see the Prince again. Without a doubt Mihrishah and Poppy would not provide us with another meeting place, and yet I felt certain our paths would cross. I dreamed of what I would say to him and how he would answer. Hours that seemed like moments passed as I recreated every word and movement of our morning together. The memory of his eyes held me spellbound. His remembered touch still brought a blush to my cheeks.

Sitting in the small circle of light cast by a single oil lamp, I passed the evening and part of the night. The household had retired. Occasionally, sounds from the Golden Road broke my reverie, but I quickly drifted into my own world again. At last I decided to go to bed. Reaching for the lamp, I heard a sound. It seemed to come from the balcony. When I went to investigate, I saw a faint light down below in the courtyard.

"Adele or one of the servants must have left a lamp out there," I thought. I turned to go, but just then the glow swept across the darkness like a falling star. Someone below in the garden had moved the lamp. Instantly I thought of Kiusem. Perhaps she had sent assassins to kill us in our beds, yet I did not alarm the household. Instead, I picked up my light and went downstairs.

As I crept through the main salon, it echoed an ominous void. Only the night wind stirred to enchant the flame of my lamp. On I went toward the courtyard, terrified of what I might find, yet unable to stay away. When I reached the archway I found the light was gone. In its place was only the gentle murmur of the fountain and a jasmine breeze against my skin.

Suddenly, a hand clamped over my mouth. Another grabbed my lamp and threw it to the tulip bed where it sputtered and died.

"Call out and we both die," a man whispered, his lips pressed against my ear. Then I felt his grip slacken, his hand slide from my lips down over my throat to my breast. "Your heart races, beautiful one." He turned me around in his arms. "It is I, Selim."

Chapter 20

The eastern sky showed only a faint glimmer of morning light when I left Selim's arms and crept from the courtyard to my bedchamber. Moments later, while I was still wrapped in the wonderful aura of having dared the unthinkable and found success, a knock sounded at the door, frightening me so that I almost cried out. Then there was a second knock, and with that I hurriedly slipped into bed and feigned slumber. Not an instant after closing my eyes, I heard the latch and then the sound of an infant's cries. Mahmoud's nurse, Seriphina, had brought my son to me for his morning meal.

"Hanoum Sultan." The woman spoke softly even though I had begun to stir, aroused, as she might have supposed, by Mahmoud's complaint. "He has the appetite of a Grand Turk," she said, chucking the child under the chin as she placed him in my arms. "May Allah protect him."

"Thank you. Seriphina," I smiled and sent her

away so that my son and I could sleep through the morning together.

That afternoon when I finally arose, I ordered a cold luncheon of *pastromani*—a kind of beef prepared from cows with calf and then preserved in barrels—and white bread and Moldavian butter. Having given Mahmoud three meals that day without eating a thing myself, I was weak from hunger and lacked the patience to wait while something could be cooked. By the time Lydia appeared at the door of my bedchamber with a tray, my mouth tingled in anticipation.

"Bring it to me," I said sharply, cross from deprivation.

"You should have eaten something this morning, Hanoum Sultan," Lydia chastised me as she pulled away the velvet cloth that covered my tray. Under it was a bowl of yogurt and a glass of tea.

"Where is my meat?" I demanded, realizing an unfortunate substitution had been made.

"You will have it," she responded, unperturbed by my pique. "But you need some liquids first and these curds to enrich your milk and sweeten your disposition."

"The stuff is foul. Bring me meat and I'll be more agreeable."

"Later. First this." She set the tray on the floor and taking up the bowl, she shoveled a spoonful into her mouth. "It's wholesome enough," she announced after assaying its purity. "And I mixed it with honey. If you close your eyes, you will think it a sherbet."

"I will think nothing of the kind. Europeans were not meant to eat such an odious porridge."

"It is not for your nourishment. Your body feeds the Prince. Now eat."

I began to obey, lifting the spoon with a sigh. "While I am at this, you may go for my other tray. By the time you return, the yogurt will be finished."

"Yes," she laughed. "Washed away in the water closet. I will wait."

My ruse having failed, I downed Lydia's concoction

with the singular purpose of getting on to the more agreeable victuals. Then, still ravenous from my night's activities and Mahmoud's demands, I devoured enough pastromani to fill a Janissary on the march and a quantity of bread equal to the Grand Vizier's allotment for three days.

Lydia shook her head in amazement. "How you can eat and still be as lean as a willow. To look at you, no one could guess that you bore a son just two months ago."

"Mahmoud takes everything from me, Lydia. But when he chews his own food, I will have to abstain from such feasts or I will wear them as flesh upon my hips."

"Just as well." Lydia took up my tray and started toward the door. "You are too slight to be a Sultan. Remember, others judge you by your appearance, and it should be more substantial. Only this morning Mihrishah Sultan came to call. When I told her you were asleep, she seemed quite troubled, concerned about your health, I believe. She encouraged me to improve your diet. 'Such a slender body can have little strength,' she said."

"Is that why you brought the yogurt?" I asked, amused.

"Perhaps it is. But Mihrishah is your friend and a wise woman. She knows what is best."

"Yes, Lydia. She knows what is best, but the question is, best for whom?"

"Ah, then you have reason to suspect her of treachery?"

"No, not really," I responded, remembering Mihrishah's anger of the day before and wondering if she believed Selim might find me less attractive if I were plump. "But she and I had a falling out yesterday. She is terribly angry with me just now."

"Then I am confused, beautiful one." Lydia left her tray by the door and returned to my bed. "Mihrishah Sultan did not come alone to your suite this morning. With her she brought four slaves,

musicians that have served her well for years. She
has given them to you as a present. That is not the
act of an angry woman."

"Perhaps it is her way of making amends," I suggested. "They will play for us tonight and return to
her service tomorrow, I suppose."

"No, Sultan, they are your slaves forever. But it
seems strange that Mihrishah would part with them.
They are her favorites, all of them grown wealthy in
her service. I cannot help but imagine their first
loyalty will always be to her."

"Do you think they are spies?"

"It is possible, Hanoum Sultan. If Mihrishah is as
angry as you say."

"No, Lydia. She would not do such a thing."

"Just the same, I will watch them closely," she
insisted.

I thought of Selim and this new risk he could be
running if he came to my courtyard again. "We have
nothing to hide from Mihrishah," I said guilefully.
"Still, you have always been wise in the ways of the
harem."

"Then you will take my counsel?"

"Yes, what do you advise?"

"We should open a window to Mihrishah's suite if
she has one in ours. I have friends among her slaves.
One of them could be purchased."

"No!" I protested. "That is out of the question.
Mihrishah is an ally. I cannot spy upon her."

"May I remind you that you have a son who must
be protected," Lydia said sternly. "If these musicians
are Mihrishah's eyes and ears, all is not well between
you. Can you afford to be ignorant of her moves when
she is watching your own?"

"Is this part of the Ottoman way?"

"You might say so, Hanoum Sultan. The mother of
a prince must keep a constant vigil."

"Very well. Hire someone, but take care whom
you approach. It would be disastrous if Mihrishah discovered our efforts."

"You need not worry, Sultan. I will be careful."

She turned again toward the door, but as she bent down to pick up the tray, I stopped her. "Send someone for that. Come with me to the *hammam*." The events of the night before and now the sordid discussion of spies had left me feeling sullied in body and spirit. I wanted to be cleansed, but more than that, I needed to sit in the steaming bath and ponder my new and more perilous situation.

When I was naked and seated in the *hammam's* antechamber, Lydia slipped jeweled *takouns* onto my feet. "You need not assist me further," I said.

"Then you will bathe unattended?"

"Yes. I want to think."

"There is oil in an urn near the fountain." Still wearing her *entari,* for she never undressed until I entered the hot room, Lydia replaced her *pestemal* in the cupboard. "Enjoy your bath," she said as she bowed and departed.

Alone, I entered the bath and for a few moments allowed its sensuous atmosphere to enliven my images of Selim and our nocturnal rendezvous. As I sponged warm water over my breasts and loins, I enjoyed the memory of his touch, of the vibrant life that trembled within him, yet hard as I tried, I could not conjure in my mind's eye the image of his face. Night had been his veil, of course, and my own, but there were stars in the heavens and torchlight from the Golden Road. I had seen his smooth countenance as he whispered his passions. I remembered delighting at how his mustaches enhanced his youthfulness so that he seemed little more than a child.

In the luxury of my solitude I could afford complete candor, and after a short moral struggle, I admitted that I did not love Selim, though the pleasing sensation I experienced in the afterglow of our passion wore love's disguise. I had to weigh carefully the rewards against the dangers I ran in going to his arms. One always had to consider begetting a child. Women of the harem knew ways to avoid that. I could learn from them. And there was the court abortionist. But Lydia assured me that while I suckled one infant, I could not conceive another, and so the problem was not a pressing one.

Discovery was possible, though the tunnel, designed to allow me to flee the palace in times of danger, offered a perfect avenue for our clandestine interludes. There were Mihrishah's spies to contend with, if they were spies, but that was not an insurmountable obstacle. Even if Abdul Hamid were to discover our liaison, I knew he would not act against us. In the first place, Islamic law requires four eye witnesses to an adulterous act before guilt can be established. Certainly, we could be more circumspect than to make love in such a crowd. But there was also the fact that Abdul Hamid saw Selim and my son, Mahmoud, as the true strength of his legacy to the Ottoman people. If he acted against us, he would clear Mustapha's path to the throne and spell ruin for the dynasty. As for Kiusem, she did not frighten me. I agreed with Adele. The woman was too dull witted and brutish to be a threat.

As I dried my body with a *pestemal* and began to smooth on a fragrant ointment, I noticed the texture of my skin had suffered none of the detrimental effects I had expected after a year of hot baths and perspiration. The French belief that water springing from the skin enlarges the pores and ruins the complexion was not true. The heat, together with oils and massage, had worked only benefits, and I wondered if I should ever grow old with such a regimen to preserve me.

I did feel particularly beautiful that afternoon as I lolled in the bath. I was much more at ease than I had been in days, and I knew that Selim's visit contributed greatly to my sense of well-being. Mihrishah Sultan had warned me the year before that I would discover for myself the appetites of a woman, and now I had. Surprisingly, I did not feel any terrible pangs of guilt, though I should have, for certainly I had sinned. Within my reach was a small wooden-handled bell with which I could summon a servant to fetch my rosary. As I looked at that bell, a small pearl of moisture rolled down its steam-glazed brass surface, and I knew I did not want the beads. I had no desire to commune with the Holy Mother or to confess a mortal sin I would certainly repeat if given the opportunity.

An unrepentant sinner, I thought to myself, and then remembered the smiling face of Marie de La Fontelle. How often over the years had I seen her being led away from some gay party or concert on the arm of a handsome young man who would soon offer his masculine parts for her pleasure. Her conscience was never pricked by the sins resulting from such interludes, and in all other ways she seemed a good Catholic woman with a generous heart. It appeared to me that she could completely disregard one of the Ten Commandments while observing the others, and I wondered if I could master her method without becoming corrupted into a godless animal.

While I sat next to the bath fountain thinking on such a metaphysical plane, I felt a cool current disturb the sea of warmth that surrounded me and I turned to see who had opened the door.

"Good afternoon, Aimee. The servants told me you were here." It was Adele, a *pestemal* knotted at her waist and a towel wrapped around her coiled locks. As was our usual practice, she addressed me in Ottoman and I responded in kind. "I looked for you in the sitting room earlier, but Lydia told me you had gone out."

"Yes," she said as she took off her wrap. Then she sat down on the bench next to me and rubbed her eyes. They seemed tired and heavy. "It was the morning for my Persian lesson," she explained.

"I should have gone with you," I said guiltily. "But I slept poorly last night, and I decided to remain in bed."

"That was wise. With Mahmoud, you need your rest."

"And it seems I am not alone. You look exhausted. Was the lesson so difficult?"

"No," she responded as she ladled warm water over her shoulders. Her nonchalance seemed studied, and I sensed that she was troubled. Her eyes refused to meet mine. "My sleep was disturbed last night too, Aimee," she confessed reluctantly. There followed a long hesitation.

"Do you want to tell me what happened?"

At last she looked at me and I could tell that she knew about Selim's visit. "How did you find out?" I asked, fighting the panicky thought that everyone in the harem knew the truth. "Did someone tell you?"

"No," she answered and drew a calming breath. "I heard noises in the courtyard last night."

"Adele," I interrupted her, thinking of Mihrishah's spies. "Please, let's talk in French. I don't want to be overheard."

"Of course," she replied, and then she sighed deeply before she continued. "As I said, I heard noises outside and they frightened me, but I didn't want to sound an alarm, and so I found my jeweled dagger, the one Ibrahim gave me, and I stepped into the darkened hallway. Just as I did, you came out of the sitting room with your lamp. I whispered your name, but you didn't hear and so I followed you."

"Then you saw him?"

"Saw him!" she exclaimed. "I almost killed him. When you ventured into the courtyard, I was at the foot of the stairs. He grabbed you, and in a trice I was at the threshold ready to bury my blade in his back. The very instant when my dagger was at its zenith, ready to plunge down, I heard him reveal his identity. Had he remained silent one heartbeat longer, he would have perished for it."

"Thank the Holy Virgin you heard him speak," I said, quite unsettled.

"Yes." Adele picked up a corner of her *pestemal*

and dabbed beads of moisture from her brow and upper lip. "I fell back quickly," she continued, "and lingered in the darkness of the salon only long enough to know your intentions. Then I ensconced myself at the top of the stairs where I could keep watch through the night to guard against your discovery by any unwitting servant."

"You did that?"

"Someone had to protect you," she said sharply. "You must have lost your senses to take such a risk. If anyone else had seen you, the entire harem would have known about it this morning, and now you would be in a weighted sack at the bottom of the Bosporus."

"Perhaps you're right," I conceded.

"Perhaps! It's a certainty. And as for Selim, his women would have found him strangled with a silk bow-string when they brought him his morning tea. But the devil take him, he knew what he was doing. What about Mahmoud? If you and Selim were caught and executed, I couldn't get him away from here, and how many hours would he live in the same palace with Kiusem and her maniacal son? You can risk your own life if you choose, but do not allow your foolhardiness to endanger that beautiful child." She was breathless at the end of her outburst, and I was moved by her passionate concern, more aware than ever of the love I felt for her as she displayed her devotion to my son.

The glowing copper of her face glistened with perspiration. "Let's go to the cool room and have a sherbet, Aimee. This heat is making me tired."

"Oh it's the heat, is it?" I laughed. "And I thought the guilt for that was entirely mine."

"I don't want you to feel guilt," she said as we covered our nakedness and moved into the next chamber. "But I fear for us all if you allow Selim to come here again. With Kiusem and her minions watching everything that happens in the harem, they will find out sooner or later, and that will be the end of you." Adele rang the bell and when a servant appeared, she requested refreshments.

I said nothing as we were served our ices. Then, when we were alone once more, I began, "Adele, I think you're wrong."

"Wrong about what?" she asked. "That Abdul Hamid will find out?"

"Wrong about several things," I replied. Then I went on to explain what I had figured out concerning the dangers of discovery.

"As for Kiusem and her lackeys," I concluded. "I hold them in the same contempt that you do. The woman is a vile sapphist with little time for anything else but her favorites. She is uneducated and bestial in every regard from her venereal delights to her bloated physique and gaudy appearance. I do not doubt she works in alliance with the Janissaries, but most certainly she is their tool to control Mustapha. I cannot believe, as Poppy does, that she bargains with them as an equal or even as their superior. I have heard too much about the Janissary Agha. He is clever and ruthless. Kiusem is not his match, nor is she ours."

"Your arguments are persuasive," Adele confessed. "Abdul Hamid cannot afford to denounce you if he entertains any hope that Selim and Mahmoud will revive the empire. Perhaps Kiusem will prove no problem."

"There is something else," I admitted. "Lydia believes Mihrishah Sultan has installed four spies disguised as musicians in our household."

"But why? Mihrishah is your ally."

"Yes, but yesterday I could see that she fears I will win Selim's heart and undermine her control over him. If her musicians are spies, she may hope to learn through them some compromising tidbits to discredit me in his eyes. Perhaps she believes you and I are lovers, or that I practice witchcraft."

Setting aside her sweetened ice, Adele asked, "How can you allay her fears? A split between you two only strengthens the hand of those who want war."

"All I can do is go to her daily, just as before. I'll assume the blame for yesterday's disastrous audience and never mention Selim again. Eventually she'll forgive me. Our friendship is as valuable to her as hers is to us."

"And you won't see Selim?"

I hesitated. "He's coming here again tonight."

"But Aimee—"

"You said yourself that I needed a man."

"I know I did, but not this one."

"He's the only one there is."

Chapter 21

The luxurious Ottoman spring warmed gradually into summer. I continued to take coffee with Mihrishah Sultan, though she did not seem as friendly to me as she once was. She could not have known about her son's frequent visits to my courtyard, but she must have realized that she was losing him and harbored ill will toward me for my part in initiating his independence.

Poppy worried constantly about Mihrishah's change of heart. I could see whenever he spoke on the subject that he was very fond of her, but he respected me for my education and worldly experience and placed his trust in my judgment about matters of state.

With intelligence gathered from his network of informers, he kept me abreast of Ottoman affairs, especially the fact that all was not well in the hinterland. Catherine of Russia was on the move along the lower Dnieper River. She intended to conquer the entire Ottoman Empire and return all of Byzantium to Christian hands. War was essential to her design, but if the first blow were struck by the Turks, so much the better for Catherine. Then, when she let loose her juggernaut, she could do so in the name of Christianity and self-defense.

Abdul Hamid understood this well. And Catherine had an effective spy system, though an unwitting one, within the very walls of the Grand Seraglio. They were the notorious Kettlemen, a clique of Janissaries, notables and bureaucrats who had wide commercial interests in the Ottoman domain. For almost every article of goods manufactured in the factories of the Porte, one of the Kettlemen provided supplies and claimed a profit. A declaration of war would mean a hungry market for everything from saltpeter to oar blades. And so war was good business for the Kettlemen.

Every new affront by the Russians strengthened the Kettlemen's position. Where they once met in secret, now they let it be known that they assembled each Tuesday afternoon following sessions of the Divan. Their meeting place was a large table in the Janissaries' Third Kitchen. It was from that evil sanctuary that they took their name, originally the Kettlemen of the Third Door. This culinary reference came from a tradition peculiar to the Janissaries of bestowing titles based on the duties of the kitchen to symbolize the importance of the Grand Turk's food as the soldier's only sustenance. Thus, the commander of all the Janissaries was known as the Chief Cook. His subordinates were Soupmen, Cooks, Head Scullions, Water Carriers and Black Scullions. The symbol of each Janissary Corps was a great copper kettle engraved with the corps' insignia. In battle the kettles became rallying standards. Their capture meant defeat and humiliation.

When the Kettlemen of the Third Door abandoned secrecy, they adopted as their badge a small copper pot pinned to the folds of their turbans. Over time this became stylized into an ornate half circle worn open end up. Now there were rumors of a plot to overthrow Abdul Hamid and bypass Prince Selim in favor of Kiusem's son, Mustapha, who was known to favor an attack on the Russians. On the day they planned to act, the Kettlemen would reverse their badges open side down, just as the Janissaries would overturn their full kettles as a sign of mutiny.

On a warm June evening, Adele and I sat together behind the lattice of the balcony off our sitting room. The scent of jasmine lay heavily upon the breeze. A sweating copper bucket filled with melting snow and two bottles of chilled champagne rested on a small rug within my reach.

We spoke French over the chamber music of Mihrishah's spies who sat on their haunches in the archway as they performed. A swarthy woman with large hips kept time on the *tabor,* a small drum. As she beat, the group strummed and tooted. She watched us closely whenever we conversed, but I was confident she knew none but her mother tongue. A Persian with one eye that wandered played the flute. A sallow Georgian plucked a long-handled mandolin strung with wire, and another Persian played a three-stringed violin. Their melodies were monotonous, but I suffered them to play often, for while they were assaulting our ears, I knew they could be up to no other mischief.

"This new rumor about the Kettlemen can't be true," I said.

Adele looked up from her needlepoint. "I hope you're right."

"They don't have enough support among the Janissary ranks."

"But aren't many of the Kettlemen Janissaries themselves?"

"Yes." I reached over and filled my glass. "There are scores of Janissaries among the Kettlemen, but all of them are officers. Their men won't profit from a war. Most of them have taken up crafts during peacetime. They have families to support and small shops. They want war no more than we do."

"Did Poppy tell you that?"

"No," I replied. "Selim did. He has friends in the bureaucracy who have their own ways of finding the truth. They tell him that the first call to arms will cut the strength of the Janissary Corps by more than half. The scribes who keep pay records hold that astounding numbers of registered troops are either dead or have deserted. Women and children collect their wages and never let on when a man is missing."

"The Kettlemen must know that," Adele reasoned. "But if they do, they realize we are not prepared for a war against Russia."

"Yes, I imagine they believe we'll lose part of the Black Sea."

"Catherine won't stop there. She wants Istanbul. She wants Greece."

"But the Kettlemen are Musselmen, after all. No matter what evidence they see to the contrary, they still believe in their moral superiority over the Christian world, especially one represented by a woman as scandalous as Catherine. It is impossible for these poltroons to imagine any force capable of bringing down the entire Ottoman state. They see only the risk of losses in the hinterland, a small price to pay in exchange for the profits they will enjoy from a war."

As I finished speaking, I noticed that an acrid smell had overpowered the smell of flowers in the courtyard. Then my eyes began to burn. "The wind has shifted," Adele said, drawing a handkerchief from her waist shawl and clapping it over her nose. "This smoke is dreadful. Let's go inside."

I ordered the musicians away and then told the servants to close the windows. The city was afire again, and its stinking smoke, carried on a wind off the Horn, was poisoning the night.

"The second fire in a month," Adele observed in Turkish. "I find it amazing that when I look out upon the city, any of it remains."

"The people rebuild quickly, Hanoum Effendi," young Aishe said as she pulled closed the balcony doors. "When the fires are over, work will begin, and in a short time you will not be able to distinguish the old from the new."

"But when will the fire be over," I asked, already uncomfortably warm with the windows shut. "It has burned all day."

"When Allah wills it," the servant replied simply. "Perhaps tomorrow. Perhaps not."

"We shall suffocate by then."

"No, Naksh Sultan," Lydia called out as she descended the wide steps leading from the main doorway. "Forgive my interruption, but I have just learned that we shall be spared at least part of these perditious fumes." She kissed my hand and then continued excitedly. "There is to be a cruise tomorrow. Poppy just left the Grand Turk. He is concerned for the comfort of his women and hopes an outing on the Bosporus will provide relief from the unsavory atmosphere of the city. The Janissaries have assured him that by tomorrow night the fires will be out, and so a cruise and a picnic at some guarded spot along the banks are to be your diversion until the air clears. You do wish to go?" she said, certain that she knew my mind.

"I would gladly go anywhere to escape this dreadful smoke," Adele added through the cloth over her face.

"Then all of us shall go," I said. "Even the musicians."

Chapter 22

In Musselman realms, the faithful begin each day in darkness so that by sunrise they can be on their knees to the Almighty. Soon after that, the city comes alive with commercial activity. Markets are opened, bureaucrats are at their writing tables and guildsmen are at their crafts. On the second morning of the fire, the Grand Turk's women were about to board their royal barges for a cruise on the Bosporus.

As with every event in the harem, our departure was marked by prodigious ceremony. Kiusem Sultan led the procession. She emerged late from her apartment, cross and unpleasant, a hapless servant adjusting her jeweled headdress as eunuchs bustled *qadins* of lesser station out of their mistress's way.

Mihrishah Sultan stood second in line, dressed all in white, with a crown of flowers adorning her black hair. In contrast to Kiusem, who was overburdened with gems, Mihrishah wore only one necklace, the Bursa sapphires, traditional possession of the Sultan Valide or the woman who next would assume that title. The sapphires were a breathtaking historic treasure from the days before Istanbul was the Ottoman capital.

As one royal matron passed the other on the Golden Road, they exchanged glances like lance blows. Kiusem's despicable consort, Safiye, with her trembling whippet in tow, followed close behind her mistress. The unnatural harlot brushed my arm as she passed but in no way acknowledged my presence. Neither did the two sultans who preceded me in the procession. Of course, I expected no more from Kiusem, but Mihrishah's behavior suggested a deepening rift between us and I noted it well.

At last Kiusem adjusted her veils and began to move forward, passing through the Shawl Gate and out of sight. Instinctively, I turned back for an instant. Seriphina was behind me, Mahmoud safe in her arms, Adele by her side. All was well. I covered my face and stepped outside.

The smell of smoke was stronger beyond the gates. It blended unfavorably with the unmistakable scent of nearby horse stables. But I would have suffered the stench of both without complaint if I had been able to see the fire or the animals. Instead, when I reentered the world, ready to be thrilled and dazzled by all that I had been denied for so many months, my hungry eyes met the beautiful but all too familiar blue sky. Below it, I beheld a long double wall of bleached white linen from which the green booted feet of eunuchs protruded, as they supported wooden staves to which the fabric was attached.

Seeing the obstruction, my spirit faltered. But still I hoped that from the barges we might be able to view some of Istanbul. There I was not disappointed. Our linen cocoon broadened as we approached the marble dock. Beyond it, under a yellow dome of smoke resulting from the past night's blaze, I could see the bustling shoreline of Pera just across the Golden Horn. The Kislar Agha ushered Kiusem Sultan and her entourage aboard the first of the vessels as I took in the view. Then Mihrishah and her women nested under the white awning of the second. They were enclosed by a delicate lattice outside of which were stationed twenty-four rowers who, at a word from their commander, pushed off from the dock and put their oars to good purpose.

"Your barge approaches, Naksh Sultan," Poppy said, signaling me forward. Then he nodded to Lydia and she assembled the rest of my household.

"This is your first excursion, is it not?" the eunuch asked as we waited together.

"Yes," I replied. "Excluding my visit to the Hippodrome for the celebration of Mahmoud's birth. You spared the linen on that occasion and I commend the economy. Being forever cut off from the world is becoming tiresome."

"It is the Ottoman way," he said simply. "Now if you will look there." He pointed east toward two magnificent barges with red awnings, each crowned by three shimmering gilt lanterns. "His Highness Abdul Hamid is in the first of the vessels," Poppy explained. "He alone may have twenty-six rowers and a scarlet canopy."

"Then who is in the second barge?" I asked. "It seems the mirror image of the first."

"It belongs to Abdul Hamid as well. He will be carried in one on the way out, and on the return voyage he will use the other."

"What is the reason for that?" I asked, puzzled by the extravagance.

"It is the Ottoman way, Sultan. Two barges are required to carry the Grand Turk." Untroubled by the inadequacy of his answer, he took my arm as I stepped aboard the waiting craft. "Enjoy your voyage, Sultan. After we arrive at the picnic site, I will call upon you. There is an interesting bit of news you should hear."

"Come aboard and tell me now," I encouraged him.

"No. I must supervise the loading." He waved his arm toward eight more barges strung out in a wavering line as they waited their turn to take on passengers. "This afternoon I will tell you."

Seriphina stepped aboard behind me, Mahmoud beginning to complain of hunger. As we made our way to the entrance of our enclosure, we passed a half-dozen brawny oarsmen, every one of them scrupulously studying his boot tops, never daring to take one look at the Grand Turk's women. Once inside and settled on a cushioned bench near the bow, I removed my veil and put Mahmoud to my breast. Adele and Lydia joined me a few moments later, and when everyone else was aboard, the barge groaned into motion.

Within a few moments a sea breeze cleared the smell of smoke from my nostrils, and I felt refreshed. Although we were enclosed, the confining lattice proved no obstruction to the fresh air, and it allowed a clear view over the heads of the oarsmen to the multitude of activities occupying the population along the waterway. To one side I could see high wooden towers constructed at the water's edge where fishermen kept watch so they could signal below to their comrades when schools of fish approached awaiting nets.

Farther along, a single boatman maneuvered his craft to a collection of floating gourds which marked the location of a string of underwater pots. Pulling one aboard, the man harvested four crabs, their extended claws grasping for a piece of their captor. Undaunted, he shook them into a tightly woven basket near his feet.

Picturesque villas lined the shore. Most of them were built of wood with a similarity of architecture distinguishable only by a narrow base. Each floor was cantilevered over the one below so that every level had more living space than the one supporting it. The resulting inverted stairsteps to the third or fourth story were lined with windows and created an airy, lighthearted effect but for the fact that every villa was marked by one section completely enshrouded with shutters or lattices. When I realized that women lurked behind those barriers, a strange melancholia overwhelmed me, and I wanted to call out to them.

Working diligently, our oarsmen carried us beyond the residential shoreline to a well-manicured green that made up part of the grounds surrounding one of the Grand Turk's summer palaces. Several fine Arabian stallions waited near the pier as Abdul Hamid came ashore. Then he and his attendants mounted the animals and rode away while preparations were being made for the women to disembark.

Following the Sultan's vessel three uncanopied barges unloaded their human cargoes of over two hundred eunuchs and grenadiers. Members of the first group carried staves to support the billowing linen wall with which they fenced off a huge enclosure to insure our privacy. Before a single woman touched her foot upon solid ground, the grenadiers stationed themselves outside our rural harem, weapons ready in case some unfortunate passerby might venture too near the Grand Turk's treasure.

More eunuchs scurried off a fourth barge and hastily assembled open air pavilions within the enclosure so that we would not have to endure the hot sun. Rugs and cushions were spread about. Closed tents were provided for the demands of privacy. Tables were set up to support a fine array of refreshments, and then Kiusem Sultan and her entourage came ashore.

As soon as everyone had been unloaded, noon prayers were in order. Surprisingly, the eunuch fence held firm in spite of the sacred hour. Perhaps the eunuchs were granted a special dispensation from the Shiekh-al-Islam for omitting their religious duty on such an occasion.

Following the ritual, Abdul Hamid made his appearance. Among his women he eliminated much of the pomp usually associated with his presence. That day it was understood that every member of the harem was welcome to behold him, though none dared speak unless she was addressed.

First, he paid his respects to Kiusem Sultan and presented her with a small gift. In honor of her position, he spent a few moments with Mihrishah Sultan. As he moved about within the enclosure, every woman watched him intently, his presence creating a tension that I had never felt before in all my months in Istanbul.

As was the proper order of events, he sought me out next. Approaching, he smiled warmly. "Peace be upon you, Naksh," he said formally.

"And upon you be peace, Your Highness." With little Mahmoud in my arms I knelt before the Grand Turk and he allowed me to kiss his hand.

"We will hold our son," he said eagerly. I placed the boy in his arms. Then Abdul Hamid pulled a handkerchief from his belt. "You have given us a precious gift, Naksh. One that can never be duplicated in value, but we have crafted a simple present for you as a token of our appreciation."

"There have been so many gifts already," I said, pulling away the silken cloth. Inside was a fine chain on which was strung a delicately wrought gold medallion inscribed with the Islamic creed. "You made this yourself?" I asked, very impressed with the workmanship.

"Yes," he admitted, smiling. "It is a feeble effort, but every man must have a craft."

"It is very beautiful," I remarked honestly as I placed it around my neck.

"Enough. It is merely a token." He took up one of Mahmoud's little hands and kissed it. "And now it is time our son mounted his first horse." A look of concern must have clouded my face for Abdul Hamid laughed gently. "Do not worry, little mother. He will be well cared for."

Abdul Hamid was right, of course, and I smiled my acquiescence. Before he moved on to his other women, I took the opportunity to present my household. Adele, properly enshrouded with veils, received the Grand Turk's special compliments. After her, each

of my women knelt reverently before him. Dear stern
Lydia was so moved by his presence that her eyes
welled with tears when he spoke to her.

The presentation complete, Abdul Hamid departed,
his son cradled in his arms. From time to time he
stopped to exchange a few words with one of his
women. I watched as he allowed each one to look
upon the Prince's face. Many of them noticed how
tenderly their Padishah carried his son. They saw the
love that shone in his eyes, and quickly made signs
against the evil eye. More than once during his interviews, a concerned *qadin* pressed a token into Abdul
Hamid's hand. He then gently laid it upon the infant's
tiny breast. I quickly surmised that these were charms
to ward off the evil one, perhaps the horn of a stag
beetle or an amulet containing a verse from the Koran.

To the superstitious, Abdul Hamid courted disaster
by openly demonstrating such unbridled joy in his
newborn son. His imprudent display could easily
arouse the envy of someone less fortunate than he,
and from envy sprang the evil eye. Benighted as the
idea seemed, I had to admit to there being some reason at the root of it, for from my pavilion I could see
clearly that Kiusem Sultan never allowed her gaze to
wander from my child and his doting father. Envy was
there in her face—envy and hatred. But I comforted
myself with the knowledge that she lacked the wit to
do any of us harm.

After Abdul Hamid quit the confines of the linen
wall and carried Mahmoud off with him, tensions on
the green eased noticeably, and many of the women
began to amuse themselves. Lydia and I played chess.
Adele sought out a group of dancers she had met who
were teaching her their erotic arts. Everywhere one
could hear laughter and conversation as all of us enjoyed the clean air and unusual environment of the
wilderness. Fruit, soup, meat and pilaf, nut cakes,
chilled sherbets and squares of rice-jelly were served.

Feeling full and relaxed after a good meal, I sat
alone in the shade of my pavilion sipping a sherbet

while I watched some girls, none more than ten years of age, wade in a stream that ran through the meadow.

"They are beautiful children, are they not, Naksh Sultan?" Behind me I could hear the miserable panting of a dog and I knew Kiusem's consort, Safiye, had approached. Repulsed by the significance attached to the woman's praise of the young girls, I did not turn or respond. During the silence that followed, I felt the heat of the dog's reeking breath upon my neck.

"May I join you?" Safiye spoke again.

I turned, no longer able to ignore her or her quivering beast. "Peace be with you, Safiye." I nodded my head, but offered no formal sign of welcome, not even a smile.

"And with you, Sultan." She tied her animal to one of the stakes supporting our canopy and drew a cushion near mine. As she sat down, a wave of disgust swept over me when I noticed that the chemise under her *entari* was without fastens, allowing it to fall open as she moved, exposing her rouged breasts.

"This excursion has been very pleasant, Naksh Sultan. Do you not agree?"

"Yes," I responded, turning away. "It is good to escape the smoke of the city."

"But more important, it gives us an opportunity to become acquainted. You so rarely leave your apartments and you never call on Kiusem Sultan. We see very little of you."

"Yet, I feel I have seen too much of you already." My eyes indicated her exposed bosom.

Safiye laughed nervously. "But surely you cannot be offended." She pulled at her chemise but her appearance remained indecent. "After all," she went on, "you saw me at Mahmoud's forty ceremony." She made reference to the ritual performed on the fortieth day after Mahmoud's birth. On that occasion everyone of importance in the harem attended the communal *hammam* where I presented the child to the assembly. Then the midwife bathed him and broke a duck egg over his skin so that he would become accustomed to the water. "I was naked then." She smiled lasciviously. "Just as you were when you paraded past all of us holding your son in your arms."

"Somehow the bath is different," I said, drawing away as her leg brushed against my thigh.

"You were very beautiful." Her voice softened. "Abdul Hamid is a fortunate man. He gave you that medallion, did he not?" She reached across my shoulder and took the golden disk in her fingers, but as she did, she allowed her hand to rest against my breast and linger there.

"Here," I hastily lifted the chain from my neck and handed it to her, realizing with horror that the woman was making a sexual overture.

"Your servant, Lydia, told me he made it with his own hands," she continued. "Giving it to you is a great honor."

"He is a kind man." I could tolerate the creature's disgusting presence no longer. "Now, if you will excuse me, I wish to walk." I began to get up, but Safiye put her hand firmly on my shoulder forcing me back to the cushion.

"You find my company offensive?" she asked angrily.

"Yes, I do. Sapphists disgust me."

"Your superiority is born of ignorance, beautiful one. Half of your household is of the sapphist persuasion, yet you suffer them to bathe you and remove your hair and attend to your most intimate needs. Has lovely young Aishe ever scraped the depilatory from between your legs with the edge of a shell? She is one of us. But of course, you did not know that she and Guselli have been lovers for a long time. Do you ever enjoy Aishe's touch when she oils your skin? Perhaps you are one of us and you need only be shown the way." Her hand clung to my shoulder like a poultice as she spoke.

"You are lying about my servants," I said, freeing myself from her loathesome grasp.

"No, Naksh Sultan. I am not lying. There is much

that goes on in the harem that is secret from you. Believe me."

"I would never believe somone of your sort," I responded, feeling myself sicken with the intuition that she spoke the truth.

"Because you are French you feel you are superior to the rest of us." She sneered and threw Abdul Hamid's medallion to the ground. "Yet the French travel long distances to Istanbul in order to trade with Ottomans. If we are as worthless as you think, why have they come to the palace of our Padishah?"

"There are French traders in the seraglio now?" I asked, delighted with the news, no matter how base its source.

"Yes," she responded, gloating like a jackal over the victory she identified with my ignorance. "And they will present their wares to the harem within the month. Are you not amazed, beloved of the most high, that an unclean creature of my station knows of this while you do not? Does it chill your heart with fear that I may know of other, more important matters while you remain in darkness?"

I was slow to respond to her taunts as I retrieved Abdul Hamid's medallion. "You surprise me, Safiye," I confessed at last.

"It will not be the last time you are surprised." Low, ominous laughter oozed out of her as she got to her feet and untied the whimpering cur that adored her.

After the two of them departed, I set out quickly to find Adele, but before I had traveled ten steps from my pavilion, I heard Poppy call.

"Naksh Sultan!" I turned to see his corpulent mass moving toward me, a satisfied look brightening his face, testifying to the fact that the outing had been a success. "If you will walk a bit more slowly," he panted, "I shall accompany you." He dabbed a handkerchief against his moist forehead.

"Of course," I responded. "I am delighted to have your company." We walked on at an easy pace toward a group of dancers at the far end of the green.

"There is interesting news," he began, obviously pleased to be delivering it. "French merchants have come to the seraglio, and Abdul Hamid has agreed to a sale in the harem."

"Oh?" I said with nonchalance.

"But, Naksh. I thought that such an event would please you."

"I learned about it earlier, no thanks to you, and in a most embarrassing way."

"But how? The arrangements were made only last night. No one could know."

"Safiye told me just a few moments ago."

"Kiusem's Safiye?" Poppy asked, genuinely disturbed.

"Yes."

"It is impossible." His eyes searched the horizon above the linen wall as if seeking an explanation. "I have told only one person other than you, and she would never confide anything, no matter how trivial, to Safiye or Kiusem."

"Mihrishah?" I asked.

"Yes. We spoke of it together just after noon prayers."

"There is the source then," I said, surprised that Poppy did not realize it. "A spy in Mihrishah's household overheard you."

"Never!" Poppy was vehement. "I know every one of them. They are all loyal to Mihrishah."

"There must be someone," I persisted.

"A spy?" he muttered, still not believing the obvious. "But if not that, then something much worse."

"What do you mean?"

"It is difficult to say," he replied pensively. "But whatever the explanation, Safiye has told you much more than she could have intended. We need only decipher her message."

Chapter 23

More than a week passed before I learned the actual source of Safiye's information. My enlightenment came one midmorning while I sat at my escritoire looking over four pages of calligraphy I intended to show Abdul Hamid as proof of my improving skills. Mahmoud rested against my breast, his dark eyes heavy with approaching slumber after finishing his second meal of the day.

Suddenly, a sharp knock at the door broke the summer stillness. Mahmoud turned his head toward the sound, and Adele, who had been on the balcony reading, came inside to see who was disturbing the tranquility of the morning.

Upon my response Lydia burst into the room, throwing herself at my feet. "Your pardon, Hanoum Sultan." She hastily kissed my hand. Then turning to Adele, "And yours, Hanoum Effendi. Peace be upon you both."

"What is it, Lydia?" I asked.

"I have news, Sultan. It is about Kiusem's favorite, Safiye."

"What have you learned?"

"Take care to speak French," Adele cautioned as she walked to the door and pulled it shut.

"Safiye called at the door of Mihrishah Sultan's apartment late last night," Lydia began.

"Then she does have a comrade within Mihrishah's household," said Adele, sitting down on the loveseat near the windows.

"Wait, there is more," Lydia insisted. "Safiye received a cool reception from the eunuchs in the vestibule. They would have sent her away had she not paid them well. Only after that did they call for a servant to announce her. Then came the surprise. Mihrishah Sultan herself bid Safiye welcome. The two of them hastily repaired to the courtyard for several minutes of quiet conversation. Afterward, Safiye left clutching a silk handkerchief within the folds of which could be detected a strand of diamonds, a bracelet perhaps, or a necklace."

"Then Safiye is in Mihrishah's employ?" I was astounded. "That explains how Safiye would be privy to information given only to Mihrishah."

"So it would seem, Hanoum Sultan. But this time Safiye was the one bearing news, and whatever she told the Sultan did not please her. Mihrishah was in a terrible humor after the interview and reprimanded several of her servants for no apparent reason."

"Just as well," Adele said, sourly. "I hope her treachery brings her nothing but grief."

"More likely it will bring grief to us instead," I observed. "I don't like it."

"At least we have identified Mihrishah's people within our own household," Lydia pointed out. "They haven't learned anything of value since they arrived."

Still, Adele was not satisfied. "Can we be certain they are the only ones? If Mihrishah has dealings with Safiye, then we may assume she is in league with Kiusem. The two of them together are devious enough to use the musicians as a ruse to cover the existence of another conspirator."

As she presented that unpleasant possibility, I thought of Selim's visits to my courtyard and how I had slipped downstairs to join him. Could it be that I had been observed? Turning to Lydia, I said, "We must find out at once if there is anyone else."

Another knock at the door prevented her acquiescence. This time it was a servant to announce that the Kislar Agha had arrived to escort me to my audience with Abdul Hamid.

"Poppy should be told about this," Adele said.

"I suppose so," I responded, and then spoke Turkish to the servant. "Ask him to join us please, and find Seriphina. It is time for Mahmoud to sleep."

When Poppy entered, winded and perspiring from the stairs, Adele yielded to him the loveseat, little more than an armchair when accommodating the bulk of his frame and voluminous robes. "The Grand Turk awaits, Naksh Sultan," he admonished me.

"Yes, I know, but there is something we have to tell you." I instructed Lydia to repeat in French what she had told us earlier. As she did, Poppy toyed nervously with his worry beads, shaking his head slowly and invoking the name of Allah as we announced our conclusion that the two sultans had formed a sinister alliance.

"The evidence is there," he confessed, a bewildered expression on his face. "But to what end would Mihrishah conspire with Kiusem? The goal of each woman is to place her son next upon the throne. No matter which of the two succeeds, it can only be by defeating the other. How can they work together?"

"Abdul Hamid is an obstacle to them both," I pointed out. "Perhaps they have a plan to eliminate him."

"That would benefit Mihrishah, but Kiusem's son, Mustapha would still face the Cage until Selim is dead," Poppy countered.

"Kiusem may be willing to wait when her son is the immediate heir," I suggested.

Adele laughed sardonically. "If Mihrishah believes that, she is a fool."

Poppy turned to Lydia. "Are you certain of your information?"

She shrugged. "As certain as one can be in such matters. I pay well for what I learn, but my sources are for hire. Others may be more generous."

The eunuch sighed despondently. "I was told you had someone in Mihrishah's household, but I chose not to believe it. Naksh, what has happened between the two of you that you employ spies among her people?"

"It all started on the day Selim and I met."

"Ah yes. It is as I suspected."

"All of us should have realized before that unfortunate scene that Mihrishah will not be satisfied with less than all of her son's affection. His unseemly and unsolicited attentions toward me must have terrified her into thinking she would lose him. Ever since then she has seen me as a treacherous seducer, trying to gain power in the harem through Selim before my own son's accession establishes me as Sultan Valide."

"But she has never actually moved against you," Poppy said, more as a question.

"She placed her own informers in my household."

"No!" he protested.

"It is true, and that is not the act of a friend."

"I cannot deny it," he responded. "But since you have a clear understanding of Mihrishah's suspicions, what have you done to reassure her? After all, Naksh, your mutual interests make you and Mihrishah natural allies. I have told you many times of the rumors afoot that Kiusem plots with the Kettlemen to assassinate Abdul Hamid. His favor is the only source of your influence until your son takes the throne, and his protection against the Janissaries is essential to Selim's survival and Mahmoud's as well."

"I understand that, and I've tried. There have been

special gifts. I visit her for coffee as often as before. You've been with us. Surely you've noticed the difference in her manner."

"I confess that I have," he said sadly. "And I've spoken to Mihrishah about it. She tries not to fault you for the change in Selim, but it is difficult. Ever since he saw you, he speaks of little else but the time when he is Grand Turk and how he will surround himself with French advisers, making you the most exalted one of all. His mother merits that position, Naksh. She has stood between him and his enemies for years, and now she feels threatened."

The eunuch paused. "Your single meeting with the Prince had a remarkable effect upon him." Poppy looked at me intently as he made his last comment, and I could feel the weight of his suspicion. I had learned something of the Ottoman way by that time, however, and I knew secrecy could be maintained only by telling no one about my liaison with the Prince. Unabashedly, I met his eyes with innocence. "Selim has been too long in the Cage, Poppy. Any woman from outside would have turned his head."

A servant at the door of the sitting room interrupted our discussion. She was a Persian by the look of her, very young, with heavily lined eyes and a nervous manner.

After she kissed my hand she said, "I have come for Mahmoud."

"Where is Seriphina?" I asked.

"She is at the harem infirmary, Sultan. A sudden illness."

"I hope nothing serious."

"It is in the hands of Allah," the girl responded in a way that left me far from relieved.

"What is your name?" Adele asked, mindful that the child was unnerved in the presence of her superiors.

"Nasi, Hanoum Effendi."

"I have never seen you before," Adele continued. "Where do you usually work?"

Lydia quickly came to her aid, for the girl was quite out of her depth in our company. "Nasi has been in the kitchen for the last several months. And now you assist Seriphina?"

"Only today," Nasi answered timidly. "Now please. The baby."

"Of course." Mahmoud had already fallen asleep, and so I kissed him gently on the forehead and handed him to his nurse.

After she carried him away, Poppy insisted I accompany him to the Grand Turk's suite. Abdul Hamid was waiting to inspect my calligraphy, and his humor did not improve with delays.

As we walked along the Golden Road, an escort of eunuchs ahead of us, we were too occupied with formalities to speak further of the difficulties between Mihrishah and me. On all occasions when I traveled the harem thoroughfare, it was important that I appeared congenial and gracious. To that end I exchanged greetings with everyone who seemed even remotely familiar. Alert as I was to the faces I encountered, I was quick to see Seriphina at a distance as she returned from the infirmary, a look of concern etched on her brow.

"Peace be upon you, Hanoum Sultan." She bowed quickly and kissed my hand. "And upon you, Kislar Agha."

"Are you feeling better, Seriphina?" I asked, noting her pallor.

"Pardon me, Sultan?" she questioned. "Where is Mahmoud?"

"He is with Nasi. She told us you were ill. I hope you feel better now."

"Sultan, Nasi found me in the laundry. I was there collecting the little prince's clean clothes. She was very upset and told me Mahmoud had been stricken with fits. That you, yourself, had carried him to the infirmary and I was to hurry and join you there. Now, is Mahmoud all right?"

"Yes," I assured her, trying to make some sense out of the confusion. "We just left him."

Next to me, Poppy stiffened. "There is an evil hand in this." I looked at him. His eyes mirrored what I had only just concluded. Without another word we turned back toward my apartment.

"Allah be merciful!" Seriphina cried as she ran alongside me. Behind us, Poppy bellowed to his eunuchs that the prince had to be found without delay. I thought of nothing except my son. Once it was clear that Nasi had lied, only one explanation was possible. She was an assassin.

Screaming at all who obstructed me, I raced ahead of the others. The guards at my door heard my whirl-wind approach and threw open the portals of the apartment, but when I flew in, taking all three steps to the salon at once, I found Adele on the divan with Mahmoud sucking on a bit of marzipan and cooing contentedly in her arms.

"Oh, Adele!" I cried. "He's all right!" The next moment I threw myself upon both of them and wept.

"Praise Allah we were mistaken," Poppy wheezed as he breathlessly signaled his eunuchs away.

Almost laughing with relief, I hugged my loved ones, and as I did I noticed Adele's arm was moist. Clearly, Mahmoud had made water upon her, and in my soaring spirits I was about to joke at the fact, but when I looked at the spot, it was red with blood. Her hand was spattered, her neck and the front of her chemise. Then I realized that her body was aquiver, and that she had not responded to my outbursts or embraces.

"Adele, what's the matter?" She did not reply. "What's happened?"

"I've killed her," she whispered at last. "She's up-stairs."

"To save Mahmoud?" I asked, realizing that we had been right after all.

"Yes."

Hovering over us, Poppy muttered prayers of thanksgiving while Seriphina pleaded with him to translate our French so she could know what had taken place.

"How did you know she was an assassin?" I asked, my arms still enveloping Adele and my son. "It was not until I saw Seriphina."

"I didn't know," she said softly as she looked down at little Mahmoud and began to cry. "But when you were gone, I thought about the girl. She had seemed so nervous that I decided to go up and look in on her, perhaps offer my help. When I reached Mahmoud's door, I decided not to knock for fear I would waken him. Instead, I just eased it open and stepped inside. Nasi was standing over his cradle attentively, or so I thought, but as I approached, I saw." Her eyes widened as if a terrible scene were taking place in front of her. "She had a pillow over his face. She was killing him.

"I lunged at her and dragged her away from the child, my hands around her throat, chocking her, but she had a knife in her sash." Adele looked to her arm. "She broke free of me for an instant, but I knocked her down. I must have been mad, Aimee, wild, raving mad, but the sight of her smothering Mahmoud, half his body swallowed by that pillow." She sobbed violently, dark streams of *surma* running down her face. "I wrenched the knife from her hand and stabbed her with it. I stabbed her again and again."

She crushed Mahmoud against her as she wept. He began to protest the strength of her embrace, and I tried to take him from her, but she resisted. "It's all right. It's all right," I crooned, rocking her gently in my arms. "It's all right. Mahmoud is safe."

"She will sleep now," I told Poppy from the top of the stairs after Adele's arm was bandaged and I had given her two opium pills. "Lydia has been told everything and she will stay with her until you and I have finished what we have to do."

The Kislar Agha, his worry beads still clicking, began ascending the staircase. "As you instructed, I sent word to the Grand Turk that you were indisposed. Still, I believe he should be told."

"It's best no one else knows," I said firmly. "Only we few and, of course, the ones who sent the assassin. Abdul Hamid can do nothing. If we tell him it will only add to his worries and lead him to doubt us for allowing Nasi access to the Prince. I'm ashamed to have been so careless and frightened that someone else recognized my vunerability, but I won't aid my enemies further by putting up broadsides throughout the harem to announce what's taken place."

"Yes, I see your meaning," Poppy nodded in agreement as he heaved his prodigious weight up the last step.

We made our way to Mahmoud's nursery, and found the dead woman inside. Her wounds were as gruesome as Adele's description suggested, but aside from bloodstains on two rugs near the body, there were no other signs of the mortal struggle that had taken place. I found the dagger and placed it near the corpse. As I turned to look for other signs of the killing, my eye caught a silk pillow on the floor next to the empty cradle. Although I had steeled myself against the gore of Nasi's remains, the sight of that pillow conjured in my mind an image of my son lying dead by an assassin's hand. I began to quake.

"Hanoum Sultan," Poppy called to me. "You did not know this Nasi well?"

"I didn't know her at all, fool that I am for entrusting my son to a stranger."

"She is not among those to whom you have given presents?"

"No, nothing."

"Then look here, honored one." He held up a diamond bracelet pulled from the folds of her waist shawl. "Perhaps partial payment for the life of a prince."

"Mihrishah!" I exclaimed, thinking instantly of her meeting with Safiye and the reported exchange of gems.

"No!" Poppy countered passionately.

"Of course. Lydia told us what happened yesterday. You heard her say there was a diamond bracelet."

"I cannot believe it. I will never believe it. Kiusem's hand is behind this. Make no mistake. Kiusem and Safiye, but never Mihrishah, no matter how it may appear."

Chapter 24

When the nursery was in order, I went downstairs and instructed my guards to prevent anyone from entering the apartment. Then, while Adele continued her opiated sleep, Lydia went to the kitchen where she organized a thorough cleaning of the place, occupying all the women there so that none could wander into the salon. Our privacy thus guaranteed, Poppy and I carried Nasi's body, wrapped in the bloody rugs, downstairs and into the courtyard where we sequestered it in the recesses of the hidden passage. That night, loyal deaf mutes put her to rest at the bottom of the Bosporus.

Two days later when I awoke to the faint music of the palace band as it played its prelude to the *muezzin's* first call, Mahmoud stirred in his cradle beside me. Since the grisly episode with Nasi, I had not allowed him out of my sight, even moving his bed next to my own. Additional precautions were ordered; no new servants unless purchased outside Istanbul; only a select few allowed upstairs or anywhere near my son.

"It's time you returned to your own room with Seriphina," I whispered in French as I lifted him from his cradle and put him to my breast. "You'll be safe now, and the household must return to normal."

I drowsed peacefully, enjoying our closeness. Then Lydia came in with my morning tea. On the lacquered tray next to the glass was a single white rose.

"It was as before, Hanoum Sultan," she explained. "I found it on the edge of the fountain."

"Thank you, Lydia," I responded, ignoring her curious expression. "Do you know if Adele has risen yet?"

"Yes. She asked for her tea in the sitting room. I think she is feeling much better."

"Good." Suddenly, I was eager to see her. "Tell her I will be in shortly, and take Mahmoud to Seriphina."

Lydia lovingly lifted the child in her arms and carried him away. Because of the warm weather, I had slept *à la turque,* nude, and so I hurriedly slipped a gauze caftan on and went to see Adele. She was on the balcony looking through the lattice toward the Golden Horn. Hearing my approach she turned and the smile on her lips disappeared. "Another one," she grumbled, noting the flower in my hand. Only she and I knew it to be Selim's signal. Before dawn he had crept into my courtyard and left it to announce he would wait for me in the passage the following night. Lydia had been alerted to look for a rose before morning prayers, but she believed an informer simply threw it over the courtyard wall to arrange a meeting.

"Well you help me?" I asked Adele.

"Have I a choice?"

"After final prayers then, in the salon." I left her to the morning, wishing to avoid another argument over the risks involved.

We did not see each other for the rest of the day, but at the appointed hour, she appeared in the salon. The apartment was quiet and dark except for our lamps.

"Just an hour or two, I promise."

Adele scowled. "I'll stay awake until you return."
She looked about nervously. "Now go."

I found Selim waiting. After our first eager embrace
we hurried back through the passageway to a place
where the narrow walls widened into an alcove directly under the Cage. Selim had had his deaf mutes
furnish it as a small salon. Dried foodstuffs and casks
of water were stored there against the day when he
might have to go into hiding from Kiusem and
Mustapha.

"Come to me, Golden One," Selim commanded
tenderly as he reclined on his silk divan and spread
his arms in welcome. I lay down beside him, delighted
with the warmth of his body against my own.

"At night," he whispered, his lips against my hair,
"as I wait for the sound of your footsteps in the courtyard, I fear you will not come. I grow angry that you
would shun me so, but soon terror overrides all. I
begin to believe some evil has befallen you, that you
have been taken ill or that assassins have penetrated
the defenses of the harem and taken your life."

"Then I hear your approach and my heart soars
for I know you are safe and well, and that you love
me."

"I do love you, darling," I whispered, knowing my
fondness for him fell short of the all-consuming passion he wanted it to be. I stroked his brow and followed the silk edge of the turban along his forehead.
"You should not torture yourself so, Selim."

"I know, but as soon as you leave me, it will begin
again. Every moment we are apart my fears and my
anger grow, knowing that I am helpless to protect
you. When I am Grand Turk, all will be different.
Then you will live in the suite next to mine. I will be
able to see you simply by stepping through the door
and calling your name. You will be my closest confi-
dante, and I will listen to your wise counsel in all
things."

"Then listen now, darling," I whispered gravely.
"You must stop talking to your mother about me."

"But why?" he asked with the innocence of a babe. "Aside from you, she is my most trusted friend, and there are times when I feel I may burst if I do not speak of you."

"That pleases me," I responded, caressing his cheek. "But to Mihrishah, every word you say in my favor seems to diminish your love for her. She has come to resent and distrust me, and you know we must remain allies. She has done so much for you over the years, Selim. Surely, you can hold your tongue for her."

"I can if you think I must," he said glumly. "But when I'm Grand Turk, you will live by my side openly and she will have to accept you."

"I kissed him gently, as if to say that his dream was my own, and he responded to my lips with a passion that was half anger, half desire.

"Allah be merciful!" he cried out. I hastily covered his mouth, fearful his outburst might be heard by those above us. "Forgive me, Aimee," he whispered. "But I cannot endure these separations. How long can Abdul Hamid live? His health is failing. His flesh wastes from his limbs. Why does he not die and set me free?"

"He is an old man," I agreed. "The time will come soon, but when he dies, Kiusem and Mustapha will make an attempt to take the throne."

"Of course. But I am prepared. Our allies among the Sipahis wait only for my signal to march on the palace and secure my accession. By my oath, nothing will stop me, for when I am Grand Turk, I will have you."

His own words inflamed him. We spoke no more of thrones or allies, but yielded to each other in a ravenous embrace. He pressed his lips on my mouth. I could feel his tongue against mine, his hands on my shoulders easing away my gown. The thrill of the moment created an indescribable tension within me, a hunger much stronger than desire. His touch was tantalizing, yet unsatisfying. He was so gentle, too gentle. I grabbed his wrists and forced his hands against my breasts, my hips, even hard upon my portal of delight. I crushed myself against him, seeking, almost fighting to release the coiled energy within me.

Understanding my need, he threw me down upon the divan and pressed the weight of his body against mine, then his mouth sought my breast and lingered there, moist and warm, arousing me further. I took his head in my hands, but he grasped my arms and forced them back against the cushions. I wanted to cry out for him to enter me at once, but he only kissed my shoulders, my neck. Then he looked at me and smiled in wonder.

"You are like none of my other women," he said breathlessly. "With you I need nothing else. When I am with them, dancing girls must stimulate me. I must watch them stroke one another before my Ottoman staff comes to life. But now I need no massage, no aphrodisiac. I simply touch you and feel you move against me and I can yield up my seed."

He kissed me, then rolled over on his back. "Mount me now, darling," he commanded as he revealed his aroused manhood. "You please me like none other." His eyes closed, his hands eased my hips over him and I thrilled to the sensation of our bodies joining. "Perhaps it will be this time," I thought.

He moved beneath me forcefully, lifting me off the couch, once, twice. I grew more tense, more excited as I moved with him, feeling his rhythm. My hands pressed down upon his smooth chest, grasping his flesh. With every second, the coil of energy inside me grew more taut. Then suddenly, with one quick thrust, Selim's body collapsed beneath me, a luxurious sigh escaped his lips and he pulled me off him into his arms.

I lay beside him. His eyes were still closed, his face placid. I was proud that I had pleased him. Soon his breathing told me he was asleep. As I pulled myself away from the comfort of his arms to return to my apartment, I envied him the satisfaction he took from our interludes. Perhaps women are not meant to enjoy the act of love as men are. I found pleasure in his touch and the knowledge that I could arouse him. I felt better for having been with him. Yet, I wondered if there might be something more. The excitement I felt seemed to be anticipation. But of what? I did not know.

Afterward, when I crept into my courtyard again, all was quiet. Adele sat reading in the salon. I thought for a moment that I might ask her if she had experienced similar sensations when she lay with Ibrahim, but I felt awkward and could not think of a way to begin. We retired to our beds, and sleep came to me quickly. I arose early, refreshed. Poppy would call for us before dawn. It was Tuesday, the appointed day for sessions of the Divan, and we planned to attend.

Chapter 25

Suleiman the Magnificent reigned as Grand Turk in the sixteenth century when the Ottoman star was at its zenith. It is in his name that the Turks have invested all of the memories of greatness which sustain them through times of defeat and humiliation. Yet there are those who believe Suleiman himself planted the seeds of decay that have eaten away at the foundations so well laid by the ten Sultans who came before him.

One unfortunate precedent begun by Suleiman was his failure to preside over the sessions of the Divan, his official advisory body. In those times, the Divan met frequently and allowed those officials in charge of political, judicial and financial matters to present their concerns and grievances to the Grand Turk himself. This kept him informed of affairs throughout his domain and daily reinforced his authority as absolute monarch.

When Suleiman abandoned that aspect of his dynastic duty, he devised a clever substitute for the royal presence which still exists today. It is the Eye of the Sultan, a grill window built into the wall of the Divan chamber at a height just above the heads of those participating in the deliberations. The window is so designed that no one in the Divan can see through the grill, while at the same time, a person within the Eye can watch the entire proceedings and hear all that is said.

It was early on a Tuesday morning that Adele and I met a very uneasy Kislar Agha who led us through the labyrinth of harem corridors to the delicately tiled fountain vestibule which concealed the secret entrance to the Eye of the Sultan. Until that day, I had been the only woman Poppy had ever brought there. Now Adele was the second.

Poppy extended to us the extraordinary privilege of watching the Divan because he believed our experiences outside the walls of the harem would allow us to help him interpret the proceedings. Poppy was an intelligent man who recognized the limits of his own palace horizons and desired confidantes who could look at events with a different perspective. The interests we shared with him in preserving Abdul Hamid's reign and hindering the designs of Kiusem and the Janissaries made us truthworthy. The devotion we all felt for Mahmoud sealed our alliance.

Once inside the Eye we ensconced ourselves upon a low couch with Poppy on a straight chair behind us, while we awaited the grand procession to the Divan. Below in the chamber, white eunuchs busily made preparations for the session—lighting lamps, sweeping, dusting and straightening the cushions of the benchlike seats that hugged the walls on three sides of the room.

It was a small chamber with space for few more than a score, all of whom I had come to recognize easily from my previous visits to the Eye. Some were Kettlemen or their allies. A few openly wore the badge of the cabal upon their turbans. Others had spoken out in favor of reform and against a precipitious attack upon the Russians.

Among that group was the renowned Grand Admiral of the Navy, Ghazi Hassan Pasha, the only heroic figure to have emerged from the disastrous Battle of Chesme in 1770. During that debacle the Russians, with English assistance, destroyed almost the entire Turkish fleet and attempted to seize Istanbul. It was Hassan, leading four thousand volunteers from among the city's lowest orders, who undertook to break the encirclement. His success won him the grand admiralty and the eternal gratitude of the Sultan and his subjects.

Adele had met Hassan Pasha the previous winter while she was living with Ben Raza. She was especially fond of the fine old man because, like her husband, he was an Algerian by birth who gained his knowledge of the sea as a corsair. "Such men can be trusted among their own kind," she said several times, referring to Ben Raza's unswerving devotion to Baba Mohammed. I prayed she was right, for although Prince Selim was the living symbol of the reform movement, Hassan Pasha was its strongest champion. He had the Sultan's ear and the people's hearts. When he spoke against war, his words were heeded.

As I watched through the Eye, I saw the last of the white eunuchs finish his work. Not a moment after the chamber was empty, Poppy whispered, "My people have uncovered a dangerous rumor. It is said that the Chief Cook of the Janissaries intends to be present at the session today."

"Is that unusual?" Adele asked.

"Yes. Unusual and very dangerous," Poppy replied, his worry beads clicking a staccato tattoo behind me.

"Does his appearance have anything to do with Abdul Hamid's negotiations with the Russians?" I asked, knowing that representatives of Catherine had been residing within the seraglio walls for the past two weeks.

The eunuch nodded his head slowly. "I fear so. It is said that the Kettlemen hope to commit some insult to offend the Russians in order to nullify the fragile agreement upon which Abdul Hamid has placed his hopes for peace. There have been reaffirmations of the Treaty of Küchück Kainarji. Abdul Hamid has again recognized Catherine's right to intervene on behalf of Christians dwelling on Ottoman lands. The Kettlemen may use it as a pretext for a call to arms."

"And so the Chief Cook comes to the Divan in order to speak against the Russians?" I questioned. "This seems an unlikely forum. After all, Hassan Pasha will speak for peace and challenge the Kettlemen's arguments on every point."

"The Chief Cook is no fool," Poppy said somberly. "He knows Hassan Pasha well. But my people say Hassan has been marked for death. I sent a warning to him last night but have heard nothing since."

Just then two pages opened the doors to the chamber, signaling the start of the session. From that moment on we could not speak above a whisper.

Adele squeezed my arm when she saw Hassan Pasha among the first to enter. "Thank the Holy Virgin," she sighed. "He's alive." Poppy's hand rested upon her shoulder for an instant, then upon mine. All of us shared her relief.

"The man with him in the great conical turban with the gold rings is the Grand Vizier, Halil Hamid Pasha," I whispered.

"The wily one?" she asked, remembering what I had told her.

"Yes, a true son of the bureaucracy, coming up through the ranks by back-stabbing and toadying. Understandably, such occupations do not foster a strong character."

"But Abdul Hamid values his counsel," Poppy added, as incredulous as he always was at the Grand Turk's confidence in the self-seeking vizier.

Walking with all the pomposity they could muster, the remaining high officials of the Divan slowly filled the room, great game birds displaying their plumage to the assembly. Each wore a costume that was meticulously prescribed by laws which determined hue, sleeve length, fur appendages, turban height and shape and even the cut of the beard.

"There he is," Poppy leaned forward to single out the fellow. "By the tears of the Prophet, he has worn his swords. That is Suleiman Agha, the Chief Cook of the Janissaries."

At last I gazed upon our nemesis, the leader of the palace guard. He was a giant of a man, at least as tall as Captain Pasha Ben Raza, standing like a solitary minaret among the squat figures which made up the rest of the assembly. From his lined face, I determined he must have been fifty years old, yet his body belied it, for it was that of a young warrior. Suleiman was an awesome figure, his black eyes steady and piercing, his bearing confident, his countenance sober. Upon his head he wore a large turban shaped somewhat like a champagne bottle. The front of his robe bore crossed spoons, the insignia of his position. Emerging from his belt were the tools of his profession, two short-swords, their handles meeting one another at his chest.

"He has worn his swords to the Divan," Poppy repeated. "This does not augur well for the day."

The Grand Vizier took the floor as soon as everyone was in his proper place. After he had acquitted himself of his ceremonial duties, he recognized the Chief Cook.

"Very unusual," Poppy mumbled. "They are two serpents in the same nest."

The Grand Vizier sat down again directly below us and out of our view, just as Suleiman Agha stepped to the center of the forum. "The blessings of the Almighty upon this assembly," the Chief Cook began, carefully avoiding the traditional Ottoman salutation of peace. "Distinguished viziers, pashas, kadiaskers, defterdars and members of the Nisanci, I have presumed to enter this honorable chamber today because my heart cries out for justice."

"Justice is found at the feet of our Padishah," called a voice from the assembly.

"That was Hassan Pasha," Poppy whispered.

Suleiman Agha had not expected a challenge so soon and his ire rose, but he did not yield to it. Instead, he slowly wrapped his manicured hands around his sword handles and began to pace. "Negotiations have been completed with those infidel dogs, the Russians," he went on. "It is said in the halls of the seraglio that Abdul Hamid has reached agreement with representatives of the godless whore of the north. No more armies will march on our northern sanjaks. No more Turks will die at the hands of bloodthirsty barbarians. In exchange for these blessings, we must sacrifice only a small bit of land here, a few thousand subjects there, access to the Black Sea at certain unimportant ports. Oh yes, and we must allow Russians to violate our borders so that they may shield their fellow infidels against Ottoman justice when they dispute us. A small price you say? Our pride, our sovereignty, our future as a great power in Europe. A small price indeed!"

With the precision of actors rehearsed in a drama, Kettlemen stood up in protest to the terms of agreement. "We are betrayed!" someone shouted. "Death to the infidels!" resounded like a chorus.

The Grand Vizier raised up his arms to restore order, but his efforts went for naught, as arguments erupted among the dignitaries and chaos reigned. Then, when peace finally settled upon the chamber, Hassan Pasha, the very image of wisdom with every year of loyal Ottoman service etched upon his face, rose to his feet and leveled an accusing eye at the Chief Cook. "By what right do you question the decision of Abdul Hamid, Allah's shadow upon the Earth? By what right do you place your judgment above that of the grand caliph of us all?" The Pasha said no more, but continued to glare at his adversary.

Suleiman Agha made no immediate response. He

looked to the Kettlemen, perhaps expecting them to shout down the old man. But no one spoke. Such was the aura of the Grand Admiral that even his enemies revered him.

"May Allah strike me dead where I stand if ever I should question the wisdom of our great Padishah when his decisions are based on sound knowledge," the Chief Cook said at last. "I eat the Grand Turk's bread and I am as loyal to him as any man. But Abdul Hamid has been misled, and it is upon those jackals who deceive him that I heap my contempt and scorn. By their lies they threaten the dynasty and with it the entire Ottoman domain."

Rumblings from his followers, as they cursed the anonymous traitors, interrupted Suleiman Agha. When the orchestrated outcries had subsided, the Chief Cook continued. "Those who have the Sultan's ear counsel us that we are too weak to protect our own people." Now, it was apparent to everyone that his words were directed at Ghazi Hassan Pasha. Tension gripped the Divan. "There are those," he went on, "who advise we are too few to meet the filthy infidels in battle, and too disunited to carry the conflict away from our own borders in a holy war against the Godless ones. To such cowards I say we are the Turks, created by Allah to be let loose upon any people who incur His wrath. We are the Turks, who have spread the name of the Almighty from Persia to the walls of Vienna, from the Ukraine to the black heart of Africa. We are the Turks, invincible in battle, and defeated only when traitors at home mislead the Sultan into judgments that humiliate us in the eyes of the world. Such lies have caused the disastrous agreement we are to celebrate today."

"Abdul Hamid and his ministers negotiated with the Russians believing the enemy has two vast armies on our northern border under the command of the butcher Potemkin. By the blood of the Prophet, I swear that is a lie. My men have just returned from the north. More than half the Russian force has been diverted to guard against a Swedish attack. They are weak. We should strike them now to regain the territories that have been stolen from us."

Kettlemen and others, deeply stirred by the force of Suleiman's words, cried out vigorously for a holy war against the Russians. The Chief Cook sensed his growing power over the gathering and pressed on. "Today's banquet celebrates lies—lies that say we are weak, lies that say our enemy is strong. But it is not too late to end the lies and confound the traitorous liars who would see the empire crumble. I refuse to attend the banquet. I urge all of you to do the same."

What Suleiman was suggesting was an unprecedented insult to the royal person of the Grand Turk as well as to the Russian emissaries. None but a few zealous Kettlemen rushed to agree.

The Chief Cook, sensitive to the mood of his audience, hastily reassured them. "Abdul Hamid will be angry, it is true. But he cannot act against us, for the Janissaries will be our shield until he has learned the truth. Then his gratitude will be boundless for we will have saved the honor of his reign. When the Russians return to their whore queen with news of our insult, no agreement will be possible. She dreams of conquest and aches for war. This will tempt her into an attack before her troops can return from the north, and we will meet her depleted armies with all the vengeful force of the sword of the Prophet."

We in the Sultan's Eye grew fearful as enthusiastic agreement erupted from the assembly. There remained only a few who were not caught up in the explosion. They were well aware of the thinly veiled accusations behind the Chief Cook's words. He had labeled as a liar and traitor the man who had advised Abdul Hamid against war, and that man was Ghazi Hassan Pasha. Such an affront to even a lowly Turkish street urchin would result in an immediate fight to the death. When hurled directly at the head of a great pasha, no one knew what would follow.

Seeing Hassan rise to his feet once again, the Divan fell silent. "If it please you, Suleiman Agha, be seated that I might speak." The two men glared at each other, Hassan too wise to become angered, Suleiman clearly aflame with his own rhetoric.

"Perhaps too many have listened to you already, Hassan," the Chief Cook bellowed contemptuously.

"Yield the floor!" shouted a voice from the assembly. Others joined in, causing Suleiman to scan the chamber malevolently. "Traitors among you will feel Allah's wrath," he cursed. "The day is at hand." Then he strode to his seat.

Hassan Pasha walked slowly to the center of the forum, the magnitude of his presence filling the chamber. His voice was deep and strong with a compelling quality. "Honorable members of the Divan, noble servants of Sultan Abdul Hamid, peace be upon you." Many returned his salutation. Then he continued. "You have heard much this morning and have been asked to believe much. I will not now repeat what I have said in this forum so many times about the condition of our armies and the strength of our mortal enemy, Catherine of Russia. I will not remind you of the defeats we have suffered at the hands of her infidel hordes. I will not ask you to look at our new weapons and powder factories, nor our modern navy, for none of them exist. We cannot face the Russians in battle and hope for victory until we have them.

"But believe me now, for I speak the truth. Catherine has brought Sweden to its knees. Her armies swell with new recruits. Defeat and death wait for us beyond the Dnieper, and those who call for a holy war against the Russian infidels know it well. Do not be deceived. Their lies are pretty and easily embraced, but they are lies, and we must praise Allah that these death merchants do not yet have the Sultan's ear. Those who preach war are traitors, traitors who will reap vast profits from the bones of fallen Turks."

"Whom do you call traitor, Hassan?" Suleiman shouted, jumping to his feet in outrage.

"Every man who seeks war for his own gain is a traitor against the Ottoman domains, against his Padishah and against Almighty Allah." Hassan's voice thundered through the room.

"Is there nothing you can do to aid Hassan?" Adele asked. "There may be violence on the floor of the Divan."

"I am sorry, Hanoum Effendi." Kislar Agha shook his head slowly. "It is in the hands of Allah."

As invisible as the wind, we watched as debate on the floor deteriorated to shouting between the Kettlemen and those supporting Hassan. Then suddenly, it became apparent that all of this had taken place according to Suleiman's diabolical design, for amid the confusion he drew his short-swords and clanged them together, their deadly song demanding silence.

"Too much has been said here today. Most of it I will ignore, but by the blood of the Prophet, no man will call me a traitor and live. Hassan Pasha, you son of a jackal, defend yourself!" At that, the Chief Cook threw down one of his swords at the feet of the Grand Admiral.

"I will not do battle in the halls of the Divan," said Hassan calmly. "Keep your filthy blade that knows only the taste of Ottoman blood."

"You are not only a liar, but you are a coward as well," Suleiman ranted. "Members of the Divan, see how your Grand Admiral runs from me as he does from the Russians." The Chief Cook's taunting ploy was so transparent as to merit ridicule, but among a race of men who take pride in their Ghazi past and cherish the trappings of the warrior, refusing such a challenge was an indefensible act.

Hassan looked around the room and recognized the doubt Suleiman had planted, doubt that would become contempt if he did not respond. He bent down and picked up the blade. In spite of his years, it was clear that the man was a warrior. "I have no fear of death, Suleiman, not so long as it is for a purpose. I am old. You will slay me quickly just as the Russians will destroy our armies. But when Abdul Hamid learns what has happened here, I will earn my place in paradise, for my death will be the cause of your own."

Suleiman slowly began to circle Hassan. "The Sultan will learn of your death from my own lips, but he will do nothing, for I have the strength of the Janissaries behind me. Soon enough he will discover that you are a traitor and a coward. Paradise is not for your kind, Hassan. Prepare yourself for the fires of hell."

With the speed of a lightning bolt against the night sky, Suleiman lunged at Hassan's belly. The shock of his action brought me to my feet, terrified. From my hiding place I was about to bear witness to the slaughter of our most important military ally, and I could do nothing to stop it. Then, in the dreadful silence that followed the first exchange, I saw that the old man, with the instincts of a seasoned fighter, had parried the blow, bringing his own blade down across Suleiman's right arm to draw first blood.

"He will save himself!" I half whispered. Then I fell back upon the couch, causing its wooden legs to slide noisily along the tiled floor. In an instant, the attention of the assembly focused on the Eye of the Sultan. Adele and I froze where we sat.

"It is our Lord Abdul Hamid," someone gasped. "The Grand Turk is present."

Suleiman was transfixed as he stared at the grill window. Then he found his tongue. "Perhaps you are right, Hassan. This is not the place for us to settle our differences. Praise Allah no one was hurt," he stammered as he clutched his crimson arm and marched out of the chamber.

No one moved, no one spoke. All believed that Abdul Hamid had witnessed the entire scene from the Eye and knew the identity of those who had supported Suleiman. The Janissaries might shield their leader, but would they protect every Kettleman who had provoked the Grand Turk's displeasure? At that moment, the silence was pierced by the high-pitched voice of the seraglio *muezzin* calling the faithful to noon prayer. Poppy grabbed Adele's arm and mine, and we fled from the Eye of the Sultan.

Chapter 26

When we were safely away from the Sultan's Eye,
Poppy left us to inform Abdul Hamid of what had
transpired and that everyone in the Divan believed the
Grand Turk was present during the session. We re-
turned to our apartment to find a very hungry
Mahmoud, far from satisfied with the fruit juice
Seriphina had given him.

With my child, Adele and I repaired to the French
sitting room, both of us disturbed by what the Chief
Cook's new challenge could mean to our position.

"There can be no doubt that Suleiman intended to
take Hassan Pasha's life today," I said as I settled
upon the loveseat and put Mahmoud to my breast.

"One is tempted to accept the Musselman belief in
destiny after a morning like this," Adele replied nervously. "Hassan might be dead right now had we not
gone to the Eye as we did. The noise of that couch as
you fell upon it saved his life."

"Saved it? Or perhaps just extended it a few more
days. The Kettlemen have always known he was their

enemy. They want him dead because he has become an obstacle to their plans."

"Then you believe they may be preparing to move against Abdul Hamid?" She began to pace back and forth behind me.

"Poppy said he'd heard new rumors, and there is something else."

"What is it?"

"The attempt upon Mahmoud's life. I know what evidence we have. Our woman in Mihrishah's household saw Safiye go to her and come away with the diamonds. The very next day we found the stones in the possession of the assassin. Does this mean that Mihrishah is now in league with Safiye and she conspires with Kiusem as well?

"To believe that Mihrishah has gone over to Kiusem would require believing her a fool. While she may be a jealous woman and an uneducated one, she is not a fool. On the contrary, she has managed to keep her son alive for over twenty years while others have tried to do away with him, and she has arranged to make Selim's captivity as stimulating as Ottoman traditions allow."

"You suspect that Kiusem, not Mihrishah, is behind the attempt on Mahmoud's life?" Adele walked around the loveseat, pulled up a chair from the card table and sat down facing me.

"Yes," I responded. "She is the only one who could benefit from Mahmoud's death. Poppy saw that at once. You see, if the Kettlemen assassinate Abdul Hamid, Selim will take the throne, but the Janissaries object to him because of his desire for reform. They may force him to remain in the Cage and throw their support to another heir.

"Kiusem believes they will choose her son, Mustapha, but the Chief Cook might prefer to be rid of him and his mother, for he knows they are power mad. Instead, he could drive Mustapha into the Cage as well, or even kill him, and put Mahmoud on the throne, knowing an infant could be easily controlled.

The only way Kiusem can be certain Mustapha will become Grand Turk is to kill Mahmoud."

Adele was puzzled. "If you are correct, what was the purpose of the elaborate charade with the diamonds? Kiusem could not have been certain we would see them."

"True. I imagine she hoped we wouldn't. Nasi could have been successful and escaped with her booty, though I doubt she would have gone far before Kiusem had her killed. I'm beginning to believe we have underestimated Kiusem's intelligence. She knew there was a reasonable chance that Nasi would be unmasked before she assassinated Mahmoud, and she saw the possibility of recouping that loss by incriminating Mihrishah in the plot."

"If Safiye went to Mihrishah's apartment on Kiusem's instructions so that she could make it appear she had received a diamond bracelet, Kiusem must know we have a spy there," Adele said. "Otherwise we would never link the diamonds to Mihrishah at all. Of course all this is just conjecture. We have no proof. And it seems impossible that a woman as boorish and uncivilized as Kiusem could be so clever."

"Still, it is just as unlikely that Mihrishah would try to kill Mahmoud or that the Chief Cook would challenge Hassan Pasha as he did unless it were part of a plot against the Grand Turk." I looked down at my infant son as he took his sustenance from my body. "Mahmoud's royal inheritance," I paused. "His destiny has been the most important thing in my life since the day he was born."

"I know that," Adele said softly. "He will make a fine monarch."

"If he lives," I added sharply. "But I'd sooner he were a goatherd in the hills of France than an heir to the Ottoman throne murdered in his cradle by Kiusem's assassins."

"You've always known that was a possibility."

"Yes, but I believed my enemies were inferior. I never dreamed that a woman like Kiusem could outwit me, but now as we unravel her recent handiwork, I am fearful I may fail. If I do, my son will die. Look how close to success she came with Nasi. Had you not been there—" Tears filled my eyes as I stroked Mahmoud's little arm.

"All we can do is be more vigilant," Adele said.

"No, we can do more than that," I countered. "We can leave this place."

"Escape?"

"Yes. I know it can be done. You've seen the chest of gems Baba Mohammed gave me. There isn't a Turk alive who wouldn't sell his soul for a handful of such stones. Anything is for sale in the Ottoman domain, even freedom if one can pay the price."

"I think you should leave," Adele agreed. "And I'll do everything within my power to help, but this sudden change of heart surprises me. Are you certain this is what you want?"

"No. I want to stay and watch over Mahmoud's interests until he takes the throne. I want to educate him properly and see to it that he avoids the Cage."

"Do you believe that when Selim is Grand Turk, he will allow Mahmoud more liberty than he himself enjoyed?"

"I do if Selim and I remain close. That's one of the reasons I continue to see him in spite of the risks. Of course, it isn't the only one. I'm very fond of Selim, but that won't matter if Kiusem and the Janissaries succeed. Then Mahmoud's life is all that's important, and he'll be much safer in France."

"Perhaps I should go to my villa for a few days and lay plans for your escape," Adele suggested. "Arrangements will be made more easily from the outside."

I hesitated, reluctant to make the first move toward changing my son's future. "No, let's wait a while longer. We need more information. I don't want to throw away Mahmoud's right to the throne if our speculations are correct, and I still have trouble accepting the idea that Kiusem is capable of such cunning. Poppy must find out what she and the Chief Cook are planning. Perhaps he could capture one of the Kettlemen and encourage him to talk."

Adele raised an eyebrow and looked at me critically. "Torture him?" .

"Yes, if he must. My son's life may depend upon what I decide to do. I must know what the dangers are."

Chapter 27

The next morning I arose eager for what lay ahead. It was the day of the harem sale, a fine occasion on which the goods to be displayed were imported from France.

Although such sales were rare, they were not without precedent. So a traditional ceremony had evolved dictating a procession to the throne room where merchants would present their wares. Because men were present, we could not show ourselves. Instead, all of us sat behind a screen that permitted a clear view of what took place in the chamber but did not allow anyone to see through it in the other direction.

Fifty of Abdul Hamid's women attended the first presentation, where we sat upon long upholstered benches behind the façade. Protocol dictated that Kiusem Sultan be seated directly in the center of the group. I sat beside her on the left, Mihrishah Sultan on her right. Everyone else found places along the benches according to their rank. Standing behind each was a eunuch who acted as purveyer. Whenever his mistress wished to make a purchase, she ordered him to fetch it. All of us brought large sums of the slipper money Abdul Hamid bestowed upon women who pleased him. Dancers of his harem were notorious for their wealth because he especially enjoyed their provocative movements and graceful figures. None of them had amassed the fortune of a sultan, of course, but a talented dancer could have purchased Marie de La Fontelle's estate near Nantes and still have reserves to sustain her in noble style for the rest of her life.

As we sat waiting for the sale to begin, Abdul Hamid entered the throne room, the *aigrette* on his turban sweeping the air as he walked to his royal couch. The ornate gilt ceiling caught flickering beams from the lamps and carelessly tossed them earthward, showering light upon a wide array of goods.

Adele on my left was dressed in a *feridjie,* the shapeless black garment by which Turk women conceal themselves when they go abroad. With Abdul Hamid's permission, she would act as my purveyor as well as her own. She could speak to the merchants in their native tongue, and she was not forbidden chaperoned male contacts as were the women of the harem.

"These new styles are not as pleasing to me as the rococo style," she observed, pointing toward a chaise, the simple lines of which gave it a stark appearance when compared to the elegant furnishings of our sitting room.

"It is very popular in Paris," I replied, remembering the formal salons of the French capital. "Though I think Turks would prefer something with more flair."

Behind me I heard the obsequious whisper of Kiusem's eunuch as he spoke to his mistress. "Naksh Sultan," she addressed me when he had finished. "You and your woman have extensive knowledge of the things here. You must advise me of the best bargains."

Adele bristled at Kiusem's reference to "your

woman," but I chose to ignore the comment. "Of course," I replied. "I will tell you what I can." From our vantage point we could see many items of value. Bolts of fabric rested on a table to our left, satin prints, laces and beautiful lengths of velvet. A great number of mirrors were displayed, many clocks and a table full of watches with finely wrought covers. Silk tapestries lay about the floor, most of them devoid of human faces, so designed in consideration of Mussel-man mores. Casks and cases of wine, now acceptable even to Mufti because Abdul Hamid had developed a taste for it, were stacked behind the ranks of furniture. Next to them were boxes of what appeared to be tulip bulbs. Wheeled tables displayed music boxes, snuff boxes, pill boxes, fans, mirrors and porcelains, all decorated with delicate artwork.

A surge of laughter from the *qadins* interrupted my praise of French miniaturists when the merchants entered the chamber. My spirits were dampened when I saw they were not dressed in European fashion. Instead, they were bundled into Ottoman gowns, ill-fitting ones with wobbling turbans and great long sleeves that dragged the ground.

Still, they were uncut males—the first, except Abdul Hamid, many of my harem mates had seen in years. Their presence caused hungry rumblings from behind the screen.

"My purse for the tall one!" a lively seamstress hooted for the rest of us to hear.

"They should see Frenchmen in tight britches and silk stockings," Adele sighed. "Imagine! An entire race of women who have never enjoyed the sight of a good pair of legs."

"I do miss that," I agreed, thinking of all the firm thighs and tight buttocks I had admired in Paris once my appreciation for the masculine form was awakened.

"Marie used to say you could judge a man by the shape of his—" I stopped abruptly. When the two merchants had finished their presentation to the

Grand Turk and walked toward the screen, something
about the taller one arrested my attention. His strides
seemed unnatural, too long for his limbs, forcing his
shoulders to roll a bit from side to side as he walked.
He appeared awkward. In an endearing way he reminded me of François de Marmont, who walked that
way when he was agitated. I remembered his hurrying
toward me one Sunday, eager to announce that he
had mastered the bore at the cannonworks and had
supervised the finishing of a barrel.

"Are you all right?' Adele asked. "Your color has
left you."

"It's nothing. Just homesickness." I slipped into
French. "For a second, one of those merchants reminded me of François."

"You haven't spoken of him in a long time."

"I rarely think of him any more. It's just seeing all
these things from home."

"Honored ladies of Abdul Hamid, Allah's Shadow
upon the Earth." The Dragoman of the Porte, a fair-
skinned Greek of middle age, had stepped forward to
address us. "May I present Messieurs Paul and François Flachat."

"You know, Adele," I said wistfully. "In spite of
all the time that has passed and everything that has
happened, I can still feel pain when something re-
minds me of him." Adele extricated one of her arms
from her *feridjie* and squeezed my hand.

With the Dragoman's introduction, the merchants
made their low and sweeping ceremonial bows. As
they did, the poorly wrapped turban adorning the
taller fellow toppled to the floor. Muffled laughter
came from the women's side of the screen as he scurried forward to retrieve it, stopping not three paces
away from me, where he stood in silent embarrassment, his turban in his hand.

It was only then that I saw his face clearly.
"Adele!" I whispered in shock.

She still held my hand, her fingers closing tightly
upon it. "Don't speak." Her voice was low and calm.

Her reaction told me there was no mistake. He was François de Marmont. "The man must be insane to do this," I said in quiet astonishment. "He was so afraid of his father he could not defy him, but here he is in the Levant willing to risk the wrath of the Grand Turk."

As I spoke, I thought I saw François cock his head. Then his eyes danced and he took a step toward the screen. "Silence," Adele cautioned me.

It was impossible but true. François de Marmont stood so near I could almost touch him were the screen removed. A rush of emotions assailed me as I accepted the fact of his presence. At first the most important thing was that he had come for me—a testimony to his love and proof he was a man of honor. But still, I could not forget that his lack of courage had driven us apart and so altered my life it could never be the same again. His appearance now did not erase his previous weakness or wipe away my bitterness. Overriding that feeling was my awe at his accomplishment. He had learned where I was, traveled such a distance and managed to gain entry to the most guarded vault in the Ottoman domain. He had found determination at last.

"I'm amazed," Adele said. "François here! It never occurred to me he'd come after you."

"Nor to me. At best I thought he might shed a few tears when he learned *Belle Gloire* had gone down. "I can't imagine how he found out I was in Istanbul."

"Too bad his sense of timing is so unfortunate. Had he only been willing to go to such lengths while you were still in France."

"He was a coward!" I said. "And I'll never forgive him for it."

"Still, making the trip to Istanbul shows a certain strength of character I thought he lacked."

"I can't believe he did it."

François and his comrade began their presentation by indicating to waiting eunuchs which articles should be carried forward for our inspection. I watched him speaking to one of the purveyors with the aid of the

Kislar Agha as interpreter. Although I tried not to admit it, I was deeply moved that he had risked so much to find me. It seemed a justification for the confidence I had once had in him.

"Somehow we should let him know he's found us."

"I suppose so," Adele said reluctantly. "At least one good thing can come of it. You'll decide once and for all to leave here, though I wonder if marriage to François will really suit you."

Her words startled me. "I'll never marry him." The idea seemed preposterous. "After what he did to me— I couldn't. But after what he's done to get here, he's entitled to some peace. He's not insensitive, and I imagine he's been burdened with a terrible feeling of guilt ever since he learned what happened."

"You have a good heart, Aimee. I don't know if I could think so kindly of him."

"It isn't easy," I confessed. "There have been times when I wanted to see his head on the Imperial Gate, but hatred is a poison to the soul. Now, I suggest you go to him as if you wanted to make a purchase. Let him know his efforts have been appreciated, and send him on his way. Our obligation goes no further than that."

Adele adjusted the gauze mask over her face and went around the screen. François was with the Kislar Agha near the display of clocks and watches, with Poppy still acting as his interpreter. Adele approached them, a shifting and unrecognizable hillock of black silk. The sale to one of the eunuchs completed, she said something and Poppy took his leave.

I watched intently and imagined the exchange that was taking place from François' shocked expressions.

Suddenly François became agitated. At first, I supposed no one else would notice, but after a short time, I heard one of the women behind me comment upon the strange behavior of the foreigner. If he kept it up, he would be discovered in his charade as a merchant and put to death. And who knows what would happen to Adele as a result.

"Sweet Mother of God, let him be silent," I whispered in a panic.

"You are trembling, Naksh." Kiusem Sultan spoke with a compassion not suited to her. "I hope you are not ill."

Overcoming my fear, I managed to say something about a slight chill. "You must take care, Golden One. The plague has already taken hold in the city." She was referring to the predictable summer pestilence in Istanbul that took thousands of lives. There was little prevention and no cure for the dread disease.

"Thank you for your concern, Kiusem," I replied, knowing how delighted she would be if I were to fall victim to the plague. "But it is all this excitement, the sale, thoughts of home, nothing more."

"And it has not been so long since the birth," she added, refusing to say Mahmoud's name, so odious was it to her. "Perhaps your strength has not returned."

"Perhaps," I replied, breaking off our intercourse.

Across the room François and Adele were engaged in discussion. Fortunately, he had managed to gain control of himself and was now behaving like a merchant. They moved away from the clocks to the wine casks, then on to the laces. Every time they stopped, François made notes in his ledger. As I watched, I hated him more than ever for coming to the Levant and opening wounds that had begun to heal. Yet the intensity of my own wrath made me fearful that I still loved him. "Impossible!" I said aloud.

"You spoke, Naksh?" Kiusem asked amicably.

"Your pardon, Sultan. It was nothing."

At last the moving *feridjie* that concealed Adele returned to the screen. "I have made all the purchases," she announced in Turkish as she sat down.

"What did he say?" I asked quietly in French.

"He was not pleased to be sent away," she replied as she pulled the gauze mask from her face. "He refuses to leave Istanbul until he sees you."

"Did you tell him it couldn't be done?"

"Yes, but he was unmoved. He said many people

told him getting past the Gate of Felicity couldn't be done either, but here he was selling watches to the Sultan's harem. He insists that we find a way or he'll break in and kidnap you."

"And he'd do it, I suppose. No matter how dangerous that would be for us." I watched him as he fondled a porcelain chamberpot. "What are we going to do?"

"This much is settled," Adele said. "Tomorrow I will leave the palace by litter on the pretense of wishing to make some special purchases. François and his comrade, Monsieur Flachat, have friends at one of the goldsmith shops within the covered market at Hagia Sophia. I am to meet him there with the arrangements for your meeting."

"But there will be no arrangements," I said firmly. "With affairs coming apart here in the palace, I can't waste my time conspiring to see a man on the outside. You must get rid of him."

"I don't believe I can," Adele replied, shaking her head as she looked out at François. "He's become a zealot, I'm afraid. Now that he's tasted the freedom of defying his father, he's ready to challenge the world. Nothing can be denied him, or so he thinks."

"Then I'll offer him a substitute, but I won't have him in Istanbul."

"What substitute?"

"Money," I responded flatly. "He has always been willing to sell himself for wealth. Now, instead of marrying for it, he'll just have to leave the Levant."

"I hope he can be bought," she said. "But I doubt it. He's afire to save you, whether you want him to or not, and from the look of determination in his eyes, I almost believe he can do it."

"The man is hopeless," I responded, sighing in disgust. "When I really needed him, he failed me, and now—" I paused as a new thought struck. Of course. Why hadn't I seen it immediately? "I must find a way to see him, Adele."

"What?"

"Yes. He couldn't have arrived at a better time.

Just yesterday we talked about trying to escape. How much easier it will be if we have an accomplice. If he's as determined as you say, he'll get us out."

"Then you've made your decision. You definitely want to leave the palace."

"No," I responded truthfully. "Poppy has yet to find out what the Kettlemen are brewing. If they can be foiled, we will stay. I owe that to Mahmoud."

"But François expects to marry you. That's why he came all this way."

"His expectations concern me only so long as they bring him to our aid. If we choose to escape, he will be useful. If we decide to stay, I'll send him back to France a richer man than when he left. His heart may be broken, but that is not a fatal injury. I can attest to that."

"There still remains the problem of arranging a meeting between you," Adele pointed out. "He insists upon it."

"And he shall have it," I said, as the pieces of a plan began to slip into their proper places in my mind.

"But you can't leave the palace," Adele protested.

"You know, Adele, I believe women make excursions from time to time. Lydia has heard rumors about it, though for us the risks are too great. François will have to come to me, and I think I know a way." I pulled at the sleeve of her *feridjie*. "He'll wear one of these."

"And walk through the Gate of Felicity? Such a giant would be found out in a minute."

"You're right, but there are other ways to get in. Lydia has told me that at night certain indiscreet young women sometimes call at the gate near the Chief Physician's Chamber. There they meet pages from the Janissary school who are housed at the rear of the Third Court. These liaisons are forbidden, of course, but the guards are less than vigilant about such matters, remembering well their own days of painful abstinence and the relief such angels of mercy occasionally brought to them."

Adele smiled as she grasped the heart of the plan. "This is more exciting than the time we smuggled a cow into the Abbess's library while she was at dinner. I'll lead François to that gate, both of us in *feridjies*. In the darkness, he could easily hunch over and pass as a woman. Then, once we are inside the walls, we will meet you."

"The Revan Kiosk would be a good place. I am the only one who goes there now. The other women of the harem don't enjoy its solitude, and Abdul Hamid prefers the Baghdad."

"I'll go to the market tomorrow as planned," Adele went on. "And tomorrow night I'll bring him to you."

Just then Abdul Hamid rose from his divan and walked toward the door, signaling that the audience and sale were over. Kiusem then began the procession back to the harem. I took third place in line, satisfied that our plan was a good one, yet troubled by my eagerness to see François again.

Chapter 28

Within the walls of the Third Court is a sprawling and complex community. Aside from the Grand Turk's living quarters, those of the black eunuchs and the throbbing warren that is the harem, the Third Court houses religious shrines attended by Abdul Hamid: the Hall of Circumcision, where young princes at the age of thirteen ceremoniously receive the first painful wounds of manhood; the throne room; many luxurious formal gardens; the Chamber of the Chief Physician; and the Palace School where pages are educated for duties in the Janissary Corps or the bureaucracy.

Extending along the east wall there is also a broad green populated with ancient trees and manicured shrubbery which provides the setting for two jewel-like structures, the Revan and Baghdad kiosks. Both were built in the seventeenth century by Murad IV in the Persian style to commemorate his Anatolian campaign which ended Persian encroachment in that region. The Revan Kiosk is also known as the Room of the Turban for its unusal shape in the form of a cross with a high dome at its center. The round chamber within is lighted by two rows of windows which overlook extensive gardens and a reflecting pool.

It was within the Revan Kiosk on the appointed night that I waited long after the *muezzin's* last call to prayer for François' arrival. I did not know how I would react when I saw him. Part of me wanted to rush to his arms. At the same time, I realized that my anger over what had happened in France had not subsided.

As is customary among Turks who go abroad at night, the two black-clad forms who entered the kiosk carried lanterns. "Quickly! Extinguish them!" I ordered while François and Adele were still clear of the windows.

They followed my instructions. For a few moments I heard the sound of rustling fabric, the removal of *feridjies*. Though I stood in the moonlight off the pond, the others were still in darkness when Adele spoke. "Be certain he leaves before first light. By day his disguise will be useless because of his height, and they'll be looking for an intruder. There was some trouble."

"Were you challenged?" I asked, fearful of discovery.

"Not exactly," she replied. "All will be well until dawn. He will tell you what happened. I'll go back now." Then she went out the door.

Her departure seemed to break a spell that had held François immobile. He stepped into the light, but still he did not speak. His eyes were upon me too long, the chamber too silent. I felt naked under his scrutiny. "Why do you look at me so?" I asked at last.

"You are so beautiful, Aimee," he replied emotionally, "even more beautiful than I remember, and you are well. Seeing you as you are, healthy and unharmed, my prayers have been answered." He rushed to me and would have enveloped me in his arms, but

my pride prevailed over all else and I presented only
a hand. He took it tenderly and brought it to his lips.
"Over all these months, my darling, I've thought only
of you. My father knows the truth. My betrothal is no
more. I am free. Will you marry me?"

"When did you tell your father?" I asked, ignoring
his proposal and controlling my desire to weep.

"Just as soon as I learned what had happened to
you. Nothing mattered to me after that but finding
you and bringing you home."

Somehow, that was the wrong answer. In the secret
recesses of my heart, I had hoped François had followed me to Martinique on the next available ship
after settling with his father. Instead, he had found
the strength he needed not from love but from guilt.

"If I had arrived safely in the Antilles instead of
being shipwrecked and kidnapped, would you have
come for me?" I wanted my voice to be as harsh as
the Abbess's, but tears in my throat made me sound
like a child.

"Aimee," he said earnestly, "none of that matters
now. Through God's mercy you have been spared.
We can go back to France and live together just as if
none of this had ever happened. I was wrong to let
you go, I know I was. But if you'll give me a chance,
I'll make you forget this dreadful year. I'll bury it
under two score of happy ones. I'll love you until the
day I die. Our lives will be just as you wanted them to
be. Nothing need be different because of this."

It was all so simple to him. I was still alive. I had
not been beaten or broken by my captors. I looked
the same, and therefore I was the same. Whatever
unpleasantness I had endured could be wrung from
my heart like dirty water from a cloth.

"Say you'll come back with me, Aimee," he
pleaded. "Say you'll marry me. I know I hurt you,
but you must forgive me. I love you."

He took me in his arms, but my rage against him
was stronger than my affection. "I'm not the same

woman who left you in France," I said coldly, pushing him away.

"I know you've been through a terrible ordeal, darling," he said tenderly. "But whatever happened, after we leave here we never need speak of it again. It won't make a bit of difference to me."

He can forgive my being raped. Sweet Mother of God! How I wanted to hurt him for his masculine condescension. "It may not make a difference to you," I said, trembling with fury, "but it does to me. I have a child."

"You can't!" he blurted out after a shocked hesitation. "It's impossible!" The astonishment and disbelief in his face grew more intense as he looked at me, desperately trying to find the ravages of childbirth. "It's impossible!" he pronounced again. "Impossible!"

"It's true, François," I said more gently. Somehow telling him about my son had purged my anger, as if the poison had been flushed from a festering wound. "Come, let's sit down."

We went to the window seat opposite the reflecting pool. The breeze through the mullioned windows bore the scent of jasmine and the sea. "His name is Mahmoud," I explained softly. "He is the son of the Grand Turk. He'll rule the empire one day."

François did not speak, nor did his eyes meet mine. Only the wind in the trees on the green whispered as we sat in the moonlit chamber. Now that I had told him, I wanted to help him understand how Mahmoud's existence had changed my life, but the time was not right, François would have to accept one part of the truth before he could accept its deeper meaning.

The long and thoughtful silence that followed my revelation must have been one of soul-searching torment for him. I know it opened my eyes. As I sat beside him, I admitted something to myself. I had hated François for over a year because I believed it was his weakness that drove me to exile and captivity. But I had been wrong. First, because he did not force me to leave France. I chose to go in spite of him.

And second, this captivity among an infidel society, though preceded by terrifying experiences, was the most challenging and exciting period of my twenty-two years. I did not regret my change of circumstances.

Ironically, the weapon I used to bring François the most pain during our reunion, Mahmoud's birth, had brought me the greatest satisfaction of my life. Sitting beside François, I remembered the rush of excitement when I announced the first pains to Lydia. The walnut birth chair was ceremoniously carried down the Golden Road. All of my servants gathered around in the salon as I sat down upon its horseshoe-shaped seat from which I did not arise until the midwife lifted the skirts of my *entari* and brought forth my infant son. True to his Musselman paternity, he was late to arrive. My labor was long and arduous, but every woman there tried to assume some part of my agony. I shall never forget the sympathy on their faces as they clutched their amulets and chanted, *"Allah akbar,"*—God is most great—through the unending hours of my accouchement. At times the rhythm of their voices seemed to fill my brain and transport me over the crests of pain. *"Allahakbar! Allahakbar! Allahakbar!"* My soul screamed it with them until the worst subsided. Then, when the midwife delivered me of the child, all of us wept for joy at the sound of his first healthy cry, sharing the miraculous moment of birth and uniting in its release.

At the news he had a son, Abdul Hamid ordered splendid celebrations, the like of which had not been seen in Istanbul for half a century. There was a great tulip festival upon the seraglio grounds where specimens of the European gold were displayed in amazing profusion and illuminated by colored globes of light, some of them mounted upon the backs of turtles who wandered among the blossoms enhancing their beauty.

At the center of the display the Grand Turk ordered the construction of a fanciful kiosk made of spun sugar. Guests strolling through it broke off pieces to eat or keep as mementos of the occasion. Among the boxwood hedges were hung hundreds of caged nightingales who serenaded the throng.

Afterward, wrestling matches were held at the historic Hippodrome, constructed during the reign of Constantine who consecrated to his new God the city that once bore his name. Surrounded by my women, I watched all the festivities from a latticed enclosure, quietly adoring my child and accepting the honors due the mother of an heir.

Such was the ordeal with which I chose to punish François. Yet as I watched him in the moonlight, I could not help but wonder if he thought more of his own suffering than of anything I might had endured. He had made sacrifices, defied his father, denied the wealth that would have come with his marriage, traveled to the Levant only to discover that the woman he loved had lain with a swarthy infidel and born a child. I wondered what was in his mind. Perhaps he would have had me take my own life rather than be violated.

"Do you hate me very much?" he asked at last, ending my speculation. "You must hate me for causing everything that's happened to you." His voice was hardly above a whisper, his eyes filled with grief and tears.

"I did hate you," I confessed. "But I don't any more. What's done is done. Perhaps it was preordained. I don't know, but I do know we must build our lives upon what's happened. It cannot be forgotten."

"We'll build that life together, Aimee, if you'll still have me. Your son can be part of it if you choose. I'll get both of you out of here and back to France. Then we'll be together." The emotion of his words, the determination that emanated from him, caught me off guard. He drew me to him and took me in his arms.

"François, there are things you should know. Things I must tell you before we go further."

"Could you love me again?" he asked as he kissed my neck.

"I don't know," I answered truthfully, confused by the rush of sensations accompanying his embrace.

"You must love me, darling." His lips against my skin aroused a desire for him I once thought was dead. I yielded to it, reveled in it, no longer an inexperienced, frightened girl, no longer needing to resist him. I did not know if I loved François, but that did not matter. Nothing mattered except his arms around me, the eruption of his manhood within my body. I would tell him later that I might not choose to leave Istanbul. I would tell him later about the plot to assassinate Abdul Hamid. Later I would tell him everything.

Through the night I lay in François' arms unable to sleep, the glow of our lovemaking still burning upon my cheeks. When I turned to see his face, we smiled like children who shared a secret. A few moments before, he had given me what my body had craved for so long, and now I wanted him again.

"Do I please you, darling?" he whispered.

"Oh, yes," I sighed as his hands slipped over my hips and down my stomach finding the hidden place that responded so quickly to his touch. He eased his body along the length of mine until his lips also found the place.

Immediately, anticipation began to grow, tingling in my limbs and surging upward. The rush of it frightened me and I started to protest. In an inkling the tension crested in an explosion of sensations like fireworks, and I lay helpless, at François' mercy, unable to do anything but cry out in ecstasy. As the moment passed, I tried to tell him of the pleasure he had given me, but he kept on with his tongue. My excitement began and he kept on with his tongue. My excitement began again and crested quickly again. I pleaded for him to stop. Over and over, these explosions came so rapidly, shaking me until I was exhausted.

As I lay satiated, thinking that at last I had found the wonders of love, François rose to his knees and lifted my hips to his. When he entered me, I felt the excitement anew, and we made the beast with two backs until both of us had spent ourselves.

The night passed that way. We slept little and spoke of few things other than love. Some time in the early morning, François managed to tell me what had happened the night before as Adele had led him to the Kiosk. They had had no difficulty at the gate, because three women joined them as they entered, women who had been there before and were familiar to the guards.

Once inside, however, they were accosted by a page who assumed they were for hire. He threatened to cause a disturbance when they rejected his advances. Fearing discovery, François drew a knife from the folds of his *feridjie* and ripped open the fellow's throat. The page's body rested in the shrubbery near the Chief Physician's Chamber. It would go unnoticed until morning, but then the Janissaries would find it and search for the assassin.

That made it imperative for François to leave the palace before dawn, but we fell asleep at last and lay together until I heard the *muezzin's* sunrise call. "François! Quickly! You must get up. It's light!"

He awoke in a second, realizing our danger. "When will I see you again?" he asked desperately as he pulled on his britches.

"I don't know, but stay near the goldsmith's shop in the covered market. Adele will find you there as soon as we have a plan."

With the *feridjie* over him, he was ready to leave. I slipped on the one Adele had left behind. "I'll lead you to the gate," I assured him. "But from there you must find your way through the woods and away from the palace."

"I'll follow the water's edge," he responded confidently. "It should lead me out of trouble."

We found the gate open, a convenience to departing ladies of the night. The only guard was outside a few paces away upon his prayer rug for morning devotions.

"Move quietly, darling," I cautioned. "The sentry will not interrupt his prayers for you. If he does, he'll have to start from the beginning again."

We could not kiss or embrace because of our disguises, but our hands touched. I watched as he slipped past the guard and into the forest.

Chapter 29

When I returned to the apartment, Adele was reclining upon the divan in the main salon, Mahmoud in her arms sucking upon a cloth doll dipped in sugar and poppy juice to forestall his hunger.

"Poor darling," I sighed. With the first thought of his need, I felt an almost painful tingle as the milk of my breasts started to flow. I had to press my hands against them to prevent a deluge. "Pass him to me quickly," I said as I sat down opposite Adele on the couch.

"Are you all right?" she asked anxiously.

I paused to put Mahmoud to my breast. "Yes, I think so."

"It's very late. Did François get away before dawn?"

"No. We fell asleep. I didn't awaken until sunrise."

"He told you about the page?"

"Yes, but he got through the gate before the body was found. I don't know if they've come upon it yet."

"They'll find it soon. It's good he cleared the gate."

She hesitated, then looked at me quizzically. "Do you want to talk?"

"I think we should. Tell me, did he seem different to you?"

"Yes," Adele replied. "He appears to have much more confidence, a will of his own. Perhaps it comes from defying his father. He always seemed something of a boy to me while we were in France. Now he's more of a man."

"You're right about that," I agreed, laughing to myself at the accuracy of her appraisal. If he was nothing else, he was certainly a man.

"I can see by your face that you still find him attractive." She smiled. "Do you love him?"

I could not answer her directly. Instead, I looked down at my beautiful Mahmoud, his eyes closed peacefully as he suckled. Of course, I loved François. I wanted to spend the rest of my life in his arms. I never dreamed a man's body could bring me such joy. I already ached to have him again. Still, there were so many obstacles to our love. I did not yet dare to dream we might find a way to be together.

"Aimee," Adele said softly. "Do you love him?"

"That's a question I can't afford to answer right now. Mahmoud's welfare is my only consideration. I can't let anything else interfere until I know he is safe."

"Has Poppy learned anything?"

"Nothing yet. His people are watching the Kettlemen closely, but they are a cunning lot."

"Has he taken a prisoner?"

"No. He reasons that if one of them disappears, the others may change their plans. Then whatever information we gain would be useless to us."

"Sensible," Adele said thoughtfully.

"Yes," I replied. "But if events begin to move too quickly, if anything should happen to Hassan Pasha or Selim, he'll have to go ahead. Better to force them to alter their course than curse ourselves for doing nothing when it's too late."

"It must have been difficult to tell François that you may not go back with him."

I shifted Mahmoud to my other breast. "Is there tea?"

"Yes." She reached to the floor behind the divan and poured a glass. "It's still hot."

I took it from her. "Have you seen Lydia? I'd love some bread and butter."

Adele rang the bell and a servant appeared. "Yes, Hanoum Effendi."

"Ask Lydia to bring some bread and butter for the Sultan."

"And some honey as well," I added.

When the servant had departed, Adele asked, "Did you tell him you might not go back, Aimee?"

"No, the time wasn't right. But there will be another meeting. There is a lot he doesn't know yet."

"It won't be easy. We can't use the same means again. They'll be watching the gates closely after they find the dead page."

"I know, but I promised you'd contact him at the goldsmith's shop when we find a way."

"Whatever you say." She appeared to disapprove. "Understand me, Aimee. It wouldn't matter if you did deceive François until the last and then send him packing. That would be no worse than he deserves after what he did. But he just isn't a man to be toyed with. If he doesn't grasp the sort of danger we're in with the Janissaries and Kiusem, he may not accept your refusal. He may actually storm into the harem with a band of hired Europeans and try to kidnap you."

The idea terrified me. François would be killed. "He'd fail, of course."

"Yes, but he'd be captured and forced to talk. Abdul Hamid might not act if he learned about you and Selim, but with François it would be different. Everyone in the palace would know you had a lover. I hate to think about what would happen. You've heard the grisly history of the Grand Turk Ibrahim."

Adele referred to a bloodthirsty Sultan of the seventeenth century who, upon hearing that one of his concubines had been unfaithful, tortured his entire harem. Failing to uncover the guilty woman's identity, he had them all put to death, ordering them tied in sacks and drowned in the Bosporus.

"Abdul Hamid is no Ibrahim," I reminded her, though I was chilled by the horrible possibility she had forced me to confront.

"No," she agreed. "But Abdul Hamid would have to take some action if François were to flaunt your infidelity to the world."

"I'll see he doesn't do that. Next time we meet, I'll tell him everything."

At last Lydia entered with my food. "Peace be upon you, Hanoum Sultan. And you, Hanoum Effendi." We returned her greeting as she placed the tray upon the divan. Then, seeing Mahmoud had fallen asleep, she took him from me. "Seriphina is waiting for the little one," she said lovingly as she carried him away.

I hungrily reached for the tray, pulling away the velvet cloth that covered it. There beside the bread and fresh pot of tea was a white rose. "It must have come this morning."

Adele laughed ironically. "It's either feast or famine. Last night François, tonight Selim."

I set the flower aside and attacked the bread and honey. Adele joined in my repast, the morning drifting by as we continued our discussion.

Toward midday, when Seriphina had carried Mahmoud up the stairs after his second meal, there were sounds in the vestibule. Adele and I were still reclining on the divan, when Poppy came in unannounced. He paused at the top of the stairs for an instant then plunged into the room, a blue-clad halberdier close upon his heels.

Halberdiers are the peculiar palace inmates upon whom the duties of woodcutter have been bestowed. Their name comes from the battle axes mounted upon long staffs carried whenever they escort harem women outside the palace. For the most part however, they are occupied with the task of providing fuel for the seraglio's hundreds of fireplaces. Chosen for strength, they are frequently very large, rarely blessed with more than the intelligence of a goatherd and are the butt of many cruel palace jokes for their unusual attire. The duties of a halberdier take him everywhere in the seraglio, even into the harem, yet he is a fully-tooled male and forbidden to look upon the Grand Turk's chosen women. For this reason he has attached to his hat two long artificial curls which dangle beside his eyes and prevent him from stealing an imprudent glance. Also, he wears a wide round collar of a stiffened material which is adjustable to stand upright when he enters the harem, thus cutting off the view directly before his eyes. These two devices, the chastity curls and the collar, render the poor devil very close to sightless and allow him to go about his work in the women's quarters without violating the privacy of the ladies.

Because of this imposed sightlessness, halberdiers have great difficulty in getting around. When the Kislar Agha entered our apartment, the halberdier, his arms full of wood, had no idea he was about to encounter three stairs. He missed the first, twisted his leg on the second and fell headlong against the eunuch's back, bringing Poppy crashing to the floor.

"Poppy!" I cried. "Are you hurt?" Adele and I hurried to him, but the thunder of his fall attracted my guards who rushed in and helped him to his feet.

"Pick up the wood," he snapped angrily as he adjusted his turban.

When the floor was free of debris, Poppy ordered the guards away. "Are there any servants upstairs?" he asked impatiently.

"Only Seriphina with Mahmoud," I replied. "But come and sit down. You took a terrible fall."

"I will sit down, but only upstairs. We must talk in a place where no one can overhear us."

"Just as you say." I grew fearful, assuming by his

manner that he had uncovered another spy in our household.

"See that the guards are alerted." There was anger in his voice. "No one should be allowed to pass."

Adele attended to that as Poppy and I walked toward the steps.

"Hanoum Sultan." Lydia appeared from the kitchen. "May I serve the Kislar Agha refreshments?"

"See that all the servants are removed from the main salon and allow no one up these stairs," Poppy ordered.

Lydia was unaccustomed to taking orders from the Kislar Agha and looked to me for confirmation.

"Do as he says." Lydia, following instructions, directed the halberdier to deposit his wood in the receptacle near the fireplace. "Why you deliver firewood in the heat of the summer, I do not know," she said disgustedly. "But since it is here we will keep it." When the fellow made no move to obey her, she repeated herself. "Over there, foolish one, or are you deaf as well as blind from those curls?"

"Go woman!" Poppy roared. Lydia responded only with a piqued expression. "Go and leave that man where he is!"

"Hanoum Sultan?" she pointedly asked my permission.

"I do not understand either, Lydia, but you had better go."

With my consent she started toward the kitchen. "Eunuchs," she said, throwing up her hands with a shrug.

Poppy spoke in French. "Now if you please, let's go upstairs."

"What is it?" I demanded. "Do you think my household is no longer safe?"

"We will talk upstairs!"

"Should this fellow come along?" Adele asked as she joined us.

"Yes," Poppy grunted disgustedly. To the bearer he

spoke in French. "Follow us." The halberdier stepped right along, and from that I inferred he was no ordinary woodcutter, but a special bodyguard in disguise, one who understood our secret cipher so that he could work with us to protect Mahmoud.

"What have you found out, Poppy, that you feel we have such need of protection?"

"You will learn soon enough." He waved us forward impatiently, then grabbed the halberdier so that the awkward fellow would not fall again.

"Take your hands off me, you filthy gelded bastard!" The voice from behind the high collar was muffled but unmistakable.

"Sweet Mother of God!" I exclaimed. "It's François!"

"Silence!" Poppy looked about desperately. "Hurry, all of you. Up the stairs before anyone discovers."

Once we were safe in the sitting room, Adele returned to the salon until Lydia was free to guard the steps. Poppy seemed about to explode from the effort of climbing the stairs in a boiling rage. He marched to the balcony to verify that no one was hiding there.

"I'm sorry, darling," François whispered through his collar. "They caught me in the woods. I told them nothing, I swear it. But the eunuch found my watch and recognized your portrait inside."

"Don't worry," I tried to reassure him. "Here, get rid of that wood." I pointed to a box next to the fireplace, but he could not see it until I snapped down his collar.

"What does this mean?" Poppy demanded in Turkish when he had recovered his wind. He pulled François' watch from his sash and presented it. "This man is your lover, is he not?"

"Yes," I responded, knowing a lie could serve nothing.

"He was within the palace walls last night, was he not?" I hesitated. "He was within the palace walls. A page is dead. He killed him."

"Yes."

François could not understand our exchange and when he was free of the wood he started to speak.

"Don't say anything," I warned him. "Please. Sit down and leave this to me." I went to the desk and turned the chair out. He did as I asked.

"You must be mad, Naksh," Poppy went on angrily in Turkish. "Running such a risk when Kiusem is preparing to take the throne."

"Why did you bring him here then?" I asked. "Certainly, this is the worst place for him."

"I did not know where else to take him. He wouldn't be safe in the dungeons below the Central Gate. Janissaries could find him and force him to talk. I might have killed him, but I knew from the watch he was important to you. Naksh, you must force him to leave here. Praise Allah he was not captured by the Janissaries this time. When they discovered the dead page, they sent out extra patrols, but he eluded them and the gardeners caught him."

"And they brought him to you?"

"Yes, they are in my purse, but I don't completely own the Janissary guards. This madness has got to stop before they become involved."

I could see that Poppy was desperately worried that my discovery could lead to the ruin of the entire reform movement. He nervously clicked the chain of François's watch. "I will send him away, Poppy. But you must realize that I did not ask him to come here. If I refuse to leave with him, he may attempt to kidnap me."

"Then we must kill him," Poppy said unequivocally.

"No! I will not allow it."

"Then what will you do to get rid of him?"

Behind me the door opened. It was Adele. Lydia had taken her place at the bottom of the stairs.

"Everything is quiet down there," she said in French.

Just then the voice of the *muezzin* arrested us. "I must go at once," Poppy said anxiously. "They are expecting me at the mosque. What should I do with him?" He nodded toward François contemptuously.

I looked to Adele. "He'll stay here with us," I said. "Adele will come to you this afternoon when we have a plan."

"Get rid of him, Naksh," he admonished gravely. "Remember, you have chosen the Ottoman way."

Chapter 30

Adele escorted the Kislar Agha away, leaving François and me alone. "What will happen now?" he asked, showing no sign of fear for his own safety. "What did you tell the eunuch?"

"I told him you'd stay here until tomorrow. I don't know what will happen after that, but somehow we'll get you away from here."

François shook his head. "I am such a fool. It is I who should be getting you away, and here I sit in this ridiculous disguise, a prisoner in your harem."

"The disguise is a good one." I said as I walked around the loveseat and put my arms around his shoulders. "How did Poppy get it so quickly?"

"Poppy?" François paused. "You mean the eunuch? My God, that man is strong and quick for such a giant. He had no trouble. After he determined who I was, he ordered his lackeys away and sent for a guard. When the poor bastard came in, the eunuch thrust out his arm and grabbed him by the throat. In a second the guard was dead. This is his uniform. His body left the palace wearing my clothes."

"That was clever," I observed. "It's a blessing Poppy's on our side." I bent down to give François a reassuring kiss, then eased onto his lap. He winced in pain. "I'm not that heavy, am I darling?"

"No, but get up." When I did, he rubbed his thigh. "It was those guards who captured me. I took several nasty whacks from their staves."

"I have just the thing for you." I turned toward the door. "While we're here, we may as well take advantage of everything we can. You'll have a bath *à la turque.*"

"What? You mean one of those steaming hot rooms with the fountains? No I won't. I saw one in Sophia. So much heat isn't healthful, especially in this climate with the plague running rampant in the city."

"Nonsense," I responded. "It will ease your pain. Now wait here a minute while I make the arrangements."

I slipped out of the room and went downstairs. There I found Adele. "What are you going to do with him?" she asked.

"He needs a bath."

"No, I mean how are you going to get rid of him?"

"I don't know."

"Then listen to me for a moment. I may have an idea."

"Wonderful! What is it?"

"You could go and visit my villa for a few days. I'll send for my own barge to take us there, my own eunuchs, but you'll need a bodyguard. François has the uniform. Do you think Abdul Hamid would let you go?"

"I could plead fear of the plague. Even Kiusem mentioned it yesterday. Yes. But what would happen once we got there?"

"I'd see that my eunuchs gave you and François some privacy. After all, they are sworn to protect my virtue, but not everyone else's. At least you'd have a few days together."

"But what if something happens here while I'm away?"

"I'll come back to the palace. If anything happens that I can't handle, I will send you word."

"All right."

"Then it's settled," Adele concluded.

"Yes. Will you see to it that Poppy gains Abdul Hamid's permission?"

"Poppy won't like your leaving the seraglio with François," she reminded me.

"I know, but tell him not to worry. I've chosen the Ottoman way."

"Is that true? Are you going to stay?"

"I don't know, and now is not the time to decide. Just tell Poppy what I said. It will reassure him. Now go. I'll talk to Lydia. She'll clear the apartment of servants and see to it the stoves are lit under the *hammam*. That's as good a place as any to tell François what he has to know."

"You were gone a long time," François said anxiously when I returned to the sitting room.

"There was much to attend to, darling, but I'm sorry. I know how difficult it is to wait."

He had tried to make himself comfortable on the loveseat, but his sore limbs troubled him, and he groaned as he stood up.

"Come." I slipped an arm around his waist. "The hot water will help you."

He continued his protests as we went downstairs, but I brushed them aside and led him to the *hammam's* antechamber. The pleasure he took in helping me undress quickly opened his European mind to the oriental bath. A devoted convert to the Turkish custom, I required no inducements, though I found an abundance. The very textures of his skin excited me— his wild, natural state so unlike the fragile alabaster of the polished Selim.

When we entered the hot room, I seated François

next to the central fountain, eased away his *pestemal* and poured water over his aching shoulders. "It is said that in the public baths men must keep their private parts covered at all times," I observed as I ladled water over him.

"By God, they had better!" he responded, indignant at the thought of bathing with strangers.

"It is different with women," I smiled.

"You mean to say they walk about with nothing on?"

My *pestemal* still hung around my hips. I pulled it away. "Just like this, all of us." I was amazed at my own boldness and amused that François seemed not to know where to rest his eyes.

Then he slipped his arm around mine. "You too, Aimee?" he asked, quite interested. "You allow other women to see you as your are?"

"Just as I am!" It was so pleasing to play with him this way that I had to laugh.

"Remarkable," he sighed and wrapped his other arm around my waist, pulling me to him. "I tell you, Aimee, every bone in my body aches or I'd take better advantage of this situation than I have." He smiled apologetically.

"Does the heat help? I asked.

"Yes." He raised his arm, testing it. "It helps a lot." I stepped to the other side of the fountain and picked up an urn of oil. "Do you mind if I ask you a question?" he asked sheepishly.

"No." I poured a bit of oil into my hand and began to massage his shoulders.

"I'm no Parisian dandy," he began. "But I know something of women and a bit about you. There was one night in Nantes when you and I lay together."

"That night is best forgotten," I said soberly.

"Maybe so, but I remember every moment, every sensation. You're different now." He hesitated. "Something is missing." His eyes indicated what he meant.

"Oh," I blushed.

"Yes, your little blond thatch is gone. What did they do with it?"

"They took it off when I first arrived. As I understand it, no civilized woman in Istanbul has any hair except on her head. Most men shave their heads too because they always wear turbans."

"You mean men take off the hair around their . . ." He hesitated.

"It is said they do."

"How is it done?"

"For men, I don't know. Perhaps they shave or maybe they use tweezers."

"Sweet Jesus! Tweezers!" François rolled his eyes and shuddered.

"Let me rub your back," I said softly. "We'll talk no more of Turks just now."

He responded favorably to my massage. Slowly the pain in his muscles abated. He forgot the humiliations of the morning and allowed his hands to caress me lovingly as they had the night before. Soon we retired to a couch in the cool room.

Though François began almost at once to caress my breasts and arouse me, I took his hands in mine, kissed them, then encouraged him to lie back.

"You rest now, darling," I said softly. "It's my turn to please you." I kissed the smile upon his lips and gently closed his eyes with my finger tips. Along with the passion François had awakened in me the night before, I felt a sense of gratitude for his giving me such magnificent sensations. Now, I looked forward excitedly to bringing him similar pleasure.

I fetched more oil from the bath and again massaged his chest and shoulders until I felt him relax. Then I poured a bit in my hands and rubbed it into his feet, working it slowly into each toe, his soles, his heels, his ankles. Next I attended to his limbs, enjoying the firmness of his muscles as I rubbed away his pain. Moving upward, I reached his manhood, which was no longer in repose. What he had done for me the night before, I did for him then, feeling him grow stronger with each touch of my lips and tongue, feeling my own excitement grow with his.

"Come, let me love you now, darling," he said tenderly as he took me by the shoulders and drew me to him. He had not touched me in the same ways he had the night before, but my body was ready for him just the same. My pleasing him had pleased me as well, and we loved each other hungrily until both of us were satisfied.

We slept a short while and awoke in each other's arms, but soon I grew anxious, knowing it was time we talked seriously. "There's food here," I said. "Joints of lamb, fruit, champagne." I wrapped myself in a dry *pestemal*.

"Bring it here," François commanded exuberantly. "I haven't eaten since yesterday."

He fell upon the tray while I opened the wine. Then after his first desperate hunger had been satisfied, I began to talk to him about the Ottomans.

It was a long story beginning in 1683 when Turkish troops numbering close to two hundred thousand went down to ignominious defeat at the hands of a much smaller Austrian force. That date marked the Ottoman's last attempt at conquest. From then they knew only defense. Debacles followed one upon another, and always it seemed for the same reason: the empire lacked effective leadership.

As I described the conspiratorial atmosphere within the seraglio, I was struck by that critical deficiency. For nearly one hundred years, no one holding the reigns of power demonstrated the insights necessary to change the Ottoman course. It was an empire built upon conquest and expansion, now forced to exist within contracting borders and limited resources. Yet no one considered new principles of government, new methods of defensive warfare, new sources of revenue. Everyone still looked to the past for solutions to every problem.

"Reform and innovation are the only hopes for the

Ottoman dynasty," I concluded as François and I sipped champagne.

"You've been here only a year, Aimee," he observed. "But you speak as if you were born an Ottoman."

I smiled at his insight. "No one is born Ottoman. It isn't like being French or Greek or Turkish. People choose to be Ottoman by accepting a certain way of life, particular customs and loyalties. The most devoted Ottoman I know is Algerian," I explained, thinking of Hassan Pasha. "Look at many of the Sultan's highest officials and you will find Georgians, Circassians, Greeks or Africans—all of them Ottomans now."

"And you count yourself among them, don't you?"

"I don't know," I admitted. "Perhaps my son has made me one. He is the living future of the dynasty. His French blood and my guidance could make him the leader the Ottomans need. He could be an innovator with the strength to challenge the Janissaries. He could create a new order."

"But you told me that there are other heirs who will precede him to the throne, and you mentioned a woman."

"Kiusem."

"Yes. She has tried to kill him and may do so again. Certainly you must fear for his life?"

"Of course. There's no doubt in my mind that soon Kiusem and the Janissaries will try to overthrow Abdul Hamid. If they succeed, I'll have to flee or they'll kill Mahmoud."

"And if they fail," François said gravely. "If you defeat them, you intend to remain here, don't you?"

"I don't know, darling. I thought I would until you came. But whatever happens, no one else must find out about your coming here. No one else, ever. We can do nothing to create any doubt that Abdul Hamid is Mahmoud's father. You understand that, don't you?"

Before François could answer, there was a knock at

the *hammam* door. "Hanoum Sultan." It was Lydia's voice.

"A moment." Then I turned to François. "You understand," I said emphatically.

"Yes, darling," he assured me.

Relieved, I encouraged him to cover himself. "Come in."

I presented Lydia to him and she bowed respectfully. "Hanoum Sultan." She addressed me in Ottoman, but her eyes were big with wonder as she examined my companion.

"Please forgive this interruption, but Mahmoud hungers. Can you go to him?"

"Of course," I replied with a smile. "Ask Seriphina to take him to my bedroom."

"Yes, Sultan."

"You spoke to her about François?" I asked.

"Yes, Sultan. Just as you instructed me. She knows who he is."

"My son needs me now," I explained when François and I were alone again. "I suckle him myself."

"Still devoted to Rousseau," he observed.

"Ah, so you read *Emile?*"

"Yes. After you left, I read many of the books you recommended. It made me feel closer to you." He hesitated. "I want to see the child."

"I'm glad."

After dressing, we went upstairs. "Seriphina!" I called when François and I stepped into my boudoir. Mahmoud, wrapped in a light quilt sewn with gold, lay upon the bed. "Seriphina!" I called again toward the closing door to the dressing room. The nurse stopped and slowly reentered the boudoir.

"Your servant, Hanoum Sultan." She bowed slowly and tried not to smile, but her eyes were full of happy laughter which quickly spread across her face in a playful grin.

"This is Seriphina." As I presented her to François, she bowed again, still smiling. Anatolians delight in a love story, and it was clear Seriphina was taken with the idea of our adventure. Of course, she never considered the dangers involved, only the romance. "Call upon me, Hanoum Sultan. Call upon me for your every need." She kissed my hand and bowed again to François. Then as she turned to leave, she looked back for a second. "Your lover is magnificent, Hanoum Sultan. Perhaps a second son in his likeness?"

"You'd better go now, Seriphina." I tried to sound stern.

"Your servant, Sultan." She laughed happily as she slipped out the door.

"She approves of you, darling," I said, but as I turned to François I could see he had heard nothing. His eyes were on the small bundle on the bed.

"He's dark," François observed cautiously.

"Yes, but there is something of me in him." I lifted Mahmoud in my arms.

"It's your mouth."

Mahmoud nuzzled against me hungrily. "I really must feed him now. Will it bother you?"

"I don't know," François responded honestly.

"Here, let's lie down together." I took his hand and led him to my canopied bed. When we were settled, he with his arms around me, I loosened my *entari* and opened the front of my chemise. As Mahmoud took my breast, I waited for some sign that François had truly accepted us. At last he moved a bit and I felt him relax. He reached out and touched Mahmoud's tiny fist.

"He's so small," François whispered. "So small and perfect." Then after a long silence he added, "the boy's half French, Aimee, and too young to be Ottoman of his own choosing. France may be the place for him. Don't close your mind to it."

I sensed a bond had formed between François and my son by the time I carried the slumbering Mahmoud away to Seriphina's care. That bond was important. I hoped it would help François understand and accept whatever sacrifices we might have to make for the child.

When I returned to my boudoir, I brought a chilled bottle of champagne. François was pensive and tender as I lay down beside him. "You've changed very much in the year we've been apart," he said without criticism.

"And you've seen the reason for it. My son's destiny is an awesome responsibility. But you've changed too, darling. Even Adele noticed it in the short time she spent with you at the sale yesterday. This past year must have been a difficult one for you, yet you've told me nothing. I don't even know how you found out I was in Istanbul."

François, leaning back on a pillow propped against the headboard, took the glass of wine I offered. "That was purely by chance," he explained. "Chance or perhaps fate . . ."

BOOK THREE

served as a relic.

"Take this away, Adele," I said and passed my pistol into her other hand. She looked at it strangely, as

Chapter 31

François' story began in Nantes. He spent the months after Aimee's departure working at the Wilkinson cannon works. His indecision about his betrothal tormented him. He longed for Aimee, yet he dared not act against his father's wishes because the family's finances floated upon the promised rewards of his marriage.

One fall evening when Wilkinson's laborers were ferried into town from the factory, François, still dressed in trousers and the jerkin he wore at work, joined some of the men for drinks at a tavern near the docks. He enjoyed their company—many were quite knowledgeable in their craft—and they had taken to him despite his station, for François had shown himself ready to do a man's work and he asked no deference to his rank.

The tavern that night was unusually quiet considering its roisterous clientele. The men discovered that a single woebegone sailor had enthralled the company with a lengthy narrative.

"Who is the poor devil?" François asked the barmaid.

"Don't know his name," she replied. "But he has quite a story. Set sail from Nantes early in the year and was taken by Barbary pirates. The bastards chained him to a galley oar. Would've died there too if Spaniards hadn't boarded her after a chase and freed the Christians."

"A galley slave?" one worker scoffed. "I can't believe there's a galley still afloat. This is the age of sail."

The storyteller stopped at that challenge. "There's galleys all right." His voice was like a rattle from the tomb. "If you'd ever sailed from Marseilles you'd know about 'em, but I'm the man who can tell you here." He pulled back his sleeve to reveal a withered arm cut to the bone with shackle scars. "My legs is tattooed by the irons as well. Damn them Musselmen bastards and their chains. My legs and my very soul from the tortures I seen. By God! It's good to be back in France where a Christian man is safe. With God as my witness, I vow I'll never take ship again until them Barbary pirates has been swept from the sea."

"Hold there, man," another seaman spoke up. "Them corsairs is devils, I'll grant. But they infest the Mediterranean mostly, and there's more than one pond for a Frenchman these days. I just made a passage from the Antilles and never saw a pirate from the day we left the islands until we reached France."

"Then send your woman to light a score of candles at the cathedral tomorrow and give thanks to all the saints," the storyteller said bitterly. "My ship, *Belle Gloire,* set sail for the Antilles in March, and I tell you now that not a wretched soul aboard ever saw Martinique."

François bolted to his feet. "What was that you said? What was your ship?"

"Belle Gloire," the sailor replied, comprehending instantly the fear in François' voice. "I'm sorry, mon-

sieur. Did you have a friend on board?" François could not speak. "At least tell me his name," the sailor pressed. "I would've known him. I could tell you if he died bravely." The fellow made his way to the table. "Was it your brother?"

François collapsed across the table and wept, burying his face against his sleeve. "It was no member of the crew," he sobbed. "It was a passenger, a woman. Oh God! It was my Aimee!"

"But the only white woman aboard was of noble birth," the sailor protested. "What would you be doing with . . ."

"He's of the same," one of François' comrades pointed out quickly. "An officer in the king's artillery."

"Ah," said the sailor skeptically as he observed François' common attire. "A nobleman and an officer." The sailor stood up angrily, his chair crashing backward to the floor. "And I'm the goddamned Duke of Orleans." He turned away.

"Wait! Please!" François grabbed his withered arm.

"After what I've suffered," the sailor roared, "I'm not a man to be baited." He tried to pull away but François' grip was firm.

"Please! Was the woman fair? Did she travel with a Negress?"

"By God! She was fair," he responded. "And a real beauty. So was the black." He reached behind him and righted his chair. "For the price of a rum, I'll tell you what I know of 'em."

A crowd quickly formed around the table. The barmaid had to push her way through to bring the next round of drinks. "I don't know how you'll take to this, monsieur," the sailor began. "But the women is alive, or at least they was when last I saw 'em."

The men who had pressed around to hear looked knowingly at one another. Calloused from years of hard living, many sniggered at the thought of captured women. François ignored them. "You're certain they're alive?"

"That I am, monsieur. I was in the port of Algiers

when I saw 'em last. The infidel bastards had me doing slave labor at the docks when a grand treasure
ship set sail for the Levant. The women was part of
that treasure. I saw a black wench go aboard early in
the morning, and later the fair one came too, with a
long train of slaves and pack animals following her.
Her face was covered, but when she got out of her
litter, I saw her blonde hair and I asked the bastard
slave driver working us if she was the one who was
taken with me. He said she was the very same. She
and the black was being sent to the Ottoman Sultan's
harem."

"God have mercy upon her," one of François' comrades muttered. Others clustered around were less
compassionate.

"I must go to her," François announced boldly when
he had heard the sailor out. "I must find her somehow
and save her."

"You're a bit late for saving anything, monsieur,"
the sailor scoffed. "What with pirates and Turks, she
will a' been boffed by the hundreds by now, and all of
them filthy Mohammedans. No Frenchman alive would
want the return of such a sullied baggage."

"You've said enough, monsieur," François said
sharply. Then he pulled out his purse and threw it
down as payment. "Though you bear terrible news,
you've done me a great service, and I thank you, but
you are wrong. I want her back and I'll find her."

"Then set your sail for Istanbul, monsieur," the
storyteller told him with a filthy grin. "You'll find
your woman in the palace of the Terrible Turk."

Chapter 32

François turned for solace to the closest friend he had
in Nantes, the owner of the cannon works, Albert
Wilkinson. The hour was late when he arrived at
Wilkinson's rooms. Pounding on the door, François
tried to rouse him. At last the Englishman responded.
A man near fifty, drunken with slumber, he looked
every day of his half century. Though the two were
near equals in height, Wilkinson seemed shrunken
from fatigue as he stood in his nightshirt. It was the
time of his life when he should put away his weapons
making and go home to his family, but there was little
chance of that. The man lusted for wealth. Educated
under the exacting eye of his father to carry on the
family's textile mill, he saw greater profit in partner-
ship with the English crown. An early and vocal advo-
cate of improved artillery as the key to military success, he applied his considerable scientific talents to
improving cannon design and manufacture. With the
textile mill as a steady source of income, he devoted
most of his time to weapons experiments, enjoying a

respected position in the vanguard of artillery advancement for over thirty years.

His prowess earned him considerable riches. During those years the English had to maintain a large military presence in their troublesome colonial possessions, as well as secure their mastery of the seas with an armed fleet. Of course, the French and Indian War and the American Revolution did no harm to his trade, but no matter how much wealth he amassed, it was never enough. Albert Wilkinson always needed more. Like so many men of humble birth, he aspired to see his progeny join the noble ranks. To that end, he had purchased well-born wives for three sons and placed them in impressive manor houses where his labor maintained them in grand style.

As successful as he was in his field, such a drain on his resources kept him at the knife edge of financial disaster. In desperation, he found a way to expand his markets. During England's war with the colonies he secretly shipped guns to the French, seemingly undisturbed by the knowledge that those very weapons would soon deal death to his own countrymen.

Looking at the rugged face of the Englishman, one could not see any mark of a troubled conscience. Far from it! The man's usual ready grin and eager expression could not disguise the single-mindedness that burned within him, a single-mindedness that allowed no quarter to patriotism.

That is not to say he did not love Mother England. He spoke nothing but praise of her institutions, repeatedly condemning the French for their decadence and inefficiency. Knowing all this, François found the man a confounding embodiment of paradoxes, but one thing was certain. Albert Wilkinson was as true to his friends as he was to his family. When François needed help, he turned to him.

"François!" the cannonmaker bellowed when he opened the door. "Do you know the hour, man?"

Looking inside, François could see through the far door that Wilkinson had not slept alone. "Forgive me, monsieur," he said in French, then shifted to English, a language he had mastered at the foundry. "I would not intrude, but something terrible has happened."

"Trouble at the cannon works? What is it?"

"No. Much worse. It's Mademoiselle de Rivery. You remember my speaking of her?"

"Yes, of course. I thought she was in Martinique." The factory owner adjusted the patch over his left eye, the one shattered years before in the explosion of an experimental missile. "Come sit down."

"She never arrived in Martinique," François blurted out. "She's been kidnapped by pirates. She's in Istanbul."

Wilkinson grabbed him by the shoulders. "How do you know this, man? How did you find out?"

"I was in a tavern tonight. There was a sailor from *Belle Gloire*. He survived the pirate attack and was taken prisoner. He knows what happened to Aimee. He told me everything."

"Sit down," Wilkinson said a second time. Then he poured François a rum, took one for himself and pulled the bedroom door shut. "You learned all this from a tavern drunk?" he asked skeptically. "Then there's a good chance it isn't true."

"But why would the fellow lie about such a thing?"

"I can't say. But it's been known to happen. Did you buy him drinks?"

"Yes, and I gave him my purse as a reward."

"Then there's reason enough for chicanery. We won't believe the worst until we can check with the shippers."

The next day the worst was confirmed, first by the merchant who owned *Belle Gloire*. It was one of three vessels in his fleet. The other two had not set sail for the Antilles until mid-June, but now they were safely back in Nantes with reports that their ill-fated sister ship had never reached Fort Royal in Martinique. Earlier in the year, the merchant had heard reports of unidentified wreckage spotted late in March in the

Bay of Biscay, but it was not until *Belle Gloire* was long overdue that he suspected she had gone down. Now there was little doubt of it. He had heard the old sailor's fanciful story of pirates and kidnapping, but it mattered little to him. His cargo and investment were lost.

Hoping for more information, Albert Wilkinson sent some of his men to the docks and taverns to question sailors newly returned from the sea. Those recently completing Atlantic passages knew nothing, but three or four experienced sailors had spent the war years sailing under eastern flags. One had put in to Istanbul the previous summer and saw the arrival of a gigantic treasure ship like the one described to François by the tavern rat.

"It's true then," François concluded grimly as he sat in an inn with Wilkinson after hearing his report. "She's a prisoner in infidel hands, but I know she's alive."

"It does sound that way," Wilkinson agreed. "Lord have mercy. I'd sooner she had drowned in the Bay."

"Nonsense! If she's alive, I can save her. I'm to blame for everything that's happened. I never should have allowed her to set foot on that ship."

"But as you explained it to me," Wilkinson said. "You could have kept her in France only by marrying her, and that was impossible."

"No it wasn't. I intend to marry her now, as soon as I find her."

"Don't be foolish, lad. The woman's gone through no fault of yours, and you can't go after her. You have responsibilities to your father. The bonds of family are stronger than any other."

"I know I'll never rest until Aimee is safe. I shan't sell my soul to support my father's extravagances. I agreed to the marriage he arranged because I wanted to spare him the humiliation of penury, but look what it has cost—Aimee's freedom, her honor, almost her life. No, some things are more valuable than position. Now I can see that."

"You're wrong, son," Wilkinson counseled. "The love of a woman is a fleeting thing, like the flash of a linstock against a slow match. But family is forever. It will become your monument. No sacrifice is too great to preserve it unsullied. Forget the mademoiselle, François. She's lost for good."

"I can't forget her," he responded with conviction as he pushed away from the table. "I leave for Paris today. There I will tell my father to end my betrothal. Then it's on to the Levant."

Chapter 33

Two nights later, having spent his last cent on re-
mounts, François arrived in Paris. When he reached
his father's townhouse, he found a score of dinner
guests. The elite of Paris were gathered in the salon,
chatting gaily over chamber music provided by an ensemble seated near the garden doors.

As he made his way through the room toward
his father, the group he passed grew silent. Ladies
clutched sacheted handkerchiefs to their noses. Gentlemen reached for their snuff.

"François!" his father called to him anxiously when
he saw his son. "What are you doing home from
Nantes? My God! You smell like a goat."

It was only then that François became aware of
the stench of lathered horses that clung to him. He
looked down quickly at his dust-covered uniform and
cape but was not distressed by the evidence of his
arduous ride. "My apologies, Father, but I must speak
to you."

"Of course," the old Comte replied, eager to lead

his son away from the salon. "We'll go to the study."

When they were alone, his father turned to him. "You really are a scandal, coming into the house as you are, François. Appearances are everything. I've told you that a thousand times, yet you continue to embarrass me." The Comte drew a pinch of snuff from a small golden box he had in his sleeve and put it to his nose.

"Father, I have something to tell you." François spread his feet apart as if preparing to take a blow. "I cannot go through with the marriage you have arranged."

"Oh," the Comte replied, somewhat piqued. "Not this again."

"News has come to me of Madamoiselle de Rivery."

"You mean, of course, that her ship went down."

"Yes." François was stunned that his father knew of the disaster.

"And so the poor thing was drowned," the Comte went on. "Why will that prevent your marriage?"

"How did you know about it?" François demanded.

"Marie de La Fontelle sent word to me that she would not be receiving guests in her salon until further notice. I have met with a cool reception there ever since your indiscreet escapade with her ward, and I made inquiries to find out if this was an intentional insult. Of course, it was not. Marie has been devastated by the girl's death and is in mourning. She sees almost no one."

"Why was I not told?"

"I intended to let you know the next time you were home. It seemed silly to write. I suspected you'd brood endlessly about it, and I see now I was correct."

"You should have told me."

"Why? The girl is dead. It is a tragedy, but you can do nothing to change that."

"She isn't dead, Father. I have evidence that she's alive. She was captured by pirates off the coast of Majorca and taken to Istanbul. I know where she is now, and I intend to go there and rescue her. Then we'll be married, if she'll still have me after what I've done to her."

"I am an old man, Francois," his father began, allowing his face to assume the familiar mask of distress. "How many more of these arguments do you think I can stand?"

"This need not be an argument, Father. It is my final word."

"I see." The Comte sat down on a sleek loveseat of the latest design and straightened his brocade waistcoat. "And what of your family, your father? This folly of yours will ruin our estates and leave me penniless." He shook his head slowly and looked away. "Thank God your mother didn't live to see a son of hers with so little sense of duty. And to think you'll throw away everything to go off to the Orient after a trollop who is either dead or very ill used by the Turks." The old man sighed and raised a manicured hand to his brow. "I don't believe I deserve this."

Looking at the Comte's practiced pose, François had to struggle against the guilt it usually aroused. Yet he seemed to see his father for the first time as a man whose character and sense of purpose had been destroyed by living too long near the center of power, too close to Versailles. "You'll not be destitute, father. All you need do is give up this house and move back to your estate. You can oversee the place yourself."

"Leave Paris! Out of the question. I'd die of boredom in the provinces."

"Then I suggest you marry again, perhaps the very girl you chose for me."

"But she's a mere child," he protested.

"Exactly what I've been telling you."

"Look here, François. You can't seriously think that you can rescue this Mademoiselle de Rivery."

"I'm very serious," he responded firmly. "Ransom seems the most likely means."

"Ransom! You have no money."

"No, but I know someone who does. Marie de La Fontelle. I'm going to see her now."

"François. You can't do this," his father cried as François turned to leave.

"Consider it done, Father. I will bring Aimee back to France or die in the attempt."

Chapter 34

François flew from the de Marmont house feeling
Aimee was almost out of danger now that he had
conquered a major obstacle to her rescue—his father's
displeasure. Discovering his own mount was wasted, he
commandeered the one-horse cabriolet in the carriage
house, the last remaining vehicle in his family's possession. Driving with the abandon of a reckless dandy, he
reached Madame de La Fontelle's house quickly and
brushed aside the protests of doormen and servants
who regarded him with consternation as he demanded
entry.

Trapped in an antechamber for several minutes,
he argued with the lady's retainers, who insisted she
would not receive him, when suddenly the double doors
to the salon crashed open. Marie de La Fontelle, clad
in black and looking fatigued and cross, stood in the
doorway. Her eyes, heavy with grief, met François'
for an instant. Then recognition added contempt to
her already unwelcoming countenance. "So it's you,"
she said coldly, appraising his disheveled appearance

with a quick and critical glance. "Your father finally told you, did he? Well, at last you know what your treachery has wrought. Oh God! How I wish it were you that was dead and not my beautiful Aimee."

"Please, madame," François began. "May I have a word with you?" The hatred in her eyes was unrelenting.

"Get out of here!"

Her servants grabbed François' arms. He resisted. "Madame. I must speak to you. I have proof that Aimee is not dead. I swear to you she is still alive and I can save her."

François' words were like cold water dashed in Marie's face. She was at once shocked and alert. "Aimee! Alive!" She pointed to her servants. "Release him!" Her face was still gray with sadness, but her eyes softened. "Come in, Captain. Come in quickly." She reached for his arm.

The lady sat down in a striped satin armchair, her back straight, her body tense, as François allowed everything he had learned to spill out of him—the sailor's story, the merchant's account and the reports of a treasure ship in the Levant.

"The news of such a ship in Istanbul is proof of the sailor's story. I have no doubt that Aimee is alive. She is in the Ottoman Sultan's palace, and I intend to rescue her, but I need your help."

It was clear from the change in Marie's appearance that she had accepted François' appraisal. Listening to him, she seemed to come back to life just as in her mind Aimee had. "I know it is foolish to believe you, Captain. After all, I have seen what sort of man you are. But not even you could be so cruel as to deceive me now. How can I help you?"

"I want to offer the Turks a ransom," he explained. "Trying to steal her away would place her life in danger, and I don't want to do that."

"Of course, a ransom! I'll provide it. Monsieur de La Fontelle may be a dullard when it comes to the social graces," she said of her husband, a man whom most of her noble acquaintances and friends had never seen. "But when investing on the Bourse, he is a genius. He will give us whatever we need. What is your estimate?"

The question startled François and drove home the fact that he was completely ignorant of what lay before him—the Orient, the Turks and even the exact location of Istanbul. "I don't know," he said, almost in a panic. Then, fighting it back, he went on, "But I'll make inquiries. Somehow I'll find out everything I need to know about the Turks."

"Perhaps I can be of some assistance there as well," Marie said as she stood up and began to pace back and forth excitedly. "I know a Hungarian, Baron Arpod Von Lazon. He was personal secretary to the Baron de Toth on a mission to the East several years ago. He has spent years in Istanbul." She thought for a moment. "Come to dine with me tomorrow. I'll have him here. He should be able to tell us something."

The following evening, François, bathed and dressed in his formal uniform, was presented to Baron Von Lazon. A small middle-aged man of delicate build and features, well dressed without extravagance, the Baron seemed eager to be of service. Marie, no longer in mourning, wore a pale blue gown, a conservative wig and her famous five-strand diamond necklace. She was hardly the same woman who had accosted François at her door the night before. Seeing the change he had wrought with his news, he realized how dear Aimee was to her.

Before dining, the Baron listened attentively as François described every bit of evidence that led him to believe Aimee was in Istanbul.

"Yes," he concurred. "A ship such as the one you describe did arrive there this past summer. And its origin was Algiers. I know that much from diplomatic reports. Its purpose was to guarantee a continued flow of military supplies to the Algerian Dey and his pirate fleet. There was some talk that a European woman was among the gifts to the Sultan, but once such a woman enters the harem, nothing is ever heard of her again. I cannot even confirm that she was French."

"Tell us this, then," Marie said bluntly, "if the woman is Aimee, what sort of ransom will be required to free her."

"Ransom?" the Baron seemed puzzled. "You misunderstand, madame. We speak now of the Ottoman Turks and their Sultan. Do not confuse them with the barbarian corsairs that roam the Mediterranean like so many hungry wolves. If this woman has entered the royal harem as you say, there can be no ransom. The Sultan might give away one of his women to a deserving pasha when she has reached a certain age, but he would never take ransom for a royal consort."

Marie looked to François in desperation. "What will we do?"

"How will we get her out then?" François asked determinedly.

"In all honesty, Captain, I do not know. But I will not say it is impossible. My years in the Levant taught me that nothing there is impossible. The Ottomans are a proud race with great traditions. I have come to respect them. But the very traditions that once gave them their incredible strength are immutable and do not allow their institutions to change with the times. Still, people must live, and so they find the means to circumvent the rigid obstacles of their society. In my personal experience, *baksheesh* has been the key to open doors that by law should remain closed."

"*Baksheesh?*" François asked. "What is it?"

"An eastern word meaning money or bribes. It works well in the cities of their realm and among the Ottoman bureaucrats. Of course, when dealing with high officials, you must offer your bribes very tactfully. For example, if a diplomat were to present a petition for trade privileges to the proper minister, he would receive no response to the naked document, but if it were offered in a gold casket that was valuable in itself, the negotiations would move forward speedily. With lesser officials, smaller gifts are in order. On many occasions when I wished to see a vizier, I offered some tobacco to his secretary and neglected to collect my gold case afterward.

"Keep in mind that such subtle practices do not work well in the provinces. Open offerings of money may buy cooperation from village chiefs among the Tatars, but more often than not you will have to beat them severely before they will comply with your simplest desire. Compared even to French peasants, they are quite uncivilized."

"But how will François know whom to bribe and whom to beat?" Marie asked uneasily.

"He will need a guide, else his efforts and his gold will go for nothing. The palace bureaucracy is large and tightly controlled by a few powerful families. If he were to assault it ignorantly, every scribe to whom he paid tribute would send him on to a cousin or nephew in order to enrich his relatives, and none of the Captain's contacts would bring him closer to his goal."

"Where might I find such a guide?" François asked.

"Fortunately, I know of a man here in Paris who could be of service," the Baron explained. "His name is Paul Flachat. As a child, he traveled to the Levant every other year in the company of his father who conducted trade with the Ottomans. Now he has inherited his father's contacts and privileges with the Ottoman Sultan and carries on his father's business. I met Flachat in Istanbul some years ago and was very impressed with his command of the Ottoman tongue and his familiarity with their customs. He is completely bourgeois, of course. But he is quite bright, nonetheless."

"Men of his class are often brilliant when it comes to business," Marie observed, thinking of her husband and the wealth he provided her from his speculations.

"Yes," the Baron agreed. "And there is the tragedy

of our times. The land can no longer sustain the nobility. As we languish, our roots dying, the inferior classes accumulate wealth and power in the base pursuits of commerce."

François realized quickly that the baron was unaware of the fact that Marie's husband was of the bourgeoisie, or he would never have been so undiplomatic. "Perhaps we are wrong, monsieur," François suggested. "Perhaps the nobility should not shun commerce as we do."

"But we must, Captain," the Baron countered vehemently. "The tawdry pursuit of profit from trade consumes the mind and spirit of men, robbing them of the leisure time required to ponder the problems of a ruling class. Every great nation requires a body of individuals who, being secure in their own positions, can devote their time to looking after the affairs of those below them. The bourgeoisie could never rule France. They have no time for it."

"And we have no time for further discussion of politics," Marie said, uncomfortable with the topic. "It is the dinner hour."

After their meal, the Baron wrote a letter of introduction to Paul Flachat. "This fellow is just the man for you," he said as he handed it to François. "He trades at the royal palace in Istanbul regularly, and claims to call the chief eunuch of the harem by name. Once he even boasted that his father was admitted to the women's quarters in disguise to observe the ladies firsthand. I did not believe him, of course. But as I said before dinner, in the Levant anything is possible."

Chapter 35

The next morning was clear, with a promise of approaching winter on the wind. Not long after sunrise, François pulled up the collar of his military cape and made his way from his cabriolet to the warehouse of Paul Flachat. Once inside, he was directed by a workman up a narrow flight of stairs to the offices of the proprietor.

The door opened to his knock, revealing a peculiar looking man with the massive chest and arms of a forgeman cloaked in impeccably tailored though gaudy velvet and silk, which fit his form so perfectly that not a single button upon his waistcoat showed signs of strain. For his great girth, however, he was a short man, his head hardly reaching François' shoulder. At first, his face seemed congenial enough, excepting a pock-marked chin and a scar that drew down the corner of one eye. When he saw François his countenance soured, his small brown eyes narrowed to almost nothing and he planted himself firmly in the doorway like a stout tree stump.

"Monsieur Flachat?" François asked reluctantly, hoping this unsavory dwarf was not the proprietor.

"Humph," the fellow said disgustedly. Then he turned to look behind him. "Paul," he said, addressing someone François could not see. "There's a king's man asking for you, an officer. Should I let him in?"

"Of course," piped a high, boyish voice.

The man in the doorway grumbled angrily. "Go inside. He'll talk to you." Then he marched straight through the door, rudely forcing François out of his way.

"Come in. Come in, please," the voice called. A squat man no taller than the first approached and smiled up at him warmly. "Come." He held out an ink-stained hand in welcome. "I have some wonderful Indian tea brewing here in my counting room."

He led François into a large chamber. Against one wall were wide shelves upon which rested rows of what appeared to be ledgers. Two clerks perched at high tables worked by the daylight that streamed through three windows reaching to the ceiling. In an alcove at the back was a dark rococo desk. Upon its surface were scattered a myriad of papers, several old crusts of bread, dirty wine glasses and tea cups. On the wall next to the desk hung a beautiful cream and azure oriental rug. In front of it was a tall console upon which were displayed a few choice pieces of porcelain. As the merchant walked by, he adjusted his spectacles, lifted a gracefully formed vase from its place and stroked it as one might the delicate cheek of a child.

Flachat was a man of haphazard physique. His shoulders were narrow parentheses around a consumptive chest. A large paunch further distorted his profile, but as a counterweight, he had no buttocks at all so that his ill-fitting breeches strained in front and hung in gathers behind. His hair was quite thin and gray, like a score of transparent boot laces pulled back to a rat-tail queue.

"Monsieur Flachat," François said in a polite tone

to draw the man from his examination of the porcelain.

The merchant seemed startled at the sound and looked up. "Ah, the officer," he responded. "I love beautiful things. Would you like to hold it?"

François took it from him carefully, not wishing to insult the man by appearing indifferent to the artwork. "Beautiful." He handed it back and the merchant replaced it on the console.

"Please forgive Monsieur Dufarge." Flachat said, referring to the man who had opened the door. "He has certain peculiarities, but he is a good friend."

"Monsieur, I am Captain François de Marmont, and I am here on a mission of the greatest importance."

"An army officer," he responded idly. "Cavalry perhaps?"

"No, artillery."

"Very interesting. Please sit down, Captain. I am Paul Flachat at your service. Will you have tea?"

"Yes, thank you," François responded as he took a seat in a straight chair in front of the littered desk.

The merchant spoke to one of his clerks who served them. "It has a delicate taste, don't you agree, Captain?" Flachat sippd slowly, with great relish. "I brought it back from the Levant myself."

"It is of the Levant that I wish to speak, Monsieur." François grasped the opportunity to present his letter of introduction from the Baron Von Lazon.

"Ah," Flachat smiled as he read the letter. "The Baron is a fine gentleman. As you must know, we met in Istanbul several years ago."

"He has the highest regard for you and your knowledge of the Turks," François explained. "That is why he sent me to you." Quickly, he apprised Flachat of the situation. The merchant wrapped his hooklike fingers around his cup and listened carefully, a look of sympathetic concern comfortably resting upon his countenance.

"You wish to gain entry to the harem of the Grand Turk then," he concluded from François' account.

"Yes. The Baron told me that your own father was once inside its walls. Did that occur recently?"

"Oh no, monsieur. My father has been dead for many years. I was but a child here in Paris in those days, though I remember his stories well. He did indeed enter the harem in the summer of seventeen fifty-five."

"Then you can help me," François said eagerly.

"Perhaps, Captain. But you must understand my position. I am a businessman. Every other year I travel to Istanbul with French goods and trade them for the products of the Orient. Much of my profit depends upon the good will of the Porte."

"The Porte?" François asked.

"The Porte is another name for the Ottoman government. I do a good deal of business within the walls of the royal palace and I enjoy a favored position with their officials. Were I to assist you in kidnapping one of the Grand Turk's women, I could jeopardize not only the goodwill I inherited from my father and have nurtured over the years, but my life as well."

"I'm certain there will be risks," François concurred hastily. "But monsieur, you cannot consider leaving a French woman of breeding in such an infidel prison now that you know of her predicament."

The merchant, a master in the art of reading expressions, could see by the candor in François' eyes, the unguarded emotion upon his face, that he was not using this plea for chivalry as a ploy. He honestly believed the cause was irresistible.

"Captain," Flachat began cautiously. "I am in total sympathy with you, but you know nothing of the difficulties you would face were you to try to liberate your lady. The Ottoman palace is a fortress guarded by a corps of Janissaries who kill for sport. Thousands of people live within the palace walls, all of them there solely to do the Sultan's bidding. The women's quarters are forbidden to all men but the Sultan and his eunuchs. My father is the only man I have ever heard of who has broken that interdict. It cost him dearly for the privilege of a few brief glimpses of the ladies at their leisure. For what I would consider a fortune in gold, I might contrive to purchase for you a similar opportunity, but I can imagine no means whatever by which you could take one of the Sultan's women and escape with your life."

"You can get me in?" François pressed, undeterred by the merchant's description of the palace.

"I believe so. But every step of your path will have to be paved with gold. Among the Turks almost anything can be purchased for a price. In that they are not so different from the French, eh?"

"I am prepared to pay anything," François said flatly.

"Your pardon, Captain, but in my business I meet many people, and I know from past experience that military officers and almost all the nobility of the sword suffer from a lack of funds. You may control great land holdings, but I'll wager your family is in debt. Of course, it is none of my affair, but tell me, am I correct?"

"You are, monsieur," François admitted without embarrassment. "But you need have no fear that I will be unable to finance this endeavor. I have financial support from another source, a commercial one."

"Understand then," Flachat continued, "I am speaking in terms of one hundred thousand gold pieces. Perhaps more. Paper money will do you no good. You must have gold or precious stones to do business in the Levant."

"The Baron Von Lazon gave me some idea of how business is conducted among the Turks. I assure you I will have the resources I need. When do we leave for Istanbul?"

"In the spring," Flachat responded.

"The spring! But I had hoped it would be much sooner."

The merchant smiled compassionately. "Perhaps tomorrow?"

"Yes."

"French roads are impassable this time of year," the merchant explained.

"But we could go by sea."

"Yes, if you want to risk the same fate that the Mademoiselle suffered. The seas are no safer now than when the English were terrorizing our shorelines. Barbary pirates attack everything afloat in the Mediterranean. No. We'll go overland in the spring when I have a new shipment ready for the East."

"I cannot wait until the spring, monsieur."

"You must if you are to travel with me."

"Then I will have to find another way."

"Trust me, Captain. If you ever hope to get inside the palace, you must rely on me. Not even Louis' representatives get beyond the Second Gate there. Only I know whom to pay. I can get you in, but you must wait."

Inexplicably, François did trust the little man. "You'll keep me informed of your plans and leave at the the earliest possible time," he insisted.

"Of course. It is in our interests as well as your own to get an early start. But before the agreement is settled, there is the matter of your fare. For that I must speak to Monsieur Dufarge."

"Dufarge," François repeated. "You mean the man at the door?"

"The same," Flachat said with an apologetic smile. "He transports my goods to Istanbul. Can you return here tomorrow morning, Captain?'

"Yes, but I assure you I will pay any price to get to the Levant. My fare will be no obstacle."

"Still, I feel I must discuss it with Dufarge. We'll talk again tomorrow."

The next day when François arrived at the warehouse counting room, one of Paul Flachat's clerks admitted him. He found the merchant seated behind his disheveled desk, and standing beside him was Dufarge, impeccably dressed as before by a skilled though color-blind tailor.

"I don't believe you gentlemen were formally introduced yesterday," Flachat began after he had greeted François.

"It isn't necessary," Dufarge interrupted. "I know him and his kind. Get on with it."

"Georges, you gave me your word you'd be civil," the merchant protested quietly.

"Present our terms and you'll see what he's made of, monsieur." As Dufarge spoke he glared at François like a stalking wolf.

"Very well." Flachat turned to François. "Won't you sit down, Captain."

"Thank you, monsieur." François eased his sword out of the way and took a seat.

"I had hoped this meeting would be more congenial, but Monsieur Dufarge insists on business first. He has agreed to take you to Istanbul with us."

"Though it's not to my liking," the teamster snapped. "Understand that."

"Monsieur," François addressed him formally. "I gather you have taken a strong dislike to me, and your enmity is something I can ill afford. Please tell me how I have offended you."

"By being born, Captain," Dufarge said angrily. "Now let us finish with this."

"Monsieur?" François did not understand.

"He means by being born a nobleman, Captain," the merchant explained. "Georges has rather strong beliefs about the nobility."

François realized the fellow was a revolutionary. "I see," he responded. "I had hoped to be able to make amends for any affront I had committed unintentionally, but what would be required here would prevent me from reaching Istanbul. It appears I will have to suffer Monsieur Dufarge's displeasure as best I can." The teamster grunted, piglike, but said nothing more.

"We have determined your fare," Flachat explained. "Considering the onerous sum of gold you will have to spend in the Levant, you will be happy to know you need not pay us in that precious commodity, nor livre for that matter."

From the predatory look upon Dufarge's face, François knew they did not intend to take him along for companionship alone, but he made no comment.

"Let me preface our request with a description of the perils of the road," Flachat went on. "The fact is that between Paris and the Rhine, we literally have to fight our way. Of course, the tolls are bothersome. Every few leagues some cleric or landowner has his barrier up and we must pay our way past it in spite of the fact that they no longer maintain the thoroughfare the way they used to with the *corvée*. But highwaymen are the real problem. When my father was alive there were robbers—unorganized bands here and there, easily routed with a few musket balls. Now they are disciplined and dangerous, many of them starving deserters from the army. I'm certain you've heard of unscrupulous officers who drive their men to lives of crime by squandering the funds meant for company rations.

"Two years ago outside Strasbourg, we lost fourteen men and a half-dozen wagons in one attack. This spring, Dufarge plans to double the guards, but he fears we won't get through unless you can help us."

"I'll do all I can, Monsieur Flachat," François replied, somewhat bewildered by the confidence they seemed to have in his combat skills. "My sword arm is not the best, but I am a dead shot."

Dufarge laughed sarcastically. Flachat gave him an admonishing look and went on. "You misunderstand, Captain. Your assistance on the road will be a valuable addition to our ranks, I am certain. But Dufarge wants something more. He understands that the army has added several new lightweight field pieces to its arsenal."

"Yes." François confirmed the fact, having become something of an expert in their manufacture.

"You are an artillery officer, Captain. We assume you have access to such weapons." He paused to look at Dufarge. "We want two of them to protect our caravan."

"And the balls they hurl," added the teamster.

François was stunned by their request. The private possession of such weapons was tantamount to treason against the crown. He studied the two men opposite him for a moment. "Two light field-pieces?" he questioned.

They nodded in unison, Flachat apologetically, as if to say he knew he was asking a lot, Dufarge smirking in the belief he had thrown up an obstacle François could not or would not overcome.

"There's nothing else you would take instead of them?"

"I'm sorry, Captain," Flachat said. "But we are quite firm. For the risks you would have me take in the Sultan's palace, you must eliminate some of our risks on the highway."

"He won't do it," Dufarge said contemptuously. "He hasn't the stomach for breaking a law or two, no matter the justification."

François knew he could get the guns with little difficulty, but he wondered if turning them over to a man like Dufarge would sooner or later mean they would fall into the hands of French rebels. For centuries his family had been loyal to the king, supporting him in war and peace, deriving their noble privileges from his munificence. Since his vow to free Aimee, he had a higher loyalty, and he realized that now the time had come to act upon it.

"I'll get the guns for you, Monsieur Flachat," he said with authority. "But there will be no balls."

Dufarge pounced upon that. "The weapons will be useless baggage without ammunition," he protested.

"Balls are used against fortifications, monsieur. As I understand it, you wish to use the weapons against men in the field. For that I recommend cannister bombs."

"Will they keep the blackguards off us?" Dufarge demanded.

"I have no doubt of it. They are a recent innovation similar to one developed in Germany by a fellow named Schrapnel. Each bomb has its own secondary fuse which causes the thing to explode in flight, filling the air with lethal particles of metal and glass. The resulting deadly hail should clear our path to the Rhine."

"I'd just as soon have balls," Dufarge muttered.

"If you press me for them, monsieur," François said bluntly, "I will have to suspect your motives. There are men in Paris who would use such missiles to bring down the gates of Versailles, and I'll not be party to that."

"That day will come soon enough without your help, Captain," the teamster responded angrily.

"The bombs will do wonderfully," Flachat piped in. "Georges, they sound like just what we need." He looked back to François. "Captain, we will keep in touch with you about our plans for departure, but I hold out no hope of any date before late March. Can you have the guns by then?"

"I'll have them."

"I suppose I need not tell you they must be disguised in some way. We'll get them past toll inspectors by bribery, but we cannot travel on the open road with forbidden weapons in tow."

"Of course, monsieur. I will take care of the matter."

"Captain," Dufarge called as François was about to go out the door. "You surprised me. I thought we'd scare you off when we demanded the guns."

"Yes, I could see that," he responded crisply. "Good day to you, monsieur."

Chapter 36

Riding home from Paul Flachat's warehouse, François
determined he had only one course open to him. He
knew he would not find the weapons he needed in
Paris or in the Ile-de-France. The capital was defended only by ancient bronze pieces, some of them
relics of the War of the Spanish Succession, and all of
them ponderously heavy, wretchedly maintained and
unreliable. In fact, they were nothing more than show
pieces. All the modern weapons were placed along the
frontiers in anticipation of foreign attacks, members
of the French command being certain that invaders
could never threaten the gates of Paris.

He would have to return to Nantes. Albert Wilkinson would manufacture the guns for him. He was certain of it. After all, Wilkinson had risked treason in
his own country. Of course, François would not trade
upon the man's friendship for such a thing. He would
pay him well with Marie de La Fontelle's money. He
refused to worry about how he could repay the lady
for the thousands he was going to spend in saving

Aimee. Somehow he would find a way when Aimee was safe.

"The Comte is in bed," a servant told him when he returned home. "He is not feeling well."

François hurried upstairs to find his father under a quilt with a cloth upon his brow. 'So you're back, are you," the old man said feebly as he held out a delicate hand to be kissed.

"What's wrong, Father," François asked, knowing that his father's malaise was due to their disagreement over the betrothal.

"I can keep nothing in my stomach. The doctor will be here soon. I suppose he'll bleed me. My humors are out of balance. And all of it due to you. Your future father-in-law is calling upon us tomorrow to discuss financial matters and the dowry."

"I have no future father-in-law. There will be no dowry," François said firmly.

The Comte fell into a coughing fit that lasted several minutes. "I really must tell him you refuse to marry his daughter?" the old man wheezed as he took the glass of wine his son handed him from the bedside console.

"You must tell him. I won't be here. I leave for Nantes at dawn."

"Then you intend to abandon your father in his most desperate hour, his health gone, his income shrunk to nothing."

Francois had heard all these words before during earlier discussions of his marriage. Each time he gave in to his father's demands, the old man's health returned and he resumed the signing of promissory notes. "You'll manage somehow, Father," he said, trying to fight the sense of guilt the Comte aroused so effectively. "Now, if you will excuse me, I must call upon Madame de La Fontelle."

The old man fell back against his pillows, a look of utter desolation upon his face. "Go then. Forget about me."

"I'll see you this evening, Father."

Early the next morning, François was on the road to Nantes armed with a letter of credit to Marie's bankers there. When he arrived, he went directly to Albert Wilkinson's foundry.

"It's good to see you back, lad," the Englishman said as he slapped him on the shoulder. The two of them stepped into his office. "Does this mean you've come to your senses about going off to the Levant?"

"No, sir," François responded with a smile. "It means I need your help." He described the arrangement he had made with Flachat and Dufarge.

"I can't blame them for wanting the weapons," Wilkinson said thoughtfully. "France is in a sorry state. But do you really wish to become their accomplice in treason?"

"I have no other choice. Paul Flachat can get me into the royal palace in Istanbul. Without him I may never free Aimee."

"Then I'll help you, but you must realize I cannot afford to take such risks for nothing, not even for you. If anything should happen to me, my family must be provided for."

"Of course. I'm prepared to pay whatever you ask."

"What's this? You've come into money all of a sudden?"

"It isn't mine," François told him.

"That's the best kind to spend, my boy. Someone else's."

The two men passed the next several days discussing the design and specifications for the weapons. They also devised a means of transporting them without attracting attention. However, François left most of the actual manufacture to Wilkinson and his crew, for he still had to acquire the cannister bombs.

The Englishman knew of a munitions maker in Orleans who was known to deal illegally for the right price. That city became François' next destination after Wilkinson agreed to deliver the guns to a safe location near Paris when they were completed. He also agreed to bring a crew with him to train Dufarge's men in their maintenance and use.

In Orleans, François discovered that the munitions maker there was eager to peddle his illicit wares. His only legitimate customer was the crown, purchasing on credit of dubious reliability. Money in hand gave François considerable leverage with the manufacturer, who put aside other orders to produce the five hundred cannisters Flachat and Dufarge would need.

Even enjoying such favored treatment, François faced over a month of waiting.

Winter was hard upon the roads when he took the reins of the powder wagon and signaled the drivers he had hired to follow him with the new munitions. Armed guards flanking the shipment and generous bribes to the toll inspectors along the route got him safely to the capital with his cargo. Then, after the three wagons were locked securely in the de Marmont carriage house, François paid his escort and sent them on their way.

"It's done," he said out loud as he pulled down the brim of his tricorner and walked toward his father's townhouse. *And so easily.* Money, he realized, had smoothed his path. The values taught to him as a child did not seem to matter. Loyalty, fealty, honor, devotion to duty were of little significance when compared to the lust for wealth. Even his own father . . . He did not wish to think about his father.

It was mid-January when all the arrangements were complete. Now François had little else to do but wait until spring. To prepare for his journey, he used more of Marie de La Fontelle's funds to hire a good fencing master with whom he drilled almost daily. He spent long hours in the country practicing with horse pistol and musket to perfect his eye. He even took up reading to pass the time, though such a sedentary activity was unnaural to him. Still, no matter how he tried to fill his days, he grew more and more restless as the winter dragged on.

His father, dancing nervously on the edge of bankruptcy, yet still unwilling to abandon the expenses of his Parisian home, held him responsible for his desperate sitution and treated him coolly. Most of his friends viewed his determination to go to Istanbul as romantic folly and chided him for it. Marie de La Fontelle seemed the only person with whom he could talk, and she became his frequent companion.

Since he had delivered her of the belief that her ward was dead, Marie had resumed her gay life. Guests returned to her salon. Dinner parties were more festive than ever, and Marie sparkled with hope. She never allowed herself to think about what might actually be taking place in Istanbul. Instead, she invested her complete confidence in François and swore she would spend her entire fortune if necessary to see that his mission was successful.

Chapter 37

Late one afternoon François returned home from an arduous session with his fencing master and found Albert Wilkinson, still dressed for the road, warming himself by the salon fire.

"By God, the wind has a nasty edge on it," the Englishman complained after the two had greeted each other. "A man my age should be home with his woman on a day like this." He straightened the patch over his eye after he handed his tricorner and greatcoat to a servant.

"Sit down, sir," François said in English, indicating two wing-backed chairs near the fire. "Tell me quickly, are the guns ready?"

"Down to the shine on the last trunnion, my boy," Wilkinson said proudly. "Sweet Jesus, it's cold. Almost as fierce as last winter if you ask me."

"Let me pour you a brandy."

"There's a good fellow." He held his hands to the fire. "But could you make it a bit of rum?"

François called for a bottle. When it was delivered, he poured drinks for both of them. "Where are the guns now?" he asked as he sat down opposite Wilkinson.

"Come, lad, pull your chair close to the fire." The Englishman reached over to help with the heavy piece. "Let those big wings do their job and catch the heat around you. It's damned cold in this house." He took a drink and seemed much satisfied with it. "Now let me tell you what we've fallen into."

"Nothing bad, I hope."

"Nothing bad indeed." He ran a hand through his graying sandy hair and pulled his braid free of his collar. "We've found the perfect site to drill on with the new guns. A site, by God! It's the best bleedin' firing range I've seen this side of the Channel."

"Wonderful!" François responded, eager to see the weapons. "How far is it from here?"

"Twelve leagues, maybe a bit less. It's perfect."

"Perfect? Within Ile-de-France? There must be people about. Won't the firing give us away?"

"I know the law about bringing cannon so near the capital, but we'll never be caught. I tell you the place is perfect. It's on one of the Comte d'Artois' estates, a peasant's field, cleared generations ago but deserted. The forest is so dense around it and the new snow heavy on every bough. We'll go light on the charges and it'll be like shooting pistols into a feather bed."

"You must enjoy a healthy risk," François laughed ironically. "Nothing like committing treason on the king's brother's land. Do you want to sample the accommodations in the Bastille?"

"Not me, my boy, and I think you'll be disappointed if that's your fancy. My men have checked everything. The land hasn't felt a plow in a decade. This Artois is as popular with his tenants as the bloody pox. Every last peasant fled the place years ago to try his luck in the city. Of course, there are still a couple of gamekeepers lurking about to protect the last of the nobility."

"And who might they be?" François asked as he poured another rum for his guest. "Any nobleman will have us arrested."

"That's rich!" Wilkinson slapped François on the leg. "Sometimes I forget you aren't one of us. Of course, I've only lately learned of them myself. You can be certain there's not the like of 'em in England."

"Who are they if you please?" François asked, knowing he was about to hear another diatribe against the French upper classes.

"First, tell me this. Does you father's estate have any land designated a captainry?" He referred to special sections of property where hunting is forbidden to all but members of the nobility.

"Yes. Most of our woodland and a good part of the pasturage is captainry. Of course, no one hunts there any more. The whole family lives in Paris or Versailles now."

"Then the last of the nobility has definitely taken your places."

"I'll wager not," François responded. "We have good gamekeepers. No one hunts without our permission."

"That's precisely my point." Wilkinson slammed his empty rum glass on the console. "No one hunts even though it's their feudal duty, so the animals overrun the place. They are the last of the nobility. The well protected wild beasts!

"You French are nothing like the English who husband their land and oversee their holdings. Feudal privileges and duties were once harnessed to the same cart, as they say. Now, if no one hunts a captainry, the animal population grows out of control, destroys crops and livestock and the helpless peasants who lose their livelihoods to the beasts can do nothing to stop them."

"You paint a bleak picture, monsieur, but I can't believe conditions are as bad as you say."

"You'll see soon enough. Our firing range is within one of Artois' captainries. For us there could be noth-

ing better. We bought the goodwill of his gamekeepers.
They plan to spend the next month drinking at every
tavern in Ile-de-France that's out of earshot from our
encampment. We'll have the forest to ourselves and all
the game we can eat as well.

"Now," he said as he slowly lifted his frame from
the chair. "Did all go well in Orleans? Did you get
the cannisters and powder?"

"For the price it could have been gold, but I have
it locked in the carriage house. There are three wagons. Paul Flachat's man, Dufarge, will provide draft
animals."

"How about crews? Who'll man the guns when your
caravan takes to the road?"

"Dufarge's people are waiting. They're drivers
though, not artillerymen. I'll wager none of them know
a muzzle from a cascabel."

"They'll learn quick enough," the Englishman said
confidently. "But there's no time to lose. How soon
can Dufarge get his men here ready for a month in
the woods?"

"I'll send word to him right now. They can get here
within a few hours. I'm certain."

"Tomorrow's good enough," Wilkinson grunted.
"I'm too old to ride all night in this bloody weather.
Tell him we leave at first light." He got up and walked
nearer the fire. "Now, get somebody to take me to
my room. These tired bones could use some rest. Food
as well," he added hastily. "I haven't eaten since
dawn."

Even within sight of Paris the less traveled highways
of the countryside were in a deplorable state of re-
pair now that the *corvée* had been commuted to a
money tax. Because of the conditions, it was not until
midafternoon on the third day of travel that Albert
Wilkinson directed his small band down an overgrown
cart path through the wood to a large clearing.

Georges Dufarge had accompanied twelve of his
men, driving the powder wagon himself, in order to

be on hand to inspect the guns. On the road he and Wilkinson struck a bond of friendship wrought of common years of hard work and strengthened by copious quantities of rum. But when they saw the smoke of a cooking fire from one of the peasant huts at the far end of the field, the teamster was all business once again.

"We'll warm ourselves and have some food," Wilkinson announced in his anglicized French after he greeted a lookout emerging from the trees. "Then I'll show you the guns."

"The devil with that," Dufarge bellowed from his perch on the wagon. "I'll see the guns now. Food can wait."

"So be it." The Englishman spurred his horse and galloped off to the hut, scattering a large herd of deer and half a hundred hare—the last of the nobility. His men emerged with him a few moments later, all of them wrapped in scarves and heavy coats against the weather. Then Wilkinson signaled the others to join him where his men had drawn up two strange looking wagons.

"A couple of gypsy carts, eh?" Dufarge commented as he looked with disdain upon the outlandish vehicles.

"But deadly gypsies inside, monsieur," piped young Billy Banks, Albert Wilkinson's quick-witted assistant who was in command of the gun crews.

"Good to see you again, Billy," François said as he tousled the boy's blonde hair and clasped him warmly on the shoulder.

"You too, Captain. You're gonna love these guns." Billy had been apprenticed to the Englishman from the time he was eight. A hard worker with a good mind, he had learned almost all his master could teach him about weapons, and in the time he'd been in Nantes he had learned French as well.

"Monsieur Dufarge, may I present Billy Banks," Wilkinson said formally. "He'll be in charge of training your men."

"The boy's young for the job," the teamster observed skeptically.

"But he's equal to it," Wilkinson responded firmly.

"Train them well, young man," Dufarge charged him. "Our lives will depend on their skill."

"You'll see the guns now, monsieur?" Billy asked.

"If you please."

"Roll 'em out!" he called to the wagon drivers. In a second, the weapons rattled down ramps to the ground.

"They're beauties, Billy," François said as he approached them. Bending down, he picked up one of their wooden trails. "Light as a feather." He turned to Wilkinson. "Thank you! Thank you very much."

"It was a joy to do it for you, son."

"Monsieur Dufarge," François said excitedly. "Pick up the other one. See how light!"

He approached the sleek muzzle, its well greased contours glistening in the winter sun. He hefted its trail. "I expected it to weigh three times as much."

"But they're strong," Billy pointed out. "We bored the barrels from solid cast iron. No seams, no weak spots. They're the best weapons of their kind in France."

"And they travel in these boxes?" Dufarge looked again at the wagons, but with more respect.

"It's time we give a demonstration of one of our iron comrades," Wilkinson said, nodding to Billy. "Roll 'em back inside while I describe our new device."

Turning to the Frenchmen, he began, "In your situation, we're all agreed that speed is the key." They assented. "With one of these wagons, at the first sign of trouble, the driver signals the men inside, then maneuvers into position and pulls a lever." He pointed. "See there, just below the brake next to his perch. That releases the wagon back and drops it down to form a ramp. The gun, primed and ready, rolls down. The crew follows and sets off the charge. The first round can be fired in a matter of moments."

"The demonstration," said Dufarge, unimpressed with mere talk.

"Now, Billy."

"Yes, sir. All right boys, roll 'em out and fire!"

Each driver rapped on the wall of his wagon, waited a few seconds, then pulled his lever. The ramps crashed to the ground obediently. The guns clattered out. Purposeful gunners with glowing linstocks rushed after them and set off the match. Then two almost simultaneous explosions shook the clearing as the cannon fired their blank charges.

"We can reload and fire fifteen to eighteen times a minute, monsieur," Billy Banks said with pride, his voice filling the void left by the blasts.

"Excellent!" Dufarge was delighted. He slowly walked around the weapons and looked into the wagons. There he saw well fitted compartments designed to store quantities of bombs, wadding, slow match and linstocks, with all the equipment and supplies needed to maintain the guns. "Can you train my men to do as well?"

"If they've the wit, monsieur. We'll start work today."

"And I'll start back to Paris in the morning," Dufarge said, satisfied with the display. "Now, monsieur." He turned to Wilkinson. "You said something about a meal and a warm fire."

"I did indeed."

"Then lead the way, and I'll drink to your health with your own rum. You're a damned clever fellow for an Englishman."

Chapter 38

The men spent the month of February in the rugged environs of their forest clearing. Every day found them trying to master the intricacies of the iron comrades. At night they huddled round the hearths of the abandoned huts, dining off their illicit catches of game.

By early March Durfage's men had reached a high level of competence, requiring only daily drills on speed to master the rapid-fire technique. By the middle of the month they were spending the last hour of each day firing cannister bombs in order to gauge range and accuracy.

Near dusk one afternoon a signal came from one of the lookouts. Someone was on the main road. To avoid detection, the firing was halted immediately. The crews gathered around their warming fires for a few moments, then rolled the guns back into their wagons and began to put their gear under cover for the night.

Protesting squawks from forest animals announced a more urgent warning from the direction of the cart path. Pistols were at the ready when a coach and six broke into the open. The horses, a magnificent matched team of grays, had been driven unmercifully. Only a single driver manned the box. No footmen rode behind.

Even before the coach had come to a halt, the door flew open. "Assist me!" commanded a female voice from within. Mindful of the weapons arrayed against him, the driver swung down from his perch as soon as he could and helped the lady out. It was Marie de La Fontelle, her clothes rumpled and her bonnet askew.

"Madame!" François called as he hurried to her, stuffing his horse pistol into his belt. "Madame! What has brought you here?"

"Captain!" She held out her arms to him as he approached. "Embrace me or I'll fall."

He did, half carrying her to the gate of one of the munitions wagons where she could sit down. The other men gathered at a respectful distance. Wilkinson pushed through their ranks quickly.

"Madame de La Fontelle, may I present Albert Wilkinson," François said hastily.

"Perhaps the lady would like to step into our cottage," he volunteered. "The night air."

"I'll stay here a moment, monsieur, but if you could dismiss your men." She indicated the gallery of curious faces surrounding her.

"Of course." He ordered them to finish their work.

"How on earth did you find us, madame?" François asked.

"Monsieur Dufarge gave me excellent directions." The lady took several deep breaths, but she was slow to recover from the violence of the long coach ride. "Your father would have come, but he feared he would be followed."

"What do you mean, followed? Who would follow him?"

"But I must tell you."

"Is Father all right?"

"Yes, he's well. It is you he's worried about."

Wilkinson slipped away for a moment and returned with a flagon of rum. "Pardon the informality of the field, madame. But perhaps a sip of this will help you."

The lady reached for it without hesitation, took several swallows and handed it back with a grateful smile. "Thank you, monsieur."

"Now, madame," François pressed. "What's happened?"

"You've been proscribed, François. Someone has purchased a warrant of arrest and affixed your name to it. Gendarmes came to your father's house. They searched every closet. Now men lurk outside watching the streets in case you return."

"A mistake! It must be a mistake," François stammered. "No one would pay the thousands it costs to buy such a warrant. I have a few enemies, but all of them are paupers just as I am."

"Mistake or not," the lady responded vehemently, "you must not return to Paris or you'll be thrown into prison. It's best you leave the country at once, and while you're away, we'll try to have the warrant rescinded."

"Ridiculous!" François shot back. "I'll go to Paris tonight and clear myself. I am no fugitive."

"You'll not go back to Paris, my boy," the Englishman said firmly. "These warrants are nothing to be toyed with. For a price, good King Louis signed his name to the damned thing, and it makes no difference whether you've done a crime or not. Your sentence is fixed—the dungeons."

"But I can't stand by while someone ruins me."

"You must leave it to others to clear you," Wilkinson warned. "If it were me, I'd run. By God, I'd fly to get away from a warrant. Believe me, I've heard about them. You won't go back to Paris, François. I'll throw you in a sack and drag you out of France myself before I'll see you a victim."

In the silence that followed, Marie took François' hand. He sat down beside her on the wagon gate and

stared into the fire. "Monsieur Wilkinson," the lady
said softly, "send someone to my coach. Under the
rear seat is a case. Have it brought to me, please."

The Englishman called one of his men who did as
the lady had requested. "You'll need this for your
journey, captain." She indicated to the man that he
should set the case on the wagon gate. After he had
withdrawn, she explained. "There's gold inside. Letters of credit will do you no good in the Levant." Her
hand instinctively went to her throat. "My jewels are
there too. The stones are free of the settings and the
metal melted down."

François thought of her magnificent diamond necklace. "But, madame," he protested.

"Take it," she said firmly. "Use all of it to get
Aimee back."

Just then Billy Banks called Wilkinson aside. "Madame," the Englishman said when he returned, "your
pardon, but pick up your case and get a good hold
on it." He took her arm and began to lead her to her
coach.

"What's the matter, monsieur?" she demanded.

"There's no time. Get inside." He spoke to the driver
who was huddled under a blanket on the box. "Hold
those horses well, man. There may be trouble."

As Wilkinson hurried back to the warming fire,
François and the others could hear what had alerted
Billy Banks—frightened animals seeking new cover,
the muffled crunch of crumbling snowcrust as it yielded
to human footfalls. Under cover of darkness, men
were moving through the forest.

The clearing was large, but at the eastern edge the
men could make out something white caught in the
flickering light of their fires. François recognized it as
the broad cross of kit straps on the chest of a French
soldier. Another emerged from the darkness. Then
another, until there were ten of them, ten white crosses
against the trees.

"You in the clearing," came a voice from the back.
"Stand where you are or be shot. We are looking for

François de Marmont, fugitive. If you are hiding him, all of you are under arrest."

Wilkinson remained calm. "We're dead men, my friends. The iron comrades so near Paris make this treason, even for a gunsmith."

"My apologies, gentlemen," François said formally. "They must have followed the lady's coach."

"No matter now," Wilkinson replied, "it will be their undoing, not our own." He turned to Billy Banks. "Put men in the wagons and see they move quietly."

"What are you going to do?" François demanded.

"What we have to." Then, turning toward the approaching troops, he called out in an exaggerated English accent, "Who are you there in the dark? Do you mean to rob us?"

"We are the king's men!" came the reply.

"Move behind the fire," Wilkinson whispered to his men as they made their way to their posts. The white crosses had begun to move, shifting up and down with each stride the soldiers took. "Surely you are mistaken," Wilkinson continued, "we have committed no crime." There was no response, just the steady approach of the soldiers. As they drew nearer, their features became visible, moving limbs, weapons, faces. Wilkinson said no more. He waited.

Then suddenly he shouted, "Billy!" and threw himself to the ground. "Down! Everybody!"

Banks pounded on one gun wagon wall and ran toward the other one. Recognizing resistance, the king's men fired a volley just as the first iron comrade rumbled down its ramp. The crew darted after, swinging it into position, the muzzle at point-blank range. The next second there was a breathtaking flash as Billy took a glowing linstock from the trembling hand of his man and raked it across the fuse. Then came the explosion.

As Wilkinson had anticipated, the carriage team was terrified by the blast. They screamed and reared against their harnesses, but Madame de La Fontelle's driver held them well so that the second bomb did not drive them to panic.

"To the woods, men!" Wilkinson commanded. "Make sure they left no one behind to tend their mounts." His English gunners, many of them veterans of American warfare, followed orders without hesitation. They had fought French troops before.

In the darkness no one could see the violence the new cannister bombs had wrought, but next morning's dawn was not so merciful. Night animals were slow to leave the clearing as they gorged themselves on the remains. Pistol shots were needed to drive them off. The job of burying the dead was more horrible than anything François could have imagined. Artillery officers rarely get so close to their victims, even in wartime.

Marie de La Fontelle was shaken by what she saw when she emerged from the hut in the morning. Wilkinson hurried her back inside.

"Madame, there is something you should know before you return to the capital."

"Just a moment, monsieur. I am not one to faint at the least provocation, but I really must sit down." She took a handkerchief from her sleeve and wiped away the chilling perspiration from her upper lip. "I think I may be ill."

"The new bombs are vicious," he said sympathetically. "I've never seen the like of them." He broke a veneer of ice from the water bucket and brought her a cold mug.

She dipped her cloth into it and held it to her temple. "Do you have any rum?"

He fetched it for her, and she drank some down. "Your man is preparing the horses now," he told her. "But I must warn you. We searched the woods as thoroughly as we could. I'm fairly certain none of the soldiers escaped us, but it was dark and there is a chance."

"I'm afraid you'll have to be more direct, monsieur.

Right now I can only pray that some of those poor wretches did survive that massacre."

"Of course. The problem is that they would know you were among us. They followed your coach."

"Mother of God! Then I'm responsible for this." She walked to the window and began to pull back the animal skin that kept out the cold.

"Don't look out there again." Wilkinson grabbed her arm and pulled her away. Tears came to the lady's eyes. She did not fight them, but allowed herself to sob, collapsing against the Englishman's chest. He held her, comforted her as best he could.

Slowly she forced herself under control. "I'm all right now. Thank you, monsieur." She sat down again.

"My name is Albert."

"Yes, thank you, Albert. Forgive my outburst."

"You are a woman of surprising strength, madame."

"Marie," she insisted. "After all this we know each other very well." Her smile was warm and without pretense.

"I am concerned for your safety, Marie. If any of the soldiers manage to return to Paris, they will report what has happened. Your name will be linked to treason and murder. You could be arrested. I don't like any of it."

"Nor do I, but I have friends and money. Even if someone does make accusations, arrangements can be made. No harm will come to me."

"But how can you be certain? These are bad times for France. The king's ministers live in fear of insurrection."

"Greed still governs France," she said coldly. "I'll be alright, but poor François. I doubt I can do anything against a *warrant*."

On the day Marie de La Fontelle returned to Paris, François and Wilkinson decided to break camp. Their clearing no longer seemed a safe refuge.

Farewells were hurried and difficult. Wilkinson and his men headed toward Nantes, while François and his

French gun crews sought a new hiding place until the roads east were passable.

What they found was a comfortable inn south of Paris. There were sheds for the wagons, plenty of room for the men and Marie's gold to pay the innkeeper. When they were settled, one of Dufarge's drivers rode to Paris with word of the new location. Several days later during a heavy spring rain, he returned. Georges Dufarge was with him.

"We won't take the road for another month if this keeps up," he said as he peeled off his soaking leather cape.

François, depressed from the long wait and his other frustrations, knew he was right. "Innkeeper! Brandy!"

The two men sat on a bench near the hearth. "I could see it from the beginning," Dufarge said with a smile.

"What's that?"

"You're a man who sparks strong reactions among your fellows, Captain. Few men who make your acquaintance walk away with indifference. Flachat, for one, sees you as a true knight in the noblest sense, honor bound to rescue your lady. It's clear he intends to go to any lengths to help you, no matter his own peril after you enter the Turk's palace.

"Albert Wilkinson, of course, has risked his head to get you those guns. Then there's me. I don't have to tell you my feelings. They were clearly spoken on the day we met, though I must confess I've warmed some toward you since then. You have risked treason and a warrant of arrest to get those iron comrades and the cannister bombs. That surely is goodwill."

François smiled back at the man. "We will need as much goodwill as can be spared for our journey." And the two men drank silently together from the brandy in front of the hearth.

BOOK FOUR

Chapter 39

Safe in the sanctuary of my harem boudoir, François passed the remainder of the day and most of that night describing what had happened to him in France and on the road to Istanbul. I had slept only a few hours when the music of the palace band heralded the sunrise and its call to prayer. François lay beside me asleep, his bedcover cast to the floor.

Admiring his body, I felt the jagged scar that veered along his side, the flesh still inflamed and distorted where it stretched over his ribs. A pistol ball had grazed him when pirates tried to take Flachat's cargo as the wagons floated on barges down the Danube above Vienna. A large bruise just going to yellow and blue discolored his thigh. It had come in the Balkans where highwaymen on foot blocked a narrow pass through the mountains. Because the iron comrades were slow to respond on the difficult terrain, François charged the brigands on horseback and one of them struck him in the leg with the butt of a discharged musket.

My eyes rested upon his manhood next. Were he
awake, modesty would have forced me to divert my
gaze, but his masculine mechanism fascinated me. In
repose it hardly suggested the massive object that had
filled me with rapture. I thought it a curious appendage
as I scrutinized its various parts. In the world we live
in, to be endowed with such a badge of distinction
identifies the wearer as a member of the superior caste,
the elite. It is prerequisite to any position of power or
authority. Among the Ottomans, its absence marks a
child from birth as a slave, destined to live within a
prison of latticed walls.

In France no one may rule who lacks a male organ.
No one may serve in the military, or even own property. Considering its importance, it is a wonder that
men keep it hidden. One might suppose they would
want to display it proudly with ribbons and ornamen-
tation as one might a staff of office.

Amusing myself with the image of King Louis
marching from Versailles with his manhood rouged
and buttressed, I lay back upon my pillows and enjoyed a cool breeze off the Golden Horn as it brushed
my skin. The scent of roses from the garden filled the
room, and as I reached down for a cover against the
chill, I savored the delightful fragrance. Then, I almost shouted. *Roses! The white rose! Selim waited
for me last night.*

Even knowing I was too late, I hurried downstairs
to the courtyard, but Lydia and Seriphina were at
prayer upon their rugs. A pang of remorse clutched
me as I thought of Selim waiting hour after hour in
the darkness of the passageway. I should have remembered, but now there was nothing I could do.
We had never devised a means for me to contact him.

I returned to my room after fetching Mahmoud.
François still lay asleep. I slipped into bed and nestled against him, Mahmoud at my breast. The child
suckled peacefully, then slumbered. Soon I slept as
well.

Later that morning, François, dressed in the halberdier uniform, accompanied me to the main salon where we reclined on the divan and took some tea with fruit and bread. Adele joined us there. She had been up for several hours, attending to the details of our departure.

"We will leave within the hour," she announced as she came down the steps. "Pour me some tea, will you?" She reached for the bread and tore off a large chunk.

"Here you are." François handed her a glass.

"You don't mind if I eat some of this?" She sat down on a corner of the couch and dipped her bread into a pot of honey.

"Of course not," I replied smiling. "Now tell us what you've planned." As I asked the question, I realized I had not given our departure a moment's thought since Adele had suggested it the day before. Quite irresponsibly, I had trusted all the arrangements to her. "We owe you a great deal for this," I said as I placed my hand on her arm.

"Yes," François agreed. "How will we ever repay you?"

"You could give me your napkin," she replied lightheartedly. "This honey is a mess." Laughing, I spread my cloth over her skirt. "Yours too," she said to François. He handed his to her as well. "Thank you." She took another bite of bread.

"It has worked quite smoothly," she explained. "I sent for my barge last night. It just arrived. Poppy has already dispatched grenadiers to set up guard posts at my villa. I shan't be too popular with my neighbors after this. The troops intend to evict them and use their houses for barracks. Lydia and Seriphina will accompany us. My eunuchs will serve you while you are with me. That way no one else need be included in our secret."

"Won't it seem strange? Only two servants when I take my entire household on a picnic?"

"I have room for no more," Adele explained apologetically. "I am only the wife of a pasha." Then she smiled.

"I will travel with you as a guard?" François asked.

"Yes. You will be the only halberdier aboard our vessel. The others will travel by *caiques,* our light skiffs, and join the grenadiers outside the villa walls. After you conduct us inside, you will simply disappear. There will be enough confusion with so many people about that you will not be missed."

"You will guard our interests while we are away from the palace?" I asked, still reluctant to take such a risk.

"As soon as you are settled, I'll return here. Then, if anything develops, I can get word to you quickly."

"You've thought of everything," I said gratefully.

"I tried to. Poppy spoke to Abdul Hamid about your fear of the plague. He also started rumors that you may not be well. No one should suspect the real reason why you are leaving."

"Thank you, Adele," François said quietly as she wiped her hands and got up to leave. "You've helped me before. I'm deeply in your debt."

"You're what Aimee needs," she said warmly. "I'm glad you're here." Then she slipped away.

A few moments later, as François and I sipped tea and enjoyed the anticipation of what lay ahead, there was a commotion in the vestibule outside the apartment.

"Stand aside, you louts!" It was the bestial bellow of Kiusem Sultan. "Such orders hardly apply to me!"

"Quickly, François. Get to the courtyard. Hide yourself."

He dashed out of sight past the archway just seconds before Kiusem came in. "Naksh, you must speak to your eunuchs. I shall not suffer their rudeness again."

"Your pardon," I replied as I turned toward her, satisfied that my voice did not reveal my agitation. "They are young and often exercise poor judgment."

Kiusem entered awkwardly. Her *entari,* the color of

a stagnant pond, was less ample than her figure required and its fabric gaped around the diamond buttons at her waist. She took the stairs without grace because the jeweled hem of her gown snaked about her ankles and almost caused her to fall. As she approached, I could see the crust of rouge upon her jowls. She looked every bit an aging harlot—vulgar, bloated and loathsome. "You look so well, my dear." She pinched my cheeks rudely. "Rumors abound that you are on the very brink of death." She made the sign against the evil eye.

"I am not well," I told her. "Perhaps you should not stay. There may be contagion."

"Nonsense. I know the plague when I see it." She walked around the divan and sat down on a large cushion, her back to the courtyard arch. "Have you consulted the Italian?" She referred to Dr. Lorenzo, the chief physician.

"No," I replied, uneasy with that oversight. Behind the Sultan, I saw François peek around the archway to see what was happening.

"Just as well," Kiusem grunted. "That infidel fool knows nothing." I hardly heard her remark. The sight of François risking discovery made me nearly panic. "You do look pale," the Sultan commented. "Perhaps your frailty is due to the birth of your son. Such a long labor. It takes its toll." As she spoke, her eyes wandered to the top of the stairs. "Peace be upon you, Adele Hanoum."

"And upon you peace, Sultan." I turned as Adele started to descend.

She smiled at me warmly, then in a light conversational French she said, "François, get back into the courtyard. If she sees you, we are lost."

Impulsively, I looked toward the arch. He was out of sight, but none too soon. Kiusem had cast a glance in that direction as well, though she could not have caught a glimpse of him. For a moment her eyes met mine. I saw my own fear reflected back at me and I wondered if she sensed that something was wrong.

"You should be resting, Naksh," Adele said firmly. "The trip today is going to tax you."

"Of course." Kiusem clumsily hoisted herself to her feet. "I shall leave you at once, but tell me of this trip. You are to leave the palace?" She raised her blackened eyebrows in feigned curiosity, but certainly she knew of our plans.

"Yes," I told her. "We are going to Adele's villa for a few weeks."

"You are taking the child?" She seemed surprised.

"Of course."

"Just as well. It is wise to be away from the city while the plague rages." She wasted no more words once she had confirmed what her spies had told her. "May Allah guide your path."

"And yours, Sultan," I said, feeling a strange uneasiness as I watched her disappear.

Chapter 40

Though our plans were well laid, a sense of foreboding haunted me as our barge cast off. My uneasiness was brought on by Kiusèm's untimely visit. Fortunately, the voyage was uneventful. François stood silent and remote near the bow in the women's enclosure, his face hidden by his uniform. Adele and I hardly spoke, nor did Seriphina or Lydia. Even Mahmoud remained silent.

The Bosporus, slender artery between two seas, pulsed with commercial life. Our vessel shared the thoroughfare with fishing boats, heavy laden barges, graceful *caiques* and rafts of timber being skillfully navigated from the Black Sea to provide winter fuel farther south. This was a rare opportunity for me to see what went on outside the harem walls. In spite of a disquietude that I could not banish from the recesses of my mind, I drank in all I could.

Variety would best describe the scene. Of course, there was the panorama of the city along the shore with its minarets, public buildings and domed mauso-

leums. Most exciting were the people. Because of the
heavy traffic on the waterway and the fact that our
ponderous barge never ventured far from shore, many
other vessels almost brushed our oar blades as we
moved along. I could see their passengers clearly. Most
were men, their women safely locked away, and each
one was dressed in a colorful and unique costume, following the laws laid down four centuries before.

In Istanbul, one knows from a costume how a man
earns his bread, where he has been educated and if
he has made the pilgrimage to Mecca. The faces of
the men told a different story, but one just as revealing about the Ottomans and their empire. Every man
who came into view seemed an outsider to all the
others because of the shade of his skin, the shape of
his nose, the color of his hair or eyes.

In the past months I had often worried that because of his infidel mother, my son might be viewed
as an outsider by his subjects when he took the
throne. Now that seemed to be a foolish concern. I
looked down at the child in my arms. But for the
promise of his beauty, he seemed no different from
the others, for he bore none of them the slightest resemblance.

"There, Aimee." Adele touched my arm, then
pointed toward the Asian shore. "Just beyond that
grove of cypress you'll see my villa." From the barge
we could see only the roof, for the house was surrounded by stark stone walls defended by a line of
grenadiers.

Once inside the gate we saw a miniature seraglio,
well kept gardens, two spectacular fountains adorning
a large rectangular pool and a rambling collection of
pavilions built on the Persian style.

François clutched his halberd with authority as he
led us through the grounds, taking Adele's whispered
French instructions toward the harem, a large pavilion
at the south end of the villa. When we entered, we
found Adele's eunuchs and personal servants waiting
for her in the open courtyard. She greeted them

warmly. Then, speaking in Arabic, she explained who I was and why François and I were there.

"You can be assured," Adele explained to them, "that none of you is in any danger. If Naksh Sultan is ever discovered, I will swear that none of you was ever admitted to the harem while her lover was present."

"Your oath will do us no good, Adele Hanoum," one of her eunuchs pointed out. "We know the ways of Ottoman justice. Our fortunes ride with your own. Your secret is safe."

Expressions of awe for my station, curiosity for the fortunate halberdier and concern for their own lives marked their faces as they left our presence. Two women took charge of Lydia, Seriphina and Mahmoud.

"They won't be grateful for the risks we've forced upon them," I observed.

"No, but they're loyal," Adele responded with certainty.

"And they'll be wealthier for it. I'll see to that."

"Is it safe to unmask yet?" François asked in a whisper.

"Yes," Adele replied. She walked toward the steps at the north end of the stone courtyard while François removed his helmet and snapped down his collar. "Come, your suite is up here." She indicated a balcony above the central fountain.

Adele led us through double doors off the balcony into a lovely salon decorated in yellows and greens, with fine Algerian rugs and a canopied divan upon a dais in front of an arched window overlooking the water. "Your bedroom is through there." She pointed toward a closed door. "And the bath is downstairs."

"This is lovely," I said, noticing the wistfulness with which she looked about the salon. "You must be very happy here."

"Yes, we are," she replied in a way that let me know she was glad I understood how she felt. "Now

I'll leave you two to enjoy it together. Tomorrow I'll return to the seraglio."

"Kiusem will be surprised to see you back so soon."

"I think not. She couldn't really believe you'd allow your affairs to go unattended. While you're here, I'll be your eyes and ears at the palace."

"There will be some concern for me in the Cage," I told her, not wanting to mention Selim in front of François. "I never left word I was leaving."

"I'm certain Poppy will take care of that, but he doesn't know everything."

"No."

"Are you worried?"

"Yes," I replied, "a bit."

"Well stop. There's nothing more you can do now. Just enjoy what time you have."

"You'll let me know if there is any trouble or if Poppy finds out what Kiusem is planning."

"At once. Now enough of this. I'll see you again before I leave." Smiling happily she pulled the doors to the salon closed, and François and I were alone.

In the days that followed, Mahmoud was the only person to share our haven. We rarely left our suite unless it was to bathe. The servants came and went. We took no note of them. Our world was that salon and its bedchamber. We lay together by the hour on the divan, enjoying the breezes of the Bosporus while we explored each other, body and soul, until each of us felt we knew the other as a part of ourselves.

For a while the subject of the future was forbidden by mutual unspoken consent. François must have feared to ask me what I intended to do, believing I would not leave the Levant with him. I was afraid to ask myself the same question. My son's destiny weighed heavily upon me.

Perhaps that is why our lovemaking seemed so desperate and compelling. The pleasure of it promised no security. I could never offer a vow of forever.

Then one night about a week after we had arrived

at the villa, as we lay together sipping tea and watching the stars, François asked me softly, "Darling, what if there is a child?"

"A child?" I asked, thinking immediately of Mahmoud.

"Our child," he went on.

I knew it was impossible, for I had not yet recovered my fertility, but that was not what François wanted to hear. "Would it make you happy, darling?" I asked.

"Of course. But you know that."

"Yes. I just don't want to talk about it now. We've had such a wonderful day. Can't we simply enjoy it?"

"I thought so," he said earnestly, "but I was wrong." He set his tea glass on the floor and stood up. "If you are going to leave here with me, you'll have to tell me so. Otherwise, I'll go alone, and very soon. Every day that passes, you become more a part of me. I can no longer imagine my life without you, but I know you don't have the same feeling for me. If you did, you would have agreed to leave. I've waited as long as I can, but I'll go mad if we don't come to a decision one way or the other. I can think of nothing else. Even when I am making love to you, at the very moment when my passion explodes, I realize you may want to remain here with the Turk. I can't live with that any longer."

He stood before the window, looking into the night, waiting for me to rush to him. I could not. "You must know I love you, François. But much more than that is involved."

"I'll be a father to Mahmoud," he said simply. "Once we get back to France and I deal with that warrant, the two of us can give him a decent life."

"But here he could be a king. Do we have the right to take that from him?"

"Does he have the right to take you from me?"

"Come, darling," I begged him. "Come and sit with me." His anger and pain were more than I could bear and I wanted to be close to him.

"No. Not now. I need to think." He hesitated and looked outside at the grounds below. "I'm going for a walk in the garden. Perhaps I've been inside too long."

"I'll go with you."

"No. I don't want you to. I have to think." He turned and walked out of the salon.

Alone, I forced myself to examine my choices. Until that moment, I had been satisfied to live moment by moment rather than face the pain of giving up someone I loved. It was not until I opened my eyes to it that I admitted I could not choose. I could not live without François, but Mahmoud was a part of me too. I refused to leave him behind. Acknowledging that, my decision was made. I would escape the palace. But how? When?

Echoing through the recesses of my mind were all the arguments for Mahmoud's future—his destiny, the needs of the dynasty, Ottoman hopes for reform. I heard them calling out to me as if from a great distance, but I did not acknowledge them. Instead, I said aloud: "Selim is strong enough. He will have sons. They can reform the empire. My son is half French. He goes with me."

It was as if a weight had been lifted from my chest. I could breathe freely and think about François without pain. But a hint of guilt still tugged at me. I fought it back and refused to focus on its cause. I would run away with François and take Mahmoud with me. That was the only decision I could make.

It was more than an hour before he returned. When I heard his footfalls, I hurried to the door to meet him.

"Darling," he said softly.

"Are you all right?" I asked as I held him close.

"Please forgive me, Aimee," he almost sobbed. "I should never have said what I did. Nothing should matter to me except that we are together now, and we will be tomorrow." He kissed me hungrily and swept me up into his arms.

I wanted to tell him what I had decided, but those words would not come. "I love you, François."

"Say nothing more, darling." He trembled as he held me and I realized he was afraid I would cast him out. I had failed to let him know how desperately I needed him.

"I was a fool to try and force you to leave," he went on. "When I reached the garden I realized I was gambling with what may be our only happiness. If you send me away, I'll be lost. You don't have to decide tonight. We have plenty of time."

"I love you," I whispered again, overwhelmed with the strength of my emotions. I wanted to soothe him, reassure him. Instead I gave in to my body's demand. As he lay me down upon the divan, I grabbed his blouse and pulled him to me. Our mouths met. I ached to have him, to be filled with him, to devour him. Never had I felt so desperate.

For him, it was the same. He ripped away my gown and crushed himself against me. He was all violence and rage as he entered. I was terrified yet delirious with desire. It seemed that no matter how deep and powerful were his thrusts, I could never be satisfied. There was pain, yet I kept on. Then suddenly, I was transfixed. My emotions carried me off. At that moment, François cried out as he reached his climax. We both wept, perhaps from joy, perhaps from sorrow. I did not know which.

Chapter 41

Late that night François lay asleep in my arms when Seriphina entered our salon bringing Mahmoud for his last feeding. Gently, I eased away and slipped off the divan. Then I pulled on my gown and took my son into the bedroom where we made ourselves comfortable upon the pile of thin mattresses that made up our Turkish bed.

When Mahmoud had nestled against me, Seriphina took her leave, and I relaxed with the simple pleasure of providing him the nourishment he needed. Time passed, yet I did not sense it. For a while I thought of nothing.

Then in the moon glow I could see that he had fallen asleep, though his lips still clung to me. I was just about to carry him back to Seriphina when my eye caught a silver splash on the water near the shore. A jumping fish, I thought, but then I saw it again, and I recognized it as a human form swimming through the sea. As I got to my feet, I could hear the voices of grenadiers along the beach calling out a warning.

By the time Mahmoud was back in his cradle, eunuchs were hurrying through the courtyard of the harem carrying blankets and towels. "It's Adele Hanoum," one of them called to me. "There has been an accident."

I rushed after them into the garden to find Adele in soaking pantaloons and a chemise, her hair streaming salt water, *surma* running in jagged lines down her face.

"Start the *hammam* fires," one of the eunuchs ordered his subordinates. "Get hot tea and send for the physician."

"I do not need a doctor," Adele protested. "Just get me the tea." She pulled a blanket round her shoulders and hurried toward me. "Aimee! I must speak to you. Come inside."

I followed her to the salon of her suite. She took tea from her servants and sent them away. When we were alone she peeled off her wet clothes and put on a *caftan*. "The eunuchs told you it was an accident," she began. "But it wasn't."

"What happened?"

"We were rammed by another boat. There were Janissaries on board. They think I was drowned. I heard them call to each other and mention my name."

"Then they wanted to kill you."

"I'm certain of it." She sat down on the divan and took a drink of tea. "Somehow they knew I was coming here to warn you," she said shaking her head. "And I was so careful."

"Warn me? Is there trouble at the sergalio?"

"Terrible trouble." Her face was grave. "Poppy found out only two days ago."

"Why didn't you send for me then?"

"We did. Two messengers."

"I saw no one."

"I know. Their bodies were found by fishermen. Poppy came to me this afternoon when they were discovered. I decided to come to you myself as soon as it was dark."

"Tell me what's happened."

"It's Selim." She paused. "Where is François now?"

"Asleep upstairs."

"Good. He doesn't have to know this. Selim must have lost his mind when you left. The Grand Vizier went to him with an insane scheme to assassinate Abdul Hamid, and he agreed to it."

"How do you know this?"

"Selim couldn't keep the plan to himself. He told his mother."

"And she told Poppy?"

"Told him! She ran to him in a panic. Mihrishah may not always be trustworthy, but she has an instinct for survival. She knows the vizier is in Suleiman's purse now. As soon as Abdul Hamid is dead, Selim will claim the throne. Then the Grand Vizier will denounce him for regicide. Mustapha will rally support throughout the empire to avenge his father's death. The Janissaries will have the people on their side when they murder Selim and declare Mustapha Grand Turk."

I was astonished. "Surely Selim can see what lies ahead as well as his mother can."

"He can now. Poppy and Mihrishah both explained it to him. He's beside himself with fear, but it's too late to call a halt. He has written some damning letters. The Grand Vizier has them. And money has been paid."

"How could he be so stupid?"

"Because of you, Aimee. He told Poppy everything. All about the passageway, your meetings. The night he waited for you and you didn't come, he thought you were dead or that you had forsaken him. Then he learned you had left the palace. All he could think of was getting you back, and the only way he could do that was to eliminate Abdul Hamid and become your master himself."

I shook my head slowly, sick with guilt at the

disastrous turn of events. "I'm the stupid one, not Selim."

"You should have recognized his weakness," Adele said soberly.

"And now there's nothing to do but go back and try to set things right."

"What about François?"

"He'll come with us to the palace. Poppy will get him safely away after that."

"You could leave Istanbul tonight," Adele said cautiously. "It may be too late to do anything for Abdul Hamid or Selim. Suleiman seems to hold all the cards."

I hesitated. Perhaps this was the time to flee. "No, not yet. As long as Abdul Hamid is alive, my son is safe. Order your men to prepare a *caique*. We'll leave for the palace immediately."

Chapter 42

I woke François and gave him a brief explanation.
I told him that Adele had been attacked and we had
to return to the palace at once. He asked no questions, but I could see on his face that he feared what
our leaving the villa could mean.

Once we were aboard Adele's *caique*, he planted
himself near the bow, his halberd ready, but not
solely as a disguise, for we feared more Janissaries
might wait off shore to intercept us.

"I still don't understand how they knew I was
leaving," Adele said, troubled that she had been
found out.

"Who else knew your plan?" I asked wondering if
a spy had penetrated our inner circle.

"No one. Only Poppy. He arranged for me to leave
from his apartment. I went through the eunuchs'
quarters and out the Shawl Gate with the proper
documents and the costume of a scullery. He had
hired a *caique*, one of the larger skiffs that usually

ferry passengers to Scutari. I didn't order the oarsmen
to turn south until we were on the Asian side."

"But still you were attacked," I repeated. "Someone else must have known about it. Whom did you
tell?"

"No one," she insisted. "Poppy took care of all the
details himself and gave me my instructions personally. He came to our apartment this afternoon. None of
the servants were about. Of course, just after he arrived Kiusem came in. She's clung to me like a
poultice since I returned to the palace, always acting
very clever and aware, but this time I know she just
wanted to find out the reason for Poppy's visit. We
had coffee and entertained her for some time. Poppy
told me what I needed to know in French. It was only
a couple of sentences. Kiusem didn't even notice."

"What did he say exactly?"

"He said, 'You'll leave after dark. Come to my
apartment and I'll get you out through the eunuchs'
quarters.' "

"There's no clue in that for an Ottoman ear. He
didn't mention a gate or a name?"

"No. Nothing. Someone would have to know
French to have understood."

"Then he must have had reason to tell someone
else who took the information to Suleiman."

"He told no one. Two messengers were dead. We
knew there was no one we could trust."

"The boatman?"

"He knew nothing until we were on the Asian
side."

Panic was beginning to build within me as I
grasped for every possible source of the betrayal, resisting what was becoming obvious. But the truth was
inescapable. I thought of the morning François and
I left the seraglio. Kiusem burst in on us and François
should have been hiding. But when Adele called to
him to get out of sight, Kiusem looked away from the
stairs and toward the courtyard. When her eyes met
mine, I thought she saw my fear, but it was she who

was uneasy because she believed she had been caught in a lie. "Adele," I said as calmly as I could. "Kiusem understands French."

Adele's head shifted quickly under her *feridjie.* "That isn't possible," she said flatly.

"Why not? We've been here in Istanbul long enough to learn the language, three of them as a matter of fact. Why couldn't she apply herself to learn just one?"

"But how? Who could teach her?"

"I don't know, but there seems no other explanation."

Both of us sat quietly for a few moments as we contemplated this new dimension of Kiusem's knowledge. "She just doesn't seem bright enough to have done it," Adele said, disbelieving.

"That's the most frightening part," I pointed out. "She must not be as she appears. I always assumed we could outsmart her, but it may well be that that is exactly what she wanted us to think. She's certainly kept us off our guard."

"I refuse to believe she could be as diabolical as that."

"We know this much," I said. "She knows I'm here with François. She was sitting with us at the harem sale when we first contacted him, and she knows he was in our apartment the day we left for your villa."

"And yet she didn't denounce you as an adulteress."

"No, she let me leave the palace and give her all the freedom she needed to hatch the scheme that may destroy us."

"What can we do?"

"As soon as we return to the palace, I'll go to Mihrishah and try to contact Selim. Then I'll talk to Poppy. He may know by now when the assassins will move against Abdul Hamid. We must keep the Sultan alive. If he dies, we'll never escape. Kiusem will not rest until Mahmoud is safe in the Cage or dead."

Chapter 43

The sun had risen by the time we caught sight of the seraglio. Adele pulled a red scarf from under her *feridjie* and handed it to an oarsman with instructions to tie it to the high rising bow of the boat. The fellow did as he was told, easing past François who continued to scan the waters. By the time we landed, Poppy's lookout had notified him of our signal and he was at the dock to greet us.

"Sultan?" he asked cautiously as our *caique* brushed the landing. He could not recognize me for my outer garment.

"Yes, Poppy."

"Praise Allah you are safe, Golden One," he cried as he helped me ashore. "And the prince?"

"Seriphina has him," I responded, indicating another black-clad figure still seated behind me with a bundle in her arms. He helped her ashore quickly and into a waiting litter. Lydia climbed in as well and they were carried to the palace under guard.

"What have you learned about the assassins?" I

asked in French, hoping our escort could not understand.

"I'll tell you everything on the way up the hill," he said hastily. "Come quickly. Adele?"

"Here," she called to him as she stepped off the boat.

"Walk with us, please." Poppy turned toward the palace.

"Wait," I protested. "What about François?"

"He will be taken care of," Poppy said officiously. I turned back quickly but the *caique* had already drifted away from shore with four lieutenants accompanying François away from the seraglio.

"You'll see him again when this is over," Poppy said, gently cutting off my protest. "But now we can't risk Kiusem's finding out about him."

I watched longingly as the oarsmen began turning the craft north toward Pera, François still standing staunchly at the bow. I strained to see his face, but it was hidden by his uniform. "She already knows," I said quietly, and then went on to explain what I had deduced about Kiusem. "It doesn't matter though," I assured him. "She has no intention of denouncing me. Her plan is much more ambitious. Unless we stop her, her son will be on the throne, and then my indiscretions will matter for nothing. Now, tell me. What have you learned?"

"We know they plan to assassinate Abdul Hamid on the Sabbath at the banquet after he attends the mosque for Friday prayers." He mopped his forehead and pendulous jowls with a handkerchief.

"Do you mean tomorrow?" Adele asked.

"Yes. We have a spy in the Janissary kitchen of the Third Door. He has been able to overhear some of the Kettlemen's meetings. Without him we would know nothing."

"Has Abdul Hamid decided to cancel the banquet?" I asked.

"That would court disaster. He does not know the details of the plot yet, but he would never cancel the banquet. His subjects already believe he is in ill health. He cannot afford to be thought too weak to carry on his duties or there will be unrest in the city."

"Then he will expose himself to assassins?" Adele questioned.

"Ceremony is very important among the Ottomans, Adele Hanoum. He will have no choice. But he will be well protected."

"I hope so," she said earnestly. "All of our lives depend upon it."

"Let me explain," Poppy went on as we left the forest path and passed through the Shawl Gate. "You have never seen one of these banquets. Tomorrow two hundred guests will sit down with the Grand Turk. Fifty courses will be served by pages who stand in a long line that runs from the kitchens and all along the tables right up to the Sultan himself. Servants outnumber diners three to one, and every servant tomorrow will be one of Hassan Pasha's men."

We stepped inside the harem and I pulled the gauze away from my face. "It's no wonder Suleiman Agha tried to kill Hassan in the Divan that day," I said, taking comfort in the knowledge that the Grand Admiral was in charge of the Sultan's protection. "Without him we would be lost."

"He has a corps of handpicked men, all of them completely loyal. For the past four years they have been the troops who lined the Sultan's path to Friday prayer, taking the place of the Janissaries whom Abdul Hamid no longer trusts. For tomorrow only, the Janissaries will resume their old duties. We will ask Abdul Hamid to order their reinstatement, feigning an act of reconciliation with Suleiman, but actually releasing Hassan Pasha's men to be ready as bodyguards during the banquet.

"We have reason to believe the attack will come early. When platters of food are brought to the diners, they are covered with black silk cloths lined with white. On the empty dishes, the cloths are reversed. Our man overheard the conspirators suggest that the

assassins might move when the first black silk reaches
Abdul Hamid's hands."

"Will there be one assassin or one hundred?" I
asked, unconvinced of the Grand Turk's safety.

"We may be close to finding out," Poppy responded
confidently. "Several Mevlevi dervishes attended the
Kettlemen's last meeting."

"Dervishes?" I asked, careful to be quiet as we
passed under one of the balconies of Kiusem's apartment.

"They are religious groups. The Mevlevi are one
of the most aristocratic of them, sometimes known as
whirling dervishes because they spin round and round
to achieve a state of ecstasy."

"I should think they would achieve little more
than giddiness from such a pastime," Adele observed.

"Not at all. They practice from childhood to keep
their wits through the trances by holding a nail in the
ground between two toes and turning on that pivot.
But as I said, several Mevlevi were seen at the Kettlemen's last gathering."

"Does your man know why they were there?"

"No, but we should know soon. Gardeners who are
in my purse managed to capture one of them. We
dared not keep him in the palace dungeons. The
Janissaries might discover we had him and change
their plans. They know we'll make him tell us his part
in the plot. He's in the Seven Towers now." The Castle of the Seven Towers once housed the bulk of
the Ottoman treasury, but was now used solely as a
prison, secure and terrible as the Château d'If, and
known to be a place of unspeakable tortures.

"If the assassins intend to strike tomorrow, we have
very little time," I said, giving a handful of gold sequins to each of the guards at the door of the suite.

"It will be time enough," Poppy said confidently.

"Then there is no danger your men will be merciful
because the fellow is devout?" Just after I spoke, I
noticed Adele had pulled away her gauze mask to

reveal the wonder and disgust on her face at my callous attitude.

She too had heard stories of suffering at the Seven Towers. I avoided her eyes, refusing to allow her conscience to become my own.

"I know the men there well," the eunuch responded. "No one passing through those portals should hope to find mercy within."

"You'll let us know the moment you learn anything," I instructed him.

"Of course."

"Then tell me of Selim. What is his state of mind?"

Poppy did not answer immediately, for we walked into the main salon where my servants were waiting to welcome me home. I distributed among them what coins I had, then sent them away.

Adele walked to the courtyard to make certain no one had remained behind. When she nodded that we were alone, Poppy began, but he seemed cautious and guarded. I wondered as he spoke if he were willing to tell me everything he knew now that he had discovered the secret I had kept from him.

"The Prince is fearful," he explained. "He realizes he has blundered. Now he understands that his part in the conspiracy to assassinate Abdul Hamid will allow Mustapha to lead the Janissaries against him as soon as he takes the throne.

"You should know," he went on, "that he told me of his love for you. Of course, I suspected it. Whenever I saw him he spoke little else but your praises." Poppy's smile was enigmatic. "I had no idea things had gone so far though. My eyes and ears never told me of your rendezvous." He looked toward Adele. "You and your friend keep a secret well. Too bad the man who shared it with you does not have your strength."

"I should have recognized his weakness," I admitted.

"Yes," Poppy responded. "But you cannot know the effects of the Cage upon a man. I have seen it more than once—the weight of idle hours, the imagined dangers. The Cage is a breeding place for fear. Selim is convinced that you are the great passion of his life. When you were out of reach, he lost his reason and agreed to the assassination as the only way he could bring you back."

"Does he know yet that I have returned to the seraglio?"

"Yes. He's waiting for you now at his mother's apartment."

"Mihrishah will be delighted to see you," Adele said sarcastically.

"Yes," I agreed. "Selim might have chosen a better meeting place."

"Selim makes few choices without his mother these days. She chose the location. As for Mihrishah, it is on your head that she places the blame for everything that has happened, even though her son should bear the responsibility. But it is difficult for a mother to see the faults of her child. Be patient with her if you can." Poppy's affection for the woman softened his eyes as he spoke.

Then he became more stern. "Adele Hanoum, if you remain here to supervise the guards and the servants, we will go to Selim. Remember, there may be a plot against Mahmoud now to insure that Mustapha is the only remaining heir. Be wary of anything unusual."

"I'll admit no one until you return," she responded uneasily.

After Adele helped me off with my street gown, I went out to the Golden Road and walked the short distance to Mihrishah Sultan's apartment. The tension among her servants as we entered told me that the Prince was inside. When I walked into the salon, Selim, nervous and tired, broke into a broad smile and began to get up to greet me, but his mother held his hand tightly and kept him next to her on the divan. "Aimee, you are well," he sighed with relief.

Mihrishah said nothing and made no offer of welcome. She simply clung to her son and glared.

Behind me I could hear Poppy easing himself into his chair. I knelt down on a cushion. "Things have not gone well while I've been away," I said.

"I have told Naksh about the Grand Vizier's plan to assassinate Abdul Hamid and your part in it," Poppy explained.

"I was a fool," Selim confessed almost in tears. "Now Mother and I agree there is nothing else for me to do but leave Istanbul until all this is passed."

"You must not leave the palace, my Prince," Poppy said flatly. "If you go outside these walls, you will be killed at once."

"And if I stay?" Selim asked.

"Then Poppy's men will have a better chance to protect you," I told him. "But there will be no attempt on your life unless Abdul Hamid is assassinated. That is what we must prevent. All of us are safe as long as Abdul Hamid remains Grand Turk."

"She will still enjoy the privileges of a favorite," Mihrishah said caustically. "That is what is important to her."

"My influence with Abdul Hamid has done you no harm," I pointed out.

"Your influence with my son has done him no good," she shot back angrily.

"What is done cannot be undone, Sultan," I said solemnly. "You may choose to hate me, and so be it, but just now an argument will serve nothing. Selim must remain here and wait for tomorrow. If he leaves the palace, he will be killed."

Mihrishah began to protest but Poppy prevented it. "The Cage can be a haven as well as a prison, Sultan. Selim will be safer there than anywhere else. You must believe me."

Mihrishah studied the eunuch's face for a long time, then her anger melted into helplessness. "Very well. He will remain in the Cage."

"It is the wisest course," he said, comforting her,

his voice filled with the affection that comes from years of intimacy and shared secrets.

Suddenly Selim jerked his hand free of his mother's and jumped to his feet. "I'm glad all of you have decided what I am to do. But answer me this. What if Abdul Hamid discovers my part in this? What will he do to me, Aimee? What will he do?"

"I don't know." But then a plan came to me. "Perhaps we can turn your complicity into an asset." I looked to Poppy. "You say Abdul Hamid does not yet know the details of the plot?"

"I plan to go to him with the news as soon as I leave here."

"Then let Selim go in your place. He can tell the Grand Turk that he went along with the dervishes only to uncover them."

"I shall denounce the Grand Vizier," Selim cried out vengefully.

"But what of the letters Selim signed?" Mihrishah asked. "They commissioned the assassination."

"He can deny them as forgeries or claim they were part of the deception," Poppy suggested. "Yes, the plan will work."

"If Abdul Hamid lives it will work," Mihrishah said skeptically. "But what if he dies?"

She used the question to strip Selim of what courage he had mustered. He collapsed pitifully upon her shoulder. "What if Mustapha comes for me?" he whimpered. His mother comforted him and rocked him in her arms as if he were a tormented child. "If Mustapha comes," he sobbed, "I will be trapped in the Cage like a sacrificial lamb. What shall I do then?" He looked desperately to Mihrishah, but she looked up at me, challenging me to find an answer where none existed.

"I do not know," I confessed.

"The answer is simple," Poppy said calmly, in spite of the Prince's hysteria. "If it be the will of Allah, Mustapha will rule. Then you will die tomorrow, and with you, the rest of us."

Chapter 44

The Musselman belief, nurtured from childhood, that all things happen as they have been preordained gave the Kislar Agha a fatalist's courage and a clear head during our time of crisis. I did not share it. Though I had come to doubt my own Catholic belief in freedom of will, I could not embrace the opposite point of view. And so through the long night before the Islamic Sabbath I lay awake wondering if there was anything I could do to insure Abdul Hamid's safety.

Neither did I take comfort in the revelation Poppy brought me just before the sunset call to prayer that the dervish in the Seven Towers had taken his own life before the inquisitors could learn anything from him.

"It seems a careless oversight not to notice a dagger in the hem of a robe," Adele pointed out as she sat opposite me on the divan in our salon the next morning while we sipped tea. "Do you think Poppy told us the truth?"

"I believe the dervish is dead," I responded. "But

suicide? More likely Suleiman Agha's men learned he had been captured and had him killed before he could talk. But with no proof, one can only speculate. Poppy may choose to keep such knowledge to himself. There's Selim to consider after all. He's near hysteria now. Anything unpredicted might tip him over the edge."

"Poppy seems so certain of everything," Adele observed. "Is that solely for Selim's benefit, or is he so confident we will succeed?"

"He believes it is out of his hands. Allah will determine who the Grand Turk will be when all this is over. Poppy is simply playing his role as it was written. Of course, he puts a lot of faith in his spies. Perhaps too much." I looked through the archway into the courtyard. Kiusem was on my mind—Kiusem and her deceptions. "Why is it that with so little difficulty we know everything about this assassination?"

Adele's eyes were questioning. She did not understand what I was saying. "Poppy has his people. He must spend a fortune to keep up his connections with the First Court and the bureaucracy. That sort of thing eventually bears fruit, doesn't it?"

"That's the easy answer, and I hope you're right, but discovering Kiusem's cunning was a bolt of lightning to me, and there has been no thunderclap. Something is wrong."

As we spoke, Aishe came in, her slippered feet making no sound on the rugs. "Your pardon, Sultan." Both Adele and I turned abruptly, startled by her presence. "Kiusem Sultan is waiting to see you."

"She always comes for a reason," Adele said as she set down her tea glass. "I've learned that much from all this."

"One moment," I said to Aishe. "Leave us quickly, but wait for my call before you admit her." When she was gone, I turned to Adele. "Go out through the courtyard passage. Follow it to the left until you reach the end. That is the door at the laundress's chamber. Then find Poppy and bring him here." Adele slipped silently away.

I called to Aishe, then stood up and walked toward the door as Kiusem entered. "It's a beautiful morning, Kiusem," I said in French.

"Yes it is," came the response in a strangely accented version of the same language. Kiusem smiled knowingly. "So you have caught on to my little game," she continued in her usual mixture of Arabic and Turkish.

"I do not like games."

"But you play them, do you not? Of course your skills are unpolished, though you have courage. A *man* in the Sultan's harem." She shook her finger in my face, then sat down on the divan. "Such risks for a moment's pleasure."

Somehow Kiusem looked different that morning. The dullness of her eyes had vanished and her complexion seemed much healthier. Her clothes were not overtaxed to cover her frame. They fit well and were of an ice blue color that flattered her skin tone. "Where did you learn to speak French?" I asked as I scrutinized her appearance.

"Here in the harem," she said proudly. "The Dragoman has a wife more gifted in languages than he. She visits me often. Of course, her husband knows nothing of it. He is too close to the Kislar Agha to be trusted, but she feels quite comfortable in my purse, and she tells me what she learns from him at home. That's how Safiye knew of the French merchants before you did, for example.

"I worked very hard to learn French," she went on. "You see, Naksh, you are not the only one who can master another tongue, though you think yourself brighter than the rest of us."

"You encouraged me to believe that," I responded, realizing that Kiusem had played the role of a fool for my benefit.

Kiusem laughed heartily. "Yes. At last you can see it." She waved a jeweled hand toward a cushion at her feet. "Sit down, Naksh. Now that the charade is over, it can do no harm to tell you all." I did as she suggested.

"I have lived in this harem most of my life," she began, smiling with satisfaction in the knowledge that she had deceived me totally. "And I have learned many lessons, but the most valuable is that no one is an ally. Those who seek alliances beg to be deceived.

"It was clear from the preparations the Kislar Agha made for your arrival that he intended to recruit you to Mihrishah's cause. Perhaps she had something to offer you. I doubt it. Certainly, I expected no friendship from a potential rival for influence with the Grand Turk, and so I decided to reduce the danger of your interfering with my plans by leading you to believe I was unworthy of your concern. In that I found you very cooperative. Tell me, do all Frenchwomen have such high opinions of themselves as you do?"

"I hope all Frenchwomen are not so easily duped," I replied. She smiled, savoring her victory after a year which must have cost her dearly in self-esteem. It could have been no pleasant task to allow a younger woman to usurp her place with the Sultan while she masqueraded as an aging harlot, devoid of charms. "I do confess I never expected you to learn French. Why did you go to the trouble? Certainly not to be able to talk to me. I was struggling to learn your language."

"Your arrogance was encouragement enough," she responded. "You and your women spoke it like a secret code, assuming ignorance in those around you. When I saw your heavy eyes and faded complexion last autumn, I realized you were with child and a genuine threat to my son. Here in the harem it is difficult to keep secrets, but you had an advantage with your unknown language. I decided to take away that advantage, and I must say it was a very wise move.

"You can thank me for your holiday with the Frenchman, you know. My people followed Adele the night of the harem sale. We knew she led him to the Third Gate for your rendezvous. The Janissaries would have caught him the next morning had I not sent word to the Chief Cook to keep his patrols out of the woods."

"Of course," I said, genuinely amazed. "You were sitting next to us at the sale. You must have heard us talking. You knew about François from the beginning."

"Now you see. Your holiday to Adele's villa suited my purposes, or I would have exposed you. But what better way to keep an enemy off guard than to send her away with a lover. You were a danger to me. Your influence with Prince Selim could have ruined my plans."

"You know about Selim?" I exclaimed, distressed.

"I have eyes in Mihrishah's house. I know you met him there when he crept in from his secret tunnel. I also know Mihrishah took to her bed after you left. It is no great leap of the mind to imagine from such a reaction that the Prince found you attractive. You must have had other meetings. No doubt he confided in you his plans for reform of the government. It pleases me to imagine Mihrishah as you sat in her salon seducing her son away from her day after day."

The panic in my throat subsided as I realized she did not know the tunnel also led to my suite.

"Certainly," she continued, "he would have let you know that he planned to take Abdul Hamid's life had you been here. And you would have dissuaded him. No doubt he was as eager to possess you as to rule the Ottoman domains. Your leaving the palace as you did pushed him to a commitment. He had been slow to take the final step sending written orders to the dervishes before that."

"And so it will be the dervishes," I said. "That is why you had the one in the Seven Towers killed."

"Yes," she replied, pleased that I could see her design.

As I looked at her in the new light of her cunning, I noticed the *surma* around her eyes was not smudged and heavy as it usually was, and I realized the lengths to which she had gone to create an image of brutishness. Without gaudy rouges she had no jowls, no creases in her neck. She was an attractive woman, almost beautiful, were it not for the cruelty in her eyes.

"You look different today, Kiusem. I can see now why Abdul Hamid loved you."

"You notice everything now, little Naksh. Like a child with a Chinese puzzle. Once you learn the secret, it seems so easy to you."

"And I will always remember who it was that showed me the way it works."

"But still you do not know all." She smiled without showing her teeth. There was something of a cat in the way she waited for me to reveal my ignorance again.

"Perhaps I know more than you think." I hoped she was unaware we had found out about the banquet.

She stood up and walked across the dais, the folds of her *entari* falling gracefully from her waist. "Do you like this color?" she asked as she turned and unbuttoned the diamonds that held the silk together.

"Very becoming," I replied.

"Still, you have not understood." Her smile was frightening. "So you know more than I think you do. Do you know I have a pistol?" She reached under her chemise and pulled it out.

"I do now," I responded as calmly as I could. "Are you going to kill me?"

"No." She smirked at my lack of perception. "At least I hope it will not come to that. But when I tell you what is going to happen, you may try to stop it, and that would leave me no choice. However, if you are reasonable, we might even go and watch."

"Women are not admitted into the banquet room," I said as if taking a trick at cards. "You see. I do know something."

"There will be no banquet today." Her face glowed with excitement as she enjoyed our mistaken conclusion. "Poppy's ears in the Janissary kitchen have been no secret to us. The Kettlemen let his spy overhear a plan. It sounded believable, you must agree with me there. After he brought his report to the Kislar Agha, my men took him. His ears hear no more. They are filled with the Bosporus."

"Then all our preparations were for nothing," I said, sickened by our stupidity.

"If you mean arranging for Hassan's troops to pose as pages at the banquet," she sniggered playfully. "That is hardly for nothing. Disguising themselves in those lovely red uniforms will keep them occupied."

"You know every bit of our plan," I cried in frustration.

"Perhaps I do," she responded indulgently. "But that is because the Kislar Agha makes one grave error. He fails to realize that anything or anyone he purchases is also for sale elsewhere. When I need one of them, I simply offer a higher price. It is the other side of that coin that is my biggest obstacle. I have never been able to penetrate your defenses." There was a hint of respect in her voice as she made that confession. "Of course, you pay your servants well, just as we all do. And you see to it they have gifts at the appropriate times, but most of them came with you from Algiers. They are grateful that you gave them the chance to serve the Grand Turk, and they believe your son is destined to rule as the caliph of us all. They are genuinely loyal and out of my reach. Incompetent Nasi was the only exception."

"Then you were behind the attempt on Mahmoud's life!"

"Of course I was. Mihrishah could not benefit from your son's death. You disappoint me, Naksh. I thought you would see through that deception easily, but Safiye was right."

"Safiye?" I felt myself blush with humiliation to have been outwitted by such a person.

"Yes. She thought you would be ready to believe anything of Mihrishah, even that she would kill Mahmoud, because of her jealousy over Selim."

"She was right," I admitted.

"The business of the bracelet was only a precaution. Of course, Safiye never went to her apartment.

She just put the story in your spy's mouth with a few gold coins. At the time I wanted Mahmoud dead in order to end your influence with Abdul Hamid. But Safiye realized there was a possibility of failure and wanted to turn such a misfortune to our advantage. She is very clever."

"And I was a fool."

"Do not be too hard on yourself," Kiusem counseled. "Mihrishah's love for Selim is unnatural! Much more than what is proper between a mother and her son. Recognizing it, you cannot be blamed for believing the worst."

"You speak about others and their unnatural love. What of your relationship with Safiye? It is an abomination."

"Perhaps. But I enjoy it and it binds her to me. She cannot be bought."

As Kiusem spoke, I thought I heard the sound of the stone being moved from the entrance to the passageway in the courtyard. Kiusem may have heard something as well, for she hesitated.

"You have told me a great deal this morning, Kiusem," I said, trying to distract her. "But still I do not know how you intend to assassinate Abdul Hamid."

She played with the pistol in her lap and smiled. "It will be at the parade. If we are to watch the event, we must leave soon."

"You intend to murder him on his way to prayer."

"No. He can pray for his people one last time. The dervishes will strike as he returns to the seraglio. It would have been difficult for them to get through the guards along the route if Hassan Pasha's men were on duty, but Abdul Hamid himself replaced them with Janissaries. Their Chief Cook, Suleiman Agha, has good reason to want my son on the throne."

"Then you intend to kill Selim?"

"I will have no hand in it! The Janissaries would never tolerate a reformer of his ilk. It's for that same reason I have no dread of your son. Under your tutelage, he would make sweeping changes in a system that has served the Ottoman domains well for more than four centuries. The Janissaries would not support him."

"Is Mahmoud safe now?"

"In spite of my failure with Nasi," Kiusem said confidently, "you can be certain that if I wanted Mahmoud dead, he would be dead." As she spoke, hard lines formed around her mouth and eyes. I felt compelled to believe her. "Enough talk now, Golden One." She waved her pistol toward the door. "I have a *palanquin* waiting at the Shawl Gate."

"The gardeners will allow us to leave the harem so easily?" I was astounded that she owned them as well.

"No. For now they are in the Kislar Agha's purse. But my good friend, the wife of the Dragoman came to call this morning. Her sister accompanied her. While they enjoy my garden, you and I will slip into *feridjies* and leave the palace in their litter. It is a simple ruse. Their bearers will carry us to the steps of Hagia Sophia. We should be able to see everything from there."

"I do not care to see it."

"You will go with me, Naksh." She did not wave the gun again, but it was there in her hand, finishing her thought. "I want to watch you when he dies."

"You must hate me," I said, seeing the passion in her eyes.

"Let us say simply that I intend to make you pay for the contempt in which you have held me. Now, let us go to my suite. Safiye is waiting with our disguises."

Chapter 45

As we left my apartment, Kiusem explained the unfamiliar guards outside. "They are mine. One of your slaves may have been listening to our conversation. No one will leave here until Abdul Hamid is dead."

I said nothing in response, hoping the guards were confirmation that Kiusem did not know about the hidden passage. There was a chance Poppy or Adele had returned to the courtyard and overheard the plot. I was almost certain that while Kiusem was talking to me I had heard the scrape of the stone over the entrance.

Safiye waited for us in Kiusem's salon. Her dog lay sleeping on the divan. "She knows everything?" Safiye asked her mistress eagerly. "She knows how we have outsmarted her?"

"She knows," Kiusem responded, as if to a beloved child. "Now call for some tea. We have time to relax before leaving for the parade."

When a servant brought in the drinks, Safiye took the glasses from her. As she handed one to me, she whispered, "I should be the one to accompany the Sultan to her victory."

I was in complete agreement with her, anxious to quit their company and send a warning to Abdul Hamid. But Kiusem interrupted.

"That will be enough," she said, unperturbed. "We have talked this through. It will be sweeter if she is there to watch him die. Be satisfied that your deception with Nasi and the bracelet took her in."

Safiye sat down on a cushion in front of her mistress and draped an arm across Kiusem's lap. "She actually believed Nasi was in Mihrishah's purse?" Kiusem stroked her hair tenderly and smiled.

The two gloated over their cleverness while they finished their tea. Then Kiusem and I slipped *feridjies* over our clothes. "I will return as soon as it is over," the Sultan assured her companion. Safiye kissed the hand presented to her and we left.

Kiusem's eunuchs accompanied us to the Shawl Gate where we passed out of the seraglio without difficulty. "The gardeners do not know the identity of the women who visit me," the Sultan explained. "It is the simplest of tasks to travel incognito in Istanbul. The costumes our men require of us make it impossible to tell one woman from another while they are abroad. A wife may pass her own husband as she walks with her lover and the cuckold will not recognize her."

As we rode along smoothly in the charge of skilled bearers, I looked through the sheer curtains to see her eunuchs escort our litter after we entered the busy thoroughfare leading to Hagia Sophia. A boisterous crowd lined the street, waiting to catch a glimpse of the Grand Turk when he returned from the mosque. The eunuchs wickedly cracked hippopotamus hide whips and cleared our path. When we reached the mosque, one of them approached the rank of Janissaries on duty and presented a medallion. Upon seeing it, the fellow became deferential and cleared his comrades from an area along the street so that our litter could be placed there.

"The medallion is the seal of the Grand Turk," Kiusem said. "It means that we are his honored guests for the proceedings. The Janissaries do not know who we are."

"I had no idea leaving the palace could be so simple," I confessed, hoping I would live to take advantage of the discovery.

"You must remember, Naksh," Kiusem said with condescension, "most of us have lived in the harem for many years. You cannot expect to learn everything there is to know without an apprenticeship."

Just then a sherbet vendor in his dripping turban of snow passed our litter. Kiusem called to her eunuchs. "Do you care for one?" she asked me, as if we were on a picnic.

"No," I replied, refusing to admit my thirst when Abdul Hamid's life was in such jeopardy.

"Nonsense, child. The dust from this crowd fills the air, and it is very close inside this litter. You will have one." She instructed her servant who presently handed in two chilled cups. I uncovered my face and drank mine quickly. It smelled of roses and was delicious.

Across the street, the Janissaries stood casually. They were uniformed in red boots, ballooning blue britches and peculiar white bonnets with long drapes in back to simulate the sleeve of the dervish blessing the Christians who at one time made up the Janissary Corps.

"Look!" Kiusem said excitedly as she pointed out the window. "The Mevlevi have made their appearance."

In the distance I could see a disturbance among the crowd as a group of dervishes began their whirling dance. "The assassins?" I asked as I scrutinized the pistol in Kiusem's lap.

"Yes," she answered, full of eagerness. "They hate Abdul Hamid for even the suggestion of reform, believing it threatens their power. They were easily bought." She pulled the gauze mask from her face to get a better look, but she noticed my attention to her weapon and smiled contemptuously. "You will gain nothing by taking it. My eunuchs will kill you if you try to leave the litter."

I slumped back and looked out the window, consumed by doubts that Poppy could stop Kiusem's plan even if he had learned of it. "What's happening now?" I asked. At the entrance to the mosque, I recognized Abdul Hamid by his high oval turban with its black crown and graceful plume. Suleiman Agha, discernable in his pointed cap, bent over the Grand Turk's feet.

"The Chief Cook is replacing Abdul Hamid's boots. He wore prayer slippers while he was inside."

After he finished, I saw Suleiman take up his gigantic spoon, sling it over his shoulder and proceed toward his horse. Then another group of men crowded around Abdul Hamid. "Who are they?"

"Officers of the Privy Chamber," she replied. From her tone I assumed she had little respect for them. "The Master of the Keys, the Master of the Stirrup, the Master of the Turbans, Swordbearer, Raincoat Bearer."

As she spoke the Grand Turk disappeared. Soldiers came up on all sides of him while he mounted his white stallion. Each man wore a high turban with huge feathers rising out of the top, all of them together creating a screen to protect the Sultan from prying eyes.

"That small group is loyal to Hassan and Abdul Hamid," Kiusem said grudgingly. "They have sworn to die for their Padishah, and today they will have their opportunity."

I noticed, closer to the street than before, the Mevlevi dervishes entering their trances. By that time the procession to the seraglio had begun. First came several dozen ministers, officers, professors of law and other persons of insufficient consequence to merit a prescribed place in the line. Each of them was on horseback and surrounded by an entourage of footmen. Each man had a distinctive costume and turban peculiar to his station. Their mounts were uniquely dressed as well.

Suleiman followed, looking sallow and stern for a man on the brink of victory. He was preceded by horse attendants and two rows of colonels who marched on foot. At the center of their ranks walked the principal of the Agha's kitchen. He wore an ornate uniform of black leather covered with great silver knobs. Around him was fastened a girdle suspending numerous hooks and supporting two enormous knives, the handles of which covered his face. Spoons, bowls and other silver kitchen utensils hung from his person in such a profusion that while he walked, he had to be supported by two aides.

Soldiers in red came next, followed by different officers of the empire. All of them paid their respects to the crowd, nodding from left to right as they moved along the street.

"That one clad in white satin is the Grand Vizier," Kiusem told me. "It was he who persuaded Selim to our cause. This is your first occasion to see some of the men who play such important roles in your life. Are they as you expected them?"

"I did not know what to expect, Sultan," I replied, taking comfort from her remarks that she was ignorant of my visits to the Eye overlooking the Divan.

A gilt chariot came next. "The Mufti must be in poor health," Kiusem observed when she saw the holy man inside the vehicle. "Unless he were ill he would walk beside the Grand Vizier." After a long pause she reasoned, "Just as well he is out of harm's way. It would not rest well with the crowd if the old man were injured, and his place is very near the Grand Turk in the procession."

I looked toward the place where I last saw the dervishes, but they had moved to the very edge of

the street and their dancing pressured the Janissaries
to move aside.

"I do not see Hassan among the officers," Kiusem
pointed out as the royal turban bearers passed our
litter. Two men on horseback each supported a scarlet
tripod upon which rested a headdress. As the men
rode along, they inclined the turbans very slightly to
the left and right. In return, the crowd and the Janissaries along the route made a great show of obeisance to demonstrate respect for their Padishah.

When I looked away from the display outside, I
could see Kiusem smirking. "Hassan must be oversee-
ing his troops and preparing for the banquet. I wonder
if he intends to dress himself as a page and serve part
of the dinner." She laughed, but her laughter was full
of tension.

The dervishes were dancing across from us, more
wildly than before. Several had extended an arm toward heaven, while the rest kept their hands upon
their breasts as they spun around. Onlookers pushed
against one another to avoid interfering with the holy
men. As they danced, the dervishes managed to move
directly into Abdul Hamid's path. Only his single line
of feathered bodyguards separated him from the assassins.

Janissaries left their posts to try to divert the
dervishes, but their actions lacked conviction. I assumed they knew where events would lead. Then suddenly, the whirling dancers stopped where they stood.
On hearing the wild cry of one of their number, they
rushed toward the Grand Turk pulling pistols and daggers from their trousers.

The crowd around us rioted. Our litter was buf-
fetted by people rushing away from the violence. Now
the dervishes engaged Abdul Hamid's honor guard in
bloody battle, but the Janissaries made no move to
intervene. Badly outnumbered, the guardsmen began
to fall. Their human wall was breeched and two assassins broke through. Pistol shots rang out so close
to me I thought that Kiusem had fired. Dervishes fell.

Abdul Hamid had slain them himself with pistols smoking in his hands. More shots followed. The Grand Turk's horse reared in terror. Miraculously, the ailing Abdul Hamid still held control. The animal plunged into the mass of attacking dervishes. From behind, the royal swordbearer charged forward, drew the weapon from its scabbard and threw the blade to the Sultan. Abdul Hamid caught it with the dexterity of a warrior. Seeing the irresistible flow of the battle, many Janissaries lent a hand to their monarch as he pursued the fleeing dervishes. Screaming people flooded the streets. In the confusion we lost sight of the Grand Turk, but Kiusem knew he had survived.

At last he rode back to the center of the thoroughfare, his subjects scurrying to avoid his horse's hooves. Kiusem glared at him through the window. Then she gasped. I saw what shocked her. The man on the Sultan's stallion was not Abdul Hamid. It was Hassan Pasha. "No wonder he was so skilled with a sword," I said in amazement, remembering his performance in the Divan. "He's spent a lifetime in combat."

Kiusem reached through the window to touch her eunuch's arm. "Take us back to the harem at once." The pistol lay in her lap, momentarily forgotten. I snatched it up and aimed it at her breast.

"You've won this one," she said calmly. I felt our bearers lift up the *palanquin* and move us forward as eunuchs called out threats and cracked their whips at the crowd. We were jostled badly by what had turned into a celebration of the Grand Turk's survival, and I feared the pistol might go off.

"Put it down," Kiusem muttered in contempt. "You have not the will to use it."

She was right. I pulled the priming and put the weapon on the floor.

"Were our places reversed, I would not have hesitated. You would be dead now."

"Yes," I responded. "That is the chief difference between us."

"And that is why my son, Mustapha, will rule while

Selim and Mahmoud languish in the Cage. You lack the courage to act, to carry the battle to your opponent. It will always be your place to respond to my challenge. One day your response will come too late." She sat back against a brocaded cushion and appeared unperturbed by the defeat of her cabal.

Suddenly, our *palanquin* lurched. One of the bearers had stumbled over a body trampled by the crowd. Not bothering to cover her face, Kiusem thrust her head out the window and cursed the fellow soundly. Then she settled down again, replaced her mask and allowed herself the release of tears.

Chapter 46

Upon our return, Safiye took the news of their failure with less grace than her mistress. She brandished a dagger as she wept with regret and threatened to cut out my heart. Kiusem intervened on my behalf, slapping the weapon from Safiye's hand and physically throwing her out of the salon. Her act troubled me, for I believed she thought me a desirable adversary—easily deceived and therefore harmless.

As I made my way back to my suite, I heard Poppy's voice.

"Naksh Sultan! Now all is well," he gasped breathlessly. "You are safe." He fell to his knees and kissed my hands. I helped him to his feet and we walked arm in arm to my apartment where Kiusem's eunuchs no longer flanked the door.

"Sultan! Sultan!" Lydia cried when we came in. "What is happening?" She rushed to embrace me as I descended the steps to the salon. "There is rumor of riots in the city, and Mahmoud has disappeared. The guards outside threatened me when I tried to leave.

Seriphina is upstairs in the nursery weeping. What is happening?"

"Calm yourself, woman," Poppy said firmly. "Mahmoud is safe. He is with Adele. Now, leave us. Your mistress will explain everything to you later."

Lydia clung to me. "If there is danger, my place is with the Sultan," she said courageously, and I remembered Kiusem's praise of my servants.

"The danger is past," I assured her. "Now do as the Kislar Agha asks. Go to Seriphina and put her mind to rest."

"Yes, Sultan." She squeezed my hand and took her leave.

"Quickly," Poppy urged. "Adele is with the little prince, hiding in the passageway. She knows nothing of our success and waits for a sign to flee the palace."

We went into the courtyard, where Poppy bent his great bulk down and knocked three times on the stone. Then he shifted it aside to reveal Adele, Mahmoud asleep in her arms, a primed pistol clutched in her hand. "Abdul Hamid lives," Poppy said simply. "By Allah's will we are saved."

When I saw my child emerge from the tunnel, content and secure in Adele's care, I embraced them both and led them inside. A rush of emotion caused my milk to flow. I took Mahmoud to me and reclined on the divan. Adele joined me there, her face revealing the tension of her long wait. Poppy fetched his chair and sat opposite us.

"Was it you I heard in the courtyard when Kiusem was telling me of the plot," I asked him. "I thought I heard the stone."

"Yes, it scraped along the cobbles as I tried to emerge," he confessed, apologizing for his girth.

"Kiusem noticed nothing," I assured him. "Praise Allah for that."

"What possessed you to send me after Poppy at the last minute?" Adele wanted to know.

"Intuition, I suppose."

"The parade was just as Kiusem described it," Poppy said. "But the outcome was different."

"I saw the entire thing," I told him. "From a *palanquin* opposite Hagia Sophia. Kiusem wanted me to witness Abdul Hamid's death."

"I heard her describe the plot," Adele said. "But how did you foil her?"

Poppy and I explained that the dervishes had attacked Hassan Pasha, thinking he was the Grand Turk. "But where was Abdul Hamid through all that?" she asked.

"Yes, where was he?" I echoed.

"He rode in the Mufti's chariot," Poppy said, proud he had orchestrated a successful deception. "Just after prayers, the holy man feigned exhaustion and was carried to an antechamber near the front of the mosque where Hassan Pasha waited, already disguised as the Grand Turk. Abdul Hamid, concerned for the Mufti's health, attended him personally. While they were hidden, the Mufti gave up his white raiments and disguised himself as one of the ulema. He remained behind in the mosque when Hassan and Abdul Hamid emerged behind a screen of body guards."

"You arranged quite a bit in a very short time," I observed, amazed at the eunuch's resourcefulness.

"It was the will of Allah," he said humbly. Still he was unable to hide his pride in the accomplishment. "You should have seen Suleiman Agha's face when he bent down to put on the Grand Turk's boots. He struggled mightily with the first one, for Hassan's feet are much larger than Abdul Hamid's. When Suleiman looked up, I thought he would fall dead from shock. Of course, he was helpless to stop the assassins or signal them in any way."

"That explains his dour expression as he rode back toward the palace," I said. "It seemed odd he was not jubilant."

"He was anything but that," Poppy laughed.

"Will he be made to pay for his part in the conspiracy?" Adele asked.

"He runs no risk of that," Poppy replied.

"His Janissary Corps is his shield," I said.

"Unfortunately so," he agreed. "It will protect Kiusem and Mustapha as well. The troops would revolt if either of them were executed, though Kiusem may have to visit the old palace for a few years of retirement, and her son may have to reside in an apartment of the Cage."

"What of Selim then?" I asked cautiously. "Did he convince Abdul Hamid of his good intentions?"

"He was splendid. His fear made him the more believable, and Abdul Hamid wanted to take his side. He even assumes it was Selim who sent word of the final change of plans. The vizier will bear the brunt of Abdul Hamid's rage. He will die slowly and without dignity."

"What of the dervishes," Adele wanted to know.

"All dead. The Janissaries saw to that."

"Then nothing has changed because of this," I concluded solemnly. "None but the Grand Vizier will be made to pay."

"It seems that is the will of Allah," Poppy responded without regret. "But I would say there have been changes. For one, I have learned a great deal about our adversaries, and so have you. Perhaps the next time they challenge us, we will be more prepared."

His words reminded me of what Kiusem had said —that I would never do more than react to her challenges until the time came when she finally triumphed.

"You are right, Poppy. I have learned from this," I said, realizing that unless I fled the Levant with Mahmoud and François, Kiusem and Mustapha would be a constant danger.

"There is something else, Sultan." Poppy's tone was somber. He reached into the folds of his sash.

"A gold *louis*," I exclaimed, surprised to see a French coin.

"Yesterday, when the Frenchman left you, he was taken across the Horn to Pera and delivered to Paul Flachat. Two days from now, the merchant begins his return journey to France. Your lover will accompany him."

Poppy's words stunned me. In the panic of recent events, François had not entered my mind, but now the thought of his leaving brought a new panic. We had not yet made our escape plans. I began to protest, but the Kislar Agha stopped me.

"Listen to me, Sultan," he said boldly. "I know the man is dear to you. I know also that the walls of this harem are not high enough nor strong enough to keep you here unless it is your will to stay.

"Now is the time for you to discover what is in your heart. Tomorrow just after sunrise prayer, you will leave the seraglio. The guards at the Shawl Gate will be told you are Adele Hanoum. Your bearers will take you to the covered market. There you will present the coin at the shop of a certain goldsmith, hoping he will melt it down and fashion it into jewelry. He will invite you to the rear of his shop to show you some of his work. Accept his invitation. The Frenchmen will be waiting for you."

Mahmoud squirmed in my arms, and I shifted him to my other breast. Perhaps this would be my only chance. "François would like to see the baby," I said cautiously. "May I take him with me to the goldsmith?"

Poppy smiled sympathetically. "You are a beloved friend, Naksh, and I would love to help you further, but I serve the Grand Turk before all others. Mahmoud is his son. He will stay in the palace."

Chapter 47

Next morning the air was cool and heavy with the sea's moisture when Poppy and I descended the Fifty-Three Steps to the lower terrace of the harem. Slaves shuffled close to the walls like cloistered nuns. A *palanquin* waited at the Shawl Gate. There were two extra bearers with a chest I had packed the night before.

As the vehicle carried me through the alleyways formed by stalls and shops overflowing the covered market of Hagia Sophia, I thought of François waiting for me at the goldsmith's shop and of how happy we would be together. But even as I hurried to him, an image of Mahmoud came to my mind. A tentative smile lit his face as he looked up from my arms. Then he nuzzled against me seeking nourishment.

I could not have both of them, I admitted at last. François could not remain in the Levant. Kiusem knew about him and would reveal his identity when the time suited her. Mahmoud could not leave. Poppy would see to that.

Looking through the sheer curtain of the *palanquin,* I could see in the dim light of the high window gratings a well organized merchant city under a single roof. We traveled along a major thoroughfare of the metropolis for some time, passing avenues which branched off in both directions. Along each one there were neat stalls and shops where a great diversity of goods was displayed. At last my bearers took me down such a street, the avenue of the goldsmiths. The *palanquin* stopped. A eunuch came to the window and pulled back the curtain.

"The coin, Hanoum Effendi," he requested formally. I placed it in his hand. He stepped away, returning a moment later. "The artisan is honored to accept your commission. He bids you enter his establishment to view some of his work."

The gauze clung to my face as I spoke. "I am most anxious to see it."

The eunuch opened the litter. I stepped out and was ushered past the goldsmith's display to the back of the shop where a suspended Persian rug formed a partition creating a tiny salon. The eunuch pulled it aside for me. Behind it, François stood waiting.

I felt the rug drop back into place after I passed it. I removed my mask. I studied François' eyes and he mine, each of us looking for a different sign. Neither of us spoke.

"You aren't going back with me," he said.

"No, darling. I must stay here. Mahmoud will need me."

"But I can't stay in Istanbul," he protested. "It would be too dangerous for you."

"I know."

In the silence that followed I began to feel the pain that I knew would only grow worse as the days without him became years. Everything ahead suddenly seemed as cold as the grave. Living without François would not be life at all.

"Is there nothing I can say to make you change your mind?" His voice trembled as he spoke, but it was I who first succumbed to tears. Then we collapsed upon the cushions on the floor and wept together.

In the emptiness that remained I gave François a packet of letters.

"Will you see these are delivered?"

He looked at them. One was addressed to the Abbess in Nantes, another to Marie de La Fontelle and the last to my only family living in France—my cousin, Marie-Josephe Rose de Beauharnais. Marie Rose was of my blood, and she should be told of my fate.

As François read her name, I remembered that years before, the fortuneteller who had so accurately predicted my future also prophesied that Marie Rose would one day rule France. At the time the prospect seemed outrageous, but now, after all that had happened, it was quite possible.

I had written two other letters the night before, one to Adele and the other to Poppy. They remained tucked in my shawl. I would not need to send them.

"Nothing for me," François said miserably. "Through the rest of my life I have nothing to remind me that you were real, that this actually happened. The eunuch even took my watch. I have nothing."

I slipped my hands under my *feridjie* and unclasped the chain around my neck. It held a key to the chest I had brought. In it were more than half the jewels the Dey had given me when I left Algiers.

"This is for you, darling. You will need what's inside that case when you return to France. There is the warrant to deal with and your father's debts. I'll not spend the rest of my days believing you married that little girl from Paris for her family's money."

He smiled bitterly. "You'll forget me soon enough, Aimee."

I wanted to cry again, but there were no tears left, and no words to soothe the pain both of us felt. I touched his cheek one last time, kissed him gently and replaced my mask. Then I left him in the dim light of the goldsmith's shop.

Before my bearers hoisted my *palanquin,* I ordered those with the chest to stay behind. A feeling of peace took possession of me in the sunlight. Through the window I beheld the wonders of Istanbul, perhaps the most magnificent city in the world, a perfect union of East and West. There was Hagia Sophia, built to celebrate Christ and now a Musselman shrine. In the distance was the Hippodrome, a Roman contribution. Farther along the road was the magnificent Suleimaniye, Sultan Suleiman's mosque and mausoleum, constructed by the great Sinan, a Christian architect whose work became the definition of Ottoman style.

Istanbul, created by Constantine. Justinian, Theodosius, Mehmed and Suleiman were among its rulers. My son, a child of two worlds, would follow them. The thought both frightened me and filled me with joy.

Excitedly, I pulled back the curtain of my litter and called to the eunuchs. "Tell the bearers to hurry," I instructed them. "I am needed at the palace."

GLORIOUS BATTLES OF LOVE & WAR

Romances of Strange Lands and Distant Times

Read about the dazzling women and bold men whose passion for love and excitement leads them to the heights and depths of the human experience—set against flamboyant period backgrounds.

Look for Richard Gallen Romances from Pocket Books→

___ 83504	**SILVER LADY** Nancy Morse	**$2.50**
___ 83524	**SWEET NEMESIS** Lynn Erickson	**$2.50**
___ 83560	**THIS REBEL HUNGER** Lynn LeMon	**$2.50**
___ 83561	**SAVAGE FANCY** Kathryn Gorsha Thiels	**$2.50**
___ 83562	**THIS TENDER PRIZE** Nancy Morse	**$2.50**
___ 83366	**THE FROST AND THE FLAME** Drucilla Campbell	**$2.50**
___ 83636	**TOMORROW AND FOREVER** Maud B. Johnson	**$2.50**
___ 83564	**TANYA** Muriel Bradley	**$2.50**